Codename Lazarus:

The Spy Who Came Back From The Dead

A. P. Martin

This book is a work of fiction. The names, characters, businesses, places, events and incidents are products of the author's imagination or used in a fictitious manner and are not to be construed as real. Any resemblance to actual persons, living or dead, actual events, locales or organisations is entirely coincidental

Copyright © 2016 A.P. Martin

The moral right of the author has been asserted.

Apart from any fair dealing for the purposes of research or private study, or criticism or review, as permitted under the Copyright, Designs and Patents Act 1988, this publication may only be reproduced, stored or transmitted, in any form or by any means, with the prior permission in writing of the publisher, or in the case of reprographic reproduction in accordance with the terms of licences issued by the Copyright Licensing Agency. Enquiries concerning reproduction outside those terms should be sent to the publisher.

All rights reserved.

ISBN-13: 978-1535212304
ISBN-10: 1535212306

For my wife Gloria, Mark, Jude and John for their unstinting encouragement.

PART ONE

Chapter One

Wednesday, February 1st 1939, Tunstall Chapel, Durham Castle, England.

The sound of the ancient Tunstall Organ's rendering of 'Jerusalem' all but drowned out the voices of the small choir and the sizeable congregation in Castle Chapel, the largest place of worship within the confines of Durham Castle. The dismal grey weather outside matched the sombre mood of those who had gathered to mark the loss of Dr John King in a hiking accident in Switzerland. Loss was indeed the correct term, for his body had yet to be recovered from its frozen resting place, high in the snow covered Alps. King had been a successful and popular young History don at the University of Durham and many of the young faces in the congregation, deathly pale even in the warm glow of candlelight, belonged to those he had taught.

The Swiss Authorities had expressed the firm view that King, while walking in the Bernese Oberland, had been the victim of an unfortunate accident. The evidence indicated, with little room for doubt, that a rock and snow fall in a notoriously dangerous spot on the mountain path from the Gemmi Pass to Leukerbad had swept King away down a deep and inaccessible ravine. Several of his possessions had been found scattered in the snow, close to where the avalanche had broken the somewhat rickety safety fence. Analysis had proved that this bore traces of human blood. Evidence had been submitted by Gerhardt Rösti, a very experienced local mountain guide and Inspector Peter Graf of the Swiss National Security Service, both of whom had stated firmly that the balance of probability was overwhelming that King had been the victim of a terrible accident. The formal investigation in Switzerland had heard further testimony that King, though young and fit, was relatively inexperienced in mountain conditions. Moreover, on the day of his death a freak snow storm had engulfed the area in which he was walking. Such conditions, Rösti had told the investigation, would have challenged even the most capable of Alpinists.

As the music faded, King's father, a straight backed veteran of the First World War, came forward to deliver the reading. His shoe heels clicked in perfect time, as he walked briskly over the black and white tiles laid out on the chapel floor like an oblique chess board. Perhaps it was fitting that for the few seconds before he commenced, the only audible sound was the rain beating relentlessly against the beautiful stained glass windows of the chapel. As he began to speak, in a voice conditioned by countless amateur dramatic performances, many in the congregation sensed something unusual about his tone. For this seemed to reflect a defiant optimism, rather than the expected sense of loss and sorrow. Without hesitation or stumble, he confidently read Verses 1 to 7 from Revelations, before returning to comfort his distraught wife and daughter.

A little behind the family members, in one of the sixteenth century misericord seats, sat an alert looking, grey haired man in his mid-fifties. Without doubt, this mourner had been King's most important tutor and mentor during his curtailed academic career. Professor Bernard Pym's bright, intelligent eyes observed closely the two generations of the British-German Bernstein family who were sitting just in front of him. He was aware that all of these good people had the loyalty and humanity of John King to thank for their escape from the anti-Semitic maw of Hitler's Third Reich. The parents, prematurely aged now by the stress of their very recent departure from Heidelberg, and their son, David, longer established in Britain and proudly wearing the dress uniform of a British police officer, sat straight backed and silent.

The Service of Remembrance was conducted in an understated way, of which Pym was certain King would have approved. As soon as the principal mourners had left the Chapel, the Professor took the opportunity discreetly to view the various floral tributes which had been placed on a large table to the side of the altar.

These, he noted, included a pretty bunch of snowdrops, no doubt collected by David Bernstein from some northern woods and accompanied by a hand written card from his sister, Rachel who now lived and worked in America. On reading the signature on the card, the Professor smiled as he recalled how, back in 1933, John King's passionate and persuasive campaign had convinced him to accept his half Welsh, half German friend as a postgraduate student at Oxford University. Rachel had, in fact, proved to be an excellent student and had gone on to obtain tenure at one of the better universities in New

York.

Looking further among the flowers, Pym was not surprised to see a number of bouquets with messages written in German. King had spent the last few months of his life participating in an academic exchange in Berlin, where he had made many new friends. It was soon clear to Pym that flowers had been sent both from Berlin and from his longer standing friends in Heidelberg, where he had studied for eighteen months in the early 1930s. The Professor paused somewhat longer to look carefully at two individual tributes which, for him, stood out from the rest. The first was a single red rose and the accompanying note written in German bore the heartfelt message: *'Goodbye my darling John. I will never forget you. All my love. Greta.'* The second, and perhaps the most unexpected message of all, read: *'Rest in Peace, John. You will always be my good and honourable friend. Erwin Kalz.'* Pym nodded his head in acknowledgement of the writer's discretion in not mentioning his rank. Arguably, for King to have received a message of condolence from a serving Major in the German *Abwehr* would have been in poor taste.

Moving out of the Chapel now and into the grey half-light of a North East afternoon, he could not help but conclude that this had been the most difficult part of the operation so far. And, he reflected with real concern, if it was difficult for me, how much more difficult is it going to be for Dr John King to have his own memorial service described during our meeting tomorrow in London?

Chapter Two

Saturday, 24th June 1933, Heidelberg, Germany.

The young SS officer and the rangy, fair-haired man looked equally shocked and baffled that things between them could have come to this. As the German picked himself tentatively from the floor, trying in vain to maintain what dignity he could, the Englishman was taken in the unforgiving grip of two SS soldiers. Briefly their eyes met, full of sadness and incomprehension, for they both knew instinctively that this would change everything.

The day had begun so well for King. Lazy clouds floated across the azure sky and mid-summer sunshine reflected off the calm waters of the river Neckar, as it flowed sedately through the ancient university city of Heidelberg. He had planned it as a day of celebration; a day of some sadness to be sure but, hopefully, a day of *Auf Wiedersehen* rather than *Adieu*. For this was John King's last day in Heidelberg, a city which he had come to like very much, and his last outing with his University friends and colleagues who had become his family in Germany. A fit and athletic looking six-footer, King stood out among the group of several young men and women which had met just before noon at the far side of the Carl Theodor Old Bridge. Their plan, such as young people do plan anything, was to enjoy a farewell walk along the Philosophenweg. Whatever local tradition dictated, however, this was not intended as an occasion for deep thinking. On the contrary, the group of King's best friends in Heidelberg chatted happily and noisily as they progressed along the pathway, high above the river and overlooking the old town with its famous *Schloß*.

'I don't know what you two think,' said the overweight Konrad Schulz, as he paused to wipe the first beads of sweat from his pink forehead. 'But I'm not that surprised that Joachim hasn't appeared.'

King looked in surprise at his friend, before replying, 'I'm not sure I understand you, Konrad. It's true that I've hardly seen him since the Elections but he knows this is my last day and I did expect him to turn up.'

'Well I agree with Konrad,' replied Rachel Bernstein firmly. A pretty, studious looking young woman, wearing horn-rimmed spectacles and with thick black hair tied up severely in a long ponytail, she raised a hand to silence King before attempting to explain. 'I know that you're good friends with him, John. And Joachim can be interesting company. But I suspect that there's always been a part of him that's hidden. He's seemed such a loner, who doesn't quite know how to fit in properly with others.'

'I know what you mean,' conceded King with a shrug. 'He did sometimes behave as though all he wanted was fully to belong to something; to have real meaning in his life. But you know, he and I had some really enjoyable times and I do think he's a good man and I count him as my friend.'

Rachel came closer to King and linked her arm through his. 'Oh John. Of course you should see him as your friend. It's just that most of us think that there's a side to him that maybe none of us knows.'

Just as Rachel had finished speaking, a boisterous group of *Hitlerjugend* came into view, marching towards them around a bend in the path. As they approached, King immediately felt Rachel tense beside him. 'Relax,' he said, smiling and running his hand through his unfashionably long hair. 'They're just boys playing at soldiers.'

'That's easy for you to say, John,' replied Rachel with uncharacteristic vehemence. 'But one of my best friends was badly beaten up by such a group last week, just because she's Jewish.' The next sentences were spoken in staccato, reflecting her high emotional state. 'In broad daylight. In the Heumarkt. It was right by the University. No one tried to help her, although she said there were lots of people about.'

King glared at the group of boys marching noisily past, as if he were daring one of them to take issue with either himself or his friend. Their attention was, however, fixed firmly on the business of trying simultaneously to keep in step and to avoid bumping into one another. When the last of them had passed, King turned to Rachel. 'I'm sorry... that was unthinking of me. I know things are getting much worse now and I fear that they'll not get any better. What will you do Rachel? Will you leave Germany?'

The young woman sighed deeply and looked out over the

glistening river below, a peaceful, almost idyllic scene. Eventually she turned back to King and replied softly. 'I honestly don't know, John. On the one hand, this is my home and has been the home of my family, at least on my father's side, going back generations. On the other hand, many of my Jewish friends are no longer allowed to study and, since the Election, the anti-Jewish propaganda and violence are increasing steadily. I may be only half Jewish, but I'm very proud of that part of me and I can only see things getting worse here. I've seriously thought of trying to get to England and from there to America. There's none of my Mama's family left in Wales, but she does have some distant relatives who emigrated from Wales to New York before the First World War. Without help, though, I don't think it would be possible. I mean, where would I go in England? And what about my studies?'

King tried to imagine what he would feel like, were he to face being driven out of his home and away from all his family and friends by the Nazis. 'Would your parents and brother leave as well?'

Rachel gave a harsh laugh. 'You must be joking. Papa would never leave Germany. He fought in the Great War, remember. He was even decorated for valour. He can't believe that what's happening now is anything other than a temporary aberration. Of course, Mama was born in North Wales and is very conscious still of her roots. She definitely brought David and me up to feel part Celt. But she'd never leave Papa and, as I've said, he's here to stay.'

'And David?' enquired King gently. 'Oh David?' she replied with some exasperation. 'All he wants to do is become a policeman! It's crazy! Can you imagine that? Doing the dirty work of the Nazis? Even he's coming to recognise that he'll never achieve his ambition here. So, yes, I think he might jump at the chance to leave with me.'

'Then you must let me help you both, Rachel,' offered King without a second's hesitation. 'My parents have plenty of space for you. I'm certain that you could stay with them until you got yourselves sorted out. And I'll speak to Professor Pym, my supervisor at Oxford, about you transferring your work there. My dad might be able to pull some strings to help David with his career goal too. I promise that I'll be in touch as soon as I get back home.'

Rachel smiled sadly at King's earnest expression and squeezed his hand affectionately. 'That would be wonderful, John. Thank you.' In her head, of course, she thought that her chances of leaving Germany were very slim. In her heart, however, she really believed that if anyone could and would help her, it would be this earnest, fair-haired Englishman.

As the group continued on its way, the path ahead of them was made golden by the dappled sunlight. Walking in silence and in more reflective mood now, King looked back over his last weeks in Germany. The imminence of his departure and the thought of having to leave some places and people behind certainly depressed him. But, now that he had thought directly about it, he had to admit to himself that he was glad that his eighteen-month research stay in Heidelberg was coming to an end. The prospect of returning, both to the familiarity of Oxford to complete his Doctorate and to the taken for granted freedoms enjoyed in England, filled him with eager anticipation. For although he had met many cultured and pleasant people during his time in Germany, he found himself more and more repulsed by the Nazis and horrified by the rapid expansion both in their numbers and their influence on daily life.

Things had, he reflected, certainly moved quickly since the *Reichstag* fire just four short months earlier. The suspicious blaze had taken place barely a week before the day of the Election and King shared the view, held by many of his more liberal friends, that it had been caused by the Nazis in order to provide a major platform for Hitler. While the Nazi Party had not won an overall majority in the Election, the specious incrimination of a Communist for the arson had given Hitler a rationale, however dubious, to justify the arrest of more than eighty deputies, all of whom opposed his party. With horror, King had quickly realised the consequences of this action. Because those arrested were now unable to vote, Hitler had effectively manufactured a pro-Nazi majority in the *Reichstag*.

Within three weeks of the Election, the now doctored *Reichstag* had passed the 'Enabling Act', which basically gave Hitler the power to make his own laws without reference to any elected body. Many of King's left leaning and Jewish friends were terrified of this legalised dictatorship and, he had recognised bitterly, with very good reason. Within weeks, swastikas were flying from almost every public building, trade unions and any opposition to the Nazis had been either banned or crushed and anti-Jewish violence was on the increase. 'Dirt and shame books' were being publicly burned and the universities, including Heidelberg, had begun to purge themselves of Jewish and unsympathetic professors and students. Many of King's Jewish and Communist friends had already been banned from the University Library and suspended permanently from its lecture rooms. Indeed, that very week King had been outraged to learn that his friend and tutor Professor Daniel Berg's position as Professor of Modern History at the University was under threat.

Despite these terrible developments and the resultant increasing division of Germany along political and racial lines, King was pleased and proud that almost all his closest friends had turned up to bid him farewell. The one real surprise was that Joachim had not appeared. For much of his time in Heidelberg, King had thought Joachim Brandt to have been among his closest friends. They shared such diverse passions as the historical analysis of the German 'Second Empire' and beer. Their friendship had been cemented when, initially as a joke, they had each agreed that they should find something to love about the other's country. Joachim had introduced King to the music of Richard Wagner while, in return, the German had been educated in the quintessential English pursuit of cricket. It is odd, thought King uneasily, that I've seen nothing of Joachim these last weeks. But never mind, at least I'll see Professor Berg at the restaurant and hopefully Joachim will turn up there as well.

The friends had enjoyed a perfect picnic, produced, as if by magic, from the various knapsacks which they had carried and by late afternoon they were contentedly walking back across the bridge and on towards the 'Old Town'. As usual, the twin white towers of the *Brückentor* entranced King as they basked in the warm sunshine. He led the group through the brown sandstone gate at the end of the bridge and on into the lengthening shadows of the 'Old Town' itself.

King had invited those who did not want to make the steep climb up to the Philosophenweg to meet the hikers at six in the Universitätsplatz. From there, they would proceed together to a farewell meal at King's favourite restaurant in the city - the *Weisser Bock*. As the group walked happily across the Marktplatz and on towards the agreed meeting point, King was not surprised to see trestle tables erected beneath a particularly huge swastika which flapped lazily in a gentle breeze, as it hung from a first floor window of the town hall. Brownshirts and other more sinister looking party officials, identifiable only by tiny lapel pins in their generally unfashionable suits, were busy handing out leaflets to the passers-by. These identified both the latest list of proscribed books and the faculty members, who had recently been dismissed from the University. Just to the right of the *Herkulesbrunnen* was a huge brazier which was burning fiercely and a long queue of ashen-faced people had lined up, to take turns to throw their copies of banned books onto the fire. King and his friends looked uneasily at one another as they hastened past the looming brown sandstone mass of the *Heiliggeistkirche* and out of the square into the Hauptstraße. Despite its grand name this was a narrow street, flanked on both sides by tall, gaily coloured buildings, many of which housed the more fashionable shops, inns and offices of the city. King and his friends barely had time to adjust their eyes to the deep shadows cast by the buildings, when they found their way blocked by yet more SA troops. Rather less menacingly, this group was organised into a marching band which was lumbering, painfully slowly, in the direction of the University. Passers-by looked on at the heavy, sweating Brownshirts, as they wheezed their way through various favourite Nazi marching tunes. King noted that by no means all the spectators looked happy at this rather tuneless interruption to their early evening stroll through the Altstadt.

'Let's turn into Keltengasse and go up to the Universitätsplatz by way of Merianstraße,' suggested Konrad, with an exaggerated grimace. 'I'm not sure I can stomach much more of this cacophony.' King was equally glad to have left the band's efforts fading into the distance, as the group made its final approach into the large square, across which the 'Old University' building faced that of the 'New University'.

His face broke into a wide smile as he recognised Professor Berg waiting at the agreed meeting place by the fountain. He rushed over and warmly greeted the older man. 'I'm delighted to see you, sir. It's very good of you to come.'

Looking every inch the dapper professional, Berg raised his hat to the girls in the group before responding, 'Not at all, my boy! I would not have missed this for the world.' As King began to steer his friends and his mentor in the direction of the *Weisser Bock*, he found his path obstructed by a man in the uniform of an *Untersturmführer* in the SS.

'John, I'm sorry I couldn't make the walk, but as you can see I now have other duties,' Joachim Brandt explained in a manner intended, but not quite succeeding in communicating his new found status. While it had been several weeks or more since King had last seen Brandt, he was nevertheless stunned at his friend's transformation. Dressed now in the sinister black of Himmler's feared organisation, his friend looked very different from his once habitual drinking partner. Though slightly shorter than King and now with closely cropped, dark hair, with his unusually dark eyes and fine features, Brandt was equally handsome. 'I can see you are a little surprised at my new status, John?' suggested Brandt eagerly.

'Yes, Joachim. That's very perceptive of you. I am indeed surprised,' King replied evenly, 'But no doubt we can talk about things later and you can explain what's been happening with you. The main thing is that you're here now, so let's all go straight to the restaurant, I'm starving.'

As King approached Brandt in order to shake hands, he noticed the smile fade rapidly from his friend's face, to be replaced immediately by an expression of outrage and disgust. 'But surely John, you do not mean to socialise with types such as these?' Brandt indicated Professor Berg and Rachel Bernstein with a dismissive gesture of his black-gloved hand.

'Of course I do, Joachim,' replied King calmly, but firmly. 'Rachel is a good friend of both of us and my debt to, and respect for Professor Berg is so great that a farewell meal without his presence would be unthinkable.'

Brandt, perhaps conscious of the sharp looks being exchanged by his platoon of soldiers, began to shake his head, as if having to instruct a rather slow-witted student in the basics of his subject. 'John, John. That is not a good idea. You must surely realise how Germany is changing, and changing very much for the better. It is important that you respect this process and what it means. And,' he concluded in a more menacing tone, 'you should respect my uniform.'

Before King could answer, Professor Berg and Rachel began to detach themselves from the group of friends. 'We have no desire to cause difficulties for you, John. Perhaps it would be better if we say our goodbyes now.' Berg sounded more resigned than angry, as if this was yet another example of what was to become his lot in the Führer's Reich. In a provocative attempt to establish his mastery of the situation, Brandt moved quickly towards Berg and began to push him roughly away. As he did so, he sneered disrespectfully, 'That's right, old Jew! Get out of here. You have no place in the new Fatherland!'

    King had little recollection afterwards of what had happened. First he noticed the graze on the knuckles of his right hand and then he saw Brandt struggling back to his feet and wiping away both the dust from his uniform and the blood from his lip. Half a dozen jack-booted SS soldiers immediately surrounded the group, two of them seizing King by the arms. 'Shall we arrest them Herr *Untersturmführer*?' asked one particularly brutish type, with evident relish. Clearly for him, the thought of being able to rough up a group of students and a couple of Jews offered by far the most attractive entertainment imaginable for a Saturday evening. 'No,' barked Brandt loudly as he blinked away his shock and incomprehension, before saying much more quietly, 'That will not be necessary.'

    Moving to face King and looking him directly in the eye with an expression full of confusion, hurt and anger Brandt whispered, 'You know I could have you and all your friends arrested for hitting me? With one word from me, you would all be on your way to one of our special camps for the antisocial elements in our society.'

    Looking at his friend, a feeling of great sorrow came over King as he realised what he had done. 'You gave me no choice, Joachim. Surely you must see that?'

    A hardness and a fury came into Brandt's eyes as, having seemed to come to a decision, he replied, 'I had hoped that you would have respected my choice to act for my country in the best way that I see fit. I can see now that I was wrong. Our friendship is now over. But one thing I can and will give to you is my solemn promise that you will live to regret what you have done today.'

    Before King could reply, Brandt turned his back on his former friend and with an icy 'Release him!' issued his orders to his obviously disappointed squad. The soldiers who were holding King, reluctantly shoved him back towards his friends, but only after each had delivered a hefty blow to the Englishman's upper body. They then followed Brandt as he marched quickly out of the square, pushing interested bystanders roughly aside as they went.

King stared after his friend, shock and genuine sadness etched into his expression, while his visibly shaken friends breathed heavy sighs of relief. It was not until the group was comfortably seated in the familiar and normal environment of the restaurant, that King was able to speak. His voice shaking with emotion and his face a picture of dejection, he turned to the Professor and Rachel. 'I'm so sorry. I don't know what came over me. It was unforgivable. You could all have been put in real danger by my actions.'

'You acted from your heart which is pure, John,' replied Berg quietly. 'I would be the last to criticise you for that.'

'Yes,' added Rachel more brightly, in an attempt to lighten the mood of the group. 'And nothing happened anyway.'

King was not yet ready to draw a line under the confrontation and, uncertainty written all over his face, asked of no one in particular, 'But what's happened to him?'

'I don't know,' replied Konrad Schulz sadly. 'I didn't want to say anything earlier, but according to one man in my building who's something big in the local Party, membership of the Nazis rocketed just after the 'Enabling Act'. The long standing members call them 'March Violets' out of disregard. I suppose it's inevitable that we'll all know at least one or two of these people.'

'That may be so, Konrad,' said King, shaking his head sadly, 'but I would never have expected that of Joachim. He was never particularly political …'

'But he did always want to be somebody, to be accepted, respected and fully part of something. He always feared being the outsider,' suggested Rachel. 'Maybe this is his way of having a purpose and truly belonging.'

King nodded his head sadly, as if reluctant to understand this rationale for his friend's membership of the SS. 'But why, then, did he let us go?' asked King, hope returning to his face. 'Maybe he can be helped out of such a dark place. I'll go after him and try to bring him back.' King was about to stand up when Professor Berg placed a restraining hand on his arm. 'Wait, John. Just listen to me. Joachim clearly valued his friendship with you very highly. It must have taken quite some strength of feeling to disappoint those thugs who were with him. You could see they just wanted to arrest us all and God knows what they'd have done to us in their cells.' A shudder went through the group as the Professor continued, 'But he has, I'm afraid, embraced his new ideology completely. He's a leading member of those who are denouncing me to the University authorities as unfit to retain my post.' Seeing the disbelief on King's face, he quickly added, 'He has put his friendship with you above his clear duty once, John. I think you would be unwise to expect him to do it again.'

Chapter Three

Wednesday, 16th March 1938, St John's Wood, London.

Despite the ever-lengthening shadows, the early evening sun still managed to shine gently across one corner of the green outfield of 'Lord's Cricket Ground'. Professor Pym, who was staring from his window into the growing twilight, was of medium height and build and was wearing a tweed jacket and corduroy trousers - the classic uniform of an off duty don. Squinting out into the last of the sunshine, he found it easy to remember the many happy hours he had spent on the benches in front of the Pavilion which loomed in all its grandeur to the right of his apartment block. He had never regretted keeping on his mansion flat in St John's Wood after inheriting it from a distant uncle who had died in 1921, while in Colonial Service in India. It had served both as his frequent bolt-hole from his professional life as Professor of German History at Oxford University and as his residence of choice, during both the cricket season and his frequent study trips to the capital. The insistent ring of his telephone rid his head immediately of fond visions of Hutton, Washbrook and Hammond and, having placed the receiver to his ear, he heard the calm voice of the building concierge announcing that his guest had arrived. 'Show him right up, if you please, Mason,' he replied politely.

Taking one more look around the room, Pym caught sight of the game pie which had been prepared by his faithful housekeeper. This prompted a sudden pang of hunger which he deflected by decanting the bottle of 1925 *Lafite*, its rich, fruity bouquet wafting invitingly into the air. The most discreet of knocks told him that his guest had arrived and he opened the door with a broad smile. 'Quex, it's good to see you. Come in and sit down,' said the slightly younger-looking host, as both men shook hands with real affection.

Sir Hugh 'Quex' Sinclair, Chief of the British Secret Intelligence Service, smiled at the man with whom he had served for two years of the Great War on HMS *Renown*. During their service together, Sinclair, a professional Royal Navy man, had been impressed with the younger academic's grasp, both of naval strategy and of man management on-board a battle cruiser in wartime. They had remained close friends and colleagues and had together watched with appalled fascination Hitler's rise to power.

'The latest word is that Hitler has definitely made up his mind to annexe Austria, possibly as soon as this month,' Sinclair said, as he gratefully received both his first glass of the *Lafite* and a hearty slice of the game pie.

'And his popularity at home is likely to soar,' Pym added with a heavy sigh. 'The reoccupation of the Rhineland was bad enough, but this is likely to whet his appetite for even more. Just how far will Chamberlain allow himself to be pushed? Does Hitler really have what amounts to a free hand to do what he will? I'm increasingly concerned that if we want to make sure that Britain's interests are fully protected, we're going to have to act sooner rather than later.'

'Well,' Sinclair replied carefully, 'given Chamberlain's obsession with sound finance, even in the current circumstances, we certainly won't be able to rely on him to expand the SIS adequately. Also, let's not forget my deep suspicion that all is not watertight with that organisation. I'm doing what I can to root out any bad apples, but it's a deuced slow and sensitive business. All things considered, I think that we have to give some serious thought to our 'irregular' concept. Do you agree, Bernard?' Sensing his friend's discomfort, Sinclair gave him some thinking time by ostentatiously enjoying the bouquet of the wine.

At last, Pym was ready to respond. 'We both know that Chamberlain is most likely to deepen the policy of appeasement to Hitler. Also, we are agreed that this is based on a total misreading of the Führer's intentions and character. And we must not forget that the PM is desperate to avoid the cost of full rearmament, which a more realistic appraisal of Hitler must inevitably involve. So, yes, I think maybe we have to take our idea a stage further, otherwise it may soon be too late.'

Sinclair sat upright in his chair, as if to emphasise his next point. 'The information MI5 is receiving regularly from Putlitz at the German Embassy is unequivocal – we must stand up to Hitler, otherwise we will face a Europe dominated by Fascism. I really don't understand the reluctance of the Government to recognise the value of the information which our agents are continuing to supply. Do they actually believe that these people simply make something up out of self-interest, if there's nothing genuine to report?' He shook his head in sad bewilderment, as if in hope of contradiction by his old friend.

'I'm afraid you're right,' said Pym sourly, endorsing his friend's opinion. 'Chamberlain has always been more prepared to take risks with defence than with finances. So, we develop our plan and I attempt to recruit a principal for our mission?'

'Yes. But remember, this is emphatically not an official operation. Your man must be made aware of that before he commits. How long do you think you will need to recruit?'

Pym responded quickly to his friend's serious expression. 'It's early days, Quex. I have a few initial ideas and, all being well, I think I'll be ready to approach my target in a month or two.'

'So you already have someone in mind, Bernard?' asked Sinclair hopefully. 'Oh yes', Pym replied to his friend's anxious question. 'In many ways I wish I didn't. But I think I may have the perfect man for the job.'

Chapter Four

Tuesday, May 17th 1938, The Universities Club, London.

The cement bas-relief of Sir Isaac Newton gazed down as if in judgement on John King, as he made his way down the steps from the front door and across the entrance hall of the Oxford and Cambridge Universities Club. As an Oxford man, and having taken advantage of the Club's facilities on more than one occasion, King had a reasonable idea of its layout. Once past the doorman, he crossed the Staircase Hall and from there, bounded up the main dogleg stairs towards the Committee Room and his scheduled appointment.

Since receiving the Professor's message, King had tried to guess the purpose of the meeting. After all, the world of academic history was sufficiently small to ensure that he and Pym met regularly at conferences. Moreover, the Professor, a long standing member of the MCC, had already invited him to attend a day of that year's Lord's Test Match. To receive such an urgent request and to be entreated not to mention it to any of his family, friends or colleagues was quite out of the ordinary.

King's knock on the door was answered immediately by a genuinely warm invitation to 'Come in, John,' and he briskly entered the room, a broad smile lighting up his face. The sole occupant carefully placed his favourite pipe on the table and leapt to his feet, hand outstretched in greeting.

'John! It's very good to see you again. How are you? Thanks for coming. I've arranged for us to have sole use of this room to ensure that we'll not be disturbed.' King immediately felt his hand taken in the still familiar paw-like grasp of Professor Pym, his old university tutor and mentor. The younger man was very happy to note that, unlike so many men well into middle age, it seemed to him that Pym had lost none of his vigour. Neither had he lost much of his hair, though it was now a steely grey and his eyes twinkled with joy at the sight of one of his star students.

'I'm fine, sir. Thank you. And I must say you look in the pink. It was a bit of a surprise to receive your summons last week. I expected to see you again for our annual day at the cricket – we'd agreed the

Saturday of the Second Test hadn't we?'

A smile of regret passed briefly over the Professor's face, as if in his mind's eye he could see England taking on the West Indies at his beloved Lord's. However, he quickly returned to business. 'That's right, John. But something rather urgent has come up. Anyway, please tell me how things are up in Durham and what are you working on at the moment?'

'All's very well in Durham, thank you, sir and I did as you asked and told none of my colleagues of our meeting.'

'Thank you, John. I know it may sound somewhat melodramatic, but it was an essential precaution,' said Pym quickly. 'But I interrupt…. Are you still interested in the Second *Reich*? I seem to remember an excellent piece you had on 'The Kaiser after Bismarck'; *The English Historical Review*, wasn't it?'

'Yes it was and indeed I still have that major interest,' replied King with the undisguised enthusiasm of a scholar who relishes nothing so much as a discussion on his favourite research topic. Having answered the Professor politely, however, King fixed him with a confused look before continuing sharply. 'But hang it all, sir, and with all respect, there must be some other motive for our meeting now, apart from offering me a cup of tea, that is'.

As soon as he had asked the older man directly about the purpose of the meeting, King immediately felt better. He had heard on the academic grapevine that a new post was being created in the History Department at Oxford University and he was concerned that Pym wanted to sound out his interest in it. In fact, unlike the certain response of almost all his contemporaries, his interest in the possibility of a position at Oxford was non-existent. Over the past three years, he had settled very well into his life in Durham, where he was viewed as a hard-working and popular member of staff, of whom great things were expected. Indeed, he was rather unusual in that he was a gifted academic, but totally without any sense of separateness from ordinary people. He was just as happy discussing Newcastle United with his college janitor, as he was debating some arcane academic point with a colleague. King's ease of manner and innate sociability, not to mention his tall, sporty physique and his pleasant and open face, ensured that he was very popular with the ladies. This was not, however, to suggest that he was a ladies' man; his almost complete lack of any awareness of his attractiveness to women served only to draw them even more to him. Indeed, in certain circles in Durham he was regarded as something of a catch and, whilst not lacking female company, he was very content with his current status as single and a member of Durham University.

Pym smiled enigmatically at the younger man, 'You always were very perceptive, John. And, yes, I do have a specific reason for asking you to meet me here.' As the Professor busied himself with pouring the tea, he began once more to question the fairness of involving King in the proposed mission. A lifelong bachelor, Pym had never had the pleasure of being a father. He did, however, permit himself to take an almost paternal interest in the progress and development of one or two of his ex-students, including King. In some ways, he reflected, John King had not changed since his arrival in Oxford a decade earlier as a callow eighteen year old. He could still be unnervingly naïve and his spirit was arguably far too Corinthian for the modern world of the Thirties. But he was also very perceptive, a rational thinker and analyst and not without courage. It was his recognition of King as perhaps too generous of spirit that led Pym to begin the conversation in a rather uncharacteristically hesitant way. 'Tell me John,' he asked gently, 'I wonder if you'd share with me your general views on the rise of Fascism and of Hitler?

Of all the questions that he had expected to hear, for King this was way down the list of likely contenders and he was, consequently, rather taken aback. Quickly realising that he may have taken two plus two and made five, with his theory about the Oxford post, King noticeably relaxed. It did not, after all, look as if he would have to decline politely any overture from Pym about that.

'That's actually an interesting question for me, sir. The 'Second Empire' remains my principal area of study, but I have to say that I'm becoming increasingly interested in the contemporary history of Germany. I've been giving much thought to my experience in Heidelberg in '32-33, the recent *Anschluss* and the situation in Czechoslovakia. I've concluded that Fascism in general and Nazism in particular are the greatest extant threats to the maintenance of peace and I'd also argue that we need fully to understand them in order to be able to resist them.'

'I think I'd agree with every word of that, John,' interrupted Pym with enthusiasm. 'Tell me then, what do you think of the political prospects for Europe over the next couple of years?'

'Well, sir, it's very hard to believe that Hitler will be satisfied by his reoccupation of the Rhineland in '36 and his more recent gobbling up of Austria. It beggars belief that the British and French didn't send him packing when his troops crossed the Rhine! Neither was I surprised at the invasion of Austria, as my friends there had been telling me for some time that the Austro-German Agreement was designed to effect both the release of Nazis from Austrian jails and the inclusion of National Socialists in Schuschnigg's Cabinet. In return, of course, Hitler was to have supported Austrian sovereignty. But the events of the past few weeks have shown what value the assurances of the Führer are worth! Anyone with even the vaguest appreciation of Hitler's writing would know that it's eventually to the East that he'll turn to seize the *Lebensraum* he requires for his 'Third *Reich*."

The ancient grandfather clock ticked quietly in the background as Pym poured another cup of tea for himself and his guest. After a moment's pause he asked sharply, 'So you don't think that Herr Hitler will be satisfied by his latest conquests, John?'

King found it difficult to reconcile the turmoil and danger, which he could see beginning to envelope Europe, with the calm, unchanging atmosphere in the Club. 'I'm afraid not, sir. We already know that the Czechs are fortifying their borders with Germany and that the opposing *Sudeten* Germans are part funded from Berlin and getting stronger by the month. In my view, it's highly likely that Hitler will want, as an absolute minimum, the incorporation of the *Sudeten* Germans into his *Reich*. Of course, he might also want the total destruction of Czechoslovakia as a sovereign state to provide space, resources and manpower for his expanding empire.' King paused to sip his tea, before continuing, 'From there, anything's possible. Poland is ripe for conquest and the Germans are clearly building up army, navy and air-force strength. To believe these are for defensive purposes only is ludicrous.'

'You paint a very gloomy picture, John,' observed Pym archly. 'Do you really believe this will happen?'

'Not will, sir. But most definitely could,' responded King with eager emphasis. 'A key factor, of course, will be the attitude adopted by ourselves and the French. If Britain and France stand firm and call his bluff when he next moves to acquire territory, we could yet face him down. Sadly, I fear that this is not at all likely... now were Churchill to become PM....' King left this thought hanging between them, before reaching his conclusion. 'Neither France, nor Britain seems in any way ready to oppose Hitler; America is clearly uninterested and while Stalin is waiting to advance westwards, given half an opportunity, there is sufficient territory to be shared with Germany to prevent immediate conflict. When we also recognise that the League of Nations is ineffectual, it leaves a very bleak picture which suggests to me the inevitability either of war with Germany, or of a morally base peace.'

'You say a 'morally base peace', John.... Surely the people of Britain and France wouldn't wish to revisit The Great War, or something likely to be even worse. Is peace not the desired outcome?'

'Of course peace is desirable, sir. But is it so at any cost? Things were becoming grim when I left Heidelberg in '33. But consider more recent events. Look at Hitler's introduction of conscription and massive rearmament. Look at the Nuremberg Race Laws and the tightening of his racist policies. Look at the so-called labour camps, into which anyone who disagrees with Hitler is consigned, many to a painful existence or even death. Can we really have an honourable peace with such a madman?' King looked deep into the eyes of his mentor and was pleased to see a fire burning there, every bit as determined as that in his own.

'I can't disagree with any of your analysis, John. Indeed, I would go further and say that, undoubtedly war is coming.' Pym's habitual smile and light-hearted demeanour had all but vanished from his face as he fiddled thoughtfully with his pipe. 'I think, John, it's high time that I told you a little bit about my, how shall I put it.... non-academic work.'

****

High grey clouds covered the sun when King, having emerged onto Pall Mall from the Universities Club, headed towards Trafalgar Square. His original plan had been to go straight to the nearest Tube station after the meeting, get to Kings Cross as quickly as possible and to catch the first train back to Durham. However, what Pym had said to him in the previous two hours had left his head spinning. He needed time and peace to think through the extraordinary proposal that his old mentor had made. Despite his lack of any real religious conviction, King decided that he should gather his thoughts in the relative calm and anonymity of St Martin-in-the-Fields. He made his way along the edge of Trafalgar Square, passing in front of the National Gallery and taking a quick glance at Nelson atop his column. Thanks to its Georgian design, the interior of the church was bright and welcoming, even on what was becoming an increasingly dull afternoon. King was grateful that there were very few other visitors at this time of the day and he sidled into one of the dark brown pews to reflect on the events which instinctively he felt could change his life forever.

Pym had, in fact, taken the best part of an hour to explain to King the 'little bit' about his 'non-academic work.' He had begun by informing King that anything further that was said that afternoon should be regarded as falling under The Official Secrets Act and had obtained the younger man's formal acceptance of that condition. He had then outlined how he had served as a consultant to the Secret Intelligence Service on German issues since 1918, a revelation that had fully captured King's interest

'Well, John, I think we're both agreed that war with Germany is inevitable.' King had nodded his head without hesitation as the older man continued. 'Given that this is the case, I'm sure that you'd also agree that we must take every step to hinder German activities, insofar as they threaten Britain and her security.'

'Of course,' King had replied. 'That goes without saying.'

'What I'm going to propose speaks exactly to that goal,' Pym had said with an enigmatic smile. 'Tell me, John, do you know anything about Nazi sympathisers in Britain?'

King had met his mentor's gaze as he had replied, 'Well, of course I am aware of the British Union of Fascists which had a pretty respectable vote in the London County Council Elections last month, around 8000 votes if I remember rightly.'

'Yes,' Pym had interjected, 'but thankfully none of their candidates was elected to office.'

'Then there are surely whole sections of the British aristocracy, from the Duke of Windsor down, which are very sympathetic to Hitler. Let's not forget that he and Wallace Simpson left Britain for Germany on a Nazi ship last December – a great propaganda coup for Goebbels.' King had paused a little to consider his next suggestion, before continuing confidently. 'Then there are sections of the press which are supportive of both British and German Fascism. Rothermere fawned over Hitler in '34 and his *Daily Mail* has supported the BUF ever since. In addition, many in academic life have pacifist tendencies, so may simply want to leave the Nazis alone and be left alone by them.'

It had been clear that King had by no means finished his exposition, when Pym had interrupted with a question. 'Would it surprise you, John, that we estimate the number of active sympathisers - not pacifist appeasers you understand, but those who are positively enthusiastic about Hitler and Fascism - runs into tens of thousands in Britain today?'

King had recoiled in shock. 'Surely that can't be true, sir. That must be an exaggeration.'

'Not at all,' Pym had replied gravely. 'In fact, I'm afraid that the real number could be far higher than that. Now, of course not all such sympathisers would be active in furthering Germany's interests. They may well remain passive supporters.... but a fair proportion will not.'

'But in the event of war, which we both feel is inevitable, that could be absolutely catastrophic,' King had said quietly, almost to himself.

'Yes it could be, John. Unless we put plans in place to neutralise, or better still, to make use of such people, as and when necessary. Of course, plans have been drawn up in the event of war to interview and classify foreign nationals, especially Germans and Austrians. Those deemed a risk would be interned... but I am talking about Fascist sympathisers who are British.'

King had studied the older man thoughtfully, before beginning to argue, 'Then, surely we'd have to do the same thing with them...'

'Well,' Pym had countered quickly, 'consider this argument,

John. If we round up significant numbers of Nazi sympathisers and intern them, then in all likelihood those remaining would be driven further underground to maintain the flow of information to Germany. They'd then be even harder to track down. What if, instead, we decided to leave them in place and run them ourselves....' This is the crunch, Pym had thought to himself, either he'll see it, or he'll miss the point.

It hadn't taken long before the Professor could afford himself a smile as his *protégé*, almost thinking aloud, had said, 'You mean they think they're sending sensitive and valuable information to Germany, but all the time they're simply giving it to us?' King had rubbed his chin, while evaluating the proposed plan. 'It's elegant, enables us to control and direct the flow of information and, at the same time, identify where sensitive leaks are appearing. But the Nazi sympathisers would believe that they're doing their bit for the Third *Reich*. It's a brilliant scheme, sir. But what's it got to do with me?'

'Before I answer that, John, consider also that if our man wins the trust and obedience of the people he is running, we may actually get leads to authentic German agents who are operating in Britain. This could be a key element of our counter espionage strategy both in the run up to the war and after war is declared.' Pym had sat back in his chair and watched King's face, as it had revealed his dawning realisation of the potential scope and value of this operation. Finally, after having filled his pipe once more and enjoyed the first puffs of his favourite tobacco, Pym had put the crucial question, up to which this whole discussion had been leading. 'How would you like to be the person both to run these Nazi sympathisers for us and perhaps even root out enemy agents?'

Having seen the look of total disbelief on King's face, the older man had hastily continued. 'Before you say anything, John, just hear me out, please.' An astonished King had given a barely perceptible nod of consent and Pym had continued. 'You will agree that we need someone who can present himself to potential informants as to all intents and purposes German...as bilingual and as someone who understands German culture and mores, especially those of the Nazis. You most assuredly fit perfectly this part of the bill. At the same time, you'd raise no suspicions among more loyal sections of the population, a great advantage for any German agent, real or fictitious. We need someone who is not emotionally or privately involved and who can go undercover without causing too much of a stir. I hope you will forgive me John, but I did commission a full review of your private life before approaching you.'

As King made to interrupt, the older man, fearing that he was about to object strongly to this invasion of his privacy, prepared for the worst. 'Hang on a minute, sir,' said King, his hand raised in emphasis. 'I haven't spent any significant time in Germany since '33 and a lot has changed since then. Yes, I have a few academic colleagues and friends there, but getting periodic letters from them and following the news is not the same thing as witnessing Nazism at first hand.'

Relieved at the nature of King's objection, Pym asked thoughtfully, 'You make a good point, John. What, then, would you suggest?'

'Well, that really depends on your projected timescale, sir. I believe that, ideally, I'd need to live and work in Germany for some months to prepare for this task,'

'Hmm. Yes, I can see how that might be necessary and also might work well,' replied Pym carefully. 'As an academic, you could easily take a sabbatical in Germany for 'research purposes,' without causing suspicion or raising questions among your colleagues, neighbours or friends. You could use this time to try to find out as much as possible about how the German security services operate. I'll give some thought as to how this might be facilitated. But, John, if you do take this on, you must recognise fully that, once your mission begins in Britain, you would be operating under an assumed name and, as far as all your friends and family are concerned, John King would be dead.'

Pym had noted with concern the shock this brought to his erstwhile student's face. 'Are you really sure that's necessary, sir? Surely parents could be told...'

'It's absolutely necessary!' Pym had interrupted harshly. 'There can be no exceptions at all. But, please, allow me to finish. You're young and fit and we could easily teach you all other aspects of your tradecraft.' Despite his slight concerns about his mental toughness, Pym had concluded his argument decisively. 'Surely you can see, John, how you look to be a perfect match for our requirements...?'

King had shifted uneasily in his chair. He had clearly not agreed with his friend and mentor, but was struggling to explain his reasoning. 'I can accept the logic of your argument, sir. But, dash it all, what I don't understand is that there surely must be a professional SIS operative who fits the bill every bit as well as I and who would have the advantage of being fully trained in such operations already.'

'You are, as ever, to the point and correct, John,' had come the flattering reply. 'But there is one final fact that I haven't told you, which I'm sure will alter your view. You see, we strongly suspect that SIS has been penetrated by The *Abwehr*. This is not definite, but in these circumstances, we have no option but to operate on the assumption that it is true. So you see, this operation will have to be 'off the record' and not part of the general work of SIS.'

'What would that mean, exactly, sir?'

'I can't dissemble, John. It will mean that, apart from myself, only one other person, a retired SIS operative, will be involved fully in the operation. This person will be responsible for your training in tradecraft and when that's complete, he will initially act as contact between the two of us.' Pym had been studying King's reactions to these revelations, especially for any signs of fear. While he had noticed evidence of concern that he was up to such a task, he had not seen any indication that the younger man was scared to take on the mission. Taking heart from this, the Professor had continued, 'You'll be alone, my boy. Your family will believe you to be dead. You'll be working closely with enemies of Britain, but as far as the forces of law and order and the secret services in Britain are concerned, you too would be an enemy of the state. If things were to go badly wrong, you could find yourself being pursued both by the British and by authentic German agents. However, in discussing this with you I'm speaking with the full authority of Sir Hugh Sinclair, Head of SIS. I know it's a heavy burden that I'm asking you to take up. But I honestly believe that it's vital to keep a very close eye on the enemy within, in order that we may be able to neutralise any threat both before and after war comes.' Pym had been well aware that, were his proposal to be declined by King, now was the most likely time that this would have happened. He had sighed heavily as he had removed his reading glasses to clean them with his handkerchief, unable to do anything more than await the decision of his chosen candidate.

****

King was abruptly brought from his reflections on the conversation with Pym and returned to the present by the busy preparations being made all around him for the regular 5PM Evensong. He politely declined the order of service and hymn book which were offered to him and, with a smile at the young curate, slid out of the pew and made his way to the main entrance of the church. After experiencing such a summersault in his own life, King was somehow shocked that the world seemed to be carrying on exactly as normal. The rush hour traffic was clearly building up around Trafalgar Square and, putting his hand into his jacket pocket, he felt the piece of paper with the address of the hotel arranged by Pym. The older man had insisted that King should take the evening in order to think things over and that they meet again the next day.

****

King did not enjoy the most restful of sleeps in the far from luxurious hotel. He had turned over and over in his mind the arguments which the Professor had deployed to convince him that he was the right man for this particular task. He had also found the time to laugh at his own notion that Pym had wanted to test the waters, with regard to a post at Oxford. My God, he had thought with no little irony, would that the conversation had been as easy to deal with as that would've been! In truth, King was not convinced, either that he was up to the job, or that he was actually prepared for the sacrifices that it would entail. It was not, he instinctively knew, because he was frightened of the degree of risk involved; like most men in their late twenties, he tended to see himself as indestructible and any associated danger constituted more of an attraction than a reason to decline the proposal. Neither was he unprepared to give up his life at the University in Durham. He was very happy there, enjoyed teaching his students and had a wide circle of interesting and committed friends. But he was also sufficiently aware that, in times of crisis, people had to make sacrifices.

As he lay in bed, analysing the situation, he came to the conclusion that his concerns were partly about his suitability for the job.

Most important of all, however, were the possible effects on his parents. He was fairly certain that, in his shoes, his father would understand the call of duty and would put the interests of the nation before his own or even his family's. On the other hand, the effect on his mother of faking his own death was not something that he cared to have on his conscience and he resolved to discuss this more fully with Pym at their meeting the next day.

****

Unsurprisingly, given his state of agitation, King arrived early for his appointment with Pym in St James's Park. He sat with his back to the Bandstand, gazing over the Blue Bridge and watching the succession of office workers and government bureaucrats as they made their way towards the Treasury and Foreign Office buildings. On such a glorious Spring morning, with the sun reflecting on the water and the ducks making their noisy circuits of the lake, King half believed that the events of the previous twenty-four hours were but a dream. However, the purposeful approach of Pym from the direction of Buckingham Palace served as sufficient reminder of the reality of the situation in which he now found himself.

'Good morning, John,' Pym greeted the younger man warmly, before asking sympathetically, 'I don't suppose you slept so well last night, my boy?'

King smiled thinly, 'Not really, sir. I must admit that I've had more restful sleeps!'

Pym went on to reassure King that such a reaction was perfectly normal. 'In fact,' he said decisively, 'had you immediately said yes to this proposal, I would've had serious doubts as to whether you were the right chap for the job.'

'But that's exactly my concern, sir,' the younger man said miserably. 'It's not that I'm in a funk about it, though of course I recognise the potential dangers. It's more that I'm worried that I don't have what it takes to succeed in the mission and I'm very concerned about the effect that faking my death might have on my family, especially my mother.'

Pym shuffled uncomfortably on the bench and gazed silently towards the Royal residence. Eventually he turned to the younger man and spoke with great sincerity. 'I understand your position, John. For myself, I debated long and hard the fairness of asking you to carry this burden. You know that I've always taken a keen interest in your career and your welfare. Believe me, I wouldn't be asking you to consider this proposal unless I was certain that you could carry it out successfully, that you're by far the best man for the job and that the job is essential to the interests of Great Britain. As to the issue with your family, that unfortunately is part of the deal. We couldn't compromise on that at all. I'm sorry, John. But there it is.'

Deep in thought, King nodded his head slowly before turning to his old mentor and asking quietly, 'How soon do you need a decision, sir? How long do I have to think about it?'

Pym looked even more in pain, as he replied sadly, 'Not long at all, John. We need a decision pretty quickly, because if you turn us down we'll have to start our search for a likely candidate all over again.'

'I see,' replied King gravely. 'Then I'd better give you my answer now, sir. No point in prevaricating.' Pym tensed as he waited for the younger man's decision, all kinds of thoughts swirling through his mind. Part of him would certainly be relieved, should the invitation be declined, but he despaired of having to find someone as suitable and who he would trust as implicitly as he trusted this man. Eventually King continued, 'I've given this sufficient consideration, sir and I'm keen to accept your proposal. I'm aware of the certain, likely and possible consequences of this decision, but my mind is quite made up. I can make myself available at your convenience.'

Pym's face flushed with pride and gratitude and his eyes had a certain moisture about them as he shook King's hand. 'I'm delighted, my boy. Your country is grateful to you, even though it may not yet realise it.'

Chapter Five

Monday, September 12th 1938, Kent, England.

The months following the decisive meeting at the Pall Mall club had passed for King in a welter of meetings, briefings and planning. Only now, sitting on the *Golden Arrow* train, as it sped from London to Dover, was he able to reflect a little on the process by which his old life had been sloughed off like a dead skin.

Once the plan for him to spend up to a whole academic year in Berlin had been agreed, things had gone relatively smoothly at Durham University. This was undoubtedly eased in no small measure by Pym having provided sufficient funds to enable King to request a year's study leave in Germany. As the available grant could more than cover the cost of a replacement for King's hardly onerous teaching duties, his Head of Department had had little reason not to approve the application. With the assistance of a highly placed colleague at the Board of Education, King had been placed at the top of a list of British nominations for an academic exchange with Germany. As this scheme had been devised in order to promote better mutual understanding between Great Britain and Germany, his proposal to produce an analysis of 'Mutual Security and How to Achieve It' was very much welcomed by the German officials. In fact, King had been offered Visiting Research Fellow status at Berlin University and could look forward to some limited official support in his work. When he had met with King to discuss the cover story for his presence in Germany, Pym had enthused, 'This has worked out extremely well. Indeed, your project and your status in Berlin may well afford you some opportunity to find out at first-hand how their security and espionage organisations are structured and operated.'

Embarkation at Dover was a typically lengthy, but nevertheless straightforward process and it was a beautiful September day as SS *Canterbury* steamed sedately across a very calm Channel. Leaning on the ship's rail and looking back on the white cliffs as they faded and then finally disappeared in the emerging sea haze, King felt a first pang of homesickness. The ferry was fairly busy, with a mixture of various European nationalities en-route home and British couples off to France for a late holiday, buoyed no doubt by the Prime Minister's recent promise of 'peace in our time.'

It scarcely seemed possible to King that it was just over a week before that he had been enjoying several days at home with his parents at their fine residence in the Gloucestershire countryside. After a distinguished military career, Henry King had succeeded in reinventing himself as a country solicitor and pillar of the local Amateur Dramatic Society, while Amanda still taught part time at the local primary school. King was immensely proud of his parents, whom he loved and respected deeply as fundamentally good and decent people. They had been undemanding and essentially tolerant in raising both him and his sister, encouraging them both, without favour, in their respective life and career choices. Indeed, King often reflected that he undoubtedly owed his love of study, of history and of ideas to both his parents, who, in equal measure, had encouraged him first to go up to Oxford and later to choose an academic career.

On his first evening at home and over a fine dinner of roast beef, Amanda King had enjoyed relaying the latest family news. 'Cordelia is blissfully happy,' she had gushed, 'and George simply dotes on his sons.' King had immediately felt a brief stab of guilt that he had not made more effort to see his sister and her husband before he would leave for Germany. After all, Portsmouth was not so far away and George had been enjoying a couple of weeks leave, while his command, HMS *Sheffield*, was enjoying a minor refit in the Naval Dockyards there.

'Oh and we had a lovely letter from Rachel. She says she's very settled in New York and still loves her apartment and her teaching post at Columbia.' King had remembered with great pride and love how his parents had, without hesitation, taken in Rachel and David Bernstein after they left Germany in the winter of 1933-4. 'And young David is in the last year of his police training in Lancashire. Such a lovely and gentle young man, I do wonder sometimes if police work is quite right for him.'

'Nonsense, my dear!' King's father had interrupted in a not unkindly way. 'It's one of my greatest pleasures that, in some small way, I could help him achieve his career goal. He's just the sort of sensible and intelligent chap that we need in the forces of law and order.'

He had not discussed the European political situation with his father until his final evening at home. Then, after dinner and over brandy and cigars on the terrace, King had asked his views on the Prime Minister's recent visit to Hitler's *Berghof* mountain retreat in

Berchtesgaden. In response, Henry had simply snorted with derision. 'The man's a disgrace to his office. If the French and we abandon the Czechs, we'll hand Hitler an enormous propaganda coup, which would dwarf the significance of his reoccupation of the Rhineland. If we don't stand up to him now, he'll demand more and more concessions until he has hegemony over all of continental Europe.'

In many ways, after dinner was King's favourite time of the day. He loved listening to all the nocturnal shuffling and hooting, which replaced the merry birdsong of the day and he enjoyed the various garden scents, which became more pronounced as the dew settled. Gazing out over the garden, as dusk finally gave way to night, King had tried to imagine the inner battle his father must have fought to come to this conclusion. In common with the overwhelming majority of his contemporaries, who had survived the horrors of four years on the Western Front, his father had always demonstrated an iron willed determination that no generation should be sacrificed in the same way as his own.

'You really think it's that bad, Pa?' In answer, King's father had fixed him with a sad smile. 'I'm afraid so, John. God knows I had hoped that you and your contemporaries would be spared after The Great War, but we have to face facts. Spain has clearly been a test bed for the Wehrmacht and the Luftwaffe and our serial capitulation in the face of Hitler's demands simply empowers and emboldens him. It certainly does not, and never will, satisfy him.'

'You're absolutely right, Pa. Chamberlain, with his scurrying around, is only postponing the inevitable. Giving Hitler more time to strengthen himself is pure madness. We should take him on now, not let him decide when he's ready to take us on.'

On hearing this, King's father had shifted uneasily, as if unwilling to ask the obvious question that had been troubling him, since he had learned of his son's plans to stay in Berlin. At last, he had been unable to hold back any longer and asked with real exasperation, 'Then why on earth are you about to take part in this 'academic exchange' of yours? You must surely realise that the Nazis will simply want to use you, a visiting British academic, as a propaganda tool?'

As the two men had stood, side by side in the increasing gloom, enjoying their cigars and one another's company for what King had feared might be the last time in years, he had felt a real urge to confide in his father the true nature of his business in Germany. However, on this point Pym had been absolutely firm. 'Under no circumstances whatsoever, should you give even the vaguest hint of your true purpose in going to Germany,' he had said with all his authority. 'However strong the temptation may be to explain; you may not do so.'

King had not consciously intended to communicate anything of his mission but, having held his father's gaze for a full minute, he had finally replied. 'I know that's a real danger, Pa, and you're not the first person to have pointed that out to me. Believe me, a couple of my friends've been rather more blunt in their comments. But on this question, I must ask you to trust me. I do believe that my visit there may serve those causes and interests that we both hold most dear.'

There had been something in his son's expression and tone that had dissuaded Henry from pursuing the matter further. Indeed, the briefest of nods from the older man had been all the confirmation King had required to know that some important message had passed between them.

King had planned to leave after breakfast on the following morning and he was delighted when he drew back the curtains of his bedroom and saw the sun shining brightly on the contrasting greens of the lawn and the huge oak tree, standing sentinel at the bottom of the garden. It had been a perfect day to pull back the soft top and put his beloved MG through its paces along the country lanes on its final circuitous route back to Durham. His mother, naturally, had been a little tearful as he had taken his leave, but there had been something in the firmness of his father's handshake and his knowing smile that had reinforced their unspoken communication of the previous evening.

****

The formalities at Calais took somewhat longer than King had envisaged and it was a relief when he found himself comfortably seated by a picture window in a quiet compartment of the fast train to Paris. The fields and villages of the Pas de Calais hurtled by in a hypnotic whirl and, exhausted by the tensions of the previous days, he soon fell into a deep sleep. A little more than an hour after the train had left Calais the call for the first sitting in the dining car was issued and King, roused from his sleep, rapidly became aware that he had not eaten since his final London breakfast meeting with Pym. Without delay, he made his way to the Dining Car, where a waiter in a starched white jacket showed him to a small table for two on the left side of the carriage. The silver cutlery and crystal glassware glinted invitingly in the light of the small chandeliers which were hanging from the carriage ceiling. The crisp white linen of the table cloths and the rich velvet curtains at each window completed the impression of a long narrow drawing room, incongruously moving at speed through northern France. The Dining Car became pleasantly busy during the course of his meal, but while he enjoyed the babble of several languages, he was also happy that no one came to sit at his table. His hunger satisfied, he made his way back to his carriage seat stopping only for a brief cigarillo in the corridor.

****

At last, the train rumbled into the Gare Du Nord in Paris, accompanied by clouds of steam and a series of ear shredding squeaks. Bang on time, King reflected happily. I should be at my hotel by eight at the latest. His reservation was at the classically elegant Hotel Lancaster on the Rue de Berri, just one hundred metres from the Champs-Élysées itself. With luck, he thought as he cheerfully waited for a taxi to take him to his hotel, I may even get a room with a view of the Eiffel Tower. This was not to be, however, and King smiled ruefully as the Chief Desk Clerk *'avec beaucoup de régret'* was only able to provide a room on the fourth floor, which 'enjoyed' a view into the inner court of the hotel. After quickly unpacking what little was required for an overnight stay, he returned to the Reception Desk to enquire about suitable music clubs to visit. 'My preference would be for jazz. Do you have any recommendations?'

'Ah, Monsieur! Vous aimez le jazz?' the Chief Desk Clerk sounded pleased and distraught in equal measure. *'Mais, Monsieur,* had I but known this, you would certainly have been offered a room with a view of the Tour Eiffel! *Je suis désolé!* But I will make this up to you. You must go to 'La Grosse Pomme' in Rue Pigalle. Tonight the Quintette du Hot Club de France is playing with Grappelli and Rheinhardt. And there is something else very special about tonight. But that will be my secret for now. Tell the doorman there that Henri at Hotel Lancaster has

recommended the club to you and they will look after you.' King was astonished by the transformation of this formal hotel functionary into a smiling jazz enthusiast and he liked what he saw. 'That's perfect, Henri. Thank you very much.'

King calculated that, given a brisk pace, he could walk from his hotel to the club in half an hour. As it was barely nine o'clock on a warm, early autumn evening and he did not want to arrive before ten, he decided to take a longer route and perhaps call in somewhere for a drink on his way. As he walked, he thought fondly of the new cohort of eager students who would be getting ready to leave their homes for the first time and begin the exciting journey of undergraduate study at Durham. It would be the first time for some years that he would not be joining them and doing his very best to ignite their interest in History. Having enjoyed a glass of wine in a smart little bistro, a further fifteen minutes of easy strolling in the heady Parisian evening took King to the Rue Pigalle. The last of the light had left the western sky as he eventually found the inauspicious entrance to 'La Grosse Pomme', guarded by two huge doormen. To King's surprise, dozens of people were milling about, obviously hoping to gain admission and it was with some trepidation that, in far from perfect French, he said as clearly as he could, *'Bonsoir Messieurs! Henri à l'Hotel Lancaster m'a conseillé de visiter ce club du jazz.'* To his great pleasure, King saw the faces of both doormen break immediately into huge grins. *'Vous avez de fortune, Monsieur. Il n'y a pas de place ici ce soir. Mais si vous êtes un ami d'Henri…. entrez s'il vous plait.'* King slid gratefully between the doormen, with the voices of many outraged would-be patrons ringing in his ears.

The club itself was small and extremely lively, the audience excitedly anticipating the night's entertainment. One of the shorter sides of the principal room was taken up with a stage, down the middle of which a stairway descended from the ceiling. He was very much looking forward to the performances, especially that of the American singer Adelaide Hall, for whom the club had been opened and named by her husband. As King was shown to his place at a tiny side table, positioned mid-way down the room, he saw only one other person seated there; a rather elderly man in immaculate evening dress.

'Bonsoir, Monsieur,' said King's neighbour, with a smile full of

gold teeth. *'J'espère que ce soir sera formidable.'*

'I'm sorry,' replied King, shrugging his shoulders and holding his hands up in a gesture of helplessness. 'My French is not so good.'

'Do not worry, Monsieur', replied the older man in good English. 'I was merely saying that I hope tonight will be memorable, as it is Miss Hall's farewell performance here.'

'Really?' asked King, aware now of what Henri had kept secret. 'But I thought she was very popular here?'

'Oh, she is, Monsieur, but she and her husband have sold 'La Grosse Pomme' and are planning to move to London.' King's table companion was clearly relishing his ability to impart the most current gossip and smiled conspiratorially as he continued. 'The rumour is that Miss Hall has been the subject of unwanted amorous advances from someone who claims to be of the European aristocracy. This man has apparently threatened to kill Miss Hall and himself if she does not return his feelings. *Et violà! Paris, c'est fini!*'

Before King could respond, Django Reinhardt, Stephane Grappelli and the rest of the Quintette du Hot Club de France took to the stage and began their first set of the evening. Suavely dressed in tuxedos and bow ties, the three guitarists, double bass player and violinist made music which soon had the whole room swaying and tapping their feet. As they were breaking into 'Ain't Misbehavin'', a stirring of the audience to his right drew King's attention. To his amazement, the next table which had carried a clear *'Réservée'* sign, was now being occupied by a glamourous group including Maurice Chevalier and Marlene Dietrich. Just before midnight, all the lights in the club were extinguished and the Quintette began the opening bars of 'I Can't Give You Anything But Love'. All eyes in the house were trained on the top of the stairs leading down to the stage. He would never forget the moment he first caught sight of Adelaide Hall, illuminated by a single spotlight and dressed in a fantastic costume of multi-coloured feathers and sequins, as she swayed down the steps and began to sing. Some two hours later, after much wonderful music and unforgettable cameos from Chevalier and Dietrich in honour of the final performance of Adelaide Hall, the American began to sing her finale; 'Stormy Weather.' In light of the current political situation in Europe, King could not help but reflect with sadness on the appropriateness of that farewell song.

By three in the morning the club finally managed to encourage its last patrons, including King, to leave and to make their unsteady way to their respective beds. It took him a little less than an hour to return to the Hotel Lancaster and after hastily scribbling a note of profuse thanks to Henri, which he left at the desk, King finally closed his eyes on what had been a memorable day.

Chapter Six

Tuesday, September 13th 1938, Paris, France.

A mere five hours after finally finding his way to bed, a somewhat bleary eyed King found himself alone in a First Class compartment of the *Nord Express*, as it stood steaming and hissing on platform three of the magnificent Gare de L'Est. The station had experienced a doubling in size in the early 1930s and, even in his less than wholly alert state, King had been impressed by its airy and light entrance foyer with its superb curved glass roof. As he settled in to prepare himself for the journey to Berlin, he issued a silent prayer that no one would join him in his blessedly conversation free space. The fine champagne and cognac which had flowed throughout the previous night's entertainment had not only put a dent in King's finances, but had also left him nursing a fearsome headache.

The first part of the journey was uneventful and King took the opportunity to catch up on a little sleep. He was awakened by the border police as the express entered Belgium and later, as the train waited in Brussels, he gratefully took his chance to stretch his legs on the platform. When he returned to his compartment, King was a little disappointed to see that he was no longer alone. He had been joined by a tall, slightly built, fair-haired man in his late thirties, wearing gold-rimmed spectacles, dressed in civilian clothes and, he noted with distaste, a small swastika lapel badge in his suit jacket. The sight of the Nazi badge caused King to regret that he had allowed Professor Pym to reserve him a seat in a First Class compartment. I bet one gets a better class of passenger in Second, he reflected ruefully.

The two men nodded politely but, to King's relief, they did not exchange words as the train steamed grandly out of Brussels. The nearer he came to entering Hitler's *Reich*, the more King began to feel a mixture of excitement and tension. On the one hand, he was repulsed by everything that the Nazis believed and practised, especially the cynical racism, casual violence and overbearing militarism. On the other hand, in some ways he was looking forward to experiencing Berlin at first hand and felt a grim determination to use his time there productively and wisely.

'What is the purpose of your visit to the *Reich*?' demanded the officious-looking German border guard, as he peered suspiciously through his thick-lensed glasses at King's passport.

'I'm here by invitation to participate in an academic exchange,' replied the Englishman brightly and in perfect German. 'Here are my official invitation and my credentials from the appropriate Ministry of the *Reich*.' King smiled as the official, having read his papers, stiffened and saluted.

'Thank you, sir. I hope that you have an interesting and educational time in Germany. Heil Hitler!' The guard took the briefest of glimpses at the identification documents which were proffered by King's travel companion, before handing them back and exiting the compartment with such speed, that it seemed he feared contamination.

'So, Herr...?' asked the German, making it clear that he wanted to know King's name. 'You are a visiting academic, come to observe and learn from we Germans?'

Not wishing to give offence, the Englishman smiled and said noncommittally, 'It's Dr King and I'm certainly hoping to learn much about Germans and Germany while I am here.'

'Well, Herr Doktor, there is much to admire about the new German *Reich*. By the way, my name is Major Kalz and I would be pleased to offer you any assistance during your stay in Berlin. But what exactly is the purpose of your visit there?'

As soon as King explained that his work in Germany would involve issues of mutual security between Britain and Germany, he observed that Kalz demonstrated an even keener interest. He listened patiently as the Major argued that, 'Of course, there is no reason for disagreement between Great Britain and the *Reich*. It is in Britain's interests to have a strong Germany and Germany has no interest in the British Empire. We two great and related nations can coexist in peace, as your Herr Chamberlain clearly believes. The real threat, of course, comes from the East and Stalin's barbaric hordes. Surely you would agree with me Herr Doktor?'

'I can see some merit in what you say, Herr Major,' replied King evenly. 'However, I must also caution you that there are many in Great

Britain who are concerned with Germany's policy towards Czechoslovakia.'

'Pah!' snorted the German dismissively, 'you mean Churchill and the rest of his equally marginalised followers? They surely count for next to nothing in the great scheme of things. The München Agreement has settled this question of the German minority. But come, my friend, let us not argue. Let me give you some advice for your stay in Berlin.'

King was happy to allow Kalz to spend the greater part of the next hour offering advice on where to eat, what to see and what to do in Hitler's capital city. The German was also keen to learn where it was that King lived in Britain. Once it had emerged that the Major had spent some years in Britain, they were able to exchange stories and memories both of London and Oxford. The time went by unexpectedly quickly and pleasantly with his urbane fellow traveller and King was surprised to see that the train was slowing down to enter the main station at Köln.

Kalz seemed also to have been taken aback by the train's arrival and he quickly reached into his briefcase for some paper and a pen. He hastily wrote his name and telephone number, before passing the paper over to King and announcing that he had reached his destination. 'I should have liked to continue our very interesting conversation, Herr Doktor. Regrettably, however, duty takes me to Köln for a few days. So I must leave the train now. However, I should be back in Berlin by the week after next and it would please me very much if you would get in touch with me then. I would be very happy to offer you any assistance in my power, in order to help you with your work.' Kalz offered his hand and King immediately reciprocated, pondering whether such a contact would be extremely useful to his mission in Berlin, or extremely dangerous to his security there.

****

Despite his knowledge of contemporary Germany, King had to admit that he was not at all prepared for the degree of palpable triumphalism that greeted him on his arrival at the Lehrter Station in Germany's capital. Huge flags were hanging from every available point on the concourse roof and a military band played jaunty marching tunes. The *Anschluß with* Austria and now the reincorporation into the *Reich* of the *Sudetendeutsch* with its associated humbling of France and

Britain, had clearly left many Germans with feelings of pride in the seeming invincibility of their Führer.

King had a late afternoon meeting with the Administrator and a couple of the teaching staff of the History Department at the Humboldt University of Berlin, in order to collect the keys to the flat which had been arranged for his stay in the city. As he had time to spare and it was a pleasant afternoon, he decided to deposit his cases in the left luggage office and to walk to the University. His journey took him over the River Spree and down towards Königsplatz, where he saw the Siegessäule with the glittering bronze sculpture of Victoria atop its stone column. King wondered with a pang of nostalgia whether he would ever be able to return to his academic life and his interest in the military victories and their consequences, which were celebrated by this rather garish monument. Shortly after leaving the square, he took a left turn and the unmistakable Brandenburger Tor came into view. As he approached his destination, he could not help but be impressed with the grandeur of the city and the happy mood of the people who were thronging the pavements and streets. Once inside the University buildings, which occupied a central position on the fine boulevard Unter den Linden, he was disappointed by their evident Nazification. Party posters, swastikas, and photographs of the Führer adorned almost every available surface. Having introduced himself at the reception desk, King was asked to take a seat for a moment and informed that someone from the Department would be down presently to meet him. He didn't have too long to wait, as some ten minutes later a tall, attractive woman in her mid-forties came down the stairs into the reception hall and approached the still seated academic. 'Heil Hitler!' she began with a rather thin smile. 'Welcome to Berlin Herr Doktor King. I am Fräulein Müller, Administrator of the Department of History.'

'Thank you, Fräulein Müller and, please, call me John,' he replied while offering his hand and fixing her with what he hoped would be his most winning smile. The woman seemed very relieved that his answer had been in excellent German, shook his hand and indicated that he should follow her up the stairs.

'This way, please Herr Doktor, your colleagues are most anxious to meet you.' Fräulein Müller led King up to the third floor and across a bridging corridor to a building which was set behind the main administration block, through which he had entered the University. 'The History Department occupies the top three floors of this building,' explained the Administrator. 'The Departmental Office is just along this corridor on the right.'

On entering the office behind his guide, King was immediately greeted by two smiling men, both of whom offered what he now feared was the obligatory *Hitlergruß*. The first, a dapper man of medium height and build, with a shock of silver hair and furtive, weasel-like features, introduced himself as Professor Brunner. The second man was much taller and younger and, King had noted, a less than enthusiastic performer of the Hitler salute. Smiling shyly, he offered his hand and said in very good but accented English, 'Hello I am Dr Schwarz. I'm delighted to meet you.'

King immediately warmed to the younger man and began to hope that his time here might not be so lonely. After the introductions and some polite enquiries about his journey from England, Fräulein Müller gave him the keys of the centrally located and fully-furnished flat. King was touched to learn that she had even had the thoughtfulness to provide an initial supply of basic household essentials for him. Thanking the Administrator, he joked that he had brought half a suitcase of tea in his luggage. 'Ah, you English,' chided Professor Brunner, with a not altogether pleasant smile. 'Where would you be without your tea?'

'Your flat is on Ludendorffstraße, which is just over half an hour's walk from here. I hope you will find it to your satisfaction, Herr Doktor,' said Fräulein Müller with an anxious smile. 'Dr Schwarz has kindly agreed to escort you there today and to make sure that you settle in.' King smiled at Schwarz, before admitting that he was very tired and would be pleased to set off for the flat as soon as possible. Everyone agreed that this was for the best and, having agreed to meet again at 10.30 the next morning for a fuller discussion and induction, King and his colleague set off for the flat.

Schwarz seemed preoccupied during the walk and restricted himself to pointing out the most obvious and famous landmarks. After just over thirty minutes of steady walking, the two academics arrived at the entrance to number 66 Ludendorffstraße. King could clearly sense the discomfort of his young colleague and therefore made it clear that he was happy to let himself into the flat and to find his own way around it. Schwarz seemed relieved and, with a nervous smile said, 'Professor Brunner instructed me to ensure that you're settled in the flat. As it happens, I've an urgent engagement, so I'm very happy that you don't need me to do this. But please, you'll not tell the Professor of this?'

King laughed and reassured his colleague. 'Of course not. It's my wish and you're simply conforming to that. But, here, I can't go on calling you Dr Schwarz. I'm John to my friends, of which I hope you'll soon be one.'

The young German seemed very pleased and replied warmly, 'That's my hope too, John. And I'm Andreas. I look forward to seeing you tomorrow. But now, I really must go.' With a final smile of apology, he turned and walked quickly down the street.

Some thirty minutes later, a mentally and physically exhausted King finally managed to close the door on Berlin and, especially, on Frau Bauer, the indomitable *Portierfrau* of the block. He had been intercepted by the elderly, yet supremely observant woman as soon as he had, as quietly as possible, closed the front door and turned towards the stairs. After providing his older interrogator with a reasonably detailed autobiography, King had been delighted to see her eyes glaze over as soon as he responded to her question about the purpose of his stay in Berlin. He had begun to outline his role at the University only for her to cut short his explanation with an imperious wave of her short plump arm and to insist that he follow her into her *Büro*. The old woman may have seen this as a desirable work space but it was, in reality, merely a tiny, flimsily constructed cupboard, which had been placed across a corner of the spacious hallway. King could hardly fault Frau Bauer's hospitality, however, as no sooner had he squeezed himself into the office than he was offered a glass of schnapps by way of welcome. Moreover, she had insisted that a couple of the younger residents would bring his suitcases from the station, 'if you would be so kind as to give me the receipts for them.' In some ways, King was to reflect later, this was a perfect introduction to Berlin and Berliners. He was to find the city's residents similarly pleasant, generous and engaging company, but he was never able fully to reconcile those positive qualities with their ability to witness and to remain silent about appalling acts of inhumanity.

Chapter Seven

Autumn 1938, Berlin.

The first weeks in Berlin passed quietly, as Pym had advised would be appropriate. 'Don't rush your fences, my boy,' he had said, in his quiet yet authoritative way, during one of their last meetings in London. 'Let your information come to you. If I know anything of the Nazi mentality, they'll be unable to stop themselves boasting to you of their organisation and achievements.' He had also taken very careful notice of the Professor's advice that he should leave no sensitive information in his flat. 'The University is providing you with this accommodation, so I think we must assume that the authorities will have it both frequently searched and kept under regular surveillance.'

King, a man who valued his privacy and found it abhorrent that his 'home' could be violated in such a way, nevertheless genuinely enjoyed his first weeks in the city, learning to find his way around, establishing his office at the University and gradually getting to know his colleagues. Both Schwarz and Brunner were the staff with whom he had most contact and his first impressions of each had been confirmed. Brunner seemed a slippery and untrustworthy character, whereas Schwarz seemed a genuinely liberal and free thinking academic, who was eager to discuss a wide range of issues. Unsurprisingly, King had spent more of his leisure time with the younger German and his somewhat Bohemian circle of friends than with any other group.

One Thursday morning towards the end of his sixth week in Berlin, when the late October sky had taken on a steely grey colour which hinted at the winter to come, King was stopped by Fräulein Müller, as he sauntered into the Department. 'Excuse me, Herr Doktor, but there is a letter for you.' He had been trying, not altogether without success, to wean the Administrator away from addressing him so formally and he wondered whether this reversion to a more distant style reflected her reaction to the letter. 'It was left here earlier today by a very official looking man. I do hope that you are not in any kind of trouble, Herr Doktor.'

King looked fondly at the Administrator's anxious face and took immediate steps to reassure her. 'Oh I don't think so, Anna. I've been very careful not to drop any litter and to keep my shoes well shined,' he said with a cheeky wink as he took the letter and set off up the stairs towards his office. As soon as he let himself into the small corner room, with its connecting door to Schwarz's office, King threw down his briefcase and coat onto one of the two worn armchairs and flopped contentedly down into the other, studying the envelope with interest. He was intrigued to see neatly printed on the envelope the initials 'OKW' and '76-78 Tirpitzufer, Berlin', which he already knew was the address of The *Abwehr*, Germany's Military Intelligence organization. The slight sense of anxiety which he had initially experienced was quickly eased, when he saw that the contents of the envelope comprised a short handwritten note and some sort of invitation card.

'*My dear Herr Dr King,*' began the note written in perfect Gothic lettering. '*It was a great pleasure to converse with you on the Berlin train and to learn of the purpose of your visit to the Reich. It would give me great pleasure to invite you, as my guest, to a Reception which is being held, in order to celebrate the Munich Agreement and the wholly justified reincorporation of Sudetenland into the Reich. The Reception will take place in the Columned Hall in the HQ of the OKW, Bendlerblock on November 2nd at 7.30PM. I do hope that you will be able to attend and I look forward very much to further discussions with you. Heil Hitler!*' The note was signed 'Major Erwin Kalz, OKW, Berlin', and the gilt edged invitation card informed King, both that he should confirm his attendance and that formal dress or uniform was obligatory.

On the day of the Reception, King was surprised and touched to learn that Fräulein Müller had arranged for him to be picked up at home in one of the University's cars and chauffeur driven to Tirpitzufer. 'It is a proud day indeed for the Department and for the University, Herr Doktor,' she had cooed as she brushed away an imaginary speck of dust from his tweed jacket. 'Now, are you sure that you have your formal dress organised?' 'Yes, I have Anna, don't worry,' replied King, as he reflected sadly that because so many Jewish professionals were no longer permitted to practise, many had been reduced to selling their possessions in order to survive. To his discomfort, it had proved much easier and cheaper to buy rather than to hire a full dinner suit.

Frau Bauer was beside herself with excitement, as the uniformed chauffeur pulled up in a perfectly polished, gleaming black Horch, with its huge front wheel arches and characteristic bug eyed headlights. 'Now you behave yourself, Herr Doktor. This could be the making of you!' she exhorted King, as she ushered him out of the house and into the waiting car. As the car pulled away from the kerb, he smiled as he noticed that Frau Bauer was surrounded by her fellow *Portierfrauen* from the neighbouring houses.

The crowds on the pavement stopped to stare as the Horch cruised down Hermann Göringstraße, past the Reich Chancellery and on across Potsdamerplatz. The traffic was building up as they turned into Tirpitzufer, the cold grey waters of the Landwehr Canal on their left and the huge stone frontage of his destination, the Bendlerblock, looming in the distance on the right. It was clear that this was a major event and King began seriously to consider who might also be in attendance. The Wehrmacht Chiefs of Staff would be there for sure, but perhaps also more political figures, such as Himmler, Goebbels, Hess or even Hitler himself. For one naïve moment, King wished he was equipped with some device that, with luck, could wipe out the whole foul lot of them in one redeeming blast.

The Horch took its turn in the parade of meticulously polished cars which were queuing to disgorge their invited guests at the entrance to The Bendlerblock. As they drew nearer, King could see both a phalanx of uniformed officers, saluting each new arrival, and the huge red, black and white swastika flags fluttering in the arc light beams above the main entrance. Finally, it was his turn to step out of the warmth of the car and into the cold autumn air and the dazzling artificial light, which illuminated his path up the steps to the main entrance door. He was vaguely aware of the cheers of the crowd and the light marching music which was being played by an immaculately uniformed military band. He kept his eyes firmly forward and, having shown his invitation, was able to pass inside the door and be directed towards the cloakroom, where he deposited his overcoat.

'Herr Dr King?' asked a fresh-faced adjutant with an expression that changed from concern to obvious relief at the Englishman's nod of the head. 'It's a relief that I've found you at last. There are so many people here in dinner suits. It's quite overwhelming. Please follow me. Major Kalz is awaiting you in the Columned Hall.'

The adjutant led the way through the throng of men, all in uniform or formal dress, and their partners in their glittering finery.

They crossed the large reception area and made their way through a huge doorway into a rectangular hall which boasted, at first floor level, a gallery supported by huge stone columns. Massive flags were hanging from fixtures which were positioned just underneath the magnificent glass ceiling and a podium, already set up with a microphone, was positioned on the gallery at the far end of the hall. White-jacketed waiters, carrying trays of champagne or canapes, made elegant pirouettes between the crowds of guests who were clearly both hungry and thirsty. Over the shoulder of the adjutant, King caught sight of the tall, fair haired figure of Kalz, in the full dress uniform of a Wehrmacht Major. He was deep in conversation with an army officer, whose uniform bore the unmistakable gold shoulder boards and red striped trousers of a full General. His heart was thumping crazily in his chest, while his escort awaited a suitable break in the conversation. At the first suitable pause, he coughed discreetly in order to attract Kalz's attention. 'Excuse me Herr General, Herr Major. May I present Herr Dr King.'

Kalz turned around to face the Englishman, a beaming smile on his face, 'My dear Herr Dr King. How good it is to see you again. Please, allow me to introduce you to my commanding officer, and Stein, another round of champagne, if you please.'

'Yes sir,' responded the adjutant with a salute, before rushing off to find the nearest waiter. Kalz placed a proprietorial arm on King's elbow and, while leading him towards the waiting officer, announced 'Herr General, I would like to introduce Herr Dr John King from the University of Durham in England. The Herr Doktor is here as part of an academic exchange between Great Britain and the *Reich*. His particular interest concerns issues of mutual security for our respective nations. An admirable subject, I am sure you will agree.'

King could scarcely believe his ears as the older German murmured his agreement and introduced himself as General Hans Oster. As soon as he heard the name, King was transported back to one of his many briefing sessions in Pym's St John's Wood flat. 'We really could do with you picking up as much information as you can about The *Abwehr*, John.' His old mentor had gone on to explain that SIS knew relatively little of its workings, but was confident that most, if not all agents sent from Germany to Britain would initially be run by that body.

'The *Abwehr* is run by Admiral Wilhelm Canaris and his Deputy is General Hans Oster, so do listen carefully to any gossip or opinions about these men that come your way. Almost anything you can bring back would be useful. But don't, for heaven's sake, jeopardise your mission by seeming to be too interested. You'll have to be circumspect.'

Suddenly, it all fitted into place for King; Kalz in plain clothes returning from some sort of assignment in Brussels; the fear of him shown by the German border guard; his genuine interest in his reasons for travelling to Germany and the invitation to an event such as this. It was now crystal clear to King that he had enjoyed an incredible stroke of luck in meeting a Major in The *Abwehr* and he greedily anticipated the flow of information that could come his way.

Every inch the career officer, around fifty and with bright, smiling eyes which seemed to King to penetrate his innermost thoughts, Oster addressed King directly. 'Well, Herr Doktor, you certainly have an interesting topic of study. I'm sure that you have found many in Germany who are prepared to expound on this subject.' King immediately recalled the advice offered by Pym that, with German officers and officials, flattery is often the most effective strategy to get them to talk. 'Indeed I have, Herr General,' he replied, 'but none in such a senior position as yourself.'

Oster gave a brief nod in acknowledgement of such an obvious truth, before continuing in a tone which stated loud and clear that he was a man who was used to being listened to. 'What Europe needs is a strong Germany. We live in a very different world to that of 1918 when the Fatherland was crippled by the terms of the Versailles Treaty. The real threat to a civilised and peaceful Europe now comes from Stalin. A strong Germany which is able to withstand the Soviet Union and a strong Great Britain which can continue to maintain order throughout its Empire; these are surely in the interests of both our great nations.'

'I said much the same to Herr Dr King when we met on the train, Herr General,' interjected Kalz with a challenging, but not unfriendly look in the direction of the Englishman. 'But I had the feeling then that our guest was not in full agreement with our views.'

King recognised that he would have to choose his words carefully lest he alienate the Germans or appear wholly implausible.

'Well Herr General, like you I have little positive to say about Stalin, with his almost total disregard for humanity and his routine use of terror. I'm certainly not one of those naïve intellectuals who see developments in the Soviet Union as representing an advance for mankind.' Both Oster and Kalz nodded vigorously in response to this, but before he could continue an orderly approached Major Kalz, saluted and said something discreetly into his ear. 'I'm afraid that we shall have to postpone this most interesting conversation, gentlemen, as the *Reichsmarschall* will be arriving shortly. We should make our way to the reception area Herr General,' suggested Kalz, with what seemed to King to be little enthusiasm. The General nodded curtly, as if irritated to be taken from an engaging conversation in order to carry out a distasteful duty. 'I hope we have the chance to continue this discussion another time Herr Dr King,' said General Oster suavely. 'In the meantime, enjoy the rest of your evening with us in OKW.' With that wish the General, closely followed by Kalz turned away towards the Reception Hall and King was left to his own thoughts.

He barely had time to take his second glass of champagne and a couple of canapes from a passing waiter, when a steady stream of guests began to enter the Hall. These increased numbers brought with them a palpable buzz of excitement and King decided to leave the centre of the floor to those who were eagerly anticipating the delivery of some Nazi rant. Feeling very much an unbeliever among the zealots, he politely made his way towards one of the near corners of the Hall, from which vantage point King, because of his height, would have a good view of the Party star in action.

Nothing could have prepared him for his first view of *Reichsmarschall* Hermann Göring, a Ruritanian plenipotentiary if ever he saw one. A dazzling white uniform braided with gold, whose look was rather spoiled by the double breasted jacket having to strain over his sizeable girth. Here was a man who had clearly gone to seed, his face a round, soft-looking pudding which showed obvious signs of his well-known predilection for narcotics. It was only the sight of the Iron Cross decorating his left breast pocket that reminded King that he was looking at what remained of an authentic German hero of the First World War. After waiting for the applause to die down, Göring began to speak:

'Men of the armed forces and women of Germany! I have

spoken on many occasions, in many different places and on many different subjects. But today is a very special occasion. Today, I speak on a day when Germany can stand taller and prouder than at any time in living memory.'

As Göring warmed to his theme, King could see that a dapper-looking man in the full uniform of an admiral, who he took to be Canaris, Oster and the most senior staff of the Wehrmacht were standing immediately behind the corpulent *Reichsmarshall*. To King's mind, they all looked less than enthusiastic members of Göring's audience. In contrast, those in the crowd wearing the jet black of the SS and, to his surprise most of the women present, displayed the light-in-the-eyes-look of the true believer. King grudgingly had to admit that, for all his grotesque appearance, the *Reichsmarshall* knew how to manipulate an audience. In particular, he was a master of the planned pause, which offered just the right number of opportunities for the audience to join in with their ritual outbursts of 'Heil Hitler!' and 'Sieg Heil!'

'For many months, the peaceful Germans of the Sudetenland have been abused and mistreated by the bullies of Prague. Well, I can now state categorically that, thanks to the fearless and astute statesmanship of the Führer, this is now at an end!'

Göring was working himself into a frenzy now and seemed grateful for an opportunity created by a particularly enthusiastic round of the *Hitlergruß* to quickly produce a bright yellow, silk handkerchief from his jacket pocket. Having dabbed his sweating brow, at the same time exercising considerable care not to smudge his all too obvious facial make-up, he raised an arm to silence the audience before continuing, 'Our grateful thanks must also go to the organised and efficient military, who carried out *Fall Grün* with exemplary skill and bravery.' At this compliment, the hall echoed briefly to dozens of military boots being stamped on the floor. 'However, as the Führer has stated, we will never step away from a fight, if it is in the interests of Germany. So I give warning to all those powers, who may be tempted to stand in the way of the legitimate claims of the *Reich*. With the unfailing support of the Fatherland, I say to these... do so at your own peril!'

By this time, King had heard enough of this rabble rousing and felt the need for some fresh air. He was, therefore, relieved to hear

Göring say that his address was almost at an end.

'Today, fellow Germans and members of the glorious Nazi Party, is not about speeches. It is about celebrating a great triumph in the succession of victories masterminded by the Führer. But it is also vital that we all recognise that we must retain our perfect state of preparedness for the many battles ahead, which will be necessary to ensure that the destiny of our Thousand Year Reich is properly fulfilled. Sieg Heil! Heil Deutschland! Heil Hitler!'

After a brief wave and smile for the press cameras, Göring left the platform to a rapturous reception from the body of the Hall and made his way along the first floor gallery to the stairs, which descended to the ground floor just to the right of King's position. With a mounting sense of horror, yet also with a morbid fascination, King realised that, unless he moved quickly, the *Reichsmarshall* was going to walk right past him.

Once again King found himself struggling against the tide, as he attempted to move back towards the centre of the Hall just as most of the crowd was pushing for a closer look at Göring. When he finally emerged from the frenzied people, he caught sight of Kalz's back, no more than a few metres away. The Major was in animated conversation with two officers in SS uniform, one of whom King was shocked to recognise as Joachim Brandt. The other officer was speaking in a very loud voice, perhaps in order to be heard above all the *Hitlergrüße*, which enthusiastic audience members were still shouting in the direction of Göring's massive back, as he retreated out of the hall.

'We know you feeble Junkers army-types were terrified that the Czech crisis would lead to war and that you've breathed a great sigh of relief that it didn't,' Brandt's SS *Sturmbannführer* comrade was saying to Kalz in a hostile and unpleasant manner. 'But it would be a mistake to get too comfortable in your barracks, Kalz. The Führer sees war with the decadent western powers and the inferior eastern people as both inevitable and desirable. And as for you amateurs in The *Abwehr*, we in the SS await only the order to show you how best to protect the interests of the *Reich*. Believe me Kalz, not many weeks will pass before you and your aristocratic cronies will see the power of the SS.'

'Be that as it may, gentlemen, for the moment I suggest that we enjoy the evening and the peace, long may it last. And my dear Schröder,' Kalz said suavely before turning his back on them, 'do calm down and try to enjoy this rather fine champagne.'

The German's sudden turn meant that, in order to avoid being seen eavesdropping on the exchange, King had to duck sharply behind a large group of chattering army wives. Before he did, however, he managed to note both the colour draining rapidly from the Major's face and the unmistakable fury and hatred in the eyes of *Sturmbannführer* Schröder and Brandt as they glared at Kalz's retreating figure. A passing waiter received the full force of the senior SS officer's anger, as he carelessly threw his half full champagne flute onto his tray before the two of them stalked away towards the rear of the Hall.

As King appeared from behind his human shield, Kalz seemed simply to look through him without any sign of recognition. Even though the German was obviously very distracted, King realised that he could be recognised at any moment and decided to acknowledge him with a cheery, 'Well, Herr Major Kalz, listening to the *Reichsmarshall* was quite an experience for me.' The urbane manner and smooth smile were immediately restored as Kalz replied, 'Yes, I rather imagine it was. I'd be very interested in your opinion.' King was aware both that the most important thing he had heard had been the consequence of his eavesdropping the hostile exchange and that Kalz, despite his very friendly demeanour, was obviously nobody's fool. The sharp look that he shot in King's direction reinforced the point and demonstrated that he had fully recovered from his earlier distraction. King chose to respond blandly, 'I suppose I've learned that politicians the world over are much the same. They revel in their own importance and play to the audience.'

'Ah. There I can only agree with you, Herr Dr King,' said Kalz with a smile, 'They are indeed a special breed. But now, I fear I have duties to perform. I trust you have enjoyed the evening and that we will have the opportunity to meet again during your stay in Berlin.' With a military salute and the merest click of the heels, Kalz disappeared into the still dense crowd. As King replaced his now empty wine glass on the tray of a passing waiter, he failed to notice that one of the SS officers had returned to the hall. Looking up from the tray, the Englishman blinked in surprise at the sight of the inscrutable face of Joachim Brandt, staring directly at him. King had not had any contact with his former friend since that final evening in Heidelberg and, having noticed him earlier, had thought that it would clearly be better to avoid him altogether. However, now that a conversation seemed inevitable, his mind turned over memories of their friendship and the happy times they had shared, studying, dreaming, womanising and, of course, drinking. Holding out his hand, he approached his old University friend and said amiably, 'Joachim. I hardly expected to see you here tonight. What a coincidence.'

'Indeed, John,' began Brandt as he came face to face with King, studiously ignoring the outstretched hand. 'I noticed you earlier and if I were a suspicious type, I might have thought that you were trying to avoid me.

'Not at all, Joachim,' countered King pleasantly, while deliberately looking at his still offered hand. 'In fact, it seems to me that it is you who take little pleasure in meeting me.'

Brandt was evidently thrown by this accusation and for a short time seemed uncertain how to respond. It had taken all his self-control not to have King and the rest of them arrested after their confrontation all those years ago in Heidelberg. Indeed, as a direct consequence of the reporting of his perceived leniency by some of his platoon, he had had to work hard to alter a reputation in the SS as being soft on opponents of the Party. He had, since then, frequently proved his worth as a cunning and astute officer and his time in America had finally caused his fury at his friend's perceived rejection of him to dissipate somewhat. However, while part of him was prepared to rebuild some kind of friendship with King, his recently developed self-confidence insisted that the Englishman must first make some gesture of repentance for his behaviour. Despite his uncertainty as to how King would respond, but nevertheless believing that he was acting correctly, he suggested, 'I trust that you have learned since our last unfortunate meeting and that this time you will show me the respect that my status warrants.'

King gazed into the eyes of his former friend, trying to convince himself that he could still discern vestigial traces of the shy and troubled young man who had been his closest friend in Heidelberg. With growing sadness, he realised that, as often happens with friends who each feel badly let down by the other, neither he nor Joachim seemed willing or able to take the kind of selflessly decisive action that would prevent the conversation becoming ever more hostile. He simply could not find it in himself to show any sort of respect to an SS uniform and he reflected bitterly that Brandt had chosen to insist on precisely that which he could not give. Even though he was aware that this refusal would almost certainly destroy his last opportunity to avoid a final breach, King deliberately looked down his nose as he answered, 'Indeed I have learned a great deal since we last met, Joachim, and believe me, I know exactly how much respect to pay to that uniform.'

As intended, this response stung Brandt like a slap across the face and he reacted furiously, 'Be very careful. You are in my territory now and I could destroy you with a click of my fingers.'

King burst out laughing at the German's threat and suggested confidently, 'Really, Joachim? You must do your worst; you don't scare me in the slightest.'

All hopes of a reconciliation now reduced to ashes, and his face turning bright red with embarrassment, Brandt began to reach for his pistol, only to find his hand gripped by his superior officer. 'Brandt!' the man hissed urgently. 'What's going on here? This is not the place...' The sound of Schröder's voice seemed to bring Brandt to his senses and, aware now of several intrigued faces turning towards the incident, no doubt in the hope of witnessing some scandal, he immediately turned to the *Sturmbannführer* and nodded quickly. 'What on earth are you playing at, Brandt?' demanded Schröder, as he stared with undisguised hostility at King. 'And who is this, that he disturbs you so much?'

Before Brandt could respond, the Englishman introduced himself with a frosty smile. 'My name is Dr John King and I am here at the invitation of your Government to take part in an academic exchange with Great Britain.' Pleased to see both the look of confusion appear on the *Sturmbannführer's* face and that of consternation on that of Brandt, he continued icily, 'Joachim and I are old acquaintances from Heidelberg, where, I'm afraid, we parted on hostile terms. It appears that, in the intervening five years or so, the poor chap hasn't been able to get over it.'

Brandt, his face a strange combination of anger and disappointment, came nose to nose with King, shaking his head slowly,

'You have just repeated the same mistake you made in '33. Sadly, you are still incapable of recognising the new reality so I will repeat my promise to you.' A crocodile smile spread across his face as he menacingly advised, 'I will enjoy teaching you the error of your ways. Take very great care while you are here in my country. Unfortunate accidents can always happen.'

'That's enough, Brandt,' whispered Schröder urgently, as he pulled him away from the scene of the confrontation and out of the hall. 'He evidently enjoys a certain protection here and remember, you're only here on leave from America. Don't do anything stupid. He's not worth it.'

Attempting to put Brandt out of his mind, King decided that he should make use of his good fortune in once more being left alone. Ignoring the many notices instructing guests to remain at ground or first floor level and despite his awareness of the risk involved, he resolved to take the opportunity to discover what he could of the Bendlerblock and its organisation. His plan, if intercepted by an official, was to play the slightly tipsy and confused guest in search of a lavatory. But most importantly, he would have to take great care that Brandt, Schröder and Kalz were nowhere to be seen, as he made his search of the building. After a few minutes of careful reconnaissance, King had ascertained both that the third floor was home to the Headquarters of The *Abwehr* and, from a plan of the offices which was displayed at the top of the stairs leading to that floor, that Kalz was located in its Central Division, under the leadership of General Oster. King silently thanked the characteristic German attention to detail, as he committed to memory everything the plan told him of the structure of the Military Intelligence organisation. It was evident from the departmental nomenclature that The *Abwehr* was divided into three main sections. The first, King surmised was the controlling section, the so called Central Division, in which Kalz and Oster were based. The second department was the fairly self-explanatory *Amtsgruppe Ausland* or Foreign Section and the third the more prosaically named *Abwehr* I, II and III. He had no idea what these last sections denoted.

Acutely aware that had ventured deep into parts of the building which were prohibited to outsiders, he decided not to push his luck any further. Just as he was beginning to descend the stairs from the third floor, he heard someone climbing up towards him. Uttering a silent prayer that the officer ascending the stairs did not know him, he rapidly fell into his planned role. He greeted the surprised looking officer, who thankfully he had never seen, with a heartfelt, 'I'd be grateful if you could direct me to the nearest lavatory... I can't seem to find one anywhere.' The initial suspicion quickly lifted from the German's expression as he directed King down to the first floor. He did, however, end the exchange with a rather brusque, 'Guests were under strict instructions not to stray beyond the first floor. I should report this, but I can sympathise with your predicament and we'll say no more about it.' King was rattled by this narrow escape and, as instructed, made his way downstairs before heading back to the cloakroom to collect his overcoat. To his relief, neither Brandt nor Schröder were anywhere to be seen as he prepared to leave the building, which was by now rapidly emptying of guests.

    Outside, the evening was crisp and dry and, despite the long line of available taxis and a reasonable number of Pym's *Reichsmarks* in his pocket, King decided to walk home. He felt certain that he was not under any immediate threat from Brandt. Schröder had made it absolutely clear that any 'accident', so soon after their public argument, would be foolish in the extreme. The walk would give him time to reflect upon, and organise in his mind, the events of the evening and what he had learned from them. He was due to make his first report to Pym before Christmas and he hoped that some of the information gleaned would even have a wider significance than his own assignment.

    As he walked, he reflected on the bellicose attitude of Göring. It did not take him long to realise that basically the *Reichsmarshall*'s comments had been directed at the senior staff of the Wehrmacht. He recalled the disengaged faces of the military staff surrounding Göring as he had spoken. King deduced from this that there must exist among some of the senior military, significant unease with, or even opposition to Hitler's aggressive posture regarding Czechoslovakia. He further pondered the significance of the exchange between Kalz and *Sturmbannführer* Schröder. His initial thought was that it perhaps indicated a kind of power struggle between the Army and Himmler's SS organisation. It certainly suggested that the SS held a highly dismissive view of The *Abwehr* and its capabilities. Approaching Ludendorffstraße, he shivered involuntarily as he remembered the menacing boast of

Schröder that the power of the SS and its view of how to protect the interests of the *Reich* would soon be demonstrated for all to see. While he did not fully understand this, it was obvious that some plan was already in place, which awaited only the order to proceed. It seemed to King that Kalz was also perplexed by this threat and greatly concerned by its implications.

King, along with Kalz, Germany and the rest of Europe did not have long to wait for the shocking fulfilment of *Sturmbannführer* Schröder's boast.

Chapter Eight.

Wednesday, November 9th 1938, Berlin.

On alternate Wednesday evenings since his arrival in Berlin, King had enjoyed supper and conversation with Schwarz, his brother and a couple of university colleagues. The members of this loose grouping took it in turns to choose the location and this time it had fallen to the Englishman to determine their meeting place. Schwarz groaned a little when the Café Kranzler on the Kufürstendamm had been proposed by King. 'You must be joking, John. I know you're still a bit of a tourist here, but just think of the ghastly types who'll probably be there and think of the cost for Sebastian and some of the others. They're not lucky academics with tenure, you know.'

'Point taken, Andreas,' replied King quickly. 'Tell you what. I've got a decent allowance on top of my University salary so tonight's on me.' Seeing the look of doubt cross his friend's face, he hurriedly went on. 'I insist. I've really enjoyed your company over these last weeks and I think it's the least I can do. I'm sure they'll all want to hear what I made of 'Fat Hermann' and besides, I've been in the Kranzler many times. It's no more frequented by Nazis than anywhere else in the city centre. Come on, we'll have fun and I've a very special treat in store that I hope you'll all enjoy.'

Schwarz was not the type to relish surprises and in vain he tried every trick he could think of to get King to reveal his secret. Eventually giving up, and grinning like a child who could not wait for Christmas, he agreed to let the others know of the arrangements to meet in the café. King spent the rest of the afternoon feeling quite pleased with himself and really looking forward to his evening with friends. He had managed to obtain tickets for the Café Leon, where they would enjoy a review, hosted by the legendary Max Erlich. He really hoped that an entertaining evening at the Kranzler and the Leon would cheer them all up. We could all certainly use it, he thought sadly, as he reflected on the dreadful news from Paris, regarding the attempted assassination of German Embassy official vom Rath by the Jew Grynspan.

It was a pleasant, calm evening with a full moon and clear sky as, shortly after quarter past eight, King approached the Kurfürstendamm. He even thought that he could hear the plaintive calls of some unknown animals, echoing into the night sky from the nearby Berlin Zoo. Perhaps, he was to think later, they could sense the imminence of some awful event. At length, he passed the Gedächtniskirche and entered the Kurfürstendamm itself. Most of the buildings on either side of the wide boulevard were draped with Nazi flags and the windows of even relatively select shops were adorned with crude propaganda posters. Consciously trying to pay them no attention, he finally reached the Café Kranzler and made his way to the first floor salon, in which he had arranged to meet his friends. As he was to foot the evening's bill, King had planned to arrive first and he was relieved to see that none of the usual group was in the café. The salon was about half full and King had no difficulty in selecting a round table for six, which was perfectly situated in the front window overlooking the broad boulevard. He ordered a coffee from a passing waiter and instructed him that everything consumed by anyone on the table should be placed on his account.

Schwarz arrived some five minutes later, accompanied by Hans Breitner, one of his doctoral students and Elaine Duval, a Professor of French from the Department of Foreign Languages. Hans was a serious young man who invariably dressed from head to toe in black, whereas Elaine was a typically gamin and most attractive Frenchwoman. The waiter had just arrived to take the drinks order when Schwarz's younger brother Sebastian entered the salon with his girlfriend Sophie. Sebastian was a slightly smaller and fresher looking version of Andreas and Sophie was a very delicate, fine featured and nervous looking girl. Jokes about 'Fat Hermann' were forgotten, as the talk around the table glumly focused on the shooting in Paris and its possible consequences, especially for Germany's remaining Jewish population. King reasoned that, on any reading, this must be seen as the action of a single deranged individual which, therefore, should have no broader ramifications.

'You've got to be kidding,' said Andreas Schwarz with uncharacteristic hostility. 'Grynszpan's timing could hardly have been worse. He chose the exact date when the Nazis think the 'November Criminals' and Jews stabbed the army in the back in 1918. To make matters worse, it's also when Hitler's 'Bierkeller Putsch' was attempted in '23. The Führer made his usual speech yesterday and they all marched through München. Goebbels must have been rubbing his hands with delight that this shooting should happen on such a significant day in the Nazi calendar. We're in for trouble, no doubt about it. The forced removal of the Jews of Polish descent a couple of weeks ago will be nothing compared to what will happen now.'

Sophie looked terrified, as Andreas finished by shaking his head in desperation. 'Don't worry. You know he always exaggerates,' Sebastian said comfortingly, as he placed a protective arm around his girlfriend's shoulders. 'And besides, I'll look after you, I promise.'

'On the way here I did see quite a lot of SS hanging around the streets,' said Elaine, so nervously that King decided it was time to attempt to lighten the mood.

'Relax, Elaine. They were probably all out drinking themselves stupid and boasting that they were at Hitler's side in '23. Look, I suggest that we all try to put this stuff out of our minds for one night. I've tickets for us all at Café Leon. It's Max Erlich's latest review *Mixed Fruit Salad*.

'How on earth did you wangle tickets for that?' shouted Hans in excitement. 'I've heard the demand is so great that they're having to move to a bigger venue.'

'Yes, I've heard that as well,' confirmed Andreas, all thoughts of events in Paris now forgotten in his excitement. 'Thanks, John, from all of us.... it'll be a real treat!'

King was absolutely delighted that the tension seemed to have vanished and he was faced with a circle of broad smiles, his friends all nodding in agreement to his suggestion that they 'have another round of drinks here and then push off for the start of the show.'. They saw little evidence of any Nazi gangs as they made their way along the Kurfürstendamm and the group eagerly established itself in the very popular venue which was the Café Leon.

The review comprised a series of excellent musical numbers, composed by Willy Rosen, which were arranged scenically by the theatrical and comedic genius Erlich. He also added comic skits and sketches with topical and more traditional jokes which, to the delight of his audience, he always dusted off. King was hugely impressed by the spirit, bravery and talent of those members of the *Jüdische Kulturbund*, who performed regularly in the face of hatred and violence from the Nazis. He was also heartened by the level of support offered by an audience which evidently cared little for the race or religion of the person sitting in the next seat or performing on the stage. The drinks and the laughter had flowed freely for almost three hours, when the ecstatic audience finally allowed Erlich and his fellow performers to retreat offstage for the final time that evening. As it cascaded haphazardly onto the pavement, the audience was still excitedly exchanging recollections of the performance and rehearsing their favourite extracts. However, even with their generous level of intoxication and happiness, as soon as they set foot outside the Café Leon, it was obvious to the vast majority of the audience that something was very badly wrong.

The calm of a still night was constantly disturbed by strange shouts, screams and loud crashes and the air smelled of smoke and burning. To King, it brought back childhood memories of the bonfire parties which people back in England would have enjoyed just four nights previously. He rapidly realised, however, that what was happening on this night in Berlin was not such innocent and harmless fun, but rather something altogether more sinister and brutish. As the friends stood together on the pavement, preparing to take their leave of one another, a group of men in the black breeches and boots of the SS, but wearing civilian overcoats and hats, bustled past and headed directly for the nearby shop, café and restaurant fronts. Each was carrying what appeared to be a long metal stick, which they then used to smash the large front windows of many of the commercial premises. It was obvious from the start of this vandalism that premises owned by Jewish people were the sole targets. Far from the random actions of some Nazi hotheads, to King this looked much more like a calculated and targeted assault on any Jewish owned property. A second wave of thugs followed the window smashers, using white paint to daub what remained of the damaged shop frontages with crude representations of the Star of David and racist slogans, of which *'Juden Raus!'* was the mildest. Andreas recognised the uniform of a Berlin police officer, as he stood on the opposite pavement and, without hesitating, he ran across the street to point out to the official what was happening.

'I can see nothing that requires my intervention,' the policeman replied stiffly. 'I suggest that you and your friends make your way home as quickly as possible. None of this need concern you.' Schwarz was incensed by this response and with his face very close to that of the policeman shouted, 'You only have to look, man! Those thugs are vandalising property. It's your job to stop them. If not, then what are you doing here?'

A more senior police officer, who had heard this exchange, intervened to advise Schwarz firmly, 'Our role, sir, is to protect German property and German people. I can see no damage to either taking place here. I suggest that you follow my colleague's sensible advice and leave immediately.' Andreas was about to respond again, when he felt surprisingly strong arms pulling him away from the policemen and heard King urgently whispering, 'For God's sake, leave it, Andreas. You can't win. Let's get out of here.'

Schwarz continued to wave his arms and shout abuse at the police officers, as King dragged him bodily back across the Kurfürstendamm towards the waiting group of friends. By now, the first looters had appeared, their cars and vans screeching to a halt in front of the broken windows of the shops. Shamelessly, and again without intervention by the on-looking police officers, they grabbed what they could and made their getaway.

King could see the shock on the faces of his companions and decided that he should take the initiative. 'Let's get ourselves off to our homes,' he said in such a forceful manner that none of his friends objected. 'Sebastian, you and Hans make sure that Andreas gets home without any further problems. Now, Elaine and Sophie, where do you live?' The former replied immediately that she could go almost to her apartment block with the others and it was quickly agreed that King would ensure that Sophie arrived home safely.

It was clear to King that Sophie was very distressed, not only by the violence against property that was becoming more and more evident the longer they walked, but also by the risk that Andreas had run in objecting to the indifference of the police. 'But John, just think. He might've been arrested or beaten up or even worse.... And he's not even Jewish. ..It doesn't bear thinking about,' she said miserably, searching King's face with her huge dark eyes. Before he could reply, she pointed ahead and her hand flew to her mouth in horror. 'I can smell smoke and see flames over there on Fasanenstraße. A fire must have broken out. I know people who live there. Let's see if we can help.' Somewhat against his better judgement, King followed the running woman in the direction of the smoke and flames. Soon he could smell petrol and was sure that the fire was no accident. As they approached the synagogue, with its Moorish design and three large cupolas, they were both shocked at the thick column of smoke which was billowing out from the central dome. King was grateful for the police barricades which restrained the crowds to the opposite side of the street. He was sure that, had these not been present, Sophie would have rushed across the street, with no care for her own safety, towards a pile of burning *Torahs*.

It was sickening for him to witness the fire brigade hose down the buildings on either side of the synagogue to prevent the fire spreading, but leave the beautiful building, once visited by the Kaiser himself, to the uncontrolled flames. Just as appalling for King was the realisation that many in the crowd were actually enjoying the spectacle of the burning synagogue. Anti-Semitic chants and slogans began to roar through the night air, as increasing numbers of people gave in to their basest instincts. It did not take long for violence against property to transform itself into that against people. The catalyst was an unpleasant looking, small man shouting to the mob with shameful relish that a Jewish family lived in the ground floor of the building immediately behind them. No more encouragement was needed than an anonymous 'Let's get them!' to cause several hot heads to begin to break down the door. A roar of triumph went up as a middle aged man was dragged out of his home and cruelly beaten by members of the baying crowd. The sight of such senseless and indiscriminate violence caused King to recall Sturmbannführer Schröder's sinister boast. *So, this is what the bastard meant*, he thought savagely. *What I wouldn't give to have the preening swine in front of me now.*

King had been briefly distracted by the physical violence and when he turned to speak with Sophie, he realised to his horror that she had vanished. Desperately pushing his way through the laughing people, he called out her name as loud as he could, but when he finally reached the edge of the crowd he could only stand frantically looking in all directions, but with no idea of where to find her. Despondency overwhelmed him, as he realised that he had let her and his friends down. He had undertaken to get her home safely and he had failed. Just as he was beginning to fear that he would not find her safe and well, he heard a loud, terrified scream coming from a dark alley between two large apartment blocks. The attention of the crowd was still firmly on the burning synagogue, which was now well ablaze, and the beating up of more Jewish residents of the nearby apartment house. Without pausing to think, King plunged into the darkness of the alley in search of Sophie. As soon as his eyes had adjusted to the poor light, he could clearly make out the shape of a young woman, pushed back against the wall by a much larger and more powerful man in SS uniform. She was whimpering and pleading with him to allow her to go, while he merely shrugged and began to unbutton his coat. 'You have seen how we treat your churches and your holy scriptures... now you will discover how we will treat you, Jew,' he spat with pure malevolence.

King was relieved to recognise Sophie and, advancing into the alley, he shouted at the man to leave her alone and let her go. 'Relax, friend,' came the irritated reply. 'We can both take our fill of pleasure here...wait your turn.' Outraged, King grabbed the man by the shoulder as he turned back towards Sophie, spun him round and struck him with a fierce blow to the face. His fist felt a satisfying crunch as it broke the man's nose and sent him careering into the wall of the alley, from which he slumped, unconscious, to the floor.

'Come on Sophie, let's get out of here as quickly as we can,' King urged his terrified and shaking friend. However, he had failed to notice the shadow which had appeared further down the alley and which now blocked their escape route.

'Stay where you are.... both of you,' the figure growled in a thick Berlin accent. 'What's going on here then?' As the man advanced, King was able to make out the upturned plant-pot helmet and thick overcoat of the Berlin police force. The Englishman groaned inwardly, expecting little sympathy after Andreas' earlier experience and given that a man in SS uniform was spread-eagled and unconscious at his feet.

'I ... er.... that is to say. .. er.' He never got to attempt his explanation of the situation because Sophie, leaning heavily against the wall of the alley, sobbed quietly and with total resignation. 'He was going to rape me. Just because I'm a Jew. My friend saved me.'

A look of distaste crossed the policeman's grizzled face as he weighed up what the distraught young woman had just said and the evidence before his eyes. He gave an almost imperceptible nod of the head before replying in a kindly voice, 'Then you'd better let your friend take you home straight away, Fräulein. There's all kinds of riff- raff on the streets tonight.' Kicking the prone body of the SS man, he continued, 'I'll stay with him until he wakes up. And don't worry your head, if any similar types show up, I'll tell them you ran off in the opposite direction. I'm sorry that you had to endure this tonight, Fräulein. Please be careful and good luck to you both.' Sophie was crying tears of relief as King, with a nod of gratitude to the old policeman, ushered her out of the alley and towards her home.

Chapter Nine

Wednesday, November 16th 1938, Berlin.

A mere two weeks after the reception in The Bendlerblock and seven days after *Kristallnacht*, King received another message from Major Kalz. Unlike the previous note, this was delivered to his flat in Ludendorffstraße. Having carefully opened the envelope, the Englishman recognised the familiar handwriting of the Major and eagerly began to read:

'*Dear Herr Dr King,*

I regret very much that I had to cut short our conversation on Wednesday evening at the Reception, but I am sure that you would have recognised the call of duty. It would give me great pleasure to be able to continue our conversation, on the very interesting topic of your research project here in Germany and other possible areas of mutual concern. I am sure we would have a fascinating exchange of views on these subjects. I would therefore like to invite you to have dinner with me at the Adlon Hotel at 8pm tomorrow evening.

I am aware that this is very short notice. Nevertheless, I do hope that this suggestion meets with your approval and I look forward to seeing you tomorrow evening.

RSVP to the Bendlerblock.

Erwin Kalz

King was sure that Professor Pym would want him to accept the invitation and to see what Kalz has to say for himself, and in any case, he mused, I've never dined at the Adlon...it could be quite an experience.

It was another fine dry evening, though a little cold, as King set off on foot for the Hotel Adlon on Unter Den Linden. He was aware of its reputation, both as one of Hitler's and, therefore, the Nazi leadership's favourite hotels and also as the 'Little Switzerland of Germany'. The latter name, he had been told by Schwarz, was a sarcastic reference to its status as a playground for diplomats. As he approached his destination, he was impressed by the scale and grandeur of its frontage but even this did not prepare him for the splendour which greeted him on his first entry into the hotel. Saluted crisply by two liveried doormen, he passed through the main entrance and into the splendid lobby, with its vaulted ceiling, grand staircase, rich rugs and high quality furniture. All this seemed to him to make a heady cocktail of part castle, part palace, part cathedral and with a dash of country house. He was totally captivated and, as a consequence, did not initially hear the white-gloved bellboy who was urgently paging him by name. At last recognising that he was being sought by the boy, King attracted his attention with a wave of his hand. 'Herr Dr King?' the bellboy asked politely and, as soon as he received a nod of confirmation, he continued. 'Herr Major Kalz is waiting for you, sir, in the Dining Room. Please permit me to show you the way.' King allowed himself to be led, firstly to the cloakroom to deposit his overcoat and then down a long corridor which boasted a parquet floor, covered at various points with beautifully coloured Persian rugs. The arches which connected the columns on either side of the corridor and the ceiling itself all had a gentle curved shape, adding to the Middle Eastern feel of this part of the hotel. Finally, they arrived at the large dining room with its many French windows, some of which looked out onto the now deserted dining terrace. Unsurprisingly, all save one of the tables were occupied by men in evening dress or military uniform and their female companions.

Kalz was seated at one of the smaller tables by the window. The nearest adjoining table was some distance away and King wondered whether Kalz had chosen that particular table in order to enjoy a degree of privacy. The *Abwehr* Major rose with a broad smile and a warm handshake to greet his guest. 'John, may I call you that? It's a great pleasure to see you again. Come, please, take a seat. And do call me Erwin.'

'Thank you for the invitation, Erwin. It's most kind of you, although I fear that, as a mere academic, I'll be dull company.'

'Nonsense my dear fellow,' responded Kalz with apparent sincerity. 'But first things first. Would you like champagne?' Indicating the bottle which was chilling in a silver ice bucket on a stand by the window, he continued disarmingly. 'I make no pretence of being a great connoisseur, but I am told that this 1928 '*Salon*' is a very fine vintage.' King, conscious that he must keep his wits about him, nevertheless gladly accepted the offer and the wine waiter served a flute of sparkling and very cold wine to both men.

King judged it a clever tactic that the German began their conversation by making direct reference to *Kristallnacht*. In fact, it seemed to the Englishman that his host was at pains to express most solicitously the hope that he had not been caught up in any of 'that unfortunate unpleasantness.' The look of distaste, even pain on Kalz's face, as they discussed the last week convinced King that he did not sympathise with such civil disorder and damage to people and property. He was clearly no rabid anti-Semite and attempted to pass the whole thing off as the actions of the lunatic fringe of the Third Reich.

'You can't be serious, Erwin,' countered King, determined not to let his host get away with such obvious nonsense. 'I saw enough on Wednesday and Thursday to convince me that this was no disorganised rabble, or some spontaneous expression of public feeling.'

'You may well be right,' sighed Kalz sadly. 'But I would like to reassure you that such behaviour and attitudes are not approved by everyone in Germany. You must believe that. Hopefully, such excesses will be discouraged and ironed out in time and we can concentrate on building on the more noble achievements of the *Reich*.'

'Well, I'm sure that we can both agree with such sentiments,' responded King cautiously. 'But I fear that may well be a forlorn hope. It very much seems to me that the anti-Jewish policies are becoming more central to Hitler's strategy and I, for one, can see no immediate prospect of that changing.'

Kalz seemed relieved when the waiter returned to refill their glasses and to take their order, as this distraction served to defuse what could have become a significant argument between the two men. This was evidently something that he was eager to avoid, because, as soon as the waiter had left them, he turned the conversation toward the theme of his guest's ideas on issues of mutual security for Great Britain and Germany.

In fact, King was also content with this shift in the discussion for, however much he was repelled by the events of *Kristallnacht* and wanted to condemn them without reservation, he also needed to maintain a generally convivial atmosphere in order to encourage Kalz to remain in an expansive mood. Picking up and twirling his champagne flute, as if considering his response, King eventually trotted out a pre-prepared, diplomatic and relatively non-committal answer. 'Well, Erwin,' he began, 'let's first consider the proposition that neither the British nor the German people want war with one another. What evidence is there to support this? In the case of Great Britain, the generally relieved reaction to the 'Munich Agreement', despite some feelings of unease at leaving the Czechs in the lurch, suggests that there exists little appetite for war in my country. But what about Germany? I must say that when I arrived in Berlin, it seemed to me as if the population was solidly behind their Führer and his expansionist policies. The feeling of celebration and excitement was palpable.'

'But the feelings here are actually little different from those you described in Britain,' responded Kalz without hesitation. 'It was precisely because Britain and France had accepted the Führer's territorial claims, which in turn meant that a war was not necessary, that the people celebrated. Again it was relief, not triumphalism.'

King evidently looked sceptical because the German continued in a much lower voice. 'Did you know for example, that before the 'Munich Agreement', when war was a distinct possibility, the Führer attempted to generate public support for military action by staging a large parade through Berlin? And what do you think happened, John?' King looked suitably nonplussed, a reaction which gave Kalz all the encouragement he needed to answer his own question. 'I'll tell you. No one bothered to turn up and watch, let alone cheer. Hitler, apparently, was furious. It was also a disaster for those who want war because it showed clearly that the German people have no appetite for an end to peace. So, as to your first point; I believe that we can safely begin from the position that neither people wants war.'

The German recognised that he had his guest's full attention now and went on to argue strongly that many of the recent political and military actions of Germany had their roots in a desire to undo some of the most hated elements of the Versailles Treaty.

'That's certainly an argument that may be advanced from a German perspective, yes,' King admitted tentatively. 'And undoubtedly, there are those at home who believe that Britain should revert to its nineteenth century policy of 'Splendid Isolation', which would mean avoiding all continental entanglements and focusing solely on The Empire. There are still strong memories of how the Great Powers sleepwalked into war in August 1914 and many hold to a firm resolution that such a thing should not happen again. But, of course, there are also many who see Germany's rising strength bringing it into inevitable conflict, both with France over leadership of Europe and with Great Britain over colonial influence.'

'Many John, really?' asked Kalz doubtfully. 'Is it not just Churchill and his ragbag band of camp followers who are saying this? And in any case, surely any possibility of conflict would depend on the point at which Germany's ambitions are satisfied? Remember that the Führer is on record as stating that he hopes that Britain and Germany can together, in equal strength, guarantee long term peace and security. There is simply no argument with your country.'

As King was about to reply, the waiter appeared with the first course of Chicken Consommé with Anchovy Biscuits, served with a bottle of chilled Mosel wine. He had to admit that the silver service standard was excellent and he congratulated Kalz on the choice of starter. 'Let's leave the serious part of our conversation until later, John,' suggested the Major with a twinkle in his eye. 'For now, I'd like to know a little bit more about you, if that's not too impertinent.'

For all Kalz's evident urbanity, King was certain that his host, as a senior *Abwehr* officer, could be thoroughly ruthless. Nevertheless, the Englishman found himself warming to the German and happily offered a concise version of his life story, up to and including his appointment at Durham University. By coincidence, it emerged that, before embarking on a military career, Kalz had also studied history and, through much of the main course of Medallions of Lobster à la Favorite, the two men chatted happily about the Second German *Reich*. The waiter had just cleared the empty plates and shared the last of a wonderful Montrachet, when a disturbance caught the attention of both men. Clearly, the entrance of some dignitary was imminent and King could not help but notice the distaste on his host's face as he watched SS *Gruppenführer* Reinhardt Heydrich sweep into the room with his entourage. Tall and blond, he looked the very epitome of the Aryan ideal and was obviously used to being the focus of attention wherever he went. Gazing intently at the spectacle, King noticed immediately that *Sturmbannführer* Schröder was among Heydrich's group and was staring with undiluted hostility in his direction.

Kalz seemed to be discomfited by the arrival of the *Gruppenführer*, even though he was seated several tables away. This feeling was confirmed when he rapidly suggested that they forgo dessert and make for the lounge, in order to enjoy cognac and cigars.

'Of course, Erwin,' replied King graciously. 'I've eaten far too much already and I'm happy to skip the pudding.' The Major laughed with real pleasure at the use of the English term and, with a quick signal to the waiter, indicated that they would take coffee and cognac in the lounge. Kalz's plan to slip unobtrusively out of the dining room was ruined, however, when Heydrich's strange, high-pitched voice called out. 'Herr Dr King, I believe. And Herr Major Kalz. What an interesting pair of diners.'

King and his host had little alternative but to divert towards the large circular table at which Heydrich was seated, smiling icily towards them. Kalz looked far from happy, as he saluted briskly. 'Herr *Gruppenführer*. A pleasure, I'm sure.' Heydrich ignored the *Abwehr* officer and turned the full malevolence of his gaze onto the British academic. 'I understand that last week at the Reception at the Bendlerblock you had a disagreement with one of my best officers.' *Sturmbannführer* Schröder, seated at Heydrich's side, looked pleased at what he imagined was King's discomfort.

Perhaps he had not been in Berlin long enough to be cowed by Hitler's favourite, for King responded with affable charm and confidence. 'With all due respect, Herr *Gruppenführer*, it was Joachim Brandt who had a disagreement with me. Poor man, I fear he has a disagreement with life itself.'

'That's as may be,' hissed the leading Nazi through gritted teeth, his fury at King's amusing response all too evident. 'In any case, that officer is now back in the USA. But you would do well to watch your step here in Berlin, Herr Doktor. It may not be in your best interests to be so unconcerned about, how shall I put it, the people you irritate.'

Having had the last word, Heydrich clearly lost interest in

prolonging the exchange and ostentatiously dismissed both King and Kalz by turning his back on both and engaging his fellow table guests in conversation. After a quick exchange of glances, the Major and his English guest continued on their way out of the dining room.

As they approached a small table in a far corner of the lounge, the waiter appeared, carrying a tray which held a beautiful porcelain coffee service, a bottle of fine old champagne cognac with two enormous balloon glasses and a box of fine hand-rolled Hoyo cigars. As soon as the contents of the tray were on the table, the German indicated to the waiter that he would no longer be required. 'I had thought that this would suit us admirably,' Kalz said diffidently as he invited his guest to take a seat. 'But I fear that I may have just lost some of my appetite. What on earth was that all about?'

While King did not possess a Gothic imagination, he was also happy to be out of the presence of Heydrich, who in some inexplicable way radiated an aura of evil. Sensing that the evening might end fairly quickly and unsuccessfully, King decided to play down the whole episode. 'Oh, it's nothing, Erwin,' the Englishman began lightly. 'I had the misfortune to run into an old acquaintance of mine from Heidelberg at the Reception the other week. We had not parted on happy terms and, unfortunately, he hadn't got over it. And it seems that one of Heydrich's dinner guests could not resist telling tales out of school.'

'And this friend, is he in the SS now?' asked Kalz with evident concern.

'He has been since 1933, when we had last met... that was ..' King smiled charmingly, 'one of the issues, over which we disagreed. It looks like he might be some kind of protégé of Heydrich now. But there's no problem. You heard him say that Brandt was back in the States.'

'That's true, John,' said Kalz very seriously, 'but I must counsel you to be very, very careful that you do not make a clear enemy of the *Gruppenführer*. That could be very bad for you indeed. But, I agree, at the moment, I don't think it has come to that.'

Having poured the cognac and smiling as he held open the box for his guest, Kalz insisted, 'You really must try one of these Hoyos. They are hand rolled in Cuba, you know. To my mind, their flavour is a little sweeter than normal and I like them very much.' King settled himself into the comfortable armchair and gratefully accepted a cup of coffee, a good measure of cognac and one of the cigars. He was, in truth, still a little in shock from Heydrich's not so veiled threat, but he realised that, neverthelesss, he must focus on trying to get the most from his evening.

'You now know that I am an officer of The *Abwehr*,' began Kalz through a cloud of fragrant cigar smoke. 'Indeed, I have made little attempt to conceal that fact from you.' The Englishman nodded his head in acknowledgement, but remained silent, thereby allowing his host to continue. 'And of course, you are aware that I take a strong personal interest in the topic of your academic exchange with the *Reich* as, may I say, do both Colonel Oster and Admiral Canaris.' Smiling suavely, he then asked, 'But surely, if we talk of issues of mutual security, a key question is what kind of Europe, perhaps even what kind of world, do we desire? I have already this evening mentioned the Versailles Treaty. I'm not surprised that you, as a student of German History, have already acknowledged that it is possible to hold the view that this was a foolish and vindictive act against my country. The economic terms contributed directly to the current political status quo here and there are many forces pushing us towards barbarity. Do you not agree that, in such circumstances, it is incumbent on all men of civilised standards and goodwill to seek to keep these at bay?'

'I have to say, in all candour, Erwin, that I saw little evidence of civilised behaviour a week ago in Berlin,' retorted King sharply. Kalz grimaced as if he had been struck in the face, before replying with evident sincerity. 'Neither my organisation, nor The Wehrmacht had any knowledge of, or participation in, what can only be described as those atrocities.' In a clear reference to Heydrich, still presumably holding court in the dining room, he continued in a very quiet voice. 'I believe we have just left the company of one of those most responsible. No,' continued the German with evident passion, 'the real issue is that civilisation is at the present moment surrounded by threats, and the major one clearly comes from the East. Surely you would agree that a strong Germany, which can hold Stalin at bay, would be in the interests of your country. A civilised bulwark against the tide of Bolshevism, which is, of course the real enemy of both our countries.'

'Well as you know, unlike some in my profession in Britain, Stalinism holds absolutely no attraction for me,' declared King with feeling. Recognising that this may well be the moment for which he had been working, Kalz pounced. 'Then I wonder, John, what would you be prepared to do to help the process of creating a stronger European barrier to such barbarism?' Kalz immediately saw his guest's frown and attempted to reassure him. 'Oh don't worry, my friend. I know that you are an honourable and patriotic man as, may I say, am I. I would never ask you to do anything which is obviously against the interests of your country or which, in your position, I would not be prepared to do myself. I am merely asking if you would consider sharing with me any information that you acquire during your stay in Germany which you feel is in the joint interest of our two countries. I am, of course aware that you, how shall I put it, have a varied circle of contacts here and that you may well hear things that are of interest to us both.'

'So you had me followed then, Erwin. That's not very friendly, is it?' snapped King, before taking another pull at his cigar.

'Of course not, John,' replied Kalz reassuringly. 'But don't be naïve. You must know that we have very many informers, many of whom are concentrated in areas where we might expect to find activity which is counter to the interests of the *Reich*. You have been noticed, that's all. We don't object to your activities in the slightest. But we would, subject to the conditions I have already stated, like to make use of them.'

King immediately thought of Brunner and his suspicions that he was some kind of informer. He would clearly have to be much more careful around the University in future. Kalz was evidently expecting some kind of response and the Englishman decided to play for time. 'Well, Erwin,' he began disingenuously, 'you've taken me by surprise tonight and given me much food for thought.'

Kalz, smiling in a self-satisfied way that King found slightly unpleasant, seemed most content with this initial reply. 'Of course you must think about my proposition. There's no rush. Maybe we could meet again in a few days' time, when you've had time to consider things fully. I'll contact you then, and in the meantime, I suggest that we give our full attention to this wonderful cognac and the excellent cigars.'

The evening wound down quickly and King, in need of air, declined Kalz's offer to drop him off at his flat. As he walked home through the cold and blessedly quiet streets, he reflected on how, in some ways his mission was going better than he could have hoped. His growing relationship with Kalz and the attempt to involve him, in however limited a way, in the work of The *Abwehr* was more than he could have expected. On the other hand, the uncertain ramifications of his confrontation with Joachim Brandt and now the involvement of someone as powerful and evil as Heydrich could be disastrous for him. Feeling a little overwhelmed by it all, he was eager to discuss the evening's developments with Pym. He knew, however, that before he would meet his mentor, there was something very important that he had to do.

Chapter Ten

Monday, 21st November 1938, Berlin.

It was a cold, grey morning when King jumped off the tram as it slowly passed Anhalter Station in the centre of Berlin. This was such a classic looking railway terminus, with its huge curved roof and tall windows now draped with garish swastikas, that on seeing it, he felt that he should be excited by the prospect of the imminent rail journey. On this day, however, his feelings were decidedly mixed. On the one hand, he was looking forward to returning to his old stamping ground of Heidelberg, where he had spent such a happy time several years before. On the other, he was somewhat anxious at what he might find there. Shortly before leaving for Germany, he had promised his old friends Rachel and David Bernstein that he would call in on their parents at Christmas to say hello. He had also the idea of spending some time with his old mentor Professor David Berg. That was, of course, before the dreadful events of *Kristallnacht*, after which he felt he could not afford to wait any longer to make his journey south.

King edged off the pavement and to his consternation almost stepped straight into the path of an oncoming tram, which rang its bell in furious complaint at his absentmindedness. For God's sake, pull yourself together man, he berated himself as he made his way, more gingerly this time, towards the grand station entrance. Once inside the station concourse, King headed through crowds of people surging around the ticket office windows and the various outlets for food and drink. He found himself queueing behind a harassed-looking woman in her thirties, who was struggling to keep in check three unruly boys who were dressed identically in the black shorts and brown shirts of the Nazi '*Pimpf*' organisation for youngsters. It pleased King to note that, while they may have had the appearance of miniature Brownshirts, with all their thuggish connotations, the boys were behaving just like seven and eight year olds the world over. Pushing and pulling each other and occasionally breaking away to run around the increasingly irritated adults, a collective sigh of relief went up when the mother had concluded her business at the counter and ushered her lively children out towards the platforms.

Having purchased his open return ticket for Heidelberg, he decided to visit the buffet for a coffee and a sandwich. For a moment, he wished that he had had with him his trusty MG sports car, so that he could have tried out the new autobahns which the press was saying had revolutionised long distance car travel. However, the near twelve- hour journey which awaited him would give him plenty of time to open and study the contents of his bulging briefcase. He had promised the Head of the History Department that before Christmas he would give a lecture analysing the 'Anglo-German Naval Race', which occurred in the period leading up to the start of the First World War. Given his supposed purpose in Berlin and in view of the 1935 'Naval Agreement' between Britain and Germany, King was very keen to address the present day lessons which could be derived from the first major arms race of the twentieth century. He had planned to use the long journey to begin to map out his initial ideas for the paper.

He found an unoccupied table in the station buffet and settled himself down to enjoy his coffee and cheese sandwich. It was just turned eleven and he had only twenty minutes to wait before his train was due to leave. Food and drink consumed, he decided to buy a newspaper to read on the journey, only to reject rapidly *Der Stürmer*, the *Völkischer Beobachter* and the rest of the available German language newspapers as far too rabidly Nazi. As a more palatable alternative, he briefly considered, but decided against a two-day old copy of *The Manchester Guardian* or a week old edition of The *New York Times*. Despite his new found resolve to exercise caution, King failed to notice the small, dark-haired man, dressed in a standard grey overcoat, who hastily bought a copy of the *Völkischer Beobachter*, which he folded neatly under his arm before following him out towards Platform Three and the waiting *Reichsbahn* train.

King passed swiftly through the ticket inspection and made his way along the busy platform. The train was steaming, as if straining to be on its way, and many passengers were climbing aboard. He gave a last look towards the magnificently tall curved archway, through which the train would shortly pass on its way out of the station, before jumping athletically into a second class carriage. He managed to find a window seat, facing forward, about half way down the compartment and settled down for the beginning of his journey. Ever since his time as a student at Oxford University, King had been able to shut out any distractions and get on with even the most challenging of reading. And so it proved on this day, as he managed to read two key sources on the

'Anglo-German Naval Arms Race'. Indeed, he had only taken a few minutes away from his books, stretching his legs on the platform while the train had enjoyed a seven-minute wait at Erfurt. He was so absorbed in his thoughts on the argument, which was forming in his head and which he was looking forward to developing in his lecture, that he did not notice that some of his papers and books were not quite in the same place as he had left them. Neither did he give too much attention to the fact that the old man who had been sitting facing him had been replaced by a much more attractive travelling companion, a slim young woman in the uniform of a hospital nurse, who had a very pretty, open face and bright red hair. Indeed, it was not until the train had left Würzburg and the attendant had passed through the carriage announcing the first sitting in the Dining Car that King had looked up from his papers. He was most pleasantly surprised to find two large green eyes looking at him with amusement.

'It seems that you have a very interesting topic of study,' said the nurse with a playful twinkle in her eye. 'But you know, all work and no play makes Hans a dull boy.' This last phrase was spoken in English, albeit with a strong German accent, and King could not help but burst out laughing. Of course, the nurse had managed to see the English title of one of the many books which he had placed in a kind of barrier on the table between them and had managed to recall one of the sayings, which she had learned in English classes at school. Consciously registering for the first time her attractiveness and inwardly berating himself for being so absorbed in his work, King determined to try to make a good impression.

'Actually, it's John,' he replied brightly, 'and yes, you know, I think you're right. Now, what can we do about that? Was that the call for the Dining Car that I just heard? Maybe a little supper would be in order?'

'That would be very pleasant,' replied the nurse, with evident satisfaction. 'I may even be able to practice my English.'

'It just so happens that I'm a teacher,' replied King as she looked at him with inquisitive eyes. 'But a teacher of History, I'm afraid.'

'No matter,' came the speedy reply. 'I'm sure that with your excellent German and my basic English, we'll manage. Let's go, while there's still a chance of a free table.'

As King followed his new found dining companion, the sight of her swaying hips and shapely figure instantaneously sent all thoughts, both of the naval treaty and of academic lectures to be written, flying out of his mind. A discreetly offered *Reichsmark* note, suavely pocketed by the Head Waiter, soon found King and his companion seated at a table for two in the rapidly filling Dining Car.

Having had the opportunity to look more carefully at his dinner guest, King was stunned by her natural beauty and evident friendliness. Unusually tongue tied, he asked tentatively. 'You know, I don't even know....'

'It's Margaretha... Margaretha Maier. But that's a bit of a mouthful, so all my friends call me Greta,' interrupted the nurse with a beaming smile.

'So, may I call you....' began King hesitantly.

'Of course you must call me Greta,' came the instant reply. 'If you'd like to be my friend, that is.' This was spoken with a mischievous smile and King, unused to being wrong-footed in this way, felt his heartbeat race in excitement.

'That's fine, Greta,' he said happily. 'But do you think I'll ever be able to..'

'...finish a sentence?' added Greta, with an impish grin. 'I really don't know, John. I really don't know.' And they both burst out in happy laughter. The waiter's attention was caught by this sound and he approached the table to take their order, after which Greta looked at King with arched eyebrows. 'So John,' she asked, more serious now. 'What brings you to Germany?'

The conversation and laughter flowed for the next hour, as King briefly explained his part in the academic exchange programme. Always a self-deprecating man, he then regaled his guest with accounts of his time at Oxford and some of the antics of his students back in Durham. Greta reciprocated with a series of hilarious stories from her time working in various hospitals throughout Germany. King was very taken with the ability she shared with him, of being able to tell funny stories about, yet care deeply for those she worked with and for. He was amazed and thrilled at the ease with which they could talk to one another about all kinds of things and he realised that, for the first time in many months, he was actually having a really good time with a very attractive companion.

He was, of course, aware that Professor Pym had been absolutely adamant that, should he accept the proposed assignment, he must be extremely cautious when socialising. He had not been happy with what amounted to an instruction about how he should conduct his private life, but he had accepted that Pym was more experienced in such matters and had by and large acquiesced. This evening, however, he felt more like his old self again, fully alive and enjoying his new found friendship and even wondering where it may lead.... and, he reflected happily, all this on the strength of only an hour or two in Greta's company.

Despite his wish that the meal could last until they arrived in Heidelberg, the increased fussing by the waiter indicated clearly to King that they should vacate the table in favour of one of the waiting couples. Much to the waiter's relief, King finally acted on one of his more blatant hints and summoned him for the bill. As they swayed out of the Dining Car, partly because of the movement of the train and partly due to the effect of the wine they had shared, Greta put her hand on King's arm. At this, her first touch, an unforgettable pulse of electricity ran through his whole body and his senses shot to Red Alert. Greta, however, was looking intently through the glass section of the door of the Dining Car. From her vantage point she could see clearly into their carriage and whispered, 'Did you see that man? I'm sure he was looking through your things.'

King was only interested in his proximity to Greta and by the time he could tear his enchanted gaze away from her, he saw only the man's back, as he retreated down the carriage towards his own seat. 'I'm sure you must be mistaken. Probably he just stumbled into our table as he was walking past,' he said in an attempt to reassure her. No sooner were they both seated, than Greta, suddenly with a more troubled expression replied. 'Really, John? I'm not so sure. Do you know that man? When I came to sit here and you were still out on the platform at Erfurt, I saw that he had one of your books in his hand. I thought then that he was sitting where you are and that the books belonged to him. But he simply said that he had knocked the book off the table as he was passing and was replacing it.'

'Well, there you are then. Simple accident. Forget it,' said King, with a relaxed smile. It was clear, however, that Greta was far from convinced. 'Be careful, John, please. You must promise me. Germany today can be a dangerous place.' King was touched by the evident concern of this beautiful young German woman, to whom, despite them having just met, he felt increasingly attracted. 'Of course I'll take care, Greta,' he replied with an air of genuine seriousness. 'Please don't worry about me.'

While not wanting to make too much of Greta's concerns, King was nevertheless glad that from his seat he could unobtrusively study the man who might have been looking through his papers and books. He felt sure that, after his conversation with Kalz, this person was most unlikely to be an *Abwehr* agent. However, he had to admit that he could well be an SS or Gestapo man, put on his tail to intimidate him. He decided that he would have to take every possible precaution before visiting Rachel's parents and Professor Berg in Heidelberg. For Greta's sake, he would continue to play down the concern he felt, but when he left the train he would try to ensure that he was not followed.

Greta told King that, though originally from Erfurt, she had worked at the main hospital in Heidelberg for the last eighteen months. In fact, it was from a short visit to her parents that she was now returning, in uniform so as to be able to pay a lesser fare on the train. King reciprocated by explaining that he was looking up one of his old teachers at the University and the parents of his friends who no longer lived in Germany. He felt a huge surge of frustration as he told her that, unfortunately, he would have to return to Berlin after only two nights in Heidelberg.

King was not particularly adept at reading those tell-tale signs of immediate chemistry between people, but even he could not fail to recognise the mutual attraction between himself and Greta. Moreover, he was absolutely delighted with the development, having seen enough of the darker side of a country that, during his time in Heidelberg, he had come to love and respect. He was extremely happy that now, this lovely woman was reminding him of what Germany could be like. The train was only minutes away from their destination, when King began hesitantly, 'Er.... Greta.... er.... I er ... don't suppose......'

'Of course I'd be delighted to have dinner with you tomorrow evening, John,' interrupted Greta, before they both once again laughed with pure delight. No sooner had the pair readily agreed to meet at the Hotel Hirschgasse at eight-thirty the following evening, than the train made its final approach to the station. They gathered their belongings and, with some sadness at the end of such an enjoyable journey, they descended onto the cold platform. A chaste kiss on the cheek and Greta was gone, waving from the rear window of the last tram as it made its way through a light snowfall towards her home. King consoled himself with the thoughts that he would see her again the next evening and that he was sure that he had seen her blow him another kiss from the tram.

The cold night air sobered him up immediately and, while he had the feeling that Greta had possibly over reacted about the man on the train looking through his things, he surreptitiously looked around the few people waiting outside the station. To his surprise, the suspected man was no more than twenty yards away, lighting a cigarette, as if waiting for someone. Having already decided that, whoever he may be, this man should not know his hotel, King decided to put into action his plan to lose his unwanted shadow. He had noticed that the row of taxis, which were queueing for customers, was dwindling rapidly as people departed to their various destinations in and around the city. Suddenly, and without warning, King seized his chance to jump quickly into the last available cab. The man in the grey overcoat was taken completely by surprise and, as no other taxi was available, he had no means to follow. King smiled triumphantly at the sight of him, staring angrily at the back of the cab as it sped away through the thickening snow.

Chapter Eleven

Tuesday, 22nd November 1938, Heidelberg.

Although he had experienced vivid dreams of Greta, his possible Gestapo shadow, the friends he hoped to find safe and well the next day and long train journeys all mixed into some strange nonsensical brew, King awoke early the next day feeling fully refreshed. He looked out of his room window and saw immediately that a few inches of snow had fallen overnight. This had afforded the Old Town a peaceful and charming appearance that not even the few crude Nazi posters and sagging flags which were visible could altogether dispel. He could just make out the twin towers of the gate on the Old Bridge which began at the end of Steingasse and he found himself thinking back to his last day in Heidelberg in 1933. At that time, the mere thought of him returning to the city as some kind of British secret agent would have sent him into gales of laughter. Yet not only was this true, but he was also being propositioned to spy for The *Abwehr*. Smiling at the unexpected turns that life can take, he shook his head and made his way downstairs to the breakfast room.

King was happy to see no sign of anyone loitering outside the hotel as, fortified by a typically generous German breakfast, he set off down the Steingasse. His route took him through the gate and across the river Neckar by means of the Old Bridge. Despite harbouring some concerns over what the day might bring, he felt exhilarated as he recalled with delight the time he had spent with Greta. She really is something special, he confirmed. I can't wait to see her tonight. Glad that his trusty old hiking boots still seemed to be waterproof, he turned right towards the Hotel Hirschgasse to reserve a table for dinner and, as he emerged from the lovely old building, he carefully checked that he had not been followed.

King retraced his steps back across the Neckar and on into the Old Town, where he hoped to find Professor Berg still in his tiny, but quaint old flat on the Seminarstraße, a conveniently short distance from the University Library. This was an area which, during King's stay in Heidelberg, had been Bohemian and inexpensive and therefore popular among the less status conscious among the University staff. The twice weekly market was in full swing as he crossed the Marktplatz, the city's grand Town Hall dominating one side of the square. Had he not just enjoyed an enormous breakfast at the Grüner Baum, he would have been sorely tempted by the roasted chestnuts or the spiced sausages which were sizzling over glowing charcoals. The various smells of food, spices and wooden articles from the various stalls, combined with the clear sky and bright snow gave the square a very seasonal air. This was spoiled only by the inevitable groups of uniformed Nazi activists, who were busy distributing propaganda material. King could see by their outraged headlines that they focused on the latest 'atrocities' being committed on peaceful Germans by Poles in the Danzig Corridor.

As a precaution, King decided to take an indirect route to Berg's flat; he therefore turned down Dreikönigsstraße and made his way back towards the river. Heidelberg looked every inch the beautiful and prosperous, ancient university city and he despaired about the extent to which it had been changed by years of Fascism. As if to underline the point, turning away from the riverbank up Große Mantelgasse, he was immediately confronted by the burned out shell of one of the city's finest synagogues.

More worried now about his friends, King hurried directly to Seminarstraße and as soon as he had arrived at the familiar old building, he rang the Professor's doorbell at the main entrance. He was not unduly concerned that there was no immediate answer; after all, he was unannounced and the Professor might easily have gone out for some reason. Just as he was about to turn away and leave, the door was opened by Frau Ziegler the *Portierfrau*. As a student, King had been a frequent visitor to this building and he remembered her well from those days. Now the old lady squinted anxiously at the Englishman, as if trying to recall some long forgotten face, 'I know you don't I?'

King made to answer, before the old woman interrupted sharply. 'No! Don't tell me. It'll come back to me. I may be getting on a bit, but I pride myself in never forgetting a name.' King waited patiently for a good two minutes, before seeing first the warmth of recognition in Frau Ziegler's eyes, closely followed by what he could only describe as terror. 'You shouldn't have come here, Herr King,' she whispered in a tiny, terrified voice. 'I can't tell you anything. Please go away quickly.'

'There's nothing to worry about, Frau Ziegler. I've just come to say hello to the Professor. Look, I've brought him a present from England.' King showed a fine leather bound volume to this woman who used to seem to him so bustling and full of confidence, but who now seemed a frightened shadow of her former self. 'It's an 1843 Edition of Shakespeare's poems which I found in one of my favourite second hand bookshops in Durham. I know Professor Berg has a large collection of works by the Bard, so I thought he might like it. Is he at home?'

In response to his question, an infinitely sad look came into the *Portierfrau's* eyes and she fainted, falling heavily into King's arms. The young man managed to open the door sufficiently to enable him to struggle through and help himself, and the now recovering old lady, into her tiny ground-floor flat. He carefully lowered her down onto a threadbare sofa and fetched a glass of water which he offered to her lips. Gradually, the old German recovered her senses more fully and, with them, her look of terror.

'You must go now, Herr King. It isn't safe. What if they were to find out that I was talking to you about the poor Professor?' she sobbed. 'I have heard that they send people to terrible places.'

'Don't worry Frau Ziegler,' said King in as calming and reassuring a manner as he could muster. 'I'll leave through the back, where no one will see me. I know the way and I'll be very careful. But, please, I've come a long way to see Professor Berg. You know what he means to me. What's happened here? Is it something to do with *Kristallnacht*?' When she heard this, the floodgates opened, as if she was trying to rid herself of a dreadful burden of knowledge and King could barely keep up with her rapid and emotional outburst. 'He was such a good and brave man,' she began and, mindful of her words, King prepared himself for the worst. 'After he was dismissed from the University all those years ago, he was so accepting. Many of his ex-colleagues continued to help him financially, but he was a proud man. Most of his beautiful books, ornaments, paintings and furniture had to be sold.' Frau Ziegler suddenly stopped talking and simply looked at King. She seemed to be steeling herself to tell the whole dreadful story to this fresh faced Englishman, who she remembered with such fondness from the good days. 'You know me, Herr King, I'm just an ordinary German, as proud of my country as the next person. But what they've been doing to the Jews, it's just plain wrong. It sickens me, as it sickens all good people. I begged the Professor not to go out when we heard the noise from the street. But when his friend came to tell him that the synagogue had been set on fire and the Holy Scriptures were being desecrated, he wouldn't listen to me. He went straight down to Lauerstraße to try to save what he could. I was told later that the crowd laughed and cheered as he was beaten to death by those thugs. Such a civilised and good man, Herr King. To meet such an end. How can we continue to believe in God?' She shook her head in total incomprehension, tears flowing down her sunken cheeks. Almost as quickly as the tears began, however, they stopped, as if she had finally let go of Professor Berg and was now focused only on King. 'Now, please, you must go' she insisted. 'For some days, I've had the feeling that this house is being watched. I don't worry so much for myself these days, but you are so young.'

    For the first time in his life, King simply had no words; of hope, of consolation, or even of promised retribution. He simply hugged Frau Ziegler tightly, kissed the top of her grey head, whispered 'Look after yourself' and was gone. He followed the familiar back route out of the building, certain that no one had seen him leave. For a good hour, King wandered around in a complete daze. He had feared for his good friend and mentor, but he never could have expected him to suffer such a brutal and unwarranted end. He experienced periodic surges of almost uncontrollable anger, during which he had to struggle hard to stop himself taking out his urgent need for revenge on the first uniformed Nazi to cross his path. Eventually, without having any idea how he had got there, he found himself sitting on a bench overlooking the river. He found the timeless, sedate motion of the water calming and, while certainly not forgetting any of the horror of what he had just been told, he did manage to regain full control of himself. With this came the realisation that, as Frau Ziegler had urged, he must concern himself with those he hoped were still living and so he set off towards the home of Dr and Frau Bernstein.

    The Bernsteins lived in a pleasant, though unassuming garden flat in Obere Neckarstraße, overlooked by the famous old *Schloß*. King faced a good twenty-minute walk there, especially with snow still lying on the ground and with his preference for taking a circuitous route. It was shortly before one in the afternoon when King rang the Bernstein's doorbell, hoping against hope that here the news would be better. Even though no one answered his ring, he was sure that someone was inside the flat, because he had seen the net curtain of the front window move and a shadow cross the living room. After unsuccessfully ringing three times, it was obvious that whoever was inside the flat was, understandably, as frightened as Frau Ziegler had been. Unwilling to give up and leave, he decided that his only option was to tap gently at the window and announce himself, as quietly as he could in English. 'Dr Bernstein. It's John King here, sir. I'm a friend of Rachel and David. They asked me to come to see you, while I'm in Germany. I have a message for you from them.' He could sense, rather than see movement in the flat and decided to continue. 'Do you remember me, Dr Bernstein? I was at the University with Rachel in 1933 and I helped her and David to emigrate to England? They both stayed with my parents for a few months.'

Gradually the door to the flat opened, just enough for King to see a small, grey and frightened face peering out at him. 'John, is it really you? I thought you were in England?'

'Yes, Frau Bernstein, it's me,' he replied as gently as he could. 'Are you and Dr Bernstein all right?' At the mention of her husband's name, the old lady turned from the door and went back into the flat, where she slumped, sobbing into a chair. King immediately noted that many of the family's prized possessions and fine furniture had been sacrificed to the need to survive somehow in an unforgiving Nazi Germany. 'They took him just over a week ago. After all the trouble,' said Frau Bernstein in a flat voice. 'They said it was because of all the bad things we've done. But John, my Erich and I, what bad things did we ever do? He's a doctor. He helps people.'

King looked on with pity as she trailed off into sobbing incomprehension. 'Of course you have done nothing bad, Frau Bernstein. You must never think that. But do you know where they have taken your husband?'

'They talked about a place near München, a camp where he will have to work, in order to make up for the bad things they say he did. They took a hundred and fifty others with my Erich. They said they have all done bad things.... Dachau they called it, I think.'

King's blood froze at this information. He had heard rumours of such concentration camps during his time in Berlin and he was sure that unless Dr Bernstein could be granted a quick release, he would never leave that place alive. Over the next two hours, King tried to comfort his friend's mother as best he could, with news both of Rachel and of David. She smiled proudly at the news that her son was a serving policeman in Britain, and for a fleeting moment King was able to see a glimpse of the refined and happy woman he once knew. A native of Wales herself, although having spent all her adult life with her beloved husband in Germany, it seemed to King that she was particularly pleased to hear that her son now seemed to be more British than German. She even managed a weak laugh, as King told her that her son absolutely adored tea with milk and fish and chips.

'I wish we'd gone with them, when we had the chance,' she whispered sadly. 'But it's too late for that now.... far too late.' King took both her hands in his and said earnestly, 'No it isn't Frau Bernstein. I'll try to arrange for you to go to England as soon as possible. Would you like that? And I promise that I'll do all I can to get Dr Bernstein home, so that he can come too.'

As soon as he had said the words, he knew that he had made a promise that he had no certain way of keeping. But, looking now at the hope dawning in the eyes of his friends' mother, he also knew without doubt that it had been the right thing to say. He would worry about the practicalities and how Pym might react another time. For now, he simply wanted to offer what little hope he could to this frail lady, who had treated him with such kindness in the past.

'Do you really think we could go to England, John? Would it be possible? Can you help bring Erich home? I'm sure he will be worrying about me and his patients. Of course, officially now he can only treat Jews, but some of his old patients would still come to him in secret. They like him you see. My Erich has such a lovely manner.'

Listening to her now, and seeing the faraway look in her eyes, King had some concerns that, without the strength of her husband beside her, she might collapse psychologically. 'Do you see anyone, Frau Bernstein?' he asked gently. 'Is there anyone who can help you?' King found himself surprised by this seemingly weak old woman as she replied with something of her old spirit. 'Don't worry about me, John. I can look after myself. Just do your best for my poor Erich, I beg of you.'

'I'll do my best,' promised King again. 'But you must say nothing of going to England. Not to anyone at all. That must remain our secret.

Do you understand, Frau Bernstein? That's very important.' He was uncertain that she had been listening to him, but was reassured when she smiled sadly, nodded her head briefly and whispered. 'Of course, John. I understand totally. You can rely on me.'

The air was noticeably colder, as King made his way by the riverbank towards the Old Bridge. He had no clear idea of how he might be able to help effect the release of Dr Bernstein from Dachau. Given his own circumstances, he could see many difficulties in trying to help one or both of them to escape Nazi Germany. As he trudged through the now freezing snow, however, he was determined that he would succeed in both aims.

****

It was just about dark when he returned to the welcoming light and warmth of the Grüner Baum. Hurrying through the hotel lounge, he headed straight up to his room, where he quickly removed his boots and overcoat and promptly collapsed on the bed. The rumblings in his stomach reminded him that he had not eaten since breakfast, but the warmth of the room, combined with the nervous energy he had expended during the day, made him drowsy. Before long, forgetting totally about his planned dinner date with Greta, he was fast asleep.

Some hours later, King was turning restlessly in his bed, disturbed by a strange scratching or tapping noise and a whispered voice, of which his half sleeping brain could make no sense. Waking up, he could hear more clearly now the insistent tapping at his door and the urgent call of 'John! John! Are you in there? It's Greta!'

In an instant King looked at his watch and saw to his consternation that it was nearly ten o'clock. Oh God, he thought, as the realisation dawned that he was supposed to have been at the Hotel Hirschgasse for dinner an hour ago. 'Hang on, Greta. I'll be there in a second,' he called, as he scrambled off the bed and moved somewhat groggily to open the door, where he was greeted by a sardonic smile.

'So this is the way you treat a lady on her first date, is it, John? And I thought Englishmen were supposed to be such gentlemen. I can't say that I'm overly impressed...'

'I don't know what to say, Greta. I'm so sorry,' he gabbled. 'I've no idea what came over me. I must have been exhausted. Are we too late for dinner? How can I make it up to you?'

King was nonplussed by the nature of her response, especially the undiluted amusement in her dazzlingly green eyes. He could only gape idiotically, as she mock scolded him. 'You must be joking, John! This is provincial Germany, not the metropolis of London. At this time, we'll be lucky to find a sandwich.'

King had always felt himself to be a man of reason, not prone to flights of fancy or over emotionality and certainly he was one, for whom the concept of love at first sight belonged firmly in Hollywood. However, he was totally unprepared for the joke that Cupid seemed intent on playing on him. For, standing there in his hotel room, he, the rationalist, knew that he was very much in danger of falling for this woman, who he had met only the day before.

Disregarding his hunger and instinctively knowing he was doing the right thing, King gave in to his pressing need to share his experience of the day with Greta. 'But I do want to explain to you. It's important that you understand.' Immediately the red-headed German recognised that something terrible must have happened. She sat King down on the bed, took off her coat and sat down next to him, holding his right hand between both of hers. And he told her everything that had happened. About Professor Berg and his dreadful end; about the courageous Frau Ziegler and finally about the Bernsteins and his promise to help them in any way he could. He finished by saying that he felt almost guilty because of his happiness, amid such abject misery.

'Oh John. You're a good man and, of course, you believe that everyone should have a good life. But here, now, in Germany we don't have that luxury. You must never feel guilty for feeling happiness. It's surely the fact that some of us are lucky enough to experience good and normal things, even in the midst of all this hatred and violence, that helps keep alive some sense of belief in the human spirit. Do you honestly think Professor Berg would be glad, or sad at your happiness? Be happy in his memory, as well as for yourself.'

King felt humbled by the absolute sense which this beautiful and sensitive German nurse had spoken and said decisively, 'You're right, of course, darling Greta. Thank you for helping me to see that. Whatever others may do and however dark the future seems, we can and must maintain our beliefs and our hope. It's all we can do, after all. Now,' he smiled boyishly, leaping to his feet, 'what was it you said about a sandwich?'

King had to use all his powers of persuasion, and the promise of a hefty tip, to persuade the hotel to provide a range of cold meats, cheese, bread and wine. They enjoyed the meal, and one another's company, all alone in the Dining Room, which was illuminated only by flickering candlelight. There were, of course, more smiles and laughter, as they shared information about their lives and their favourite and their least favourite things. This time, however, there were also more serious interludes, during which they both cautiously whispered their hatred of Nazism and their anxieties about the future. Much later, and after the final candles had guttered into darkness, they made their way slowly back to King's room. As if to confirm their joint commitment to love and humanity, in the face of its opposite in Hitler's *Reich*, King and Greta spent the night locked in one another's arms, gently making love and waiting for the dawn to herald a new day.

****

King awoke with a start after another strange and jumbled dream. The sun was streaming through a slight gap in the curtains of his room and instantly he knew that Greta was not beside him. Indeed, he quickly realised that she must have left much earlier, as the side of the bed on which she had lain was cold to his touch. As he continued to move his hand in the forlorn hope that he might finally touch her warm skin, his fingers brushed against a piece of paper. He quickly sat up and read:

My darling John,

You looked so peaceful and happy this morning that I didn't have the heart to wake you up - even though I yearned for your caress!

Today, I have an early shift at the hospital and I suppose that I'll be almost half way through it before you read this.

I find this difficult to explain, but life for me seems to have taken on a whole new and a much better meaning, since we met on the train, what.... less than two days ago.

But now, I really must go. I'm not sure what the Matron would say if I turned up for work in my best evening wear, so I have to rush home to change.

Please don't forget me, my love

Greta

Having ensured that the note contained both her address and phone number, King leaned back on the pillow and smiled to himself... 'Forget you, Greta? I couldn't if I tried.'

****

After enjoying another excellent breakfast, he checked out of the Grüner Baum and made his way through the bright sunshine and cold dry air towards the railway station. It had now become habitual for him to take a circuitous route with several exposed sections and by the time he reached the railway station, he was as certain as he could reasonably be that no one had followed his progress through the city.

Once he was comfortably seated in a fairly quiet second class compartment, he was able to ponder that it had been barely forty-eight hours since he had been on the train travelling from Berlin to Heidelberg. Amazingly, that seemed like a lifetime ago, or more accurately, it seemed to belong to a different life to the one which might, just possibly, lie ahead for him. After their conversations, he felt certain that he knew enough about Greta to be sure that she had no sympathy for Hitler and his henchmen. On the other hand, King had to acknowledge that she was German and he was British, at a time when those two countries seemed to be moving inexorably towards war. As if that was not problem enough, there was also his commitment to Pym to consider. He had given his word that he would undertake the mission to the best of his ability. While that remained his firm intention, he recognised that it would be naive to pretend that meeting Greta and making his promise to Frau Bernstein would not present significant additional complications that would have to be managed. It was perfectly obvious to King that Pym would, in all probability, react extremely negatively to both those developments, as the Professor was sure to see them as making him more vulnerable. He gazed at the books and notes which were spread out chaotically on the table in front of him. Of course, he knew that this work was crucial to his credibility at the University, but he also felt that it was now a lesser priority. Above all, it was imperative both to continue to cultivate Kalz and to negotiate Pym's help to get Dr Bernstein out of Dachau.

Chapter Twelve

Tuesday, 29th November 1938, Berlin.

A Siberian wind was blowing from the East as King made his way down Wilhelmstraße towards the British Embassy and his appointment with Pym. His old Professor's presence in Germany, as the British Moderator of the Anglo-German academic exchange programme, offered the perfect rationale for a meeting which would arouse no one's suspicions. Since his return from Heidelberg, he had been grateful that Kalz had not pressed him for an immediate response to his proposition and had kept himself busy with the lecture that he was due to present to his departmental colleagues shortly before Christmas.

The direction in which he was walking meant that King had to pass the NSDAP Headquarters which, bizarrely, were situated on the same street as the British Embassy. Just as he reached the flag-festooned building, a car drew up and was surrounded immediately by a platoon of SS guards forming a cordon that blocked the pavement to pedestrians. With a sinking heart, he imagined that some star of the Third Reich was just arriving at his workplace. Ragged cries of 'Heil Hitler' were raised as Rudolf Hess, characteristically dressed only in shirt sleeves despite the cold, climbed out of a rear door of the car and rushed up the steps of the main entrance. King could not help but notice that his saturnine features were even more pronounced in the flesh than in the many photographs that were published regularly in the media. Moving on quickly, he gratefully left the small crowd gaping at the retreating back of the Deputy Führer. As he approached the elegant building which housed the British Embassy, King was surprised to see another crowd swarming around its four columned neo-classical entrance. The steps leading up to the door had been hastily blocked with simple trestle tables, behind which stood Embassy Officials who, wrapped up heavily against the cold, were clearly monitoring those who claimed to have business there. King noticed immediately that this seemed a very different crowd of people to that he had just left, gazing in awe and admiration at the next arrivals at Nazi Headquarters. Most of those in front of the Embassy were Jewish, dressed in rather shabby, but decent quality coats and all had the hunted look which King was finding increasingly familiar among those people in Germany.

'But you must let me in!' one of the younger-looking women

was crying desperately. 'They're only babies.... seven and five. You must find room for them. We've read about the plans in the *'Jüdische Nachrichtenblatt'*, so it must be true.' King never heard the official's response, as he was approached by a British soldier. 'Excuse me sir, do you have business at the Embassy?'

'Yes, I do,' replied King evenly, as he handed over the Embassy letter requesting his attendance at the meeting with Pym. 'But what on earth is going on here?'

'Oh. It's the kiddies, Sir,' replied the sergeant sadly, as he reviewed King's documentation. 'You know, sir. The plan to allow Jewish children to leave Germany. It looks like Britain's going to take some. Not many, mind. Bloody shame, if you ask me sir. We should take as many as wants to come. Help them get away from these barbarians here. But, I suppose that's too simple a view, eh sir?'

King was touched by the natural humanitarianism of the soldier, who returned the letter, saluted and said, 'That's all in order, sir. Thank you. I'll take you through the barrier, then it's up the stairs, through the door and the Reception desk on the left will sort you out.'

King took a final glimpse at the increasingly desperate-looking crowd, before thanking the sergeant and making his way into the Embassy building. The young woman at the Reception desk was evidently expecting him and immediately led him to the lift which took them to the top floor. Her high heels clicked in perfect time, as she walked briskly down a narrow corridor, before pausing and knocking at a door marked 'Meeting Room 12'. He heard the unmistakable voice of Pym bid them enter and he was soon greeted by the older man's outstretched hand. 'John! It's good to see you again. As you can see, they've laid on tea and sandwiches for us. It looks like they think we've a lot to talk about.' The young lady from Reception assured Pym that he would not be disturbed and excused herself, before gently closing the door. The room was a typical meeting facility, with ten chairs placed evenly around a board-room table. The large windows did, however, offer both a splendid view out along Wilhelmstraße and its many important buildings and a great deal of natural light. Pym sat down at one corner of the table and invited his guest to sit adjacent to him so that both could enjoy the warmth of the blazing coal fire. A portrait of a rather stern looking King George VI, dressed in full naval uniform, stared down at them from the wall above the fireplace as if he also had things to say in the meeting.

'I hope you didn't have too much trouble getting into the Embassy, John', began Pym with a faint smile. 'I'm afraid we're coming more under siege as each day passes.'

'It was no problem, sir. But what's going on out there? It seemed to me that they're all Jewish. The sergeant who let me in tried to explain, but I didn't quite catch his drift,' replied King, a genuinely concerned expression covering his face. Pym told King as much as he knew about the so called 'Kindertransport' plans, which had been designed to allow the rapid emigration of Jewish children from Germany to Britain. 'Damned disgrace that some back home don't seem to want to take any of them,' he grumbled. 'Have they no idea what's going on here, or do they simply not care?'

'I imagine it's more that they want to bury their heads in the sand and pretend it doesn't concern them,' said King sadly. 'I suppose it's easier to justify that kind of position to oneself when one has no direct experience of the Nazis and what they're capable of.'

'You may be right,' conceded Pym readily, 'I just wish we could do more to protect these people.' King seized this unexpected opportunity to remark that he wanted to discuss a similar issue later in the meeting. Pym's response was to fix him with a penetrating gaze and murmur noncommittally, 'Very well, John. But first tell me, how have things developed since your arrival here?'

King gave a full account of his reception at the University and the colleagues he had met there. In particular, he explained that there seemed to be a group of younger academics, such as Andreas Schwarz, who were wholly antipathetic to Hitler and Fascism. On the other hand, there were those such as Brunner, who he suspected of being informers for the authorities. Pym seemed to have little interest in the political views of the History Department but pricked up his ears noticeably when King told him of his chance meeting with Kalz on the train to Berlin. When the younger man offered an account of the evening at The Bendlerblock and his subsequent attempted recruitment, Pym was beside himself with agitation.

'Good Lord! This is splendid. Absolutely splendid. I never dreamed that such a thing might happen, but now the opportunity has presented itself, we must use it to the maximum.' Pym went on to confirm the suspicions, which had been aroused in King, that there was tension between Canaris, Oster and The *Abwehr* on the one hand and Himmler, Heydrich and the SS on the other. 'The view of the Nazi regime as a well-oiled and perfectly functioning machine is very far from the truth,' Pym explained. 'But it's very useful that you've been able to confirm that there are many petty rivalries and jealousies among Hitler's henchmen. This may offer some significant opportunities to us.'

The two men discussed how King's involvement with Kalz's organisation might provide a unique insight into German Military Intelligence and agreed that he should make a sympathetic, but not too enthusiastic response to the German. Simons concluded that King should not waste any time and push for more reassurances as regards the kind of information that would be sought and especially the nature of The *Abwehr* itself, before making even the most tenuous of commitments. Seeing King's uncertainty at this exhortation to speed, the Professor raised a hand, 'I'll make clear my reasons for saying that when you've finished your report. In the meantime, please continue.'

King continued by explaining that he had had the misfortune to be recognised by Joachim Brandt during the Reception at the Bendlerblock. 'Do you remember him, sir?' King urged after seeing a confused expression cross the Professor's face. 'He was a very good friend at Heidelberg, until he joined the SS in '33. We didn't part on the best of terms.' Realisation began to dawn for the older man and he slapped his thigh in irritation. 'Of course. Brandt. Now I remember. I'm not sure I ever met him, but I remember you telling me all about how he went over to the 'dark side'. God, what rotten luck!' King then described the thinly veiled threat from Heydrich and the information that he had given about Brandt's return to America.

'Well, John,' the Professor responded, 'I won't insult you by pretending that all that is good for you. But, accepting that Heydrich is a very powerful man, I think we can hope that neither you, nor Brandt will occupy his mind for long. Just keep your eyes open even more now for any threat. How did Kalz react to Heydrich?'

'He was obviously repulsed by and terrified of him in equal

measure,' replied King. 'But, other than making our meetings more discreet, I don't think it will affect him significantly. He clearly thinks that I could be a useful source for The *Abwehr*.'

'That's clear,' agreed Pym with a firm nod of his head, 'but he's going to have to hurry up.' King was greatly surprised by Pym's explanation that the timing of his faked death and secret return to England was likely to take place some months earlier than had been first anticipated. 'The way Hitler has broken Czechoslovakia and is now circling Poland makes it highly likely that we'll be at war with Germany within six to nine months. You need to come back to Britain before hostilities start in order to establish yourself among the pro- German communities.'

King was by no means happy with this sudden change of plan, having expected to be in Berlin until the summer at least. Now, it looked likely that he would be in Germany only until late January and he thought instantly of Greta and what this change would mean for their relationship. He had, of course, thought a great deal about her since his stay in Heidelberg and he found that his initial attraction to her showed no signs of fading. However, the long train journey and the necessity of him staying in Berlin, meant that any sort of reunion would be possible only when Greta had the opportunity to take a few days' holiday. She had told King in a lengthy telephone conversation that she hoped to be able to do this at Christmas. Accepting miserably that there was, at the moment, nothing he could do about this unwanted change in the schedule, he agreed to meet the Professor in the Embassy towards the end of January to finalise plans for his clandestine return to Britain.

'You look a bit off, my boy. Is there a problem?' asked Pym astutely. 'No, Professor. I was just surprised at the suddenness of the new departure time. I'll get used to it,' replied King flatly. 'Very well. But now John,' asked Pym kindly, 'you mentioned earlier that you had something else to discuss with me.... something of a personal nature perhaps?' King explained concisely what he had found when he had gone to Heidelberg, what he had been told about Dr Bernstein and Professor Berg and what he had promised the Doctor's wife. 'I want you, or rather I want Britain to do whatever it can to help these people, sir,' said King firmly. 'I would regard it as a personal favour to me.' Pym seemed taken aback by the younger man's account and sat with his head in his hands for a full minute before whispering. 'My God, John. That's terrible news. I knew Berg, of course. When we were both much younger. He was a gentle and kind man and an excellent scholar.'

'Yes, sir,' interjected King, determined to press Pym. 'It is appallingly sad. But these last few weeks here in Germany have taught me that we should, above all else, do what we can for the living. A dear friend of mine helped me to see that that's what the Professor would have wanted us to do.' At this mention of a 'dear friend', Pym gave King a penetrating look, but seemed to decide not to broach that matter for the time being. He simply dead-batted the younger man's plea. 'I'm not at all sure that we can do anything. I'm fully aware of what I said about all those poor people outside, but that is quite different. You must realise that your mission is by far the most important consideration and I will not do anything that may compromise it.'

'Then frankly sir, I have to ask myself whether the mission is worth continuing,' came the immediate response from King who, seeing the worried look on his old mentor's face, quickly continued. 'After all, surely it's precisely what we're likely to be fighting for... the value of the individual and the rights we all should be able to enjoy.'

'It isn't as simple as that, and you know it,' retorted the older man angrily. 'We can't afford such luxuries in our line of work. I really thought you had understood that.' The disappointed sigh, with which Pym ended his reply really irritated King and he pulled no punches in clarifying his position. 'Then let me make myself clear, sir. If you wish me to carry on with this assignment, then you must promise me that you will do all you can to help Dr and Frau Bernstein.'

'All right,' Pym conceded with little enthusiasm. 'You leave me little option. I promise I'll do what I can to help your friends. I should have some news for you when we meet in January. Until then, you must be careful not to do anything that might compromise your position.'

Once again, King's thoughts went immediately back to Greta. His firmly held view was that his new romance had not risked his security and, resolving to keep it that way, he decided not to mention anything about it to his mentor. He felt very uneasy about keeping this secret and he hoped fervently that he was doing the right thing. But it was now apparent that his time in Germany was going to be much shorter than planned. He had always known that his parents and friends would have to be told that he was missing, presumed dead. However, he had no idea what, if anything, he would communicate to Greta in advance of his 'disappearance'. He had been absolutely correct, he reflected wretchedly, when in Heidelberg he had concluded that his life was becoming far more complicated.

Chapter Thirteen

Thursday, December 8th 1938, Berlin.

The scent of cinnamon hung heavy in the air as King made his way to the 'Museum Island' and on towards the Christmas Market in the Lustgarten. The stallholders had returned the previous year to this location, which had been the traditional site for Berlin's Christmas Market since before The Great War. He very much liked the huge figure of St Nicholas which rose jovially above the green castellated main entrance, ingeniously made from wood but made to look like mossy stone. He was less pleased to see the long red flags centred with swastikas, which hung from tall wooden flagpoles fixed into the wooden towers. Straight ahead he could see the bulk of the magnificent Berlin Cathedral rising benevolently over the happy people, many of whom were enjoying their glühwein, grilled sausages and stollen. Others were making their selection from the vast array of intricately carved wooden ornaments, houses, figures and animals, with which to make their Christmas displays at home. No one goes in for Christmas with quite the relish of the Germans, King mused, at the same time remembering his happy Christmas period in Heidelberg, when the world and his place in it had seemed much simpler.

Kalz had nominated the Cathedral for their rendezvous and King had wondered whether he had chosen this location to establish himself as a traditional patriot and to distance himself from the Nazi regime, both of which might make the idea of collaboration more palatable. The note from Kalz had been hand delivered to his post-box at Ludendorffstraße and had instructed him to enter the Cathedral by its main door and then to take an aisle seat, half way down towards the altar on the left hand side. King had been sitting in the appropriate pew for barely two minutes when he sensed, rather than saw or heard someone sit down immediately behind him. The person moved to kneel on the low padded board and, as he sat back into the pew, King could hear the other person's breath. 'Thanks for coming, John.' He immediately recognised Kalz's voice which whispered, 'I'm sorry for the cloak and dagger stuff, but I want our relationship, if indeed we are to have one, to be unofficial. The fewer people who know about it, even in The *Abwehr,* the better.' King thought about his previous public invitation to the Bendlerblock and the Adlon, with the encounters with

Brandt and Heydrich. He probably wants to find out what I could offer as an informer, King reflected quickly, but he's aware that I've possibly made an important enemy in Heydrich. From his perspective, keeping things under wraps clearly makes sense. King nodded his head slightly to indicate he had heard and understood the message. 'In a couple of minutes I'll set off for the Sexton's Office,' continued the German. 'To find this, you must walk to the main entrance, down the central aisle then turn left and it's in the corner of the building. I've arranged for us to be able to speak there undisturbed. After I have left, wait five minutes and then follow me. Understood?' Again King gave an almost imperceptible nod of the head and Kalz returned to a sitting position in his pew.

King steadfastly stared ahead towards the magnificent neo-baroque altar as the German left his seat and made his way unhurriedly towards the main cathedral entrance. Just as he was about to get up and follow his contact, King nervously reacted to the sound of someone taking Kalz's place behind him. Despite the nature of where he found himself, he cursed silently at his own jittery behaviour as he discreetly looked around to see an elderly couple already kneeling and at prayer. Twenty to thirty people were making their devotions as King followed the instructions he had been given and, within a couple of minutes of leaving his pew, arrived at heavy wooden door marked 'Sexton's Office'. He opened the door without hesitation and stepped into a small dark room where he was greeted by Kalz. 'Come in, John. Sit down and have a cup of coffee. We'll not be disturbed here.'

Settling down in the two matching armchairs, which stood either side of a fireplace containing the glowing remnants of a coal fire, the two men eyed one another like boxers circling in the ring at the start of a bout. King noted the German's choice of civilian clothes as more evidence that he really did want the meetings to be off radar. 'I'm grateful that you were able to come,' began the host carefully. 'I wonder if you've had any time to consider my proposal.'

'Well, I'd certainly not rule it out altogether, but I think I need a little more persuasion that acceptance would not be against the interests of my own country,' reasoned King, in exactly the way he had planned with Pym.

'Of course. I understand and fully respect that position. But just consider these facts,' responded Kalz, repeating much of his exposition on the common interests of Britain and Germany and their shared hostility to the Soviet Union. He made much of the argument that Germany's most significant current international alliance was the 'Anti-Comintern Pact' which, he pointed out, was specifically directed against Stalin. He also argued that the 1935 'Anglo-German Naval Agreement' was designed to prevent Britain feeling threatened by an expanding Navy. 'Germany has no wish to find cause for argument with Great Britain, John. We are natural allies and we should each do what we can to preserve that state of affairs.'

'As I have already made clear Erwin, while there are many in my country who would have sympathy with what you've just said,' King replied firmly, 'it is impossible for me to ignore both the bellicose posturing of Hitler and the appalling treatment of any domestic opposition and, of course, the Jews. I'm not sure I can reconcile that with your view of Germany and our supposed shared interests.' King realised that in saying this he might simply push Kalz into defending the indefensible. After all, it was just possible that King himself might be some sort of Nazi plant to test the loyalty of The *Abwehr* officer. Indeed, the response demonstrated how careful Kalz felt he must be. 'Ah, there we are sailing into rather deep and treacherous waters. One must be very cautious these days, in order not to create the wrong impression. Believe me, my friend,' he continued with obvious emotion, 'I have seen several fine officers not only lose their careers, but also their liberty and even their lives as a result of speaking too openly in the wrong company.' King nodded sympathetically before responding. 'Of course, Erwin. I understand. I don't want to encourage you to commit any indiscretion.'

'I know that, John, but I do think you should know that there exist differences of, shall we say emphasis within Germany today. Of course, as you have pointed out to me, it is exactly the same in Britain. For example, there are Mr. Churchill and his followers who are convinced that our two countries must come to conflict with one another. I repeat in all candour that there are many in Germany who would regard that as a disaster, not only for our two countries but for civilisation itself.'

Pleasant and urbane as Kalz undoubtedly was, King was fully

aware that a distaste for the worst excesses of the Nazis did not compensate for the fact that they were on opposite sides of the global shift to modernity and democracy. Even if somehow Germany could be rid of Hitler and his wretched crew, the last thing that Kalz and his class would want would be a return to Weimar and a democratic republic, with all its messiness and uncertainty. They would definitely want to return to a *Reich* ruled by the Emperor, in which order and tradition prevailed and everyone knew their place. The classic Junker mentality. Feeling no compunction at all in deceiving The *Abwehr* man, King said, 'I understand what you are saying, Erwin, and I do have sympathy. But you must see that for me to have any sort of relationship with you, I would need to know a great deal more about the organisation you represent.' The Major looked sideways at the Englishman and, for a moment King's heart leapt into his mouth, as he thought that he may have overplayed his hand. However, a slow smile soon began to creep across Kalz's face and he murmured, 'I wouldn't have expected anything less of an honourable man, John. Now, let me think, what do you need to know?'

Later, in the quiet and calm of his flat, King made detailed notes of Kalz's information that Admiral Canaris had recently restructured The *Abwehr* into three main sections, named *Abwehr* I, II and III. This, the Englishman was delighted to note, filled in the missing information from his visit to The Bendlerblock. The second of these sections was perhaps of greatest interest to King, as it concerned sabotage. The Major had explained that this involved the establishment of direct contact with discontented groups or individuals in foreign countries, in order to further intelligence aims. Kalz even revealed the leader of the section as Colonel Erwin von Lauhausen, although the way he pulled his face in distaste when mentioning his name, made it clear what he thought of this particular officer. King was also told that the section dealing with Foreign Intelligence Collection operated in nine areas which, in addition to the expected Army, Naval and Air Intelligence, included Economic Intelligence and Technical Intelligence. Such information, he thought happily as he wrote, could prove valuable to Pym and the SIS as they engaged in the struggle against The *Abwehr*.

'I hope you appreciate that I have given you some sensitive information, John,' Kalz had said on finishing his account of The *Abwehr*. 'And I have done that for two principal reasons. First, as a sign of good faith, to demonstrate that I have nothing to hide from you. Second, because I genuinely think, as do many of my fellow officers, that Britain and Germany should be allies. We share too much in our common heritage and have too many shared enemies. All I ask is that we meet at least every month to discuss matters of mutual interest and concern. I would like you to share knowledge with me, which would not damage the interests of Great Britain.'

All in all, King reflected, the meeting had been very successful as he had gained some useful information. It was also certain that, given the timescale mentioned by Pym, there would be insufficient time for him to meet Kalz again, thereby avoiding the potentially awkward situation of having to offer him something of value.

Chapter Fourteen.

Christmas 1938, Berlin.

It was two days before Christmas and King had spent a pleasant morning over his breakfast thinking about his recent end of Semester lecture at the University. He had been quite surprised that so many of the senior management, not only of the Faculty but of the whole University, had been in the audience. What had pleased him much more, however, was the number of students who had attended. It had been quite an experience giving the lecture in German, beneath a huge portrait of Hitler, glowering down on him, as if he rejected every word of his thesis. In his lecture, King had challenged the conventional view that the pre-Great War Triple Entente between Britain, France and Russia had been principally anti-German in its intent, at least from the British perspective. Frissons of interest and outright hostility had passed through the audience, as he had made a well-researched argument that its major purpose was to tie Britain's traditional enemies and the greatest threats to her Empire into an alliance. Germany's misreading of British diplomacy, therefore, may well have caused unnecessary tension, which contributed significantly to the arms race and the slide to war.

King had been gratified by the interest shown in his novel thesis by the students and more junior staff in the audience, which stood in marked contrast to the diffidence and plain hostility demonstrated by many of the senior academics present. Indeed, he had been asked specifically by one student to draw out any lessons for the present time, which could be learned from his analysis. 'Well,' he had begun in answer, 'I imagine you are thinking of the Naval Agreement of 1935,' to which the student had nodded. 'We could see this as a sensible attempt to improve relations between Great Britain and Germany in rather troubling times. However, it seems to me that there are also clear risks involved, especially if each country has different expectations of the Agreement.'

'Would you care to elaborate on that point,' Professor Brunner had interrupted sharply, 'I'm sure we would all benefit from your thoughts.'

Without hesitation, King had replied, 'My own view is that, from a German perspective, this agreement was intended to pave the way for an Anglo-German alliance against the Soviet Union. For the British, however, it was concerned only to limit German military expansionism, by whatever means. Thus it has been criticised by those who support a more general rearmament of Germany as being too restrictive. On the other hand, those who fear German militarism have argued that it is too lax, because it has permitted the German Navy to expand beyond the limits allowed by the Treaty of Versailles. Given such conflicting views, I believe that there is every chance the Agreement will be broken in the not too distant future. In such circumstances, perhaps the question which should concern us all is whether or not having had an agreement, which has been broken proves to be more damaging than never having had one at all. We no doubt each have our own views on that.'

King smiled at the memory of the babble of conversations and arguments that this had provoked among members of the audience, as they spilled out of the large lecture theatre and into the Departmental Pre-Christmas Apéro Reception. Taking a final gulp of his coffee, he glanced at his watch and cursed that he had let most of the morning slip away. He put on his winter boots, grabbed his overcoat, hat, gloves and Durham University scarf and bounded down the stairs.

'Now you are quite sure, are you Herr Dr King?' asked Frau Bauer with a knowing look, as she intercepted him in the hallway. 'I'm aware that you young people don't have much time together. If your lady friend wants to stay here well, after all, there's plenty of room in your flat.'

'Thank you very much Frau Bauer,' King replied for what seemed like the hundredth time. 'But as I've already explained, Greta has arranged to stay with an old friend of hers, who now lives in Berlin. They studied nursing together.' Smiling at the old lady he promised, 'I'm sure you'll get to meet her... never fear.' At this the *Portierfrau's* previously crestfallen face lit up. 'I should think so too. After all I am in the place of your dear mother here. It's my duty to meet her and besides,' squeezing King's arm as she spoke, 'I do love a bit of romance in life, even if it's not in mine! And don't you forget to buy her something nice for Christmas.' With a cackling laugh, she finally allowed King to get on his way.

Greta's final night shift at work had finished very early in the morning and she was scheduled to arrive in Berlin during that evening. King had arranged to meet her at Anhalter Station and to help her to her friend's flat in the pleasant area of Charlottenburg. He had planned a relaxed enjoyment of the final hours before Christmas, however Frau Bauer's words sent him into a panic. 'A present. Of course! How could I have forgotten such a thing?' he berated himself. Never an enthusiastic shopper, he nevertheless ventured into many stores in search of a suitable Christmas present and had, eventually, ended up in the 'last chance saloon' of the enormous *Kaufhaus des Westens*. He gazed at the comprehensive floor directory and wondered at the sheer scale of the store, with its massive array of goods from all over the world. Fortunately, there was a temporary section of the store, which was dedicated to helping hapless men to find a suitable Christmas present for their wife or girl-friend. 'You should try this, sir,' the pretty young shop assistant said, while holding out a plain cylindrical bottle, full of a bright orange-red liquid. 'It's called 'Tigress' and it's the very latest from Fabergé. It only came out this year. Just try it,' she urged him hopefully. King had to admit that the scent was very exotic, in a spicy-oriental way. 'OK. Sold', he smiled at the delighted shop assistant, 'Now would you gift wrap it for me, please?' As he left the shop, he felt pleased with his present of the perfume, together with some tickets he had bought for the recently released Errol Flynn film, 'The Adventures of Robin Hood'.

    The train from Heidelberg was due to arrive at just after nine-thirty and an excited King, with a good thirty minutes to spare, made his way to the station by tram. After slowly drinking a coffee and a glass of schnapps in the station buffet to calm his nerves, he went out onto the platform to meet the incoming train. The passengers were a mixture of business travellers, people happy at coming home for Christmas and military personnel. At last he caught a glimpse of bright red hair and then he could see her, struggling along the platform with the most enormous suitcase. He waved and shouted for her to put the case down before running into her warm embrace. He couldn't begin to explain, but it really felt to him like he was returning home and his immediate reaction was to wonder whether this was what falling in love felt like. He really hoped it was, because to him it felt great. 'Welcome to Berlin,' he said, a hopelessly cheesy grin on his face. 'It's wonderful to see you again.'

    Greta smiled and replied softly, 'It's good to be here John. But

I've had a very tiring day. I wonder, would you mind too much if we went straight to Anna's flat?' King had noticed her pale face and the dark shadows under her eyes and replied immediately, 'Of course not. Let's find a tram. Come on, I'll take your case. It looks as if you plan to be here for a month.' The tram carriage was very crowded and King had to stand with the case near the door, while Greta managed to find one of the last available seats. Despite her evident tiredness, as they walked the final few minutes to Anna's flat she talked excitedly about being in Berlin and seeing both him and her friend again. Anna's flat was on the first floor of a small block, situated on a pleasant tree-lined road and King observed jokingly, 'Very nice, nursing must pay pretty well in Berlin.'

'Oh, Anna inherited some money from a maiden aunt who died some years ago,' replied Greta, while ringing the doorbell. 'There would be no possibility of her affording a place like this on a nurse's pay.'

An attractive, dark-haired woman opened the door and immediately exclaimed joyfully, 'Greta! It's lovely to see you. Come in please.' King, despite his strength, struggled with the weight of Greta's suitcase as he followed the two women up a flight of stairs and into Anna's flat. Once inside, they walked along a generous hallway and through into a well-proportioned living room which, he was relieved to note, did not display the standard photograph of The Führer.

King was thrilled as Greta charmingly introduced him to Anna as 'my English Professor' before excusing herself, in order to change out of her nurse's uniform. As soon as she had returned from showing Greta to the guest bedroom, Anna offered King a glass of wine. Over the next ten minutes they enjoyed a friendly conversation, in which she demonstrated great interest in his impressions of Germany. Eventually, both realised that Greta had been away far longer than a mere change of clothes would require and Anna went in search of her friend. She soon returned with a drowsy-looking Greta and, with an understanding smile, informed King that she had found her asleep on the bed. He remembered doing much the same thing in Heidelberg and instantly suggested, 'Look, Greta, I imagine you'd love to have a warm bath and shake off the journey. I know what it's like sitting there for twelve hours and the train was probably packed.' Seeing her nod in agreement, he continued, 'So I thought I'd leave you and Anna to catch up over a glass of wine. We could easily meet sometime tomorrow.'

'Oh John, you are such a darling man. You've read my mind. Are you sure you don't mind?' asked Greta, the relief in her voice palpable. 'Of course not. Let's meet at the Café Kranzler tomorrow. How does 11AM sound?' asked King hopefully. 'That's fine. I'll see you then.'

After saying goodbye to Anna and enjoying a long embrace with Greta, King returned to his flat in Ludendorffstraße. As he opened the door and entered the dark hallway, he was suddenly struck by the thought that, in comparison to the warmth and conviviality he had just left, his flat now seemed lonely and cold. Pondering his situation with this slightly changed perspective, and feeling even more excited about his feelings towards Greta, he attempted to find the release of sleep. For some time, however, he lay wide awake, eagerly anticipating the Christmas celebrations, but increasingly concerned about his fast approaching departure from Berlin. He had several times considered whether or not he should tell her that he would soon have to return to Britain, but had always decided against. He couldn't imagine any plausible explanation that would be consistent with his necessary faked death, other than the truth. Given his undertakings to Pym, to tell her this was inconceivable. It was not just because the mission was of far greater importance than himself, Greta or their possible relationship. He also had to consider what might be her reaction to such a revelation. While he knew that she was unsympathetic, even hostile towards the Nazis, she was after all German and, far from seeing King as a brave patriot fighting Fascism, she could conceivably view him as a spy, working against the interests of her own country. It would surely be very foolish and dangerous, as well as unfair, to put her in such a position. He was also painfully aware that his most recent orders, to return to Britain sooner than anticipated, meant that war was now much closer and that he and Greta would be on different sides in what could be a prolonged conflict. Deep into the night, he finally subsided into a restless sleep, his heart still clinging to the hope that he could find an acceptable solution to his dilemma.

****

Last minute Christmas shopping was well under way as King entered the Café Kranzler and managed to grab a window table for two, which looked out over the Kurfürstendamm. He didn't have long to wait before Greta arrived, looking refreshed and turning heads as she made her way to his table. He rose and they instinctively entered a lovers' embrace, during which King murmured into her ear, 'Greta, you look absolutely stunning! What'll you have, a coffee or something stronger?' Having ordered coffee cognac for two, King asked how long it had been since she had visited Berlin. He was a little surprised to learn that this was the first time that she had been in the city, since it had become Hitler's capital. They spent a little time discussing, in a discreet and rather coded way, their views of what the Nazis had done to the city, before eagerly planning how they would spend their day together.

They enjoyed a happy hour at the Christmas Market in the Lustgarten, followed by visits to several of Berlin's famous department stores. Being with Greta and the Christmas mood of the busy crowds immunised King against his dislike of shopping and he realised that he was really having fun. When they stopped to take a cup of glühwein from a gaudily coloured stall, Greta asked suddenly, 'I know we had thought to go out for dinner tonight, but will you come to Anna's instead? Her partner and her brother and his wife will be there and she particularly asked if we'd make up the party. You must have made quite an impression on her.... she's really taken a shine to you. Do say you'll come, please.'

'Of course I will,' he replied without hesitation, an entranced expression on his face. 'I can easily cancel the restaurant.'

'And don't forget your toothbrush, darling,' she said with an amused twinkle in her eye. 'You never know when you may need it.' King swept her off her feet in a fierce embrace, before asking half seriously. 'It's not black tie is it? That area where she lives looks terribly posh to me.'

'Of course it is,' she laughed. 'The butler and servants will be there too!' As she said this, she quickly picked up some snow from the window frame of the stall and threw it at King's face, before running off into the crowd. The rest of the afternoon was spent in innocent enjoyment, mingling with the crowds and really entering into the Christmas spirit. As the light was beginning to fade, however, she announced that she would have to get back to Anna's flat to help with the meal and to get ready for the evening's celebration. They parted with a long lingering kiss at the Charlottenburg tram stop and a somewhat light headed King walked through the slush back to Ludendorffstraße, pausing only to buy a couple of bottles of red wine for the party and a box of chocolates for Anna.

On arriving home, King gave Frau Bauer her Christmas present of a bottle of sweet sherry and half a dozen sweet mince pies which, amazingly, he had found in the English section of the KDW food hall. In return, the *Portierfrau* insisted that he toast the season with her and a few of her friends in her ground floor flat. He found the middle-aged ladies extremely lively company and they seemed to relish having a younger man in their midst. When he finally looked at his watch, King was shocked to see that it was almost seven thirty and he hastily made his excuses. A quick shower and, having decided that he may as well go the whole hog, a rapid change into his dinner suit, saw King rushing out of the flat barely an hour after he had left the *Portierfrau's* party. Christmas spirit was very much in evidence everywhere and, on the tram towards Anna's flat, a slightly intoxicated conductor announced to everyone that, 'In the spirit of the season and goodwill to all men, I'm not taking any fares this evening. Merry Christmas everybody!' A loud cheer went up from the passengers as bottles of schnapps and other fiery spirits were passed around the car.

It was, therefore, a very mellow and slightly tipsy King who presented himself at Anna's flat. A smiling Greta answered his ring of the doorbell and, as she opened the door, he staggered backwards. 'Gosh, but you look sensational tonight, Greta. You almost bowled me over.' She giggled girlishly in response. 'Are you sure that it's not the effect of the schnapps I believe I can smell on your breath?'

'Well, maybe I did toast the season en-route here,' he acknowledged sheepishly, 'but seriously, you look like a million dollars.' Greta smoothed the full skirt of her long black dress and, much to King's pleasure, did a quick twirl. 'It's silk and satin, embroidered with black sequins,' she announced proudly to him. 'A neighbour of mine in Heidelberg is a wonderful seamstress and she made it from a photograph in a fashion magazine that I gave her. It's a copy of an original by the French designer Madeleine Vionnet. I'm so pleased you like it. And,' she whispered, 'I'm really happy to see you in your dinner suit... your tweed jacket wouldn't have matched half so well! Anyway, come on in and I'll introduce you. The others are already here.'

Anna and her three other guests were busy lighting the candles on the large Christmas Tree and Greta introduced him first to a man of medium height, in his early thirties with, in King's view, an improbably handsome face and dark wavy hair. 'This is Guido. Anna's special friend. He works at UFA, the film studios. We all think that must be terribly glamourous.' The man shook King's hand vigorously and remarked with a smile and a self- deprecating shrug, 'It's not so glamourous being up before dawn and having to put up with the histrionics of some of the actors. Not to mention our political masters.' Anna shot him a worried glance and King immediately realised that the others must be just as cautious of him, an unknown, as he was of them. What a sad state of affairs, he thought, while resolving to be as open and uncontroversial as possible. The other couple comprised Anna's brother, Carsten, and his wife, Annaliese, who were both several years older. 'Hello, John,' Carsten said warmly, 'I'm sure I speak for everyone here, when I say that I'm delighted to meet you, especially as you are an English guest in Berlin.'

King felt immediately at home with Anna's partner and family and the conversation settled into reminiscences of Christmases past, as they enjoyed their pre-dinner glass of cold Sekt. The aroma emanating from the kitchen suggested to King that they were all in for a real treat. 'Mmmm,' he asked eagerly, 'What's that divine smell?' Anna laughed with delight, 'It's our traditional Christmas meal and you'll just have to wait to find out what it is. But now, ladies, we have work to do in the kitchen.'

As soon as they were alone Carsten began to ask King about the reasons for his stay in Berlin and what his impressions were of the Third *Reich*. He offered a rather banal account of his nomination for an academic exchange and spent some time discussing his experience of life in Berlin. To his relief, he barely had chance to comment on Hitler, before the first course of thick vegetable soup was served. With the return of the ladies, the conversation centred on Guido, who regaled the table with a host of hilarious accounts of his experiences at UFA. King was interested to learn that he seemed to have somehow managed to keep away from the heavily propagandist film making, which had become such a feature of the studio's output. Guido explained that, during the previous year, he had been involved in helping Karl Hartl direct a mystery comedy, The Man Who Was Sherlock Holmes and that he had spent most of the current year working on the musical *Carmen - la de Triana*, which was based loosely on Bizet's opera. Carsten, it turned out, was an avid reader of Conan Doyle's stories and, of course, Guido had read many of them in preparation for his work on the film. It was, therefore, little surprise that the three men spent some time debating which was the best Holmes tale. In the end, they had to agree that they couldn't separate The Sign of Four, The Hound of the Baskervilles and King's choice, much to the amusement of Greta, The Red-Headed League. 'You're clearly a terrible charmer, John,' teased Anna, to which he protested in vain that it was, indeed, his favourite Holmes story.

The main course of succulent roast duck with vegetables was served with the rich *Chateau-neuf-du-Pape*, brought to the party by King. For several minutes the conversation faltered as the six people seated round the table gave their full attention to the delicious food. 'Well, Anna,' Guido said, as he finished his plate, 'that was absolutely superb. My compliments to the chef.' In an echo of the reception given to his lecture earlier in the month, the guests rapped their knuckles loudly on the table in recognition of a wonderful meal.

'But there is more to come,' said Anna, with a smile towards her friend. 'Greta has made us Dresdner Stollen to have with the Muscat wine. But I suggest we have this only after we have sung Tannenbaum and exchanged presents. Do you all agree?' King was no great singer, but he was a reasonable pianist and offered to accompany the party in the traditional German Christmas song. Afterwards, the guests exchanged gifts, Greta being delighted with her perfume. However, it was the tickets for the new Errol Flynn film which caused the most interest.

'It's in the new Technicolor, isn't it?' asked Guido with real interest. 'At UFA the boffins tell me that that system is absolutely incredible.' 'And I've heard that the film is a pretty thinly veiled attack on Fascism,' said Carsten, implying that he would find that a good thing. Not wishing to encourage a political discussion, King replied with a smile, 'It's a traditional English tale which has been given the full Hollywood treatment. Green tights obligatory. I think it'll be a fun thing to do over Christmas.' 'I agree. Thank you, darling,' said Greta enthusiastically, before planting a lingering kiss on King's wholly receptive lips.

After dessert had been served, the table was pushed to one side, the rug rolled up to reveal the polished wood below and the gramophone player set up. 'I'm a dedicated jitterbug,' declared a rather tipsy Anna. 'Now, which of you will join me?' With that she put a new copy of the recently released *Benny Goodman Live at Carnegie Hall* on the turntable and pulled Guido up from his chair to join her. King had been to many student jazz parties and dances in the last decade and he invited Greta onto the impromptu dance floor.

After a good half hour of frenetic swing, Carsten found copies of 'Smoke Gets In Your Eyes' and 'I've Got You Under My Skin.' Moving closer to Greta as the music slowed, King felt her respond to his touch and before long they were both lost in their own world, totally oblivious to the others in the room. The warm and relaxed feeling from the food and wine, combined with the music and, of course, the feel of Greta in his arms, totally overwhelmed him. He was absolutely certain that he had never been happier in his whole life and things became even better for him some hour or so later as the party broke up with many 'Merry Christmases' and promises to meet again soon. Carsten and Annaliese set off for the short walk to their flat and the four remaining guests enjoyed a final glass of cognac, before a smiling Greta led King to their room.

*****

King was awakened by the merry peal of church bells and, somewhat dimly after the excesses of the previous evening, he remembered that it was Christmas Day. Greta's luxuriant hair was spread across his chest and, as he looked at her peaceful and contented face, he felt totally at one with the world. He smiled inwardly as he remembered their love making, which by turn had been fierce and urgent, then gentle and mellow. With a jolt, however, he realised that for the past twenty-four hours he had been living the life of a normal man, who was falling in love with a beautiful woman. Bitterly, he quickly recognised that this was an option that simply was not open to him. His stomach lurched as he imagined what it would be like to say goodbye to Greta, which he must surely do soon, in the full knowledge that they would probably never meet again. A particularly loud peal of bells caused Greta to stir out of her slumber and King's 'Happy Christmas, darling,' accompanied by a hungry kiss brought her, smiling, into full wakefulness. They decided that, because of the bright sunny weather and the covering of new snow, they would get up immediately, have a quick breakfast and go for a long walk to Wannsee, where they might even be able to skate on its frozen surface.

In common with most people falling in love, they found joy in the simplest of things; a snowball fight, as they passed the lurking monstrosity of Hitler's Olympic Stadium; looking across the lake to the sun tipped, snow covered trees of the Grünewald and finally reaching the Wannsee itself. Although snow covered, in what was for Berlin only the second authentic White Christmas since the early 1930s, few people were chancing a walk or skating on the lake's inviting and harmless looking surface. Neither King nor Greta seemed particularly keen to risk a dip in the no doubt freezing water and, by mid-afternoon the sun was fading fast, so they decided to head back to Charlottenburg. The four other people from the Christmas Eve party had been invited to a traditional family meal with Anna's parents in Dahlem and she had, therefore, offered Greta the use of her flat for the evening.

They spent a much quieter, though equally enjoyable evening alone in what was, for King, a tantalising taste of what life could have been like with Greta, had circumstances been different. After all the overconsumption of the last twenty-four hours, they agreed to prepare a simple evening meal of bread and cheese and soon had the crockery and cutlery washed, dried and put away. They spent the remaining time, until Anna and Guido returned, listening to music, discussing its merits and, of course dancing. King was pleased, however, that they opted more for the slow, romantic tunes, which allowed him to hold Greta tight, rather than the jitterbugging of the previous evening. It was in the middle of one of their slow dances together that King suddenly held Greta away from him and declared, 'You do know, don't you, that I've fallen in love with you?' Greta could see from the determined look in his eyes, that he was absolutely serious and hugged him to her. Tears forming in her eyes, she began to whisper in his ear, desperately hoping that he would understand. 'I like you, John.... I like you a lot.... a very great deal, in fact.... and I love making love with you. And if I could keep on having that I would. But I know that with you, it could become much more than that and I really don't think that that would be a good idea, do you?' The last words were said, not by way of a challenge, but as a sad and realistic acknowledgement of what they both must know to be true.

King saw immediately that what this gorgeous German nurse had said made sense, indeed made perfect sense. Nevertheless, he responded quickly from the heart, 'Why not? Why could we not just live together anywhere... you could get a transfer to Berlin. Or I could move to the University in Heidelberg. I'm sure they'd be pleased to be associated directly with the exchange programme. And when that's over, you could come back with me to Durham.' As soon as he had said the words, he was aware, both of how ridiculous they must have sounded to her and of how totally impractical they were, given the reason he was in Germany in the first place. He blinked and looked down at the floor between them, a desolate expression on his face. Greta led him to a chair and kneeled on the floor beside him, 'Oh John. You're such a dreamer. Can't you see, it could never work. We're not children, who can pretend that we can change everything. We can't. But we can live for the moment. We can enjoy our time together and, when the time comes as we both know it must, we can part as good friends.' King was not prepared to give up so easily and argued persuasively, 'But I think we can have a future together. I think it would be great.' Greta seemed even more saddened by this. 'Would it?' she asked, 'Would it really, John? You know as well as I do that next summer you must go back to England and I must stay in Germany. It's also not impossible that our two countries will soon be shooting at one another. Let's not fool ourselves here, war with Britain is a very real possibility... it nearly happened last year. And I know that you think that too. I really don't think that I could survive letting myself fall in love with you and then losing you straight away.'

King could see the honesty in her face and the tears welling up in her eyes and a big part of him wished that he had never said anything about his feelings for her. Maybe he should simply have kept quiet for a few weeks and enjoyed Greta's company, until he left for Britain. He quickly realised, however, that to have done so would have been horribly cynical and would undoubtedly have eaten away at him. He knew for certain that it was precisely because he had been serious about the possibility of a future together, that he could not have kept silent. But equally, he now feared that by articulating his feelings so clearly, perhaps he had inadvertently hurt Greta even more.

'You're not going to lose me,' King said defiantly and more in an effort to persuade himself, just as Anna and Guido returned from their family party. After a quick cognac with the returning couple, Greta and King retired to the guest room where they lay, exhausted after making love, each in some ways alone with their own thoughts and concerns.

Their tickets to see 'The Adventures of Robin Hood' were for the evening of St. Stephen's or Boxing Day and they spent the hours before they left for the cinema eagerly anticipating some genuine swashbuckling from Errol Flynn. By some unspoken mutual agreement, neither of them had mentioned their conversation of the previous evening and, much as it gnawed at him inside, King had to admit that silence was now the best policy. They both said their farewells and thanks to Anna, as they were moving for this last night of Greta's stay in Berlin to King's own flat on Ludendorffstraße. Frau Bauer, of course, just happened to be in the hallway as they arrived and clearly gave Greta her seal of approval, by welcoming her and expressing the view that, 'I'm very pleased that my charming English gentleman has found himself such a lovely German girl. It's a real pleasure to see such a handsome couple as you.' With an obvious reference to the lack of physical attractiveness of many of the most senior Nazis, she added, 'After all, so many of those we see most frequently in the newspapers are hardly oil paintings, are they, my loves?' With a final knowing nod she confided in Greta, 'I can see that you'll be the making of him, my dear.' before bustling off into her own flat humming happily to herself.

As soon as the door to King's flat was securely closed, they both burst out in hysterical laughter, before finding their way to his bedroom where they remained in one another's arms until it was time to leave for the cinema. Given the film's brand new colour system and superb action sequences, King was easily able to overlook its questionable history and join in the audience's huge enjoyment. Greta was due at work on the early shift on December 28th and planned to leave Berlin the next morning. They decided, therefore, to enjoy a late supper on the Kurfürstendamm, before returning to spend their last night together at King's flat. They were both up early the next morning, aware that this escape from real-life was rapidly coming to an end. They both held to their unspoken agreement not to raise the issue of where their relationship could go and, having also expressly ruled out any last minute declarations of undying love as too painful to bear, after King had loaded Greta's suitcase onto the train, they simply kissed one another goodbye. As he watched her face disappearing from view, he could not help but wonder whether or not he would ever see her again.

*****

Climbing up the stairs towards the door to his flat, King was moodily pondering how on the one hand, chance had introduced him to Greta while, on the other, fate was determined to take her away from him. Frau Bauer waddled out from her Büro and commiserated with him. 'Poor dear. You look terrible. Has your sweetheart gone home? Never mind, she's sweet on you, there's no question of that and you'll have plenty of chances to see her again.... After all,' she continued with her playful cynicism, 'it's not as if you do a full day's work at that university, is it love? Now my poor Gottfried, he certainly knew what a day's work was and no mistake...'.

'Yes, I'm sure, Frau Bauer and thanks for your concern,' interrupted King impatiently. 'But if you'll excuse me, I actually do have a lot of work to do.'

'Of course, dear. I just wanted to give you this. A smart young man brought it round by hand just after you and your lady friend had left for the station. I do hope you don't mind me taking it in for you. I thought it might be important and didn't want to leave it in the hallway. Might it be another invitation to one of those big political events? You might even see The Führer...'

'Thanks Frau Bauer, I'm sure it's nothing so important,' King lied, as he took the handwritten envelope from the *Portierfrau*. 'It's probably a message of some kind from the University... they did say something about an emergency staff meeting being called for just after New Year.' Such hand-delivered items, in his estimation, rarely contained unimportant news. Before opening it, therefore, he poured himself a small schnapps from a Christmas gift, given by a group of postgraduate students, he had been tutoring weekly since his arrival in Berlin. As soon as he was comfortably seated in his favourite armchair, the schnapps warming the back of his throat, he opened the mysterious letter. It was, in fact a short note from Pym, which informed him in code that he would be leaving Germany at the end of the first week in January. Pym's note asked him to visit the British Embassy on New

Year's Eve, in order to receive a fuller briefing and to make firm plans for his departure from Berlin.

King's first reaction to the orders, for that was essentially what he had just received, was that this represented an even earlier departure than he had expected, after meeting Pym only a week or so previously. In a strange way, this unanticipated change in the time remaining to him in Germany helped to crystallise his thoughts.

He readily admitted to himself that, especially now that he would not see Greta again, he was relieved that he had never given in to those siren voices in his own head, which had encouraged him to tell her the truth. It was clear now, that that would have done no good. After all, however much she may reject Nazism, would she really have deserted her family, friends and work in exchange for what, exactly? To live alone and mistrusted in an alien country while he operated in a clandestine way against her homeland? Even if he survived his mission, her life, while he was on active service, would be awful... at best grudgingly tolerated and at worst interned as a potential 'enemy alien'.

He could also readily imagine Pym's likely reaction to any suggestion that he had revealed his mission to Greta. He would undoubtedly have argued that King was blinkered by love, or lust and unable to judge rationally the most appropriate course of action. He could almost hear the difficult conversation the two of them might have had, with Pym making the obvious points about her nationality and thus her principal loyalties; about the very short time he had known her; about their chance meeting on the train, with the clear innuendo that that, itself, may not have been altogether an unplanned occurrence. No, it was obvious to King that he must carry out his duty to Pym and his mission and try to clear his mind of thoughts of Greta and what might have been. A postcard from Switzerland would almost certainly be the last that she would hear from him, although she would undoubtedly learn of his tragic accident in the Alps. His final consolation was that, believing him dead, at least she would be more able than he to draw a line under their doomed relationship and move on with her life.

Chapter Fifteen

Friday, January 6th 1939, Switzerland.

King did not feel well; there was no question about that. However much he had attempted to prepare himself for this moment, the empty feeling he now felt in his stomach was worse than he had anticipated. He consoled himself with the thought that the most difficult part of the journey would be as the train passed desperately close to Heidelberg and, of course, to Greta. While this did prove to be an accurate prediction, an hour later and soothed by a café cognac consumed in the restaurant car, King's rational mind had conclusively taken over from his emotions, and he forced himself to recognise that he was hurtling inevitably and irretrievably away from his sweetheart. Sitting over his second café cognac, he began to reflect on the rush of events that had taken place in the week since New Year's Eve.

****

He had, as requested, attended the meeting with Pym at the British Embassy in Berlin, where the plans for his unfortunate 'death' in Switzerland and speedy reincarnation in Britain as James Kemp were to be explained in detail. However, before Pym had the chance to begin, King had interrupted. 'I realise why we are here, sir, and I have no wish to seem difficult, but we do have an agreement. Can we deal with that before we discuss anything else'

Almost as if he had been aware of King's sacrifice of his feelings for Greta, the older man had been surprisingly sympathetic, making no attempt to argue. Rather he had replied with an understanding smile, 'Of course, my boy. Well I'm pleased to confirm that Dr Bernstein will be released from Dachau as part of a New Year Amnesty and that both he and his wife will be leaving for Britain within the week. It took quite a bit of string pulling, but you have what you wanted.' King heaved a sigh of relief as, in all candour, he did not know what his position would have been had Pym been unable to arrange for the emigration of the Bernsteins. 'Thank you very much, sir. I do appreciate that I am involved in work, in which sentiment really has no place, so let's call it John King's final act before he becomes James Kemp.'

Pym had explained further, that King was to arrange to take a week's leave at the University before the start of the new Semester. He was to say that he had decided to take an impromptu winter snow walking holiday in the Bernese Oberland in Switzerland. He would, of course, be required to leave his flat in Ludendorffstraße with only those items he would reasonably be expected to take on such a holiday. When King had asked what would happen to all his other possessions, especially his books and his notes and writing, Pym had assured him that these would be returned safely to Britain, to his parents or, should they not wish to keep them, they would be kept in storage until his mission was at an end. 'You must not, emphatically not bid any special farewell to anyone, John, however much you may feel that you should,' Pym had stressed. 'Do you understand? This is crucial to the whole deception and the whole mission. No one must be an exception to this rule. Is that clear?' King had been surprised by the vehemence of Pym's approach to what seemed an obvious precaution and this, together with his earlier sympathy had caused King to wonder whether or not his mentor had some knowledge of his relationship with Greta. Be that as it may, King had held to his decision that mentioning it would be pointless.

    The Professor's plan involved King leaving Berlin on Friday January 6th and travelling by train first to Bern and then onwards via Thun and Spiez to Kandersteg, his final destination in the Swiss Alps. There, a local mountain guide, known to Pym as sympathetic to Britain's interests, would fake King's death by avalanche and rock fall. He would then be driven by a member of Swiss Military Intelligence to a small civilian airfield at Thun and flown back to Britain by Lysander.

****

    'Welcome to Switzerland. I hope you have an enjoyable stay here,' said the smiling border guard as King's train crossed the border at Basel. It really wasn't until he heard these words that he realised that, in all probability, he had left Nazi Germany forever and that his work against Hitler's Reich would now be conducted exclusively on British soil. King had to break his journey with an overnight stop in Thun, a pretty lakeside 'City of the Alps', which offered a real alternative to the bustle and menacing air of Berlin. Relaxing into the orderliness, peace and normality of Switzerland, it became much clearer to him that life in Nazi Germany had become increasingly pathological. As he approached the solid looking hotel building, with its huge curved arches and romantic round tower, he smelled the appetizing aroma of food and immediately realised how hungry and tired he felt. Some thirty minutes later, after dropping off his rucksack in a wonderfully warm and clean room, he felt quite revived, as he enjoyed his first local *Rugenbräu* beer and anticipated his meal.

His journey the next day would take him by train along the Lake of Thun to Spiez, where he would branch off up the dramatic Kander valley towards Kandersteg. This was a relatively undeveloped tourist village, but one which was known to climbers, hikers and cross- country skiers. King was very grateful for the manner, in which his fellow diners and drinkers at the hotel bar demonstrated the classic Swiss virtues of friendliness and openness, combined with a natural discretion and respect for another's privacy. He had neither travelled widely, nor spent much time in the small, well-functioning country, but he very much felt at home there and resolved, if he emerged unscathed from his current mission, to get to know Switzerland better. Indeed, he realised with great pleasure that he was very close to Meiringen and the famous Reichenbach Falls, from the top of which Sherlock Holmes had plunged to his death, locked in a mutually fatal embrace with his arch-enemy Professor Moriarty. Well, neither Watson nor Moriarty will be around, King thought, with no little satisfaction, and it will be an avalanche rather than a tumble down a waterfall. But I suppose, in some ways, I am about to follow in the footsteps of the greatest detective ever. I can certainly think of worse role models.

After a blissful sleep King awoke the next morning to clear blue skies and a wonderful panorama of the Eiger, Mönch and Jungfrau mountains, which towered across the lake from Thun. He breakfasted heartily on typical Swiss fare and, after settling his bill, he strolled at a leisurely pace back towards the railway station and his connection to Kandersteg. He stopped to buy a copy of *Die Neue Berne Zeitung*, before boarding his train which, of course, left punctually. As the train effortlessly moved further and further up the valley, King noticed with some amusement that the Bernese dialect of the passengers joining the train became more and more difficult for him to comprehend. The newspaper's sports pages were not full of cricket and football, as King would have undoubtedly preferred. Rather, they were eagerly anticipating something called the 'Lauberhornrennen', which was due to take place in the next few days at the nearby ski resort of Wengen. King didn't have to read much to realise that the excitement surrounding this particular downhill ski race concerned the chances of the Swiss, Karl Molitor beating the German, Josef Jennewein and, thereby, repeating the triumph of another Swiss over a different German the year before. Here's to you, Karl! The best of British luck to you, thought King happily as he contemplated Hitler's likely fury at another sporting defeat for the supermen of Nazi Germany.

As the train curved around and doubled back on itself, in order to negotiate the considerable altitude difference between the small town of Frutigen and Kandersteg, he marvelled at the alternating mountain and valley views. It was also obvious that the snow was now much deeper than lower in the valley and he silently gave thanks for the efficiency and resilience of the largely electrified Swiss railway system. Just after noon on what was now a grey day, full of low clouds which completely hid the soaring mountain peaks which he knew surrounded the little village, King emerged from the station in Kandersteg into swirling snow. The train glided off towards the Lötschberg Tunnel and the Rhone Valley beyond. Perhaps the sun is shining over there on the southern side of the Alps, he thought enviously, as he turned his collar up and, trusting once again to his reliable old hiking boots, trudged off towards the Hotel zur Post, a basic pension which would provide for his one night's stay in the village.

Even as he walked slowly but steadily towards the hotel, it became clear to King that the railway and especially the construction of the Lötschberg Tunnel, before the First World War, must have brought considerable change to Kandersteg. He imagined that before its construction, this had probably been a simple farming community, lacking the drama of the more famous Alpine ski resorts which boasted downhill pistes for all levels of ability and courage. While the Gemmipass, at the head of the valley did give a mountain route across the Alps, this was neither one of the more famous and busy passes in Switzerland, nor even a passable road for modern vehicles. In recent years, however, many more hotels and other facilities had been built, in order to take advantage of the good railway connection to the wonderful walking and cross country skiing possibilities.

As he plodded past the local *Konsum,* a kind of small food and general store, he was approached from behind by a tall, thick-set man with a luxuriant beard and piercing blue eyes who, without breaking step, whispered urgently. 'Herr King? Please act as if I am just passing you by chance. *Grüezi!* I am Gerhardt Rösti. I am a friend of Professor Pym. I am to help with the arrangements here in Switzerland. Please meet me at the bench on the curve in the river just before the Scout Centre at three-thirty. We can sort out the details then.' Rösti very naturally began to pull away from King and, on reaching the junction with the Dorfstraße, turned to go in the opposite direction to the that taken by the Englishman.

    King was pleased that his inn was right in the centre of the village and, having completed the registration formalities, he had plenty of time to study the maps of the area, which Pym had provided. He did this whilst enjoying a hearty bowl of barley soup, accompanied by rustic bread, before he set off for his meeting with Rösti. He decided to buy a couple of postcards before taking the path along the many curves and bends of the River Kander, towards the Scout Centre near the head of the valley.

    The relatively secluded location seemed an ideal choice for a meeting which, while not essentially secret, would be better if organised discreetly. Rösti was waiting on the bench when he arrived and immediately got down to business. He was a typical man of the mountains, who spoke only what was necessary to say, though thankfully in high German rather than the extremely challenging local dialect. Having confirmed that the weather forecast for the next day predicted a fine bright day, followed by possible snow showers later, Rösti outlined the plan for King's disappearance. He should leave the zur Post early the next morning and take the path at the head of the valley up to Sunnbüel. From there, a much gentler walk of two hours across the Spittalmatte would take him to his overnight stop at the Schwarenbach mountain inn, where a room had already been reserved in his name.

    'The part of the walk up to Sunnbüel will be the hardest, but you look in reasonable shape, so I'm sure it will be no problem. You should arrive at the Schwarenbach well before dusk.' King felt unaccountably pleased with Rösti's positive evaluation of his physical fitness and replied eagerly, 'That's fine. Where will you be?' His guide explained that he would meet King at a predetermined point on the path down from the Gemmipass to Leukerbad. 'This is a notoriously dangerous place, where many accidents have occurred,' he said, crossing himself. 'There will be lots of snow and the rocks there are loose, so they can be moved easily by even a small avalanche. It will be relatively easy to make it look as if you have fallen into one of the deep ravines. It's a remote place; there will be no one around and it's not at all uncommon for people to be lost in winter. It should be easy to create this deception.'

He went on to advise that King should be friendly, but not too sociable both at the zur Post and the Schwarenbach, that he should hint at his relative inexperience in mountain walking and also make sure they know his plan to walk to Leukerbad. 'It shouldn't be too difficult to do that at the zur Post. It's the place where all the locals go to gossip.' King noticed the Swiss man's eyebrows rise in a sardonic expression as he added, 'Someone as exotic as you is bound to pique their interest.'

'Thanks for the advice and for the reference,' King smiled. 'But can you tell me what are you likely to need to fake the accident?'

'Good question. We will leave one of your English gloves, your hat and maybe one of your poles and some things which could have fallen from your rucksack.' The Swiss seemed to relax a little, as he realised that King was not the incompetent, desk-bound academic that he had feared when he had been approached to assist in this deception. 'Afterwards, we will return quickly to the Kander Valley by a different route which no one else will be using. A car will be waiting to take you immediately to Thun, from where a Lysander will fly you back to England. You will be home by early evening the day after tomorrow.' King was impressed by the organisation that Pym had put in place, but one question concerned him. 'And what kind of investigation will take place?'

'That need not concern you Herr King. You can rest assured that the authorities will make an appropriate investigation and reach the correct conclusion, that the unfortunate death by accident of a pleasant, but sadly inexperienced British walker has taken place.'

The two men shook hands and parted, as the light was fast leaving the valley. 'Good luck, Herr King. Until the day after tomorrow,'

Rösti said, as he turned towards the village and walked off in a cloud of smoke which billowed from his huge cigar. King, following the directions he had just been given, walked on past the Scout Centre before turning left on the valley road and back towards the village. He passed the ancient Ruedihus on the left hand side, followed a little later by the brand new Hotel des Alpes on the other side of the Dorfstraße. He encountered no one on his return journey and indeed, as he entered the centre of the village, he saw only the local vicar on his way to the tiny church which was located next to the zur Post. Glad to be back at the hotel, he decided to write his postcards and then rest in his room before taking an early dinner.

    Shortly after six thirty, King made his way to the bar and immediately placed his order for a hearty Swiss meal of beetroot salad to be followed by *Schabziger Knöpfli*. Having received his first cool beer, he then settled down at an ancient wooden table to wait for his food. Looking around the smoke and conversation filled bar, it was clear that Rösti had not been exaggerating, when he had described this as the meeting place for the local gossips. He had barely started his first drink when a wizened old man came to sit at his table. 'You're not local, so you'll be here for the winter sport then,' he asked (or rather told) him in a friendly tone.

    King was glad that his ear for accents in German had proved to be so good and after barely a day in the Canton of Bern, he found it possible to understand a fair proportion of the local's speech. 'Yes, that's correct,' he replied brightly. 'I'm told the walking around here is excellent. I intend to walk the Gemmipass over the next couple of days and spend a night or two in Leukerbad.' King was surprised by the snort of derision that greeted this piece of information. 'Well, the walk is lovely to be sure, but of course it's much better when you're walking towards Bern, rather than towards Wallis.' The old man's face cracked into a laugh at his own joke and King could not help but follow suit. 'Where are you from then? I just heard you order your food. You sound German, but you don't look it,' was his next question and King responded that he was British, but currently on an academic exchange in Berlin.

    'Berlin, you say.... hey, Urs! Hans! come here you two. We have a guest who lives in Berlin. He's English, though.' At this command, two even older looking men picked up their half-filled beer glasses and shuffled over to the table, eager anticipation in their faces. 'Berlin is it?' asked Urs almost before he had seated himself. 'We've had climbers here from Germany, practising on the rock face up to the Allmenalp. Didn't like any of them. Arrogant, nasty types they were. Are they all like that in Berlin? Put a fancy uniform on them and they think they're supermen.' At that his friends burst out in raucous coughing and laughter, making numerous ribald comments and gestures, which barely required translation.

'I've certainly come across many nasty types, as you put it sir, and yes, many of those were in uniform,' King replied seriously. 'But there are also kind and peaceful Germans who are as bemused at what is going on there as you and I.'

'Aye young man, I'm sure you're right,' pondered Hans, his brow knitted in concentration. 'But tell me, do you think Hitler will be satisfied without a war? None of us think so.'

King considered how he should respond and decided that these three friendly old men deserved the truth as he saw it. 'I'm afraid I agree with you, sir. As long as Hitler and his Nazis are in control, they'll not be satisfied until they've created their 'Lebensraum' in the East and that means Poland must go the way of Czechoslovakia. I can't see either Britain or France accepting that.'

Just then the owner's wife came into the bar to tell King his starter had been served in the Dining Room. 'I see you've been entertained by the three wise men of the village Dr King,' she said, nodding affectionately at the three villagers. 'Now, come on you three. Give the young man some peace to eat his dinner.'

As King stood up and made to move towards the Dining Room, Urs touched him briefly on the sleeve and said with obvious sincerity, 'Well, son, if it comes to it, take care of yourself and give those Germans a bloody good thrashing. Can't abide that Hitler and all his strutting minions.' King nodded his thanks and left the bar without replying. He enjoyed his meal in silence and, shortly after nine-thirty, took himself off to his room to ponder his imminent 'demise' and, most importantly, to write an appropriate postcard both to his parents and to Greta. Pym had been absolutely adamant that, if he was sentimental enough to want to send postcards, they should in no way hint at what was about to take place and King, therefore, produced two banal greetings which he would post, before setting off towards Sunnbüel.

King slept soundly and, after consuming another wonderful Swiss breakfast and provisioned with a picnic from the hotel, he set off for the Schwarenbach mountain inn, pausing only to post the two cards at the nearby post office. It was a gloriously sunny day, the sun reflecting incredibly brightly off the perfect covering of snow. King was very grateful for the English sunglasses, given to him by Pym at their last meeting in Berlin. At the time, he had thought that the older man's insistence that he did not leave these in Germany was a little fussy. Now he realised that the Professor had been perfectly right to insist. He made good time up the valley and, with no one else in sight, was soon tackling the uphill trail which led to Sunnbüel. Despite Rösti's positive assessment of his fitness, King found the initial going to be tough and his heart was soon hammering in his chest. A fundamentally sociable person, he had, nevertheless, always enjoyed periodic solitude and here, on this Swiss mountain path, his snow shoes ploughing on through the crisp snow, alternately in the shade of the fir trees then in surprisingly warm sunshine, he felt in his element. Part way up the head of the valley, he had a splendid view into the almost secret Gasterntal, which runs off at right angles and at a higher altitude than the Kander Valley. The almost total dryness of the snow, in contrast to the wet and slushy stuff he was used to in Britain, was a pleasant surprise to him and, after ninety minutes of measured walking, he emerged from the trees to reach Sunnbüel. He rested on a conveniently shaped rock and enjoyed the spectacular view back down the valley. He could clearly see the perfect location of Kandersteg, at the top of the valley, just where it broadens out to offer both more light and more grazing land for cattle. He could see the dark glistening Kander river as it snaked its way down through the village and the much straighter railway line, which disappeared beneath him into the ornate mouth of the Lötschberg Tunnel. A noticeable rumble from his stomach persuaded him that it was time to consume his packed lunch of cold *cervelat* sausage, bread and a bottle of beer.

Feeling suitably rested and replenished, King set off over the much easier terrain of the Spittalmatte, a wide, relatively flat landscape with the magnificent Altels peak to his left and the somewhat smaller

Gällihorn behind him and to the right. After traversing the snow covered meadows, King began the short, but steep climb and descent to the Schwarenbach Inn. Rösti had advised that this may take him a couple of hours, but he made frequent pauses in order to take in the landscape of pure virgin snow which, to his admittedly untutored eye, showed no trace of human presence. He had no idea that, much higher on the mountain-side, a solitary man with a luxuriant beard was keeping careful watch over his progress. King arrived at the inn well before dusk and was able to enjoy the final rays of the sun with a celebratory beer on the terrace. He was bewitched by the constantly shifting shadows on the mountains and the way in which the sun's rays turned from gold to pink and then, finally, to an almost red looking colour. 'Herr King. Please, you must come inside now. It is much colder,' said the inn's waitress solicitously and, jolted out of his reverie, King recognised immediately that she was right. With no little regret, he left the terrace and made for the warmth of the inn.

King was the only guest at the Schwarenbach that evening and he was able to ensure, during dinner, that his hosts knew both his plan to walk to Leukerbad and that he was of rather limited experience. He also heard much about the proud history of the inn, especially its frequent notable guests such as Mark Twain, Alexandre Dumas and, to his delight, Sir Arthur Conan Doyle. That really did seem appropriate to him as he made his way to an early bed. He had been warned by his hosts that, while the next day might begin bright and sunny, there was a possibility that the weather could deteriorate and, in the nicest possible way, he was encouraged to be up and on his way as quickly as possible.

King rose early the next day, demolished his final Swiss breakfast, packed his things and bade a fond farewell to his hosts. His path took him, once more in bright sunshine, up a steady incline which, when peaked, offered an uninspiring view of what he knew was the Daubensee, but what in effect looked like a massive snow covered field. As he skirted the frozen lake, he became aware of a significant picking up of the wind, shortly followed by the appearance of the first clouds. As he finally traversed the Gemmipass the snow began; the odd flake at first but within minutes visibility had all but vanished and he was caught in a mountain blizzard. King had studied the maps, which showed the extremely steep route that he was due to take down towards Leukerbad, but in such weather there really was no certainty that he would find the right path. Rösti had told him that, with good weather, he would be able to see the Matterhorn from his current position. Bloody Hell, he thought grimly, I can hardly see my nose in front of my face.

He was just about to set off in what, according to his compass, was the right direction when he heard a familiar voice. 'I wouldn't go that way, if I were you, Herr King. Ten metres further on and there really would be no need to fake your death. Come quickly, this way is better.' King could now see Rösti's smiling face and shouted over the howling mountain wind, 'My God! You're better than a St Bernard!' The Swiss quickly got his charge onto the correct path downwards and, the first section being sufficiently wide, they were able to walk side by side and exchange some words.

'The weather is perfect,' exclaimed Rösti with what for King was inexplicable pleasure. 'An avalanche today will be all too believable and for sure we will see no one else up here. Come on, it's only fifteen minutes down to the place we have chosen for your fall.' An extremely relieved King felt totally safe with his Swiss guide and even managed to improve his snow walking style by observing the other's technique. After a good fifteen minutes' descent, Rösti indicated that they had reached the spot and King could see immediately how appropriate it was. The path at this point hugged the steep slope of the mountain on one side and, with only a rickety wooden fence for protection, on the other gave onto a dramatic drop, which the Swiss said was at least a hundred and fifty metres down to a rocky ravine.

'Please tear off a small section off your rucksack and place the bag with one of your snow shoes, one glove and one pole just here. Then make sure that your wallet and passport are in your jacket pocket, take it off and put on this different coloured one, tear off one sleeve of your old jacket, put these with the rest of the stuff on the ground and go at least thirty metres back up the path. I'm going to set a small explosion to start the avalanche. You shouldn't hear much noise over this howling wind. Here are some more gloves, snow shoes and poles for you.' King was not happy with the instruction to leave his wallet, as it contained the only photograph of Greta in his possession, but he saw that this made absolute sense and complied without complaint. 'It's very common for avalanches to cause people to lose part of their equipment or even their clothing,' Rösti explained sympathetically. 'I'm very sorry about your wallet and personal things, but they'll be valuable in identifying you with this accident.'

The mountain guide then scrambled twenty metres above the path, where the terrain was particularly steep and the snow seemed quite loose. Expertly, he set the charges for a small detonation and moved fifteen metres away from the planned seat of the explosion. After a quick wave to King to ensure that he was safe, he detonated his small charge and the avalanche began. King merely heard a soft 'crump', but was completely stunned by the sheer power and weight of the moving snow, as it levered a rock from its resting place and pushed it down onto the path. The effect was dramatic, as more snow, together with many smaller rocks started to slide down across the path, taking with them a section of the wooden fence and the items King had left in the snow. Once the snow and rocks had ceased moving and having removed any remaining evidence of the use of a charge, Rösti descended to the path and took the piece of King's rucksack, his snow shoe, glove and his hat and sun glasses and placed them around the scene, finally smearing some of King's blood onto the nearest standing fence post. 'Now you know why I asked you to bring me that small sample of your blood,' he smiled, before continuing his explanation. 'The snow will soon cover these things and hide all our footsteps and when you don't appear at your hotel in Leukerbad, they'll contact Kandersteg and eventually send out a search party. When they find this broken fence with its blood marks, hopefully together with one or two of these items, they'll reach the intended conclusion. It'll be weeks or even months before any thorough search for your 'body' will be possible and anything could have happened to it in that time.'

Rösti took one final look at the orchestrated scene, before nodding in satisfaction and saying with an enigmatic smile, 'Now, you must complete your disappearance from Switzerland.' Recognising the sacrifice being made by the young man, in giving up his very identity, Rösti patted him fondly on the back and urged, 'Come on, my friend, it's time we were away from this spot.'

For the first time, King realised that there was a sensitive side to this apparently bluff man and asked if he had known the Professor for many years. 'I suppose you could say that,' he replied evasively. 'But that is all I wish to say on that subject, if you will forgive me.' 'Of course,' replied King a little shamefacedly. 'It was foolish of me to ask. I'm still very much a beginner in this type of business.' Rösti smiled again; he was evidently warming to this pleasant young Englishman. 'Yes indeed, but now we have a hard walk ahead of us, at a much higher level than the one you took this morning and yesterday. We'd see spectacular sights, if only this cloud would clear. Come on, it should only take us around three hours, if we walk steadily.'

The weather began slowly to improve, as the two men took a little known route, high above the Daubensee, the Schwarenbach Inn and the Spittalmatte and back towards Sunnbüel and Kandersteg. King was not surprised that they did not take the direct route down to the Kander Valley from Sunnbüel. He had, of course, climbed that way the day before, but it made much more sense to avoid the risk of meeting anyone, by descending the narrow Gurnigel down into the Gasterntal and thence to the Kander Valley. King was able to make better progress with the more modern snow-shoes and sticks provided by Rösti and they reached the designated place without mishap. The car was already waiting for King, hidden from the narrow road behind a disused farm building. The driver merely said '*Grüezi*. Please hurry, we have a good forty minutes to drive and the conditions aren't so good.'

King was about to get into the car, when he saw Rösti's outstretched hand '*uf wiederluege*! It has been a pleasure to meet you. God go with you, and if you're ever back in Switzerland, please look me up.' With a final smile, he added, 'There are many more challenging walks that we could perhaps take together.' King had time only to say a quick 'thanks for everything' before he was bustled into the rear of the car which then raced off as quickly as conditions would permit towards Thun.

An hour and a half later, King was looking down at the snow covered landscape of Switzerland, as the Lysander battled its way across the darkening skies towards England.

PART TWO

Chapter Sixteen

Thursday, February 2nd 1939, London, England.

It had been a cold but bright sunny day in Kent, when King had taken the mid-morning train from Canterbury into central London. The clouds, however, had begun to build up, as he approached the capital for the first time since he had left for Berlin the previous September. From the moment of his clandestine arrival by Lysander at RAF Biggin Hill in January, King had been staying with George McNair, a retired SIS officer, in his lovely three-bedroomed Georgian terraced house in the centre of Canterbury. McNair was an untypical highland Scot, fiercely proud of his Celtic roots, yet with a love of England and all things English. With thick, dark hair and surprisingly gentle, brown eyes, he was not much above average height, but was broad shouldered and, for his age, supremely fit. Above all, he was always ready with a smile. He shared his home with Polly, his forty-something housekeeper, who was a genuine Cockney and, in his words 'the best damned cook in the whole of this blessed United Kingdom of ours.' Under instruction from Professor Pym, both McNair and Polly had initially given King, who of course they knew as James Kemp, the space to recover from his swift departure from Germany. He had spent much of his first couple of weeks in England resting and enjoying Polly's excellent cooking. Gradually, as Pym had predicted to McNair, he had started to immerse himself again in normal life in Britain. He relished being so close to the centre of the city and spent many happy hours exploring its historic locations.

One day he had taken the train down to Dover and gazed across that improbably narrow strip of water which separated his country from the Continent and all its entanglements. Having caught sight of one of the cross channel ferries which was ploughing its way resolutely through the swell and on towards France, he had been reminded of that unseasonably warm September day, when he had taken a similar passage whilst en-route to Germany. Inevitably his mind had wandered back to Greta and a distant look had come into his bright blue eyes, almost as if he had felt that by an act of sheer willpower, he would have been able to conjure his love back into his arms here in England. A loud cry from a nearby seagull had brought him swiftly back to the here and now and, thinking about the last months, he had shaken his head in amazement. Certainly a great deal had happened, both to him personally and, in a broader political sense, in Europe. Indeed, he had wondered idly whether the old John King, straightforward academic and teacher, could ever return. But he had also known with a degree of certainty, that he now felt prepared to embark on the next stage of his assignment.

He took the tube from Victoria to Baker Street, in order to enjoy the simple pleasure of passing the fictional address of Sherlock Holmes on his way to Pym's flat. Well, the game's well and truly afoot now, he mused as he saw himself, reflected for a second in the large front window of a shop. During his first day in Kent, his appearance had been changed dramatically – 'It's orders from the Prof. I'm afraid,' McNair had said with a mischievous grin. His rather long, fair hair had been cut very short and dyed almost black, as had his newly grown moustache but, by some miracle of hairdressing known only to Polly, she had managed to accentuate what were the beginnings of grey hairs at his temples. When this was combined with the clear glass, horn-rimmed spectacles which disguised his twenty-twenty vision, the overall effect had been to make King look a good ten years older than his actual age and quite unlike himself. Polly, having wrought this amazing transformation in his appearance, had simply nodded and said, 'That'll do nicely,' before returning to the place in which she was most at ease, her kitchen.

He kept a sprightly pace down the length of Baker Street and eventually came within sight of Lord's Cricket Ground which, unsurprisingly on this winter day, looked somewhat forlorn and abandoned. Another five minutes and he was introducing himself to Mason, the long serving concierge at Pym's mansion block apartment. 'Just wait there, please, Mr Kemp. I'll ring up to the Professor right away.' After the briefest of exchanges over the telephone, King was escorted to the lift and the button for the top floor pressed. 'Straight out of the lift, sir, and the Professor is third on the left,' advised Mason superfluously, as King had visited Pym at his flat many times in the past. Still, King reflected happily, at least the disguise works. He didn't give me so much as a second glance when I introduced myself as Kemp.

The door to Pym's flat opened before King could ring the

doorbell and he was faced once again by the beaming face of his mentor. 'Come in, my dear chap. It's good to see you, although I must say, looking quite unlike yourself.' King laughed as he shook hands vigorously with the older man, who continued, 'I can see that the inestimable Polly has been working her magic again.'

'Indeed sir,' replied King with a shrug, 'Never mind Mason not having a clue who I am, I scarcely know myself.'

'Oh,' countered Pym, enjoying this easy exchange in light of the far more serious matters they would have to discuss, 'he's pretty discreet, you know. He'd never let on, even if he did recognise you, which incidentally I very much doubt.' The last words were spoken with a twinkle in his eye and an arm clapping his guest amiably on the back. King felt immediately at home in the Professor's flat and willingly allowed himself to be led into the spacious living room, with its partial view of the grass of the cricket ground. The host immediately insisted that they both help themselves to a cup of tea and a plate of the excellent sandwiches prepared by his housekeeper, before they sat down and began to talk.

'Rösti sends his regards from Switzerland, by the way John,' began Pym, as he added milk to their cups of tea. 'He's a rather reserved fellow of course, like many of his countrymen, but when they take a liking to you, there are no more loyal chaps on this earth. And he seems to have taken a liking to you.'

'I liked him too, sir,' replied King readily, 'but did the investigation into my 'death' go as expected?'

'Oh, yes, there were no problems on that score,' replied Pym with a nod of his head. 'Graf and Rösti between them prepared the ground excellently, and it appears that you also did a good job convincing the locals that you were a little naïve for those conditions. The conclusion was, as expected, 'accidental death'.'

'And how did yesterday go, sir? It was one aspect of this whole thing that I really didn't feel comfortable with,' said King heavily. 'How did my parents seem?'

'Yes, John, I know this was a most unsatisfactory part of the deception and I feel wretched about requiring it of you,' said Pym slowly. 'But you must see that there was absolutely no alternative, if all the hard work done so far was not to be jeopardised.' Appreciating King's slight nod, the older man continued, 'Your mother and sister were, of course distraught, but it's a funny thing about your father. If I didn't trust you implicitly not to have revealed anything about your mission, I could've sworn that he didn't believe you are dead.' The statement was left hanging between them for a full half minute before King replied. 'Yes. I know what you mean, sir. On my last visit to see them in Gloucestershire, I had the feeling that he thought there was much more to my trip to Berlin than a simple academic exchange.'

'Well, your father's nobody's fool,' confirmed Pym. 'It's entirely possible that he suspects something not a million miles away from the truth; that you're abroad working incognito for the good of the country, for example. But he also knows and accepts the meaning of duty and discretion. I'm certain that he'll say and do nothing to put your mission at risk.'

The two men spent the next couple of minutes enjoying their lunch and refilling their cups of tea, before King asked in a tentative way, 'I don't suppose....' Pym instinctively knew what the younger man was about to ask and quickly replied. 'Yes, John. There were flowers from Germany. The ones that interested me were those from a woman called Greta and Major Kalz. The tone of the message from the woman suggested to me that there was an aspect of your time in Berlin that you did not divulge to me.' In response, King nodded and grunted slightly, his face for a moment a picture of misery and loss. This prompted the older man to add, 'Well, I suppose that's not really relevant now. I'm sorry John, but it's for the best, believe me.' The younger man looked up and Pym could read the pain in his eyes, 'On a happier note, Dr and Frau Bernstein were there and, despite their recent ordeal, I'm sure they'll recover fully.'

King smiled vaguely and replied, 'That's good to hear, sir. Thank you for organising things.' Impressed by the younger man's stoicism, Pym asked more lightly, 'So, tell me, how are you getting on with McNair and the delightful Polly?' Meaningfully patting his stomach, and grinning in a surprisingly boyish manner, he added, 'I imagine that if you stay there much longer, it'll not only be your hair's appearance that'll be altered.'

'You can say that again, sir,' replied King, a more hopeful and enthusiastic expression on his face. 'After two weeks there the old waistbands were feeling a bit tight, so I had to get out and exercise with McNair. He's a fine fellow and I'd be delighted if he's going to be involved in my training.'

'Then you'll be pleased, John,' confirmed Pym. 'McNair is going to be your principal trainer and I know of no finer man for that particular job. Of course, he's retired from the Service now, but what he can't teach you about fieldwork is simply not worth knowing. He's the best tail I've ever worked with and if you can pick up a half of what he has to offer, that'll serve you in very good stead in the months to come.'

'That's all very well, sir,' interrupted King, a frown creasing his unnaturally old looking face, 'but no one has yet fully explained to me why the date for me to leave Germany had to be brought forward so much. I wasn't really happy about that. I couldn't say much about it in Berlin, but now I'd like some answers.'

'A fair point and a good question, John,' replied the Professor earnestly. 'And if anyone is to be held accountable for that decision, it's undoubtedly myself. Call it a gut feeling or intuition, but I felt that things might begin to happen more quickly than we originally thought. As it turns out, I think I was right.' King gave a quick nod and asked sharply, 'I take it that you're referring to Hitler's *Reichstag* speech on the 30th?'

'That's right,' replied Pym seriously. 'The speech spells out two things; first that Hitler is bent on war, whatever the other powers may think and second, that given half the chance, he'll use the cover of war to destroy European Jewry.'

'I agree about Hitler and his intentions,' countered King. 'But if Britain and France continue their wretched policy of appeasement, how is war any closer?'

'Well, there's the interesting thing, John,' said Pym gravely. 'Chamberlain genuinely thought Hitler was interested only in incorporating native Germans from Austria and the Sudetenland into the greater Reich. But the Führer's policy towards Czechoslovakia has, in the PM's own words, shaken his confidence in that belief. He's coming rapidly, but firmly to the conclusion that Hitler's drive for *Lebensraum* in the East must lead inevitably, and possibly very quickly, to war.' Pym was getting into his stride now, his face a model of concentration and focus. 'There's a great deal of intelligence and corroborating evidence, which suggests that the Wehrmacht is preparing to occupy the remainder of Czechoslovakia as soon as the Spring comes. The Poles are very worried about the Danzig Corridor and Chamberlain is minded to guarantee Poland against Nazi aggression. The economy here at home is gearing up much more realistically to the likelihood of war, with increased production of armaments. In summary,' Pym shrugged, 'it all begins to look...'

'Somewhat inevitable..' suggested King, with a reflective smile.

'Yes, John, I fear so,' said Pym flatly. 'Hopefully you can now understand the urgency to get you out of Berlin as soon as possible, well prepared and in among the Nazi sympathisers here in Britain.'

The conversation shifted direction, as Pym gave the younger man an account of the latest intelligence on Nazi sympathisers and right wing and other extremist groups in Britain. He explained that the current thinking was that actual or potential threats could come from a range of sources; Germans and other aliens, Fascist groups, communists and even the IRA. 'Of course, your focus is on Fascist sympathisers and, possibly aliens. There are many sources that might be interesting. The British Union of Fascists, for example, and other rank anti-Semites such as Archibald Ramsey.'

'The MP, you mean?' cut in King. 'That's right,' continued Pym, in his unhurried, professorial way. 'He's gathering like-minded friends around him, such as the Duke of Westminster and the Duke of Wellington. There's also a retired admiral, Sir Barry Domville, who founded a pro-Nazi propaganda organisation called The Link. It has its own organ called The Anglo-German Review. There are many possibilities for infiltration,' Pym reasoned, 'but that work isn't for you.'

King's interest in what Pym had just said was evident in his body language, leaning forward, looking the older man straight in the eye. 'Really, sir,' he said in some confusion. 'I rather thought that was exactly what you wanted me to do.' Pym took his time before answering, filling his pipe, lighting it and taking a deep satisfying draw, before explaining. 'You're right. That was originally the plan. But there are others in SIS who are involved in that work and I'm sorry to say that we still suspect that there may be a German agent working within that organisation.' King had hoped that this issue would have been cleared up before he established himself in Britain, so that he could work in concert with other agents. He nodded his head slowly and thoughtfully, 'I see, sir. So I am still going to be operating in isolation from SIS?'

'I'm afraid so, John,' Pym confirmed. 'We have a chance to establish something with you that we are certain isn't being fed back to Germany. I must stress that we don't know whether or not SIS has been infiltrated, nor, if it has, at what level. But the bottom line is that we can't afford to take the risk. Unfortunately, it'll make your life more difficult, as you'll be a German agent as far as the British authorities are concerned.'

'But an English imposter as far as any genuine Nazi agent is concerned,' cut in King sharply.

'Yes,' Pym said regretfully, 'that about sums it up. But for the time being you need to concentrate on your training with McNair. I have some ideas on how we can get you into the field, which we'll discuss in due course.'

Pym went on to explain that the finishing touches to King's cover as James Kemp were being put in place and it was likely that he would begin to operate fully in the field by May or, at the latest June. The two men parted by late afternoon after agreeing that Pym would visit King in Canterbury in early March. The main target for the next weeks, emphasised by Pym over a parting glass of single malt, was for King to learn as much tradecraft as possible from McNair.

Chapter Seventeen

Monday, February 6th to Wednesday, March 22nd 1939, Canterbury, England.

'Following, or as it is often called, tailing a target, is a complex procedure if you want to get it right and stay unobserved,' McNair beamed at King as he tapped yet another of his Senior Service cigarettes on the packet before lighting it. He was clearly enjoying the task of introducing this young academic into the dark arts of fieldwork and tradecraft. 'There are hundreds of decisions, some big, others seemingly miniscule, that you have to make during a pursuit and each one of them, if you get it wrong, could jeopardise the success of your mission.' Himself a committed teacher, King was immediately engaged by the older man's evident enthusiasm for his work and his passion for sharing his own knowledge and skills. 'As with most skills in life, James,' continued McNair, using King's alias, 'good solid preparation is key. You must get to know your target as fully as possible before you encounter him in the field. That way, you may be able to anticipate his movements and not be put into a potentially compromising situation by an unexpected turn of events. Of course, we must always be ready for that, but our aim is to minimise the chances of such eventualities leading to your exposure.'

King was fascinated by the retired SIS man's highly skilled use of his own experiences, some more successful than others, which he used to reinforce or to illustrate each successive point that he was making. McNair's eyes twinkled with amusement as he continued, 'And you must always remember that you can never be invisible.' The rugged Scot looked almost embarrassed to be making what he saw as such obvious points, but he nevertheless stressed to the eager looking King. 'I realise that this may seem absolutely self-evident to you, but in my experience it's often the simplest of errors that can undo a lot of very good and competent work.'

King nodded his head in understanding and McNair continued, 'Depending on the particular circumstances, it could well be that your target sees you.' Here McNair emphasised the key point by banging his hand on the table between them, as he uttered each word. 'The vital thing, however, is that he does not notice you. The mind is processing millions of pieces of information every second. You must do your best to ensure that, if observed, you are filed under 'of no particular interest' by your target's brain.'

King rather naïvely interrupted here, to suggest that disguises may be very useful, only to be greeted by a loud guffaw from the older man. 'Surely not the dodgy wig and false nose and beard! No, James, such things are anathema to the good 'tail'. He wants to draw as little attention to himself as possible. So it's important to look and above all, to act as naturally and normally as possible. That's part of the reason that we've waited some time before starting this training, so that you feel perfectly comfortable with your... shall we say, new appearance.'

Theory was all very well, but the Scot could see that King was eager to try his hand in the field. Nevertheless, he was determined to give his student a solid grounding in the necessary skills and procedures, and informed him that he would not go out into the field for at least two weeks. He would, however, go out every day to a remote part of the north Kentish coastline to practice shooting with a variety of handguns. 'What on earth do I have to do that for?' King had demanded. 'It's not as though I'm going to kill anyone, is it?' McNair could see the concern in the young academic's face and answered reassuringly. 'It's just orders, laddie. You know what the Professor's like. He likes to cover all bases. All likelihood you'll never have to use one of these. But in the meantime, we must do as we're told.' McNair's matter-of-fact response seemed to reassure King and the shooting and gun handling practice began.

As soon as McNair could see that his student was beginning to master the theory of tailing a target, he introduced sessions on skills in recognising when someone is lying. 'These skills are extremely important,' reasoned the ex-SIS operative. 'After all, you'll be trying to get information out of people who may well be very adept at telling extremely convincing falsehoods.'

Towards the end of February, King made his first venture into the field when he successfully followed a man to his workplace in Canterbury. He felt exhilarated, finally to be out and doing something practical after his weeks of waiting, listening and training with McNair, and returned home feeling relatively pleased with himself. The Scot confirmed his successful completion of the task, smiling warmly as he said, 'You did quite well. Our eyes and ears on site reported that you dealt well with the earlier than expected appearance of the subject and maintained a close, but not dangerously close position, as you followed him. You also made good use of the bus stop in order to maintain surveillance of the school, until you could be reasonably satisfied that the subject had, indeed, entered his place of work and had not used this as a diversionary tactic. All in all, the report states that you did well and show a promising aptitude for this type of work. In fact, the only criticism of note was that you have yet to perfect the skill of maintaining a watchful eye on your subject's progress, without doing so in an overly obvious way. But don't worry, James, that's quite a subtle skill and I've no doubt you'll develop it fairly quickly.'

Throughout the rest of February and into March, King continued to practice those skills of deception, disguise and observation that he would need in the months ahead. He had to admit that, whatever his scruples might be concerning such behaviour as stalking and spying on someone without their knowledge or permission, he was actually getting quite good at it. This self-assessment was agreed by McNair, who had readily expressed the firm view, that he would approach Pym to say that King was ready for the next stage of the operation. Events, as it turned out, made this positive assessment of King's preparedness somewhat redundant as, late on March 20th, Pym turned up unexpectedly at the Canterbury house. Descending the stairs to greet his mentor, King's cheery smile faded, as soon as he registered the determined expression on the face of the older man. With a curt nod to acknowledge the younger man, Pym began with some urgency, 'I have news which greatly affects our plans. Not only, as you know, has Hitler effectively dissolved and occupied what was the Republic of Czechoslovakia, but my sources tell me that he will tomorrow demand Danzig from the Poles. Now, what d'you think of that?'

The glint in the older man's eyes told King all he needed to know and he quickly replied, 'Then I imagine, sir, that the Government must be considering some sort of guarantee for Poland.'

'Exactly, my boy!' exclaimed Pym, 'and this means that we need you active and in the field as soon as possible. Let's adjourn to the sitting room and I can fill you in on how the operation's going to develop.' The older man ushered King into the large and comfortable room, before calling out, 'McNair! Come and join us in the sitting room, and be good enough to bring one of those special bottles of whisky.' Pym was clearly in business-like mood and, having found three appropriate glasses in the sideboard, waved them meaningfully towards McNair, as the latter came through the door carrying a bottle of single malt Laphroaig. 'Come on, man, hurry up! The war'll be over before we get the chance to wet our whistle.' McNair glanced sideways at King who merely rolled his eyes and shrugged, as if to say, 'Well, he is the boss, after all.'

As soon as the three men were seated comfortably, Pym began. 'It seems as if we're going to have to accelerate your student's entry into the field, McNair. Hitler, having more or less made Czechoslovakia part of his *Ostmark*, is now about to rattle his sabre in the direction of Poland, by making demands relating to Danzig.' McNair gave a soft whistle and took a sip of his whisky as the Professor continued. 'It really looks as if the PM has learned his lesson at Munich and is disposed towards guaranteeing Polish sovereignty. We're led to believe that this will also be the likely strategy of the French.'

'Then it all hinges on the 'Austrian corporal's' reaction. Will he cut and run, or is he now too drunk on his own invincibility?' mused McNair, half to himself.

'I think, George old friend, that we must assume that Hitler will not back down and that war is coming,' replied Pym dourly. 'My best guess is towards the end of the summer, or early Autumn at the latest. In these circumstances, it becomes imperative to get our young friend here into the field as soon as possible and this is how I propose to do it.'

At this point McNair suddenly jumped up. 'Then, begging your pardon Professor, I should leave you two to it. Best I don't know too much, after all.' Pym responded immediately and with some force, 'Sit down please, George. I want you to stay because I want you to be his day to day contact, at least at the start of the mission. You're the obvious choice, as I hope you'll both agree when I outline the plan.'

Pym began by explaining briefly the purpose of the mission to McNair, who commented thoughtfully, 'Aye, it's a neat plan alright.'

'It is,' interrupted Pym. 'But can either of you suggest what is the biggest initial problem with its implementation?' King had, in fact, been thinking about this very question for some time and had his answer ready. 'Well, sir, if I may answer that. To my mind, the biggest problems will be finding the Nazi sympathisers and infiltrating their groups relatively quickly and without causing suspicion.' King looked up to see Pym beaming at him. 'Precisely! How on earth can this be achieved in a relatively short space of time?'

'Surely, Professor,' ventured McNair, scratching his head, 'we have many of these Nazi sympathisers on our security radar. Why could sonny boy here not discreetly attach himself to several of these and see which prove to be the best leads.'

'A good answer, George, and that was indeed our initial plan. But, as you know, my worry is that this operation must not come into contact with any other involving SIS. The risk of exposure to the Germans is then potentially much greater. But,' continued Pym, smiling broadly now, 'I think I have a very neat solution to get this operation up and running in a very short space of time. What would you say, young man, if we thought that there may be a way for you to start with an already existing network of Nazi sympathisers?'

'I'd say 'lead me to them and let me get to work',' replied King with real enthusiasm.

'Then I'll explain,' said the Professor excitedly. 'As you're both no doubt aware, relations between our country and Germany have deteriorated sharply since the fiasco at Munich and Hitler's takeover of Czechoslovakia. The SIS has been keeping an eye on one or two Nazi officials who we believe are engaged in espionage, or in coercive behaviour to force others into espionage. It's highly likely that, especially given recent developments, some of these will be expelled from the country. Indeed, we already have characters by the name of Otto Karlowa, Edmund Himmelmann and Johanna Wolf in our sights. Now, let's suppose that we give these Nazis the heave-ho, what d'you suppose Jerry's going to do about it?'

'Retaliate, at a guess,' offered King immediately. 'Of course he will,' responded Pym. 'Nothing would be more certain and here's the clever bit. The Government would not really want to continue with such childish tit-for-tat expulsions, but we can definitely use such a response to disguise our real purpose. SIS has already identified a further half dozen Germans to kick out. They're all small fry, but we can use this group expulsion to add another name to the list. He's currently of no special interest to SIS, but some of my 'irregular' informers, chaps who keep their eyes and ears open, but who are not officially part of SIS, tell me he is definitely an interesting type.'

'So,' King continued, understanding the drift of the Professor's argument, 'we mix our chap up with a few others, so neither the Germans nor SIS are alerted to his importance to our mission.' Pym nodded his head, before continuing his explanation of his ingenious plot with the energy of a man half his age. 'Now, our chap is called Rudolf Gottfried Rösel, a slippery character who has been responsible since 1936 for 'Education', or more accurately indoctrination for the Nazi organization '*Landesgruppe Großbritannien*'. Basically, he's a propagandist for the Nazis and runs a pretty rabid German Information Service. Now, frankly, we couldn't care tuppence about this propaganda rag, but one of my 'irregulars' suspects that Rösel may be running some very interesting Nazi sympathisers across London and the South of England. The plan is that sometime within the next month or so we kick Rösel out, hidden in plain sight among a group of low level undesirables and, after a certain interlude, you pop up as his *Abwehr* sent replacement. It could also be that Rösel's informers may give you entry to other like-minded pro-German sympathisers, but they may well be interesting enough in their own right. So, my friends, that's the plan. What d'you think should be our next step?'

King didn't pause for reflection, but immediately suggested, 'Well sir, I need to familiarise myself with my back story and establish myself in London somewhere. And, of course, I need to shadow this Rösel while he is still here, in order to get some idea of who his Nazi sympathiser friends may be.'

Before the Professor was able to agree with King, McNair interrupted and punctured the increasingly euphoric atmosphere between the other two men. 'There is, however, one serious potential problem here, Professor. What happens if The *Abwehr* or even worse, the SS sends someone to replace Rösel? Our young friend's life may be in very great danger.'

'You're right, of course, George. But I'm afraid that's a risk he has to take. We'd do our best to intercept such a replacement, and our record is pretty good, but there are no guarantees.'

'And nor would any be expected,' replied King immediately. 'Well, that's agreed,' concluded Pym with great satisfaction. 'I suggest we all have a nightcap and turn in. We'll have a great deal to do tomorrow.'

On the following morning and after a deep sleep, King made his way down to breakfast to find Pym on the telephone. Passing him with a brief nod, he turned into the large kitchen and found McNair enjoying one of Polly's full English breakfasts. 'There you are at last, laddie. It's already gone ten. What happened? A little too much of the whisky was it?' he asked with an innocent smile, before making great show of putting into his mouth a large slice of sausage covered in lurid yellow mustard. King grimaced and sat down to pour himself a cup of strong tea, saying, 'I see the Professor's already hard at it.'

'Indeed he is,' replied McNair, with more than a hint of admiration for the older man. 'I'm surprised you didn't hear them ringing up for him. It must be nearly forty-five minutes ago now. I hope he'll be able to join us before too long.'

Just as he was making a start on his own considerably smaller breakfast, King heard the tinkle of the telephone receiver being replaced on its cradle. A thoughtful looking Pym entered the kitchen from the hall and sat down on the chair next to King. 'Well, my friends, it looks as if my information about Hitler and Danzig was spot on. He has demanded it be ceded to Germany. We've no time to lose. You have to be out in the field as soon as possible. I'll fill you in on the details after breakfast.'

Having once again adjourned after breakfast to the sitting room, the three men took chairs facing one another. Pym explained that the young man's cover would be as the nephew of Paul Kemp, a second-hand book store owner in Charing Cross Road. 'He's a good man, served with me in the last war and has helped me out at various times since then. You'll be staying in his spare flat on the premises and working for him. This role will allow you to travel extensively and keep unconventional hours.' King immediately understood the choice of

Kemp for his alias and asked, 'That sounds perfect, sir. But how much does this fellow know of my mission?'

'He knows you're working for me and that you have an interest in right-wing sympathisers. Other than that, he doesn't need, nor indeed does he want to know any more,' explained Pym. 'Unless it's a dire emergency, we'll initially contact one another via weekly meetings with McNair. He'll send you a card with a time and place and you can pass on messages to me in this way. If you need urgent help a coded phone call to McNair in Canterbury will result in him being in the Lyons Coffee House near the bookshop at 10am the next day.' King recognised happily that this barrage of information from Pym was, at last, putting some flesh onto the bones of the operation. The Professor, however, was far from finished. Passing over a thin file, he offered the advice 'Study this well. It'll give you all the information we have on Rösel. It's vital that you begin to shadow him as soon as possible. I've no idea how long it will be before he's expelled, but it'll be weeks rather than months. So get familiar with his routines and start to shadow some of his informers. If necessary, we can talk about other potential leads when you're settled in at Charing Cross Road. Finally, and most important of all, your codename for use with your informers will be Lazarus.'

'How will I go on for funds, sir? Will Mr Kemp be paying me?' King asked, as Pym started to pack up his things, clearly keen to return to London. 'And when is he expecting me to arrive?'

'For form's sake there'll be a small stipend passed through Kemp's books, but that will be bogus. No money will pass from him to you. Rather you should open an account at the local branch of Williams Deacons Bank and you'll receive a sizeable allowance of £30 per week. That's more than a Civil Service Principal receives, so it should cover all contingencies. Of course, you'll have to account in writing for your expenses, but feel free to use the money creatively. And Kemp is expecting you around lunchtime tomorrow. That should give you plenty of time to study the file on your assumed identity as his nephew, in case anyone other than Kemp should show an interest in you. And of course,' Pym suggested with a smile, 'you'll also have time to bid farewell for now to McNair and Polly. I can't stress enough to you how important your work may prove to be to the security of the realm. Good luck, my boy, and remember all that you've been taught.' King could have sworn that he could see moistness in the eyes of his old mentor as they shook hands, but, on reflection, he decided it must have been a trick of the light. 'Now, if you'll forgive me, I have one or two things to say in private to McNair.' Ever the consummate professional, Pym effectively dismissed King to his room, to allow his private conversation with McNair to take place uninterrupted.

King bounded up the stairs to his room two at a time. He couldn't wait to get stuck in to memorising the details of his new identity. At last he might begin to feel like a real person again, instead of John King with a different name. He spent the rest of the morning and all the afternoon studying the file. He was, as a consequence, somewhat relieved to hear a brisk knocking at his door. A shouted 'Come in,' resulted in McNair poking his head round the door. 'Sorry to bother you laddie, but I've something to give you.' King immediately saw that the older man was carrying the case, in which he kept his collection of revolvers. 'Oh, I don't know.....' He could get no further as McNair quickly cut him off. 'Look, son, the boss was quite insistent. Whether you like it or not, you're going to London with one of these and a reasonable supply of ammunition. Now, you were pretty good with all of these, but if you'll take my advice, you should have the Walther P38. It has the advantage of being semi-automatic and it's extremely reliable. Plus, of course,' the Scot added with a sardonic smile, 'it's also German.'

King returned McNair's smile and raised his hands in surrender. 'OK, you win. The Walther it is.'

'Good lad,' replied the older man. 'I'll sort out a holster and an initial supply of ammo for you. Now, before I forget, get on with your packing and make sure you're down for dinner by 7.30 prompt. Polly is planning to see you off in style.' Before he could say anything, McNair had disappeared and could be heard thumping heavily down the stairs. King put aside his homework and lay on the bed reflecting on how much McNair and Polly had come to mean to him. They were almost parents to 'James Kemp,' he thought, and was immediately saddened by the thought of his own parents grieving the loss of their only son. But, he reflected, if Pym was right about his father, perhaps he at least still harboured some belief that his son was alive and engaged in some sort of active service for his country. With that thought, he turned his attention to packing those things he would take to London and boxing up the rest for storage in McNair's cellar.

Some several hours later, after a magnificent meal and significant amounts of McNair's best wine and whiskey, King collapsed in bed, excited and apprehensive in equal measure about what awaited him in London.

Chapter Eighteen

Thursday, 23rd March 1939, London.

King felt an unmistakable rush of excitement as he approached the premises of 'Paul Kemp: Second Hand, Rare and Antiquarian Book Dealer' on Charing Cross Road. He had bid a fond farewell to Polly and set off from Canterbury on a beautiful Spring morning, McNair walking him down to the railway station and insisting on carrying his two suitcases. 'Now don't you forget, laddie, you can get in touch with me any time and I'll be up to London the next day,' were the last words he shouted to King, who was leaning out of the open window of his compartment as the train heaved itself out of the station.

He had a good first impression of what was to be his home for the foreseeable future, its central position being perfect for his likely area of operation, from the city down to the south coast of England. Situated several doors away from 'Colletts Russian Bookshop', Kemp's premises were quite small, but pleasantly double-fronted and equipped with moveable book shelves on the pavement, which were brought out on dry days, in order to attract passing trade. King's heart was beating rather faster than normal as he opened the door to the bookshop, thereby causing a merry tinkling of bells. He had expected the shop to be dark and musty inside and was surprised to see that the front windows offered sufficient light and sunshine to make it positively bright. The walls held an unlikely number of shelves, neatly labelled into various sections with, he was delighted to note, a distinct emphasis on History. The shop was empty and just as King was wondering whether or not he should call out, a middle-aged man appeared from the doorway behind the counter. He was tall for his age, perhaps an inch shorter than King, and of medium build, but it was his warm open smile and grey eyes that were the most noteworthy aspects of his appearance. 'Hello there,' Kemp began, 'Can I help you? Are you looking for something in particular?' As he spoke, his eyes fell on the suitcases at either side of King and he strode out from behind the counter, his hand outstretched in greeting. 'You must be James,' he said with real warmth. 'Welcome to your new home. Delighted you found it alright. London can be confusing.' He moved past King, went outside and covered the pavement shelves with woollen blankets and placed a sign in the door, which informed potential customers that he would be back in thirty minutes. 'Come along. Let me take one of your bags.'

'Thank you very much sir,' King replied nervously. 'That would be most welcome.'

'Call me Uncle Paul please,' said Kemp. 'Do it all the time, so that it becomes second nature.' King immediately felt a little foolish, having made such a basic mistake, but he found Kemp to be very reassuring and gained confidence from his calm and placid manner. He followed his 'uncle' through a narrow internal door and into a reasonably sized hallway, which was cluttered with boxes of various sizes. He counted three doors from the hallway, recognising one as a very secure external door, probably leading to a yard which would give out onto the back alleyway running parallel to Charing Cross Road. He made a mental note that this would be a useful way to enter or leave the premises discreetly. The other two doors were slightly ajar and King could see that they led to a staff toilet and a small kitchenette, for use when the shop was open. He followed Paul Kemp, as he carried one of the suitcases effortlessly up one flight of stairs. 'OK, James,' the older man said, pointing to a closed door. 'This is the door to my flat. We'll nip in there now and have a cup of tea and a sandwich. You'll be staying in the flat on the next floor up. It's not so large but it has all the amenities you need to be pretty independent. Professor Pym said that you may have to keep unconventional hours, so it's best you have your own front door, rather than share with me. I'll show you round later on, if that's all right with you. I try to keep the shop open as much as possible.'

'That's fine, si.... Uncle Paul,' said King, rapidly correcting himself with a bashful smile, after having caught sight of Kemp's expression. 'Come on,' said the older man, clapping King on the back. 'You'll get used to it. Let's get a cuppa.' Kemp moved gracefully around his kitchen, making the tea in a measured and fluid way which suggested that he was a man who neither rushed things, nor panicked. 'So, James, I assume that's not your real name of course, do you know much about book selling?'

'I would have little idea of values and such like, but I think I'll be able to find my way around the stock fairly quickly,' replied King, as he picked up his cup of steaming tea. 'Tell me uncle, have you known Professor Pym for a long time?'

Kemp set down his cup, looked the younger man squarely in the eye and burst out laughing. 'More years than I care to remember! We served together during part of the last war on HMS *Renown* and we kept in touch after the Armistice. I've helped the Professor on several occasions with his more, how shall I put this?... secretive work.' King was pleased that Kemp seemed to be a friendly man with a sense of humour and looked forward to getting to know him better. When they had finished their drink, they went up to the flat, in which King would be staying. 'I hope everything will be OK for you James,' said Kemp warmly. 'There should be sufficient towels and bedlinen etc. If you run out, let me know. Anyway, you get yourself settled in. Here's your keys for the flat, the shop door and the rear door. Come down when you're ready. I'd better get back to the book-buying public.' King barely had time to assure him that the flat was perfect for his needs, before he had disappeared through the door and was busy making his way back downstairs.

It didn't take long for King to unpack his clothes and find a lockable drawer, in which he placed the files on Rösel, his new identity, the revolver, ammunition and holster. Having made sure everything was secure, he went down into the shop, where he found Kemp busy with a customer. The afternoon, spent familiarising himself with the layout of the shop and the range of volumes in store, went most enjoyably and surprisingly quickly. He had already decided that by five-thirty he would be outside the premises of Rösel's 'Anglo-German Information Service', located off Fleet Street. He would then try to catch his target and shadow him for at least part of the evening. It was just after four-thirty, when he realised that he would have to get a move on if he was to be in position on time. Silently cursing himself for becoming too engrossed in the workings of the shop, King bade a hasty farewell to Kemp and rushed to the nearby underground station at Leicester Square. He had used a plan of the system to work out that he had only one change and should arrive at Temple Station with just about enough time to find a suitable spot to wait for his quarry. This proved easier than he had expected, as there was a small tea room on the opposite side of the road to Rösel's workplace. He took a table one row in from the window and settled down with a drink and the latest edition of the '*London Evening Standard*', which was full of Hitler's virtual annexation of Czechoslovakia and his ultimatum to the Poles over Danzig. He had been nursing his drink for almost half an hour when, somewhat later than expected, the easily recognisable figure of Rösel emerged from the front entrance of the Information Service. He was a smallish man of about five feet four inches, dark hair with a narrow moustache, well dressed in a smart suit and carrying a mackintosh and brief case. King casually finished his cup of tea, stood up from the table and unhurriedly folded his newspaper under his arm, before slowly making his way to the door of the tea room. Fortunately, the number of pedestrians on the pavement had declined from its peak rush-hour levels, so he found it quite easy to keep his quarry in sight. Pym's reports were very clear that Rösel had never used anyone to try to spot a tail, but King took the necessary precautionary measures, just in case the German did have someone watching out for him. The novice spy followed his target up Whitefriars Street towards its junction with Fleet Street, where he turned towards St Paul's Cathedral. King enjoyed the splendid sight of one of the iconic buildings of London, especially with the early evening sun shining warmly on its magnificent dome, illuminating it with a golden hue. Fleet Street itself was a bustle of people, many clearly office workers from the nearby City of London on their way home from work, so King decided to move a little closer to his mark, unwilling as he was to lose him on his first attempted shadow. He was relieved that he had closed the gap on Rösel, as his target suddenly darted across the road in front of a red London Transport double decker bus. King had no choice but to wait until the bus had passed, before he could follow. When the vehicle finally moved away, he was shocked to find that the German was nowhere to be seen. King did not believe that he could have been spotted so quickly by Rösel, so he followed the frequent advice which McNair had offered during his training in Canterbury. 'Don't panic and rush about. Give him time to reappear,' had been the Scot's instruction and, sure enough, within a minute or two the German reappeared from the doorway of a tobacconist. He paused on the pavement to light one of the cigarettes he had just purchased before hastily crossing the road again and resuming his path towards the cathedral. King smiled inwardly and reflected that his first minor crisis had been overcome.

    He had always believed that Fleet Street was one of the most vibrant thoroughfares in the whole of London, with its mixture of newspaper buildings, inns, cafés, tea shops and small traders. These all contributed to its unique quality and, indeed, it was into one of the inns that Rösel vanished. Following standard procedure, King gave the German a couple of minutes to get himself a drink and find a place to sit, before he followed through the open the doors of the 'Punch Tavern' and entered its glazed tiled entrance. The place was clearly very popular with office, newspaper and legal workers and it was already fairly busy. As he took in the barrel-vaulted skylight, the ten etched mirrors which were longer than a man's height and the ornate fireplace, King spotted Rösel, sitting comfortably on what looked to the Englishman like a very low banquette and nursing a glass of beer on a small oblong table. Ever the practising historian, King reasoned that if a man as short as Rösel could sit with comfort, then the banquettes were likely to be very old. Moving casually over to the edge of the marble bar, he ordered a half pint of best bitter. Even through the fug of cigarette, cigar and pipe smoke, he was aware of the enticing aroma of food coming from what was obviously the kitchen area of this traditional old tavern. His stomach started growling in response to his realisation that the place served food and he remembered with some irritation that, since his breakfast early that morning in Canterbury, he had eaten only a small sandwich with Paul Kemp.

King's position was good, because even though he was not directly facing his target, he could nevertheless keep him in view. He was even able to find the time to admire the dark oak panelling of the bar and what looked like original Punch and Judy themed paintings hanging on the walls. When Rösel pushed his way to the bar, some three or four people along from King and, in an accent almost free of German intonation, ordered Beef and Ale Pie, relief gushed through King. Rapidly, he repeated the German's order and looked forward to a satisfying meal.

Some forty five minutes later, and feeling much fortified by the food and drink, King unobtrusively watched as Rösel stood up, put on his mackintosh and made for the door of the inn. He had little difficulty in discreetly following the German, as he turned left off Fleet Street into Bride Lane and strode purposefully down towards St Bride's Passage. King dropped back a little as Rösel entered the 'St Bride Foundation' and disappeared from view through its front entrance. The Englishman crossed the narrow passage, so as to walk directly by the front of the Foundation, where he saw a poster promoting a meeting. The poster read:

Mayfair Book Club

Public Meeting, March 23rd 1939 at 8.00PM.

Bridewell Hall, St Bride Foundation, Bride Lane, Fleet St.

'The Future of Europe'

ALL WELCOME

The time was approaching five to eight and King, reasoning that this must be Rösel's destination for the evening, made the spontaneous decision to attend the meeting himself. As he made his way up to the main entrance to the Foundation, he had the distinct impression that two heavy-looking doormen, both of whom possessed the kind of broad shoulders that always look uncomfortable when constrained in a fitted suit jacket, were weighing him up as a potential troublemaker. Evidently satisfied that he presented no significant threat, they nodded King through, helpfully pointing the way to the double doors which led to the Bridewell Hall. The hall itself was rectangular in shape, with large windows to both sides, separated by fine wood panelling. This in turn was topped by various large oil painted portraits. King admired the simple elegance of the room, which was set out for a meeting, with at least fifteen rows of chairs, each divided by a central aisle into two sets of six chairs. These faced a simple table, behind which sat four men, one of whom was Rösel. In the far left hand corner of the room, diagonally opposite the door through which he had entered, stood the Union Jack together with the Nazi swastika. The room was about three quarters full and the audience comprised predominantly middle aged, well to do looking couples. King now understood better the interest in him showed by the two men on the door. This was clearly no rabble rousing meeting, in which violence was expected, even relished. This was a meeting of those who hold their particular political views and are confident and secure enough to express them publicly. He recognised Archibald Ramsey MP, sitting next to Rösel, but the chairman and the other speaker were not known to him.

King took his seat one row from the back of the hall on the extreme right side so that, should it be necessary, he could slip out of the hall without being noticed. The meeting comprised the usual anti-Semitic rantings from Ramsey and a very pro-Nazi speech from an

American businessman called Cedric Mason. Rösel himself drew warm applause for a carefully argued speech, in which he reiterated the view, now very familiar to King from his time in Berlin, that Germany has no argument with Britain and that these two great nations should stand together to resist the spread of Bolshevism. The meeting eventually broke up around ten o'clock and King slipped outside to watch from the shadows, as Rösel climbed alone into a taxi. He just managed to hear one of the security guards bark Rösel's address to the driver. There seemed little point in following the German back to his flat and a very tired King decided to abandon his shadowing of his target for that night.

On arriving back at the bookshop in Charing Cross Road, King let himself in by the rear door and made his way directly to his own flat, with the intention of reviewing what he had learned during the evening. He had, in fact, decided fairly quickly that those in attendance at such meetings were so open about their political sympathies that they would almost certainly already be known to SIS and thus they would be of little interest to him. He resolved that he would not risk any sort of compromise to his cover, by attending such meetings in future and would inform Pym of his decision via his first scheduled meeting with McNair. He also decided that he must shadow Rösel every day and he formulated the plan that he would work in the bookshop in the morning and pick the German up at lunchtime.

The next few days passed uneventfully, with King getting to know his way around the bookshop in the mornings and shadowing Rösel in the afternoons and evenings. He found it easy to build up a friendship with Paul Kemp and was glad of the older man's advice on how best to get around London. During these days, Rösel seemed to go about his normal business and had no encounters that could possibly have involved his circle of informants. On the second Friday of King's stay in London, however, that was to change.

Chapter Nineteen

Friday, 31st March 1939, London.

King had begun the day normally, by helping out in the bookshop during a relatively quiet morning period. Having spent over a week in London, he now felt very much at home with the serious and studious atmosphere encouraged by Paul Kemp and he quickly became fascinated by the diverse people attracted to browse among the fine stock carried on the shelves. Having been on shadowing duty since lunchtime, King found himself waiting for Rösel to appear from his office building. On this particular day, the German surprised him by leaving work earlier than normal and, rather than heading to a nearby inn for refreshment, he made his way home to his flat in Colville Terrace in Kensington. Having followed his target without problem, King had once again admired the fine looking four storey building in which Rösel lived, with its classically designed porches and large windows overlooking the tree lined street. He had discussed with Pym the fact that many Germans chose the West of London for their home and he could not help but reflect ruefully that Hitler must pay his leftenants well. This being a residential street, King was faced with the immediate problem of not being conspicuous in his observation of the entrance to Rösel's flat. At the same time, on leaving the flat his quarry could go either way down Colville Terrace, or even up the similarly named Road, Gardens or Square. For a couple of minutes King was frozen with uncertainty until, once more he was able to recall the calm and certain advice of McNair. 'Trust your instincts, laddie. You've a good nose for this kind of work and sometimes you just have to do what it tells you. You'll make mistakes, we all do. But my bet is you'd be right more often than not...' Heartened by the recollection of his trainer's advice, King reasoned that if Rösel were to leave the flat, he would be more likely to head for the nearest underground station at Ladbroke Grove, just a few minutes' walk away. He therefore located himself in Colville Square, just before it intersected the Terrace, a position which would enable him both to enjoy the screening provided by several trees and bushes, and the comfort of a nearby bench. He was, nevertheless, happy that he had to wait only forty-five minutes before his target emerged from his front door at 6.30PM on the dot. He gave himself a pat on the back as Rösel immediately started walking in the direction of Ladbroke Grove underground station. He was, however, taken by surprise when the

German took the first left down Portobello Road and began to walk away from the underground station. King did not have long to wait for the answer to this conundrum as Rösel almost immediately dodged across the road between two black cabs, and entered 'The Portobello Star' pub. I could get to like following this chap, if he keeps on taking me into all these splendid places, mused King as, having entered the tavern a couple of minutes after the German, he waited patiently for his beer. Some time later, King followed Rösel out of the pub and was relieved that, despite the onset of twilight, the streetlights ensured that he could still see the German, as he walked further down Portobello Road. This surprised King, as he had half expected his man to head off home. However, after about a hundred yards he moved smartly up to a doorway at the side of an antiques shop which was by this time closed for the night. He clearly saw the German insert a key into the lock of the door and quickly let himself into the building.

Settling himself into the shadowed recess of the doorway of a nearby shop, he saw the light go on in the front room of the first-floor flat, followed almost immediately by Rösel drawing the curtains. King felt the unmistakable tingle of excitement running up and down his spine, as he realised that this might be the breakthrough for which he had been waiting. If Pym was correct and Rösel was shortly to be deported from Britain, then the urgency of identifying at least some of the members of the German's cell of sympathisers was obvious.

At ten minutes past eight, a well-dressed middle-aged woman approached the door and rang the bell. Thanks to the street lamp which was positioned directly in front of the antiques shop, the Englishman was also able to see that the woman was rather powerfully built and somewhat masculine in appearance. King saw a flash of grey hair as the door opened to admit her, before it quickly closed again. Ten minutes later, the second person to arrive, a much older man dressed like a City gent, strode confidently to the door and patiently awaited his admission. Expecting the next group member in a further ten minutes, King had the time to recall a conversation he had had with Pym, in which they discussed the probable size of Rösel's band of informers. 'I'd imagine,' Pym had said with confidence, 'that our man will not want any group to be too large. The fewer people who know who else is involved the better.'

'Then why not meet these people individually?' King had asked, already half anticipating the answer. 'Group sentiment can be vital in maintaining morale and motivation, especially with this kind of espionage work,' the Professor had replied. 'My guess is that he'll have groups of around six people and that he'll have ensured that none of the group members knows each other outside of the context of the group. In order to maintain this situation, it's likely that they live and work as far removed from each other as possible. I would, therefore, definitely not rule out that Rösel has more than one group running.'

The final two people to arrive, again at ten minute intervals, were younger looking men, one in the clothes of a manual worker and the last wearing a uniform of some kind. Having committed a basic description of each of the group members to memory, King settled down to wait until the meeting broke up. He had agreed with Pym that he should observe as many group meetings as possible and, after each one he should follow a different member to discover where they live or work. This would enable him to try to put a name to each member in turn and perhaps work out what kind of information they may be offering to Rösel. King had a hunch that somehow the order of arrival was significant. He reasoned that if they left individually and in the same order, the first and last to arrive would spend time alone with the German. He decided to wait to see if his hunch was correct and to follow the last to leave the meeting.

While none of the few passers-by even noticed him, as he stood in the shadows of the shop doorway, he was nevertheless happy when the flat door opened at ten fifteen and the middle aged woman, who had arrived first, unobtrusively slipped out and make her way quickly up the Portobello Road. King's hunch proved correct, as each of the group members emerged from the flat in exactly the same order as they had arrived. When the uniformed man appeared as the last group member to leave the meeting place, King quietly moved out of his hiding place and began to shadow him from the other side of the road. It soon became apparent that the target was heading for the underground station at Ladbroke Grove, some fifteen minutes away on foot. Once in the light of the station, it was possible to identify the man's uniform as that of a British railways official of some kind. King found it relatively easy to shadow him, even when he changed lines at Baker Street, and was able to watch him exit the underground south of the River Thames at Waterloo. The young agent struggled to contain his excitement, as he observed the man make for a small brick terraced house in Roupell Street and enter what was clearly a railwayman's cottage. Exhilarated by his success, King waited twenty minutes, until he was sure than his target would not re-emerge and then made his way back to Charing Cross Road. On the way home, he considered the possibility that the man worked at Waterloo Station. In that case, King reflected, he may well have all kinds of useful information regarding transport and movements of goods and people.

Extremely tired, he quietly entered the bookshop premises by the rear door and made his way directly to the upper flat. He knew for sure that by six thirty the next morning he would have to be positioned outside his new target's house near Waterloo.

The alarm clock rang at a dreadfully early time, waking King from a restless sleep, during which he had been haunted by dreams of his time in Berlin. Greta featured, of course, as did a ghostly image of Professor Berg and the cynical grinning faces of Heydrich and Brandt, all combined into a nonsensical and bizarre narrative. He made a cup of tea and a couple of slices of buttered toast, which he consumed with little relish, simultaneously scribbling a quick note of apology to Paul Kemp for missing the busiest part of the week in the shop. It was cold and drizzly when King arrived at Roupell Street, but he did not have to wait long before his target came briskly out of the house at quarter to seven and began walking towards Waterloo Station. King found shadowing at this time in the morning relatively straightforward, as there were sufficient people around to shield King, but not the crowds that would no doubt appear later in the day. Contrary to King's expectations, however, the man made for a bus stop and climbed aboard the first vehicle heading towards Victoria Station. The number of passengers allowed King to blend into the crowd and, unobserved, he was able to follow the man, as he left the bus and entered Victoria Station. He made his way, without hesitation, to a row of offices next to Platform One, which were clearly identified as 'Private: Official Railway Personnel Only'. King was able to see the man pass through the fourth door of the six which stretched along the length of the Platform. To enable him to read the sign on this door, King had to pretend to be seeing somebody off on the train which was standing, hissing and primed ready for departure. He rapidly bought a platform ticket and, having told the guard that he had forgotten to give a crucial message to his wife who was on the train, he dashed down the platform. As soon as he had arrived at the carriage adjacent to the door which the man had used, he pretended to be speaking to someone through the open door of the train. Thankfully, this section of the train was almost empty and this subterfuge did not draw any unwanted attention. The guard blew his whistle and King smartly closed the carriage door just before the train started to move forward, belching steam and smoke across the platform. As the train heaved itself into motion, he was able to examine the sign on the office door and was intrigued to read 'Timetable Planning: Non Passenger Services.' Underneath was a list of three names: L. Smith, P. Jenkins and J. Watkins. But which of these was his man? As he was walking through the ticket barrier at the entrance to the platform, King spontaneously said to the now unoccupied ticker inspector, 'By the way, I thought I just saw a neighbour of mine from Roupell Street go into one of those offices...' The ticket inspector was happy for any diversion from the boredom of waiting for the passengers for the next train and answered quickly. 'Ah. You must mean Joe Watkins. He lives down there, I believe...'

'That's right,' reinforced King. 'Mr Watkins. We live quite a way further down from him, so we don't really know one another.'

'He's quite an important man here now, you know,' offered the inspector, obviously one of life's natural gossips. 'He controls all the scheduling of freight and other non-passenger services out of this station. What he doesn't know about what's being moved, where it's going and when simply isn't worth bothering with. Anyway, sir, I'd love to carry on our little chat but I'm due on Platform 6 in a minute.'

'Then I'd better not detain you any longer,' said King amicably. 'Good day.' The inspector touched his cap in salute before sauntering off towards Platform 6.

King decided that there was little to be gained from hanging around the station and made his way out onto the street by means of the main concourse. He crossed the now much busier road and went quickly into a small café to gather his thoughts over a cup of tea and a bacon and egg sandwich. It was clear that, given his job, Watkins would have access to all sorts of sensitive information which, in the event of war between Britain and Germany, could well be priceless to the Nazis.

King had frequently wondered whether, during this operation, he would spend his time duping rather unimportant people and intercepting rather trivial information that, in all honesty, was not critical to Britain's or Germany's interests. All such thoughts were now banished as he began to realise how strategically placed people could pass on absolutely vital information to an enemy.

Chapter Twenty.

April 1939, London.

Over the next couple of days King continued to shadow Rösel, without a repeat of the success of the previous Friday evening. He also had the first of his weekly meetings with McNair, who seemed genuinely pleased to see his young student again. After settling themselves, with a cup of tea and a toasted teacake, in a quiet corner booth of a simple café on the Tottenham Court Road, they had begun by discussing the news that Franco's troops had entered Madrid and that, consequently, the Republicans had no further hope. 'It's a great day for Fascism, make no bones about it,' complained McNair. 'Its onward march will have to be stopped sometime, that's for sure. But anyway, there's nothing we two can do about that. Tell me, laddie, what have you go to report?'

King had also found the events in Spain extremely depressing and had been happy to change the subject to an outline of the highlights of his initial work in London. The Scotsman gave his characteristic low whistle as he listened to the details of Rösel's group meeting and, particularly, of Joe Watkins and the nature of his work at Victoria Station. 'I think the old man'll be delighted with your progress,' he said with a smile. 'That's exactly the kind of information he was hoping for. I'm sure he'll make one or two discreet enquiries, to see if he can provide you with any further background on this Watkins. But in the meantime you've made a great start and your hunch about the first and last to arrive at the meeting was inspired. Don't forget, it's quite possible that Rösel has another group on the go as well, so keep up the good work.'

The 'good work' for the next few days amounted to helping out in the bookshop and tailing Rösel, all to no immediate avail, and King's mood was darkened even more by the reports that Franco had officially declared the Spanish Civil war to be over. He thought back to several friends, with whom he had worked and studied and who had bravely signed up with the International Brigade in 1936. Of course, they were much more left leaning than himself and seemed able to accept what he saw as Stalin's appalling and inhumane policies as a temporary necessity. However, they were good men and he sincerely hoped that they would all be able to return safely to Britain, now that their cause was lost.

Exactly a week after the first group meeting, Rösel once more led King to the flat in the Portobello Road, where he observed five different people arrive for the meeting. Realising that this must be the kernel of the German's second circle of informants, King made a mental note of the young, smartly dressed woman, the middle aged couple who seemed rather on edge, and two men in their twenties or thirties who he recognised as probably manual workers. He decided that, once the meeting broke up, he would follow the first arrival and consequently trailed the young woman to her flat in Maida Vale. The following morning, King followed her to work and was amazed to see her go into The Foreign Office.

Over the next few weeks, King continued to track Rösel and found that the meetings at the flat over the antiques shop seemed rather ad hoc. However, by virtue of their frequency and his ever improving skills in tailing, by the beginning of May King had the addresses and names of all Rösel's informants. These included a couple who owned a small hotel in Folkestone, a man working in an armaments factory, one in an airplane manufacturer, and a GPO Telecommunications worker. A middle aged lady, who he would have thought would be of no interest or value to the Germans and an elderly, obviously retired professional made up the two groups.

At his scheduled meeting with McNair at the end of April, King decided that it was time to take stock. 'I now know the names, addresses and jobs of all of Rösel's informants and I also know where they meet. I believe that I have made progress. However, I don't yet know how he arranges meetings and, given that these happen on an irregular basis and sometimes don't include all group members, this knowledge is essential for me. In addition, it's not clear how or even if group members can communicate with Rösel to request a meeting. I watched him like a hawk and I'd swear that there's no sign of a drop box.' King struck the table in the pub with such frustration that their two pints of beer almost spilled.

'You need to calm down a bit, laddie. No point getting yourself all het up,' said McNair in what he hoped were soothing tones. However, the younger man seemed to become even more angry. 'But if, as the Professor says, Rösel's going to get his marching orders soon, then we've very little time left to find out this information.'

'I agree, young fellow. But all's not lost yet,' said McNair, with an infectious grin which immediately made King feel more positive. 'We need to think this through rationally. Communication must either be by telephone or by post. Telephone is not very likely, as we know that at least three of his informants are not on the phone at home and using public phones or ones at work would be far too unreliable.'

'So it must be by post,' contributed King, as he began to see the glimmerings of a way forward. 'And you know the Professor,' added McNair. 'He's always got a trick or two up his sleeve.'

'What do you mean?' asked King excitedly. 'Tell me his plan.'

'As you know, the Professor has a small army of his so called 'irregulars', who've helped him out many times in the past. Well, it just so happens that one of these has good contacts in the sorting offices, from which three of our 'friends' receive their post and, best of all, a contact in the offices which deliver Rösel's home and office mail. They've been discreetly intercepting post now for about a week and we had our first breakthrough yesterday. Would you believe that we found a letter, written in invisible ink and in code, from Rösel to one of his informants? The code was absolutely simple and our boys cracked it in minutes. It was real schoolboy stuff,' he added with a satisfied grin, before finishing with his party piece. 'So, I'll bet you a pint of this best bitter that there'll be a meeting of Rösel's second group tomorrow.' McNair took a long draft of his beer and sat back contentedly, beaming at his young friend.

'But that's splendid. We've more or less everything. And when the news breaks that Rösel's to be expelled, for sure one of these people will try to get in touch with him. I'd stake my life on it,' said King, his spirits now fully restored.

'Well, we hope it won't come to that,' added McNair with a shake of the head. 'But yes, basically we now have all but one piece of the information we need for you to take over from the German, when he leaves. And we've a very good chance of mopping that up as well.'

King, though very happy with these developments, felt

embarrassed at his earlier pessimism and said as much to McNair. The older man just patted him on the shoulder in a fatherly way and said, in a remarkably gentle tone, 'Forget it, son. You've been top notch this past month, with very little rest and more or less isolated. It's natural that you'll feel the pressure sometimes and, by God, those times are likely to become much more frequent when you go 'live' with Rösel's informants. You always know how I can be contacted and, when you need a safety valve, you can always let off steam to me. What passes between us stays between us. Agreed?'

'Agreed,' said King with a sigh of relief, 'and thanks very much.'

It remained only for McNair to advise that Rösel's expulsion was likely to take place within the next fortnight and that Professor Pym wanted to see King before he took over the networks. He would receive notice of where and when in due course and in the meantime, he was to help out in the bookshop.

Chapter Twenty One

Thursday, May 4th 1939, The House of Commons, London.

The sun was shining wanly through the leaded windows of the 'Mother of Parliaments' as Geoffrey Mander, the veteran Member of Parliament for Wolverhampton East rose to his feet to put a question to his Majesty's Secretary of State for Home Affairs. Sir Samuel Hoare knew exactly what was coming, for Mander had been one of the first Members of the House to take a strong stand against the appeasement of Fascist dictators and, for several months, had been posing awkward questions about pro-Nazi organisations and Nazi sympathisers in Britain. After clearing his throat, the MP asked whether, in addition to the three recently expelled from the country, any further German agents had been asked to leave Britain.

The Home Secretary replied courteously that, while there was no truth in the rumours that up to fifty more Nazis were to be expelled, such people and organisations were kept under constant observation. As a result of this activity, he advised that a further nine people were to be asked to leave British shores and that three had already been named in The House. The remaining six were listed as:

Richard Hans Curt Frauendorf

Captain Adolf Eduard Julius Jäger

Ernst Lahrmann

Rudolf Gottfried Rösel

Gunther Schallies

Friedrich Wilhelm Scharpf.

****

Friday May 5th, Athenaeum Club, London

'So, you see John, our friend Herr Rösel is very much on borrowed time now,' said Professor Pym with a contented smile, as he sat back in his favourite armchair in the otherwise empty smoking room of his Pall Mall Club. 'I'm delighted with your progress over the last couple of months. You've achieved more than it was reasonable to expect. We've almost all the information we need to enable you to step into the German's shoes and begin to run his networks. And what's more to the point, I've heard no suggestion that anyone in SIS knows anything about it.'

'How long before he has to leave, do you think, sir?' asked King, while enjoying his first glass of the deep red *Lafite*, which had been generously offered by his host.

'I expect it to be a matter of days, John. But there'll be a short delay before we can put you in place,' Pym said emphatically. 'It would be unrealistic, if you appeared and tried openly to contact the members of his networks on the day after Rösel is expelled. So we need to wait and see if any of his contacts panics about not hearing from him. In that case, they may well try to get in touch and reveal their method of contact. As you know, we're pretty sure that would be by post and I have all bases covered to intercept any such message.'

'What about the flat on the Portobello Road?' King asked sharply. 'Do you think I'd still be able to use it after he's expelled?' Pym rubbed his chin thoughtfully for a few seconds before replying with conviction, 'Oh, yes. I'm sure that won't be a problem. The landlord has confirmed to us that the rent has been paid for the next year and we'll take it up after that, if necessary. It might look suspicious to his informants, if a new man appeared and insisted on meeting in a different location right away. So we'll keep things as they are for the time being at least.'

'That's fine, sir. But what happens if the Germans try to replace Rösel themselves? That might be a little tricky...'

'Of course you're right,' said Pym calmly,' but I think that we just have to play that one by ear. It's most likely that any replacement for him will take at least two or three months to organise and you should have your feet well under the table with his circle of informants by then. I'll do what I can to try to ensure any German replacement is intercepted, before he can contact the group. But, of course, I can't guarantee that and, in that eventuality, you might have to deal with the problem yourself. Are you happy with that? And did McNair sort you out with a weapon?' The Professor looked keenly at King, searching for any evidence of uncertainty, or unwillingness to take such potentially drastic action. He was gratified to hear the firm and almost instantaneous answer, 'It's yes on both counts, sir. I'm sure I can look after myself.'

'Well, you make sure you keep in touch with McNair and call on him whenever you feel the need. Don't forget that he's a good man to have on your side in a scrape because, from now on, things could well become much more dangerous.'

Pym ended the meeting by passing a thin folder to King. 'This summarises the personal details of all Rösel's, or should I now say your informants. Of course you already know them by sight from your observations of the meetings. But this report is pretty comprehensive and contains some information that you may not have. I think we all agree that some of these people look to be potentially very damaging to our interests, especially if we don't keep them under our control.'

****

Exactly twenty-four hours after Geoffrey Mander's question in the House of Commons, Rudolf Gottfried Rösel climbed aboard a Junkers passenger plane at Croydon Airport on his way to Tempelhof Airport in the centre of Hitler's Berlin.

****

Friday, 12th May 1939, Sevenoaks, England.

Martha Perrygo stood impatiently next to her occasional table and gazed out of the hall window in search of the postman. 'Where on earth is the man?' she asked angrily. 'It's typical of the sloppy way in which Britain is degenerating.' Wolfgang, her almost blind tortoiseshell cat, had heard it all too many times before and, sensing the possibility of a full scale rant, pulled himself up from his cushion by the fire and stalked off towards the kitchen and his bowl of milk.

Mrs Perrygo stepped back from the window, as soon as she heard the postman walking jauntily up the path and tunelessly whistling 'Heaven Can Wait' . At last, thought the woman triumphantly, surely he'll have sent a note with the details of our next meeting today. After all, I've so much of value to tell him. As soon as she went out of the front parlour of her neat semi-detached house in the High Street, her expression changed from eager anticipation to crushing disappointment and frustration. For she could see immediately that the longed for hand-addressed envelope had not arrived. Only a brown bill envelope lay staring up at her from the mat. 'This can't be right', she mumbled, before going to the kitchen and filling up the kettle. As she searched for a match to ignite the gas ring, a memory burst into her conscious mind. Of course! He gave us details of how we could write to him in cases of emergency or if we had some vital information. Maybe I should send him a note requesting a meeting.

For the next thirty minutes, Perrygo argued with herself the pros and cons of sending such a message. On the one hand, they had all been told that this was to be done only in extreme circumstances; for things that simply could not wait. Moreover, to her knowledge, this means of communication had never been used by anyone in the group. On the other hand, it was now much longer than normal since they had met and it was worrying her. In these circumstances, anyone would agree that it would be quite in order to invoke this procedure. After all, she did have interesting things to tell him.

There, she decided finally, I've made up my mind. I'll write to him today. She sat back in her chair, pleased with her decisiveness and ready to enjoy her tea. She could have little inkling that soon several other people would be equally pleased with her decision.

****

Tuesday, 16th May 1939, Charing Cross Road, London.

'It's for you,' said Paul Kemp with a smile, as he held the telephone receiver for King. 'I think it's the Professor,' he added in a whisper, though he had little need for such precautions as the bookshop was empty. 'I'll just put the 'closed' sign up and get the kettle on... let's take a break; it's been busy this morning.' The bookshop owner was right, for in contrast to many of the days since Rösel's expulsion to Berlin, the bookshop had been busy almost from the time they opened up that morning. King had even managed to sell a copy of Houston Stewart Chamberlain's fascistic *'The Foundations of the Nineteenth*

Century' to an affluent looking, middle aged man. Patting the book lovingly, the man had declared, 'Splendid! I've been searching for this for weeks. I'm so glad you stock such excellent material. Have you read it? I must become a regular customer here and perhaps we could discuss its major themes sometime.' There was something rather unpleasant and predatory about his sickly, unctuous smile and, despite realising that he may be one of the pro-German sympathisers that he was meant to cultivate, King rather hoped that he would not see that particular person again.

'Hello, sir. You wanted to talk with me?' asked King into the mouthpiece, before hearing an ecstatic sounding Pym on the other end of the line. 'It's happened my boy. A big piece of the jigsaw fell into place this morning, when we intercepted a letter from one of your 'friends' to our now departed German friend. It's again in invisible ink and pretty basic code …. We even know the codename, by which he was known to them - Parsifal - and it looks like they identify themselves by their first name also in code.'

'That's excellent. So, it's all systems go,' said King enthusiastically. Even though he had enjoyed the relaxation of his recent time working with Paul Kemp in the shop, he was also eager to get into action.

'Well, yes. But we shall have to discuss when you get in touch with your 'flock'. McNair will have all the details at your next scheduled meeting. It's happening, John. All that we've worked for is now going to happen.' King had rarely heard such excitement in the Professor's voice and, after happily replacing the receiver, he went to enjoy his cup of tea in the rear of the shop.

****

Some two weeks had passed since Rösel's expulsion from Britain, when McNair and King met in the younger man's flat over the bookshop, in order to draft an invitation to be sent to the members of the first of the German's two groups of informants.

Chapter Twenty Two

Tuesday, 30th May 1939, Portobello Road, London

The two men met at the junction of Elgin Crescent and Portobello Road and, with a brief nod of recognition, fell in step towards the flat. 'You have your stuff? Time will be tight as we'll only have about half an hour before the first member arrives,' King explained nervously.

'Don't worry your head, laddie,' replied the Scot. 'I've checked and it's a Yale. You'll be in there in thirty seconds.' King had to admire McNair's professionalism, as he watched the older man cross the road and deliver a totally believable performance for anyone who might be looking at him. He casually approached the door to the flat, tried it, apparently without success, and shook his head in disappointment, before retracing his steps back up Portobello Road. As arranged, King waited a couple of minutes then crossed the road himself and pretended to unlock the flat door, which McNair had left slightly ajar. His heart pounding in his chest, King pushed open the door and entered Rösel's meeting place.

There had been extensive discussions as to whether or not King should continue to use the Portobello Road flat. On the one hand, it had been argued that continuity might be reassuring to the German's informants. This might be especially important once they become aware of their controller's expulsion from Britain. On the other hand, Pym had been unsure as to whether or not some other resident German agent might seek to make use of it. In the end, it had been decided that King's first meetings with the groups of informants should take place at the usual flat, but that he would make clear to them on their first meeting that, for security reasons, they would in future meet somewhere else.

'This tactic', Pym had explained to King, 'will offer the benefit of some continuity and give plausibility to your status as the replacement from Germany. It will also give an excellent reason for us to move the group meetings to another place, where we needn't fear the appearance of any authentic German agent.'

'It would surely be better to have a look around first, sir, so there are no little surprises waiting for me,' King had said with some concern.

'There's certainly a strong argument for that,' Pym had accepted, but had immediately countered, 'however, we don't know whether or not any of our informants may come to take a look, before the scheduled meeting time. We wouldn't want them to see us doing a spot of breaking and entering.' It had therefore been decided that McNair would gain entry for King thirty minutes before the scheduled meeting. Should one of the informants arrive early, King's presence would look perfectly normal and, hopefully he would be able to use the time before the first arrival, to try to find a key to the flat, from which a pressing could be made.

As it turned out, while King had about twenty five minutes before his first arrival to find the key, he actually required much less time. He quickly spotted a Yale key, which fitted the front door, hanging from a small hook to the right of the doorframe in the kitchen. He then familiarised himself with the layout of the flat, which comprised a living and dining area, a small kitchen, a bathroom and one bedroom. The furniture had that unmistakably shabby look found in many rented furnished flats and, on first inspection, there appeared to be no personal possessions, nor any evidence of the flat having been used, since the last meeting of a group with Rösel. King paced the floor nervously as the appointed time for the arrival of Mrs Perrygo approached; he recognised that these could be the most crucial minutes of the mission to date. If he could not convince these people that he was an *Abwehr* agent sent to replace Rösel, then the whole project may collapse in failure.

In response to the insistent buzz of the doorbell, King descended the stairs to admit his first guest of the evening. As he opened the door he noted that, at close quarters, Martha Perrygo looked even more masculine than she had done, when he had observed her from a distance. There was an unmistakable look of suspicion and fear clouding her hard and unattractive face. 'Thank you for being so punctual, Martha. Parsifal always said that he could set his watch by you.' The mention of both her name and the German's codename seemed to relax her a little and he watched as she preceded him up the stairs to the flat. Over the next half hour, King greeted the three remaining informants, who became noticeably less suspicious as soon as they had entered the living room of the flat and realised that other group members were present. Firstly, Gervaise Cromwell, an older man, dapper in appearance and known by King to be retired from a senior position at the Bank of England; next Fred Beach, a much younger man, wiry and nervous who worked at the Supermarine Aviation Works in Southampton and finally Joe Watkins, the more solid looking railway controller from Victoria Station.

'Thank you all for responding to my summons,' King began. 'I'm sure you will all agree that it's essential that we carry on the work begun so brilliantly by Parsifal.'

'Yes, that's all very well,' interrupted Beach, his eyes darting from one person to the next, like a frightened bird which could find nowhere to land. 'But what's happened to Parsifal and who are you?' An audible murmuring of agreement passed through the other three informants and, emboldened by this apparent support, the young man continued. 'And more to the point, why should we trust you?'

King had discussed with Pym how best to handle such a situation and adopted the assertive approach, on which they had agreed. 'I'm sorry to have to inform you that the man known to you as Parsifal has been expelled from Britain by the British authorities. He returned to Berlin on May 5th.' Beach was now beside himself with anxiety. 'But if they've expelled him, they must also know about us! That must be the reason for his expulsion. Why have you brought us here into such a dangerous situation? We'll all be arrested.' Wild with panic, he leapt up from his seat and made for the stairs to leave the flat.

A powerful current of anxiety ran through the room and King recognised that he should act quickly, in order to prevent things getting out of control. Before he could say a word, however, Mrs Perrygo's deep voice boomed out. 'For God's sake, pull yourself together, young man!' This outburst seemed to echo around the whole flat and certainly had its intended effect of causing Beach to stop in his tracks and turn around. 'Let's just calm down and at least allow our new host to speak and explain himself.' The other two group members' agreement to this suggestion seemed to convince Beach, at least temporarily, and he resumed his place in the room.

'Thank you,' King began, gesturing to Perrygo, 'I'm grateful for your sensible words, but I understand fully the concern of our young friend here. However, I am absolutely certain that all your concerns will be put to rest when I explain the new situation.' King saw now that he had the attention of all the informants and continued in a clear and controlled way. 'Parsifal's real name is Rudolf Gottfried Rösel and he was expelled in a simple tit-for-tat action by the British authorities. I have to tell you that there is no evidence that the British were in any way aware of Herr Rösel's activities with you. He was expelled in retaliation for the entirely justified removal from the Fatherland of several agitating British journalists. He was an easy target because of his excellent work leading the 'German Information Service' in London. This flat has been kept under surveillance since Herr Rösel's departure and no evidence of any British interest has been reported.' Continuing in a sympathetic tone, King could sense that he was winning the group over. 'But we should all be cautious, suspicious even.'

At this point, King produced four small pieces of paper, on which he wrote in pencil the vital information on each group member, including name and place of work. Having passed these to the confused looking informants, he was gratified to see each head nod in agreement, as they read the information. Now in full control of the meeting, King went on to assert, 'I am your new controller and you are to know me only as Lazarus. I have been sent here from Germany by The *Abwehr* to take over Parsifal's work. In fact, I had the pleasure of several long conversations with him, after his return to the Fatherland. How else would I know all your names, where you work and how and where to call meetings with you? In case any of you are still unsure, I have one further conclusive proof. Here is the copy of *'The Times*' newspaper, dated May 5th 1940. If you look on the bottom right side of the front page, you will see the list of names of those expelled by the British and even a photograph of some of them walking towards a plane at Croydon Aerodrome. The list includes the name Rösel and I am sure that you will all recognise Parsifal on the tarmac, on the left side of the group in shot.' Sitting back with satisfaction, King could see immediately that the faces of the group members were now looking far less anxious and Cromwell summed up the change of mood saying, 'Well, I for one, believe Lazarus is who he says he is. After all, if he were some kind of British plant, why would he not have already arrested each of us? Why would he have invited us here, just like Parsifal?'

'And we certainly can't argue with *'The Times'*,' added Watkins with a smile. King acknowledged the now total support of his network, saying in a confident voice, 'You will only refer to yourself and to each another in meetings by your first names and to me by my code name. My first instruction to you is that this will be the last time we will meet here. Your work is valued so highly that my superiors do not wish to take even the slightest risk by continuing to use this flat. We will therefore, in future, meet elsewhere and you will contact me in the same way via a new post office box. Any questions?'

After reassuring the group that there was no need to change the code for communications, King informed them that they would be given details of the new meeting place in the coded message summoning them to the next meeting. There then followed a series of brief reports from each member and it was soon obvious to King that Rösel had done an excellent job in selecting his informants. He was amazed at the dynamism and commitment of Martha Perrygo, who evidently regarded it as her mission to identify and recruit individuals, whose fascist or anti-Semitic views might well cause them to be prepared to spy and commit acts of sabotage for Germany. On this occasion, she reported that several new members had joined her group and that she had great hopes that they might provide useful information on such varied matters as research into jet propulsion, radar screening techniques and British coastal gun positions. King made detailed notes as she spoke and reinforced her efforts with frequent positive comments.

Joe Watkins gave a detailed report on the movement of troops, armaments and munitions towards the South Coast. 'It really seems like Britain is finally beginning to stir itself and gear up for war,' he said with an unpleasant sneer. Fred Beach offered crucial information about the output of Spitfire engines and the likely bottlenecks in the supply chain. He also promised a detailed plan of the 'Supermarine Aviation Works' for the next meeting '.. so that the Luftwaffe can obliterate it from the face of the earth.'

The meeting finished around 10PM and King was the last to leave, half an hour later. Just as he was shutting the door he noticed, in a shop doorway on the other side of the street, a man strike a match to light a cigarette. This was the prearranged sign, by which McNair would let him know that all of the group members had left the area and that he could assume that none were suspicious enough to try to follow him.

Once back at his flat, the enormity of what he had learned that evening began fully to dawn on King. It wasn't so much the quantity of the information that would have been passed to Germany via Rösel, but its quality had stunned him. He made a full written report for Pym before finally settling down to a well-earned sleep, just as the earliest risers in the city were beginning to stir.

Chapter Twenty Three

Tuesday, 6th June 1939, Portobello Road, London.

The sun was still shining strongly from a clear blue sky, as King made his way down Portobello Road to the first floor flat for his next meeting with informants. Professor Pym had been so pleased with the report of the meeting with the first group, that he met King in person and immediately issued the order for a meeting with the second to be called. 'I'm sure you'll agree,' he had said to King, with a broad smile on his increasingly suntanned face, 'that we must prevent this kind of information falling into the hands of the enemy. If the second group is anything like the first, getting them into line with you is top priority.'

King had been provided with a key from the pressing he had taken and he quietly and unobtrusively let himself into the flat. Once inside, he silently prepared himself to greet his informants: Jane and Peter Lambton would be the first to arrive. The owners of a mid-sized hotel in Dover, they had connections with several senior members of the 'Anglo-German Fellowship' and had a wide circle of like-minded friends in Kent and Sussex. The next two members of the group were Paul O'Grady, an Irish telecommunications worker, who was sympathetic to Nazi Germany on the principle that 'my enemy's enemy is my friend' and Albert Shaw, a foreman in The Royal Small Arms Factory in Enfield. 'These may well prove to be significant sources to control,' Pym had said to King, during their briefing. 'But I would wager a pound to a penny, that the final member, Miss Stevenson, is by far the most significant in the group. Try to keep a special eye on her.'

The meeting had, in fact, followed a very similar pattern to that with the first group; initial suspicion was allayed by King's knowledge of the personal details of the group and the arrangements that had governed their meetings with Parsifal. Each member had made a brief report on those issues that they felt would be of interest to The *Abwehr* and King had instructed them to await a summons to the next meeting. He had been careful to arrange for Stevenson to be the last to arrive, so that she would be the last to leave and would have some private time with him. As he entered the room from showing Shaw out of the flat, King was able to observe that she was tall for a woman, slim with long, blond hair and a pretty, fresh face. In fact, he reflected, she looked a perfect cocktail of the 'English Rose' and the classic Aryan type, as she reached into her handbag to extract a packet of cigarettes and an exquisite silver lighter. 'Do you have anything to say to me in private?' enquired King gently.

'Well, maybe it's not so significant right now, but I think it may well grow into something that is,' she began in a rush, as King nodded his head slowly in encouragement. 'You see, I'm on very friendly terms with a couple of the senior private secretaries at work. In fact, on fine days we often go to eat our lunch together in St James's Park. It's so peaceful and pretty there.' The young woman paused to take another draw on the cigarette and push her hair behind her ears, as if she needed time to convince herself that she should carry on. King waited patiently until she was ready to continue.

'I don't have clearance for the most secret work of the Office, but they do, and one day last week they were talking about how they didn't think Britain should form an alliance with Russia.' King's ears pricked up at this, as he could imagine that a real German agent would be desperate to discover more information on this theme. 'That could be vital for our interests. Did they say anything else that you think might be important?'

'Not really…. Just that neither of them were keen on this, and that maybe many in senior positions in the Foreign Office weren't keen either.' As soon as she had finished speaking, she looked up at King as he offered enthusiastic praise. 'You've done very, very well and you were right to keep this topic back for me alone. Don't talk about it with anyone else.' Stevenson nodded her head quickly as King emphasised, 'I want you to keep your eyes and ears open, but above all, don't arouse suspicion. Time is on our side and we don't have to rush things. Use what opportunities arise, but be wary of taking too many risks.'

As soon as the young woman had left the flat, with a fleeting smile and a nervous handshake, King hastily jotted down the most important notes from his conversation with her. He had the distinct feeling that Pym would be very interested in what she had had to say.

Chapter Twenty Four

Summer 1939, London.

The summer of 1939, which proved to be the last weeks before Europe was plunged once again into total war, were a strange time for many. The deteriorating political situation, combined with the visual evidence of the preparations for war, dating from before the Munich Agreement of 1938, served to remind people constantly that their lives were balanced on a knife edge. For King this was, paradoxically a rather quiet time, during which he could reflect on what it meant to be a traitor. As an academic, he was by nature interested in seeking to develop a sophisticated understanding of phenomena and the psychology of treason had come to exercise a real fascination for him. His periodic group and occasional individual meetings with the informants he had inherited from Rösel, had provided a great deal of interesting information about the varied motivations of the informants. It was clear to King that they had greatly differing definitions and understandings of what they were doing and the reasons for doing it. For the older members of the groups, such as hotel owners Jane and Peter Lambton and for ex-civil service mandarin Gervaise Cromwell, their views were conditioned by their experience of the inter-war years and their perception of the ongoing decline of Great Britain. In particular, they seemed to be most exercised by what they saw as the defeated politics of Democracy and its evident capitulation to Socialism. He remembered one conversation with Cromwell, in which his informant seemed more than eager to explain his motivations.

'You know, Lazarus,' he had begun, in the presence of the other members of his group, 'maybe there are those who would see what we are doing here as treachery. But I see myself quite clearly as one of the saviours of our great country. Not at all a betrayer of it.'

Cromwell's brow had started to perspire and he had reached for a glass of water, before continuing. 'The point is, you see, that we patriotic Britons recognise that we are already at war. Not the war of formal hostilities and armies facing one another on the battlefield, though that will inevitably come. No,' he exclaimed more and more passionately, 'this is the war being fought now to prevent our wonderful country from declining even more. We can see how in the last two decades democracy has gone soft; it's the political ideology of the mediocre and the weak, who are content to let our country be ruled by those who receive their instructions from a Bolshevik Moscow. People worry about the so-called 'Fifth Column' here in Britain. I have to tell you that it's already well embedded here, in the civil service, trade unions, political parties, even Westminster itself. We need to recognise the way shown to us by The Führer! It's not too late to save Great Britain from its decline and to march with our German brothers against the tide of Bolshevism.' King was appalled to recognise that for people such as Cromwell, committing treason by offering sensitive information and help to Nazi Germany had become a twisted form of duty for the truly patriotic Briton.

The Stevenson woman, on the other hand, revealed nothing of her rationale for treason. Indeed, King had come to the conclusion that her motivation was rooted in her past which she kept very private. His initial sense that she would be the best placed member to provide very sensitive information was proving accurate and he put himself on alert when, in late June, he received a message from her via his PO Box urgently requesting a private meeting.

The meeting was scheduled for 7PM on Tuesday July 4th on a wooden bench overlooking the Serpentine in Hyde Park. As the day had been wonderfully warm, King took the opportunity to arrive early and to enjoy the everyday pleasure of an early evening stroll in the park. In contrast to much of the second half of June, on this day the sun had blazed down from a clear blue sky and an almost Mediterranean temperature of seventy-three had been reached. He took a table at one of the tea rooms, which served the park in summer, and sat back to enjoy his lemonade in the warm embrace of the sunshine. Surrounded by happy smiling people, he could not help but reflect on how he had now lost any connection with the simple enjoyable things in life. Walking hand in hand with a sweetheart, happy family picnics on the grass in the park or garden, energetic, though always good natured discussion and argument with colleagues.... these were all now things of the past for him. In a way, he also envied the increasing numbers of young men who could proudly display their uniform, as they escorted happy girlfriends on this peaceful London evening. They could take pride in the fact that everyone knew what they were prepared to sacrifice for their country. He, in contrast, inhabited a shadowy world, in which deception and lies were his stock in trade and where the fight had to go on unnoticed and unappreciated by the British public. For a few unguarded moments, King thought with great sadness of those he had lost, if not forever, then certainly for a long time to come. He felt guilt every day at the deception perpetrated on his family and on Greta. He thought about his old life of study and fellowship at Durham University and what then had seemed such a humdrum, unadventurous existence. He felt a great pang of loss for the students he would no longer teach, the books and papers he would probably not write and, bizarrely, his beloved MG which, having been discreetly bought by Pym on his behalf, even now sat in a garage in Oxford, awaiting his return like a faithful dog.

King was so immersed in such thoughts that he almost missed the arrival of Abigail Stevenson. He had deliberately positioned himself on a slight rise above The Serpentine, which permitted him to see her approach from any direction and was only jerked out of his reflective torpor, by the appearance of a young woman in a bright, summery frock. At first he did not recognise her, having expected her to arrive from work in the uniform of smart office wear. Evidently having assumed that he would already have been waiting, her pace slowed discernibly as she realised he was not at the planned meeting place. As soon as King had verified that no one was following his informant, he moved at a normal walking pace towards their rendezvous. He noticed an immediate expression of relief cross her face as she caught sight of him, followed by the briefest of smiles. Again he noted what an exceptionally good looking woman Abigail Stevenson was; feminine without being bland, with sparkling blue eyes and hair shining brilliantly in the evening sunshine. King sat down on the bench and, having nodded a polite stranger's greeting, he unfolded his '*Evening Standard*' and pretended to read it. The bench had been well chosen for the meeting place, because it was positioned almost directly in front of the water of The Serpentine. Additionally, it enjoyed at least forty yards of open straight path on both sides and a rather rough and steep rise immediately behind it.

'I'm sorry to call you to a meeting like this, but I have useful information on the topic we discussed the last time we met,' began the woman in a rush. 'That's fine,' replied King in a steady voice. 'Take your time. It's a beautiful evening and we have lots of time.' The young woman flickered a brief smile in his direction and, as soon as her heart had stopped racing and her chest heaving, she began in much more measured, but unmistakably excited tones.

'One of my friends, a Senior Private Secretary, was ill last week and I had to replace her as minute taker in a very interesting meeting between some senior civil servants.' King maintained the pretence that he was still reading his newspaper, but inclined his head to indicate that he had understood and she should continue. 'Well, the meeting was called to discuss Britain's attitude to a possible alliance with France and Russia against Germany. It appears that...' At this point King violently swatted his newspaper from side to side at an imaginary wasp. Stevenson immediately fell silent and saw a couple walking towards the bench, hand in hand and chatting happily. Having waited until they were well out of earshot, King once more returned to his newspaper, which was the sign for Abigail Stevenson to resume her report. 'As I was saying, it appears that the Soviets are very serious about this. There even seems to be a suggestion that they have offered up to one million men to help defeat Germany.' King had to suppress his astonishment, but responded dubiously, 'Hmm, that could be very serious, if it forced Germany to fight a two front war... Was anything said about the likelihood of this alliance being realised?'

'Yes of course,' replied his informant with some impatience. 'That's the point I want you to understand. All of the civil servants present were of the view that the British Government is lukewarm about this proposal. Basically, they are suspicious of Communism and believe that, after Stalin's systematic purges of the military leadership, the Red Army is probably not fit for purpose anyway.'

'Was anything said of the formal British response to the Russian overtures?' King demanded sharply.

'Well, I wasn't quite sure what some of what was said meant... but yes, the senior person there said that Lord Halifax doesn't want a meeting with the Soviets and intends to play for time by sending a low-level official to Moscow to delay things. Did I do right to ask you for a special meeting?'

King could almost take pity on the young Englishwoman. Even in the act of betraying her country's secrets, she looked imploringly to him for approval and affirmation. 'Of course you did the correct thing,' he said quietly and risked a short look at her, a smile of encouragement on his face. 'You have given a great service to the *Reich* and I am sure that it will be recognised in Berlin.' Without giving her the chance to reply, King smiled, stood up, folded his newspaper under his arm and simply walked away.

****

Shortly after this encounter in Hyde Park, at King's request a meeting with Pym took place at the Professor's flat. 'My God, John,' exclaimed the older man excitedly, 'If you were handling only Abigail Stevenson, the continuation of this project would be well worthwhile.'

'Yes, I wouldn't like to think what damage such intelligence could cause, were it indeed to fall into the hands of our enemies. I presume much of it is accurate?' asked the younger man eagerly.

'Well, I don't suppose I should either confirm or deny, but let's just say that I agree with your previous statement. You're going to have to manage this one particularly carefully. I'm sure the Germans will try to establish contact with such a key source before too long. Of course, we've got all possible antennae out to intercept any replacement for Rösel, but we can't guarantee that we'll be successful.'

'I'm sure that you're right, sir, but don't forget that Martha Perrygo has a wide group of like-minded Nazi sympathisers surrounding her. These must provide her with a whole range of information about what's going on in the South East and on the South Coast that might prove very useful to our enemies.'

'Of course,' conceded Pym with good grace. 'So, on the basis of the meetings you've had with them, what do you make of the others?'

'I've only met them in a couple of group meetings and I must say that Joe Watkins, the goods train controller from Victoria Station and Fred Beach, the worker at the Supermarine Aviation Works, may be crucial sources to keep an eye on. The first could give full details of train movements, which may well be useful to the Luftwaffe or to German saboteurs. The latter could provide vital intelligence concerning production levels and technical data on fighters such as the Spitfire. He seems a very edgy and suspicious type, though, who probably was the least inclined to accept me at face value as Rösel's legitimate replacement.'

Pym heaved a heavy sigh as, having placed his pipe in its rest, he rubbed his chin thoughtfully. 'It hardly bears thinking about, does it John? If just the intelligence from these few sources were to find its way back to Berlin, who knows what might be the consequences?'

'You're right, of course,' replied King, 'but I'm confident that I have them all under control for the time being. As for the others, Gervaise and the Lambtons seem well in with established fascist groups, such as the 'Anglo-German Fellowship'... I'm not sure whether their possible contacts with Germany through that route could present a danger. Frankly, I'd be happier if they were out of the circles of informants.'

'Are you suggesting that we should arrest them?' Pym asked doubtfully. 'On what charge could we do that? They're not breaking any law at present... of course, should war be declared, that would be a different story.'

'Righto, Professor. That seems reasonable to me,' replied King with a smile. 'Now, as to O'Grady, the Irish telecommunications worker, his loyalties are definitely not to Germany and I've the distinct impression that he takes his orders from some Republican cell or other. He may well have connections to those who would not hesitate to commit acts of sabotage. For the time being, however, he and Shaw, who works in The Royal Small Arms Factory, may be rather lower priorities.'

****

The dog days of the summer of 1939 continued throughout the rest of July and well into August. King contented himself with working in the bookshop and holding periodic meetings with his groups of informants in the new flat provided by Pym, above a tailor's shop in the Tottenham Court Road. In common with many ordinary Europeans, his informers seemed more concerned to discuss the developing political situation, than to offer crucial intelligence. In particular, they were keen to know if King had any information about Germany's likely intentions. Some of the informants, such as the Lambtons and Beach, were very anxious about what a declaration of war might mean for their continued participation in intelligence gathering. On one particular occasion, Martha Perrygo responded to Beach's uncertainty about German policy, by demanding of the startled young man, 'Good God, man! What would you, as an Englishman, feel if someone were to give a perfectly English city such as Birmingham, or a stereotypically English county, such as Somerset to a third rate country for it to keep and run as their own?' Beach looked at her in confusion and the older woman had made a visible effort to calm down, speaking her next words as if to a particularly dim, but timid child. 'Well that's exactly what has happened to Germany, as regards Pomerania and Danzig. Of course they must seek justice. Anyone would and if the weak British Government is so short sighted as to side against Germany, surely all right- thinking people would have to do everything they could to make the conflict short and restricted. We all know who the real enemy is.' This brought a murmur of agreement from all present and calmed Beach's uncertainty. King took advantage of this discussion to outline how he intended to run his networks in the event of war. 'Should war be declared,' he stated firmly, 'it would be too risky to continue to meet as a group. Therefore, I would not call any more group meetings, but would see each of you individually, as and when either you or I deem it necessary.'

****

A little over a week after their last group meeting, on a drizzly and cool morning in mid-August, King received another request for an individual meeting from Stevenson, which he scheduled to take place in the Tottenham Court Road flat. The rain was still pouring down out of a leaden evening sky, when the doorbell to the flat rang at precisely the prearranged time. While her stylish trench-coat and small umbrella had prevented the incessant rain from thoroughly soaking her, nevertheless Abigail Stevenson's long blond hair looked damp and the shoulders and bottom edges of her coat were very wet. She grimaced as she came through the open front door of the flat to King's cheery greeting. 'A typical English summer day, if I am not mistaken.'

'You can say that again,' she replied with a smile. 'As usual I'm cold and wet.'

King turned on the small gas fire and urged her to sit close to it before observing, 'From the tone of your request for a meeting, something urgent must have come up.'

'Yes, I'm sorry about the dramatics, but I think it has,' she replied seriously, 'though it's not to do with the Alliance issue.' Recognising the obvious look of disappointment on her handler's face, she hastily continued. 'Nothing much has happened on that front that I'm aware of. However, last week I was given some meeting minutes to file. As you'll imagine, at the moment the Foreign Office is very busy. It has, however, felt obliged to honour requests for summer leave from many secretarial and administrative staff. We've brought in a few temps to do the low level work, but the permanent staff like me have been given the more…. shall we say sensitive material.'

'I see,' interrupted King, using the pause in her story to gather his notepad and pencil.

'Of course,' continued the young woman confidentially, 'I had to be very careful. There was very little opportunity for me to have a good look at the minutes. But I was allowed into the filing room, just before lunch one day. As I was searching for the correct drawer in which to place the file, one of the staff from the outer office shouted that they were all going for lunch and could I please make sure that door to their office was locked when I left. It was just lucky timing really. I would've finished and left before they went to lunch, had I been a minute or two earlier,'

'And are they supposed to leave the filing room unattended and with someone still in it?' asked King incredulously.

'Oh no. Of course not. The Office Managers are quite strict about that kind of thing,' she replied, in what he thought was an unexpectedly defensive manner. 'But, as I have said, we're very busy and short staffed and they know me as a permanent member of staff. So, I imagine that they could see no harm in leaving me to shut and lock the door. It's a Yale lock, you see.'

'Well,' encouraged King with a smile, 'you may have been lucky. But that isn't everything. You used your luck to the fullest. You impress me more and more.'

Stevenson hardly seemed to notice the compliment, merely

continuing, 'The minutes, which I had the opportunity to study, were from a meeting involving senior civil servants from the Foreign Office and the Treasury.'

'Really? That sounds very interesting. Please tell me more.'

'Well, it appears that at the end of April, Poland approached Britain for help with the financial cost of rearming. Specifically, in May the Polish Foreign Minister Beck had asked for a loan of some £60million to purchase weapons and crucial raw materials.' King was once more astonished at the sensitivity of the information that his informant was imparting. 'The Treasury civil servant is minuted as saying that the Chancellor of the Exchequer, Sir John David, had advised Mr. Chamberlain that the idea of Britain bailing out Polish rearmament in such a fashion was 'really impossible.' His reason was that the financial position of Britain herself had been greatly affected by the costs of her own rearmament. The minutes also noted that a decision had been made on 24th July, that Britain could possibly offer some £8million, which would, however, have to be spent by the Poles on British materials. There is no record of whether or not this offer was either made, or accepted.' After finishing her account, Abigail Stevenson took out and lit a cigarette and relaxed back into her chair to await King's comments.

King finished his notes, before putting down his pencil and pad and smiling warmly at Stevenson. 'I'm sure that *Abwehr* headquarters in Hamburg will be very keen to pass on this information to Berlin as soon as possible. It could have a significant influence on the military and political strategy of the Reich.'

****

Sunday 3rd September, 1939, Charing Cross Road, London

'James! James! Come down here quickly and listen to this!' Paul Kemp's voice had about it the kind of definitive urgency that brooks no contradiction and King immediately dropped what he was doing, in truth nothing more important than the previous day's '*Times*' Crossword Puzzle and hastened down the stairs from his flat. He arrived just in time to be shushed by the bookshop owner and shown to a battered armchair by the fireplace... 'Just listen to this.' the older man hissed 'For God's sake… here we go again…'

King was transfixed as, crackling out of the older man's ancient radio set, came the unmistakable voice of the Prime Minister:

'I am speaking from the cabinet room of 10 Downing Street. This morning the British ambassador in Berlin handed the German government a final note stating that unless we heard from them by 11 o'clock that they were prepared at once to withdraw their troops from Poland, a state of war would exist between us. I have to tell you that no such undertaking has been received and that consequently this country is at war with Germany.'

Chapter Twenty Five

Wednesday, November 15th 1939, London.

The last months of 1939, together with the first three months of 1940, were dubbed 'The Twilight War' by the Prime Minister Neville Chamberlain and, alternatively, 'The Bore War' or 'The Phoney War' by the British press and people. In fairness, after a couple of false air raid alarms and the tragic sinking by a U Boat of MS *Athenia*, with the loss of over a hundred non-military lives, there was very little military, or naval action between Britain and Germany. That is not to say, however, that war had not brought changes. Some of these were very evident to King as, on a prematurely dark and damp mid-November evening, he made his way on foot down Charing Cross Road. Many theatres, public buildings and shops had their entrances protected by thick walls of sandbags and their windows taped in criss-cross patterns to inhibit flying glass. The theatres also had signs which forcefully reminded patrons that they would not be admitted, unless they were carrying the Government issue square cardboard box containing a gas mask. As he continued towards Leicester Square underground station, he could see some of the higher barrage balloons swaying lazily in the slight breeze, occasionally caught by the light of the anti-aircraft searchlights, whose crews were clearly getting in a little practice at moving their beams quickly and accurately.

Over the last few weeks, King had been kept busy by his informants who, as planned, he now met individually. The passing of the Emergency Powers (Defence) Act in August had given the authorities the power to detain anyone deemed to be a threat by the Government. Challenging the ancient right of 'Habeus Corpus', it even allowed imprisonment without trial. Additionally, any property could be entered and searched on the suspicion of the authorities that this could conceal a threat to the security of the realm. In such circumstances, it had been easy to remind his informers of the wisdom of breaking up the two networks.

After a short walk, King arrived at the station, bought his ticket to Enfield West and made his way down to the crowded platform. The state of war notwithstanding, the London Underground was still operating very efficiently and he did not have long to wait for his train. Settling himself into a window seat, he gave the merest nod of greeting to the overweight, florid looking man who sat down beside him. Rather than engage in any conversation, he preferred to retreat into his reflections on the conduct and consequences of his previous meeting with his informant Albert Shaw.

The foreman at the Royal Small Arms Factory had relished the irony of King's proposal that they, two pro-German spies, should meet in 'The Horatia' pub. This had, of course, been named after the love child of Lady Hamilton and Vice Admiral Nelson, one of Britain's most cherished war heroes. After a short underground ride to Holloway Road, King had strolled the last couple of hundred yards to the pub, entered, bought a pint of best bitter beer and sat at a quiet table to await his informant. He immediately recognised the medium build and thinning, fair hair of Shaw, as he casually entered the pub some five minutes after the scheduled time. Dressed inconspicuously in dark overcoat and hat, he had ordered his pint of pale ale and taken his seat at the table with King. The two men, as routine dictated, had spent the first few minutes discussing the banalities of the weather, fictitious family matters and the increasing effects of rationing. Once the two men were sure that neither of them had been followed into the pub and that they were attracting no interest from other customers, King had asked, 'So, Albert, what do you have for me today?'

Shaw was an unattractive, furtive looking man, with darting, narrow eyes and restless hands which were forever clasping and unclasping one another. 'And for goodness sake, calm down, man,' King had felt constrained to warn him. 'You'll arouse suspicion carrying on like that.' Shaw had smiled in response, revealing his misshapen and nicotine stained teeth. 'Sorry, but you know, since September 3rd I've become much more anxious. They could hang me for what I'm doing.'

'If we exercise just a modicum of caution, it won't come to that. We're just two old friends having a catch up in a pub,' King had said soothingly, raising his eyebrows to indicate that Shaw should continue. 'So, what's happening at the Royal Small Arms Factory? Flat out, I imagine.'

'That's just it,' Shaw had replied, before taking a sip of his beer. 'We have orders for all kinds of rifles and small arms building up, but we can't meet them. And it's not because we don't have the capacity. It's because we can't get the skilled labour. I know that half a dozen people were interviewed for jobs last week and not a single one was suitable. I tell you, I heard some managers talking in the canteen the other day and they say it's the same at the other Royal Ordnance Factories... it's bound to affect Britain's preparedness to fight.'

'That's definitely interesting, Albert. Thanks. And is there any news on the new Ordnance Factories?' King had asked sharply. In response, Shaw had nodded his head like a nervous bird. 'They're asking whether staff would be prepared to move to Bridgewater in Somerset and Bridgend in South Wales to work in the new factories which are due to open there soon. I'll tell them I'm interested and try to find out more details for you.'

King had nodded his head, 'That's excellent work. Some potentially very useful information.'

'But there's something else,' Shaw had begun with some hesitation. 'Something I'm not so sure about.' King looked at the nervous man with a quizzical expression and he continued, 'Well, since the Nazi-Soviet Pact, it seems that some of the more hard-line, pro-Soviet trade unionists are secretly encouraging industrial sabotage in the factory. It's only small scale and uncoordinated stuff for now and it has caused only minor disruption. But, who knows, with organisation and planning, it may have an effect. A mate of mine is involved, and he knows my views about Churchill and his policies.'

King immediately tensed and asked sharply, 'But you've not said anything about me, have you? That could be very dangerous. The British are not fools, whatever we may think. They'll have counter espionage agents deployed in factories now.'

'Of course I haven't said anything. But I might be able to get us both an invitation to their next meeting. I'd tell them you were a friend and sympathiser. You could see how the land lies. What do you think? Do you work now with the Bolshevik organisers? Should I organise it?' Shaw's face had glistened with beads of sweat, as he waited tensely for King's response.

Discussions had, of course, taken place with Professor Pym about the possibility that pro-Soviet sympathies among some trade unionists could, in the aftermath of the Molotov-Ribbentrop pact, metamorphose into a willingness and desire to sabotage the war effort. Communist workers might even be organised by Moscow to undertake such work. They had agreed that, if King received any contact relating to the Soviets, it might be very useful at least to try to get an idea of numbers and the names of the organisers. King, therefore, replied cautiously, 'Of course the Reds have their own network of agents here and, though collaboration has been discussed at the highest levels, nothing has, as yet, filtered down to me. In such circumstances it might be dangerous to be seen to be treading on their toes. So, on no account should you divulge your activities in the interests of the *Reich*. That would be utterly foolish and explicitly against my orders. But to masquerade as anti-Churchill sympathisers and to attend a meeting might be a good idea. Let me know via the PO Box if this is a possibility. In the meantime, you should keep your eyes and ears open and try to get a list of names of these Soviet sympathisers. The sooner we all start to work together for the defeat of Britain, the better.'

Barely a week later, Shaw had contacted King to confirm that they had an invitation to attend the next meeting of the Enfield factory's communist cell. A regional organiser was due to address the meeting, which would take place in an inconspicuous function room above 'The Goose' public house in Wood Green. Shaw had explained that the landlord was sympathetic to their aims and that Wood Green was accessible to the group members, but sufficiently distant from Enfield so as not to arouse suspicion. The meeting was due to start at 8PM and King had agreed to meet Shaw in the Tap Room of the pub at 7.45PM.

As he approached the large, red brick building a fine drizzle began to fall, causing him to turn up the collar of his dark overcoat and pull his wide-brimmed hat down further over his eyes. Shaw was waiting for him, looking his usual furtive and unwholesome self and nursing an almost full pint of ale. He looked up and nodded quickly to King, who bought a glass of bitter and joined him at his table. The room was a thick fug of various kinds of tobacco, mixed with the smell of beer and the stale sweat of the almost exclusively working class clientele. Numerous faces glared unashamedly at King as he ordered his beer, but they noticeably relaxed when he went to sit with Shaw. 'Friendly natives around these parts,' said King sarcastically. 'Now, Albert, what's the score for tonight?'

'I've told them that you're an old friend of mine, down visiting from the Midlands and they're OK with that. But they'd rather that we didn't speak during the meeting and I need a name I can give them. I can hardly use Lazarus,' said Shaw anxiously. 'Relax' said King confidently, 'It'll be fine. Just call me James or Jimmy and leave the rest to me. Did you get me the list of the local Reds?' Professor Pym had been very explicit that King should do his utmost to obtain a list of the names of those active in the communist cell based on the Factory. While the security services had kept tabs on Soviet sympathisers over the last years, they had been caught a little flatfooted by the signing of the Nazi-Soviet Pact and any up to date information could be very useful. King inwardly breathed a sigh of relief when, after a careful look to make sure he was not being observed, Shaw offered King his newspaper to read. Clipped to the bottom of page five was a small piece of paper which King carefully extracted, before making a show of throwing the paper on the table, saying with exasperation, 'All the same old rubbish in that!' After taking another pull of his beer, Shaw stammered 'All the names I could get are there, but you must realise how dangerous this is... I don't like it all. They'd hurt me badly, if they as much as suspected.'

'They won't', I'll see to that,' said King smoothly, as he expertly pocketed the paper and took a sip of his beer.

'A fellow shop steward, Nixon, has arranged to meet us here and take us to the meeting,' continued Shaw. 'I thought that was a bit odd, as I'm sure he doesn't like me. Anyway, he'll be here in a couple of minutes.'

'Then I'd better pay a quick visit, back in a jiffy,' said King as he rose to his feet and made his way through the thickening crowd of drinking, smoking and arguing men. Once inside the appallingly dingy, but thankfully deserted Gents lavatory, King made for the nearest cubicle. Holding his nose against the smell and trying not to pay too much attention to the dreadful state of the facilities, he quickly took out the piece of paper which Shaw had given him, folded it until it was about the size of a cigarette card and then slipped it into a secret compartment in his glasses case. King smiled to himself at this piece of theatrically spy-like behaviour, flushed the lavatory for the sake of appearances, though it did seem to him that few did so even when they should, and made his way back to the Tap Room.

As soon as he entered, he saw that Shaw was no longer alone; a huge, brutish looking man was perched on the edge of the seat that he himself had occupied. As soon as he saw King, Shaw rose rather stiffly and began to make the introductions. 'This is Jimmy,' he began edgily, his nervous eyes flicking from King to the man-mountain and back again with remarkable speed. 'He's a good friend of mine. Jimmy, meet….'

'No names, no pack drill, OK Shaw?' hissed the other man as he eyed King with undisguised suspicion. 'If it'd been left to me, you two wouldn't be here, but we're a disciplined lot in the workers' army. We do as we're told,' he grumbled with a harsh laugh, which indicated his obvious contempt for these particular orders. With an angry jerk of his bullet like head in the direction of a narrow door to the right of the packed bar, he indicated that Shaw and King should follow him. King realised quickly, as he made his way up the narrow and dark stairway that this must be some kind of service or back route to the upper floors, where the function rooms and bedrooms to let were located. At the top of the stairs, another narrow door opened onto the corner of a broad, well-lit landing which was crowded with men, who, King realised, must have used the main staircase from the pub's entrance hall. As they queued to enter a reasonably sized function room, an excited murmur arose from the men who were all carefully nursing their pint pots, as if they were frightened of causing a spillage on the lurid red carpet. 'Follow this lot in and take the seats immediately to your left, up against the rear wall,' barked their guide as he carefully closed the door to the back stairs. 'I'll join you before the meeting starts.' King noticed that the door was so well disguised that, once closed, it could easily be mistaken for one of the simple wooden panels which lined the walls of the landing.

The meeting itself was far from the expected tedious political fare, with many heated points being made about the ethics of actively supporting Soviet Russia in view of the Molotov-Ribbentrop Pact. 'Hitlerism is the exact antithesis of Socialism. How can we positively help towards the possible victory of Fascism?' asked one of the more articulate members of the audience. The main speaker was just about to offer his solution to this dilemma, when the rear doors of the room burst open and two men rushed in shouting, 'Special Branch! Special

Branch's here! It's a raid... get out while you can!'

After a second's stunned silence, the room was filled with the sounds of chairs being pushed hastily back onto the floor and incoherent shouting, as members of the audience desperately tried to get out of one of the two rear doors. Nixon, who had come to sit with King and Shaw, grabbed the latter by the arm and hissed, 'Come with me, you two.' King's mind was racing. It seemed highly likely that Special Branch had received some sort of tip off that the meeting was due to happen. Moreover, Nixon's demeanour throughout the whole evening had made clear the suspicions which he harboured about the two of them. Not relishing the idea of being left to the tender mercies of the likes of him, King resolved to get away from him as quickly as possible. He reasoned that the raid would probably have been launched through the pub's main entrance and therefore decided that the semi-hidden rear stairs would give him the best chance to slip out through the Tap Room and the rear entrance of the pub. To his frustration, the flow of the panicked crowd was towards the main staircase and he found himself being dragged in that direction. Ahead he could see Nixon still holding Shaw firmly by the arm. His sheer size meant that he was able to forge his way through the crowd and King took the opportunity to use the pressure of the crowd to fall further and further behind him. Eventually, feigning injury to his leg, he was able to make his way to the side of the landing just in time to see Shaw's terrified face, as he was dragged down the return staircase by the huge shop steward. King used the fact that everyone else was totally focused on getting down the stairs to edge his way towards the door to the rear stairs and, when no one was looking, he managed to slip through it. Taking the dark stairs dangerously quickly, he composed himself before emerging into the Tap Room and out through the back entrance of the pub. The sounds of shouting and cursing filled the air, as King made his way out through the back yard of the pub and climbed over its six-foot wall. Judging by the noise filling the night air, King guessed that the fleeing communists had gone straight into the arms of the waiting Special Branch and that some sort of battle was taking place on the main staircase and into the hallway of the pub. Crouching down in the pitch-black alley, King gave silent thanks for the blackout, which made it almost impossible for the police or Special Branch to find and apprehend any escapees from the pub. Nevertheless, he could hear police whistles and shouts echoing all around him and he realised unhappily that he must abandon any thought of helping Shaw and use his temporary advantage to get away quickly. He moved cautiously down the alley, until it intersected with another passage. However, in the total darkness, he had no idea which way to go. He thought that he heard some traffic noise to the right and so, aiming to reach a relatively busy road which would disguise his escape, he moved in that direction. After about fifty yards of staggering down the uneven, pitch dark passage, he came to Station Road. Without hesitation, he turned left and began to walk away from the pub, moving briskly but not so fast as to draw attention to himself. He had just begun seriously to entertain the hope that he might have got away with it, when he was pinned by the strong beam of a police torch and heard the inevitable, 'Stop where you are! Do not move! You're under arrest!'

King immediately began to run away from the police officer, who was struggling to follow quickly in the darkness. He was at least maintaining his distance from him until, unable to see where he was putting his feet as he ran, he tripped over a loose pavement slab and hit the ground hard. As he lay winded and in pain on the floor, the crazy movement of the torch beam suggested that the police officer was almost on him. Just as he thought it was all up for him, a darkened car screeched past the policeman, stopped right by him and, through the now open passenger door, he heard a familiar voice hiss, 'Get in quick, laddie, or we're both done for.' King struggled painfully to his feet and collapsed rather than jumped into the car, which sped off, even as he was still trying to close the door. 'There's a bottle of single malt in the glove compartment. You look like you could use some. Oh, and pass it over to my good self when you've had a wee dram.'

Despite his discomfort, King could not help but smile. 'But how on earth do you come to be here, Mac?' he asked incredulously. 'Not that I'm complaining, mind, but how did you know where to find me?'

McNair waved an arm expansively, as if to brush away an unimportant thought, 'Oh, leave all that until later, laddie. Suffice to say that you, the Professor and me, we're a team are we not? And team members look out for one another. Now let's get out of here while we still have the chance.'

The fiery taste of the whisky on the back of his throat greatly revived King and, much relieved, he saw that the policeman and his torch beam was now nowhere to be seen. Indeed, he could not quite understand how McNair could drive so quickly in the blackout, until it was explained to him with a guffaw, 'It must've been all the carrots I ate as a wee bairn.' The car was soon pulling into the passageway at the rear of the book shop and McNair asked, with no trace of sarcasm, 'Now, will you be needing a hand to get yourself inside?' King declined and, after offering grateful thanks, made his way painfully through the rear door and up to the sanctuary of his little flat above the shop.

****

'Thank God that's over for another day,' sighed the young police constable with feeling. 'These night shifts don't half take it out of you.'

'You can say that again, David,' replied an older police officer, as he sat down with a heartfelt groan on one of the wooden benches scattered about the station locker room. 'You just wait 'til you're as old and clapped out as I am, my lad. Then you'll have reason to moan.' David Bernstein looked up at his partner and pulled a face, to which the older man responded by throwing a wet towel over the younger man's head.

'Come on you two. Pack in the horseplay... it's not a school playground here, y'know,' said Sergeant Holmes, as he came in to the locker room. 'Joe,' he continued while looking at the older man, 'you'll have to fill in the report this morning. Our young friend's wanted upstairs by the 'Guv'nor' asap.'

Joe Atherton saw the anxious look on his young colleague's face and taunted, 'What've you been up to now, young fella? I told you that the Inspector's daughter is off limits.'

'What does he want with me, Sarge?' Bernstein asked nervously. 'Have I done something wrong?'

'We've all done that plenty of times son,' replied the Sergeant kindly. 'But this time, no, you've done nothing wrong. He just wants to speak to you, that's all. Now get along as quickly as you can.'

David Bernstein had only ever wanted to be a police officer and, having had the fortune to leave Nazi Germany, he applied as soon as he was old enough. Of course, the application to join the police force had been far from straightforward. The problems mainly concerned the disadvantage of young David's dual nationality, at a time when Britons were becoming more and more anti-German. It had been crucially important that the well-respected Mr and Mrs King, the parents of the man who had greatly assisted in his emigration from Germany, had vouched for him personally. To his everlasting gratitude, this had finally tilted the balance in favour of his acceptance and he had certainly made the most of his opportunity. He had finished his training at the Police Training School near Warrington as the best in his class and had jumped at the chance of a permanent posting in Bolton, where he had done part of his 'on the beat', practical training. He had found his newly adopted hometown to be a poor, but extremely welcoming place with its fair share of villains and crime, but also with a heart of gold. Despite his frequent moans about the cold, wet and exhausting night shifts, he loved his job and couldn't think of anything that he would prefer to do. It was, therefore, with some trepidation that he mounted the stairs to the office of the commander of the station. Inspector Haslam was a jovial, pudding of a man in his early fifties, who looked as if he had eaten a few to many of the meat and potato pasties, which were the local delicacy. 'Enter,' came the loud command just seconds after David Bernstein had tapped tentatively on the door. 'Sit down, Bernstein,' began Inspector Haslam, with a smile on his face. 'And for God's sake don't look so worried. I'm not going to eat you, lad.'

'Yes, sir. Thank you, sir. Sorry, sir,' stammered Bernstein in hopeless confusion. He was completely at a loss for the reason for his summons to see the Guv'nor. 'It's like this,' continued Inspector Haslam, as soon as the young constable was seated. 'Some weeks ago, all police forces in the country were asked for the names of officers who possess a certain skill. It just so happens that you, Bernstein, possess this skill and your name was, to my knowledge, the only name sent by the Lancashire Constabulary.' David Bernstein's mind was racing; what on earth could this skill be that he, and he alone of all his colleagues in this part of the police force, possessed? He was racking his brain to come up with a plausible answer and was so distracted that he almost missed the Inspector's next few sentences. 'As you can imagine, this war with Germany will be fought in lots of ways and in lots of locations, not all of which will involve facing the enemy on the field of battle. There are hidden and secret wars going on as we sit here and you, Bernstein, could well make a significant contribution to that kind of war effort. How would you feel about being transferred to the Metropolitan

Police's Special Branch? It would mean moving to London, of course. Would that be a problem?'

David Bernstein's mind was reeling; what on earth could he offer the Special Branch? Why him? 'Well,' repeated Inspector Haslam 'would that be a problem?'

'Problem, sir? ' whispered Bernstein. 'Oh... no, no, of course that would be no problem. But tell me, sir, why do they want me?'

'The most important thing, of course, is that you're totally fluent in spoken and written German. Added to that, you understand the German mentality and ways of thinking.'

'But I'm not sure I do any more, sir,' protested the young man. 'I've never and never will understand the Nazi mentality.'

'Of course. I understand, son. But you have the vital language skills and you've made an excellent start as a policeman here in Bolton. We'd be extremely sorry to lose you, but I think that you can do far more for the war effort with Special Branch than here plodding the beat. In short, you're going to help preserve the safety of the realm, by helping to track down and arrest Nazi agents in Britain. Now, what d'you say?'

There was, in truth, little for David Bernstein to debate; he would be proud to do what he could for Britain's war effort. 'Excellent, my lad! I knew you'd not let us down. Report to Inspector Renton at Scotland Yard in two weeks' time and make all your friends up here in Bolton proud of you,' said a beaming Haslam, as he vigorously shook the hand of his stunned constable.

****

'He's just over here, sir. The doc's with him now. But it doesn't look good.' Inspector Renton of Scotland Yard's Special Branch, the officer in charge of the evening's operation, was barely paying attention to the young constable's information. He was reflecting on events which had gone reasonably smoothly. His informant had suggested that, in addition to the regular members of the communist cell, based at the Royal Small Arms Factory in Enfield, there would definitely be a District Organiser for the Soviets present. He was, of course, the prize catch to be gained and Renton was happy that he was safely in the bag. A lean man, light on his feet and with the intelligent air of a hunting dog, the Inspector followed the constable around the corner of a back alley behind 'The Goose' pub and was confronted by a grisly tableau. The body, which was pushed up against the wall, was barely recognisable as that of a human being and the fact that it was still alive bore stark testimony to the will of some to live.

'Do we know who he is?' Renton asked the sergeant. 'Yes, sir. He's carrying the identity papers of one Albert Shaw of Enfield,' replied the officer, after consulting his notebook. Renton surmised that the Reds had probably believed that this poor wretch had been the Special Branch informant. Shrugging his shoulders and unembarrassed by the heartlessness of his thought, he smiled as he reflected that at least the heat would be off the real informer. Renton rubbed his chin as he asked the doctor sharply, 'Is he conscious? Has he said anything?' The doctor looked up from the mangled shape on the floor and wearily replied, 'He's simply been battered to within an inch of his life... his face hardly exists anymore. God knows what was used... wooden or metal implements, I imagine. He's said nothing, but is just barely conscious.'

'Look, sir!' said the young constable, 'I think he's trying to say something.' Renton looked quickly down at the ruins of what had once been Albert Shaw and saw that the officer was right. He overcame his distaste for such close proximity to the consequences of extreme violence and bent down to hear Shaw whisper, through the bubbles of blood emanating from his mouth. 'Did they get Lazarus?..... warn him.... Warn Lazarus for God's sake....' Suddenly Shaw's eyes opened and swivelled in panic as he saw Renton peering down at him. Evidently mistaking the Inspector for someone he knew, the mortally injured man continued in his delirium. 'Tell him to go back to Berlin. Tell him to get out while he can. Tell him....' A surprisingly quiet gurgle later and Shaw was dead, leaving Inspector Renton to contemplate what he might have meant by his dying words.

****

At just about the same time as Shaw was breathing his last, *Oberleutnant* Adolf Beyer was enjoying the traditional pre-mission meal at a Luftwaffe Training base near Aachen in Germany. Admiral Canaris had always insisted that officers about to embark on a field mission should enjoy the best hospitality that The *Abwehr* could offer. Perhaps this was the reason that pilots queued up to undertake the relatively tedious 'taxi driving' involved in making clandestine drops into enemy territory. The improbably young pilot of his Heinkel He46 was certainly tucking in with relish to the filet steak, which had been prepared exactly to Beyer's taste. 'The weather's perfect for the journey, *Oberleutnant*,' announced the pilot between mouthfuls of the succulent meat. 'The *Wetterdienst* reports that there should be just a scattered covering of cloud, no wind and a less than half moon.' Noticing that Beyer's appetite seemed to be waning, he added with a boyish grin, 'I'd eat as much of that as you're able, sir. From what we hear, you'll not get such steak on that accursed island.' Beyer was not really in the mood for such inane banter and made no response to the pilot, who simply shrugged his shoulders and continued to help himself to the delicious food.

Beyer's silence was informed by his great concern at his lack of adequate preparation for this mission. He knew that the preferred agent had almost killed himself just over a week before in a drunken car chase through a Bavarian forest and that he was, therefore, very much a second choice. Indeed, he had been made to feel exactly that during his dreadfully brief preparation, but at least he had been able to spend a little time with Rösel, whose networks he was to take over. He had gleaned some idea of what to expect of his informers and he had the key to the Portobello Road flat, engraved with '77PR', carefully tucked away in his left trouser pocket. It had been Canaris who had given his personal approval for Beyer to take over the mission, mainly because he had been impressed by the *Oberleutnant's* fluency in English and deep knowledge of the island race's culture and mores. Despite the obvious reservations of other officers, the Admiral had felt that Beyer was exactly the type, both to cope in what was now enemy territory and to manage these networks, of which The *Abwehr* had such high hopes. Rösel had been clear that, while each of his informants was capable of offering useful intelligence, the woman called Stevenson frequently gave acute insights and very accurate information from the heart of the British Foreign Office. However, given the current state of war, Beyer felt that the woman Perrygo, who apparently had networks of sympathisers in the south east of England, might prove to be a much more valuable source of intelligence.

Shortly after midnight, the Heinkel took off and began its flight towards the drop zone just outside the town of Ipswich. From there, Beyer was to make his way by train via Colchester and Chelmsford to London, in time for his scheduled meeting with his contact. It should all have been so routine; he bailed out in perfect conditions, exactly over the drop zone and was able to guide his parachute down towards an excellent landing spot, in a field next to the main road into Ipswich. No one will ever know quite what happened next; did Beyer simply fail to see the tree as he fell towards it, or did some freak gust of wind, rising from the fens, take him at the last moment off his chosen path, or did the dangerously small number of practice jumps he had made finally catch up with him? Whatever the cause, Beyer crashed heavily into the thick branches of a British oak tree, snapping his neck and ending his mission to England before it had even begun. The speed of his descent caused his body to plunge through the tree branches, until it came to rest on the ground, the parachute tangled up in the tree only yards from the main road.

Chapter Twenty Six

Winter 1939-1940, London

The injuries suffered by King, during his escape from the Special Branch raid, were not very serious; a badly sprained ankle, slight concussion and several superficial abrasions to his face and knees as a result of his fall. Kemp provided his meals and he spent most of his time in his flat, listening to music or catching up on his reading of classic literature. Within a week he was sufficiently recovered to be able to help out once again in the bookshop, where he was making mid-morning tea, when he noticed a pile of *Evening Standard* newspapers, neatly placed on the floor. Intending to pick them up and place them by the back door, ready to be put out with the rubbish later that week, his eyes caught sight of the following headline: 'Arms Worker Killed After Raid On Meeting in Wood Green.'

His heart pounded and his head spun, as he read the bare details of the death of Shaw and of how police were seeking a 'tall, dark haired man of slim build, in his late thirties or early forties, dressed in a dark overcoat and dark hat', in order to 'help them with their enquiries'. King immediately left the kettle to reach boiling point and whistle merrily away, stormed into the shop and, having checked that there were no customers present, locked the door. Without saying a word, he then returned to the shop counter, onto which he threw the newspaper. 'I suppose no one thought to tell me about this?' he spat at Paul Kemp. 'Where's Pym? I bloody well want him here now!'

Kemp retained his customary self-control and merely looked curiously at King. 'I'm afraid I'm not sure what you're talking about, James,' he began cautiously. 'Just calm down and we'll sort things out.'

'Sort things out!' exploded King in reply. 'Well somebody bloody well sorted out our informant, wouldn't you say?'

'Look, I genuinely haven't a clue what you mean,' said Kemp in what he hoped were his most persuasive tones. 'Maybe you should speak to the Professor.'

'Damned right I should. And immediately!' shouted King. 'I insist on seeing Pym today. And don't try to fob me off, otherwise I'll go straight round to his flat, or his bloody club and tackle him there!'

'Of course. Calm down and I'll go to phone him now,' replied Kemp quietly. The bookseller disappeared hurriedly to make the phone call and less than an hour later Pym was sitting in King's small flat. 'I'm really sorry that you had to find out like that, John,' he began, a genuinely regretful look on his face. 'But, in all candour, when we got the news about Shaw, it was such a shock and in any case, there would have been nothing that you could have done…'

'Well there you are wrong,' answered King scathingly. 'I believe that I could have given a good description of the likely killer to the police. I'm certain that it must have been that oaf who sat with us at the meeting. Shaw called him Nixon just the once, but whether or not that was his real name, I couldn't say. If you'd seen the poor devil's face as he was dragged down that flight of stairs, you also would have no doubt that the police would do well to find and interview that brute.'

'Good God, John,' Pym shot back with real exasperation. 'Have you learned nothing about the business in which you're engaged?' King stared at his mentor with undisguised hostility, as the older man continued. 'Do you really think that you could go to the police and give evidence? How would you explain your presence at the meeting and your relationship with Shaw?' Pym heaved a huge sigh, as he removed his spectacles and rubbed his eyes, as if he was suffering from a serious headache. 'As it is, someone has given a description of the likely killer, and I have to tell you that you, not this Nixon, could easily be taken for him. These are very unscrupulous and dangerous people.' Having succeeded in calming King's outrage, Pym went on to explain that The Special Branch had raided the meeting after a tip off from their source inside the communist cell. It had been a real stroke of luck that the organisers of the meeting clearly believed that Shaw and/or King had been responsible for informing to the police and causing the raid. 'They had thought that their man would have to disappear, but as it is, he can stick around and keep tabs on what's left of the group. The Police didn't catch them all, though they didn't do too badly.' After waiting a minute to allow King to digest this information, he added, 'Thankfully, we have no reason to believe that The Special Branch heard anything from Shaw that concerned you. Had that been the case, we would've had to face the distasteful possibility that The Special Branch would be looking for you and we wouldn't be able to put them off, without dangerously exposing your cover. So you see, my boy, we have enough problems without fighting among ourselves.' At this point Pym held open his hands, 'I am very, very sorry that you found out about Shaw in that way. I hope that we can put it behind us and carry on with the mission.'

When King made no response, a troubled Pym revealed, 'There's something else - a rotten stroke of luck. The *Abwehr* agent, sent to replace Rösel, was parachuted into Suffolk and was found lying dead by a tree, still strapped into his parachute. He had a broken neck, presumably suffered when he hit the tree and probably died instantaneously. He was identified as Rösel's replacement by virtue of a key in one of his pockets, which was engraved with the letters 77PR. I managed,' Pym continued dourly, 'to get hold of this key and McNair tried it at the Portobello Road flat... it fitted perfectly. There's no doubt that his death was a pure accident, but it's bad luck for us.' King could not quite see the Professor's reasoning and looked doubtfully at the older man. After a short hesitation, Pym explained, 'Had he lived, we would've picked him up, as soon as he turned up at his contact's address in London. This chap is, in fact, our double agent and that's what we would've tried to do with this new man. Turn him and get him to feed trivial information back to *Abwehr* headquarters, so that they would think all was working well with the networks.'

'But surely we can simply send messages and pretend that he's still alive can't we?' asked King hopefully. The older man simply smiled sadly at his protégé's naïveté, before replying, 'I'm afraid that's not possible. We don't know his codename, or when, how and to whom he was to communicate. Also, each agent has his own 'signature' style, when he sends radio messages. We can try to copy these when we have examples on which to base our attempts. But with this man, we've nothing to go on. So, you see....'

'..they'll send another agent, when they realise this man's dead... and we may not catch him...' said King dully. The two men agreed that, in the circumstances, King should continue to liaise with his informers, but otherwise maintain a low profile. 'We'll not be greedy again,' said Pym with surprising feeling. 'I should never have let you go to that meeting. I would never have forgiven myself, had that been you instead of Shaw.'

****

Over the last months of 1939 and the first of 1940 everything, including the war, was frozen into inaction by one of the coldest and harshest winters in living memory. Serious problems of transportation were exacerbated by the inadequate supply of essential equipment, such as snowploughs, to clear the major road and rail links. While the weather created huge problems on the 'Home Front', one consolation was that it was even worse in Western Europe, such that the possibility of Germany attacking Belgium or France was seen as very small. Moreover, British morale had received a couple of boosts; first, in early December the successful denouement of the Battle of the River Plate had resulted in the scuttling of the new German pocket battleship, *Graf Spee*. Rather than risk its emergence from a neutral port and almost certain destruction at the hands of elements of The Royal Navy, the German Commander had decided to sink the ship himself. Second, in the weeks leading up to Christmas, the lack of significant bombing of Britain's cities had caused the trickle of returning evacuees to grow into something of a torrent and the renewed presence of children had added to the sense of 'normality', which had come to prevail across much of urban Britain.

King's own personal war at this time matched that of the regular armed forces. While he kept in reasonably frequent touch with his remaining informants, there was little to report and no significant activity. As a result, he, like they, had the feeling that everyone was waiting for the real conflict to begin.

Paul Kemp had decided to travel north for the Christmas holidays to spend some time with his younger son and his family. As for King, it was at this time of year that he felt most keenly the loss of his family from his life. He also found himself remembering very fondly the previous Christmas, which he had spent in Berlin with Greta and her friends. He had, therefore, been very pleased to accept McNair's offer that he should spend Christmas in Canterbury with himself and Polly and had left London a couple of days before Christmas Eve.

After a very quiet and pleasant Christmas Day, King was surprised that Professor Pym had found the time to pay them all a visit on Boxing Day. Indeed, he was delighted, if also a little saddened, when his mentor informed him that he had visited his parents just before

Christmas and that he had found them both well and happily surrounded by their daughter's young family. Of course, Pym had explained, they still grieved for the 'loss' of their son, but he was also adamant that King did not have to worry about them. Towards the end of the evening, and perhaps influenced by McNair's seasonal generosity with his single malt whisky, Pym had taken King to one side and said, 'I really am in two minds whether or not I should tell you this, my boy. But, given the season, perhaps it's fitting that I let my heart rule my head.' King was intrigued by what the Professor had just said, but was stunned by his next words. 'I have news of Greta.'

'What?' spluttered King, 'How? How is that possible? I never mentioned her to you by name.'

'Really, John? Do you suppose that I was in total ignorance about someone so important to you? I've known all along about this particular sacrifice. But anyway, look never mind that,' replied Pym, brushing away what he saw as possible further pointless questions. 'The fact is, I have news. She is well, still working as a nurse in Heidelberg and, it seems, misses you very much. Also she is, I am reliably informed, active among those honourable German opponents of the Third *Reich*. It seems your lady friend is made of fine stuff.'

As Pym related his news, the sense of Greta's presence was almost palpable for King and he had to excuse himself rapidly, pleading the need to get some air in the back garden. A few minutes later, the French windows opened and Pym appeared, carrying another two tumblers of McNair's finest Single Malt Whisky. 'I thought I'd find you out here', he began with concern. 'Here, take this, it'll warm you up. Polly insists...' King turned to face his old mentor and could see the emotion flooding his face. 'I wanted you to know about Greta, John, because I want you never to forget exactly what you're fighting for. In the shadow world which you now occupy, it's all too easy to lose one's moral compass. Hold on to the idea of your family and of Greta. God willing, you'll enjoy a long and happy life with them all, once our job is done.'

King took a sizeable swig of the whisky before replying. 'Thank you. I understand that by telling me these things you've broken many of your own rules.' Pym made to speak, but the younger man raised his hand to stop him. 'I know that, on occasion my scruples have been a cause of concern to you and for that, I am deeply sorry. What you've told me about Greta has really pleased me and heartened me to return refreshed to the fray in the new year.' Feeling desperately wretched, Pym simply nodded his head, gave King a firm embrace and, without another word, went back into the house. He could no longer bear the sight of King's eager, yet stricken face, in the full knowledge that his protégé must never know the biggest secret of all. In September, Greta had given birth to a healthy daughter who, he had been told, bore a striking resemblance to the man he had just left in the garden.

****

Once the Christmas season was over, King returned to London and his life took up a similar pattern to that of December. Over the next three months, he kept in regular postal contact with his informers, but the extreme weather continued to prevent frequent face-to-face meetings, especially outside London. It was with some relief, therefore, that King, in company with many of his countrymen, welcomed the first stirrings of Spring. Little were they all to know what was to lie ahead.

****

'I simply can't understand it, David,' declared Inspector Renton, while throwing his pen down in frustration onto the desk. 'It's more than two months since we got the lead on Lazarus and we're no further forward. We've not had a decent sniff at all. It's as if he doesn't exist.'

David Bernstein nodded sympathetically, though in truth, since his transfer to Special Branch, he had come to regard Renton as somewhat obsessed with the agent Lazarus. Despite this tic, the younger man had generally found the Inspector an interesting and sympathetic boss and he felt proud every time he went to work at New Scotland Yard. When he had told his parents that he was transferring out of the regular police force, he could not, of course, give them any real details of his new work. His father, however, had nodded thoughtfully at his news and seemed happy at the thought that, in all probability, his new assignment would involve directly opposing Hitler and his Nazi legions. Conscious of his Inspector's frustration, Bernstein tried to respond positively, 'The weather's been terrible, sir. And with that and the phoney-ness of the war, maybe there's not much for him to do and he's just laying low.'

Renton shifted uneasily in his chair, 'You could be right, son... but let's just go over what we do know and what progress we've made since Shaw's death. Something might suggest itself.' As Bernstein was opening a dispiritingly thin folder, Renton slumped deeper into his chair, closed his eyes, folded his hands behind his head and wearily began. 'First, we have Shaw's dying words. He mentions Lazarus and that he should be warned and that he should go back to Berlin. Now, what are we to make of that?'

Bernstein, who had joined the Special Branch after the raid in which Albert Shaw was killed, presented two possible interpretations. 'The most likely explanations,' he began thoughtfully, 'are that Shaw was delirious and it meant nothing, or that Lazarus is a German, possibly a spy and he should escape while he can.'

'Excellent,' said Renton, his eyes beginning to twinkle with the thrill of the chase. Ignoring the idea that Shaw's utterings had no meaning he asked, 'So what else do we have to support the second interpretation?'

Bernstein went on to recall that a search of the dead man's flat had revealed a large collection of pro-German and Fascist pamphlets and newspapers, including publications of The British Union of Fascists and The Right Club. 'This was not, in itself, particularly unusual' recalled Bernstein, 'as many British people sympathised with Nazism, in the years up to the outbreak of war. What was altogether more significant, however, was the discovery of a series of note pads, in which Shaw had written a lot of information about his place of work at the Royal Small Arms Factory in Enfield. This was divided into sections, each of which was headed by a date. The dates were usually two to three weeks apart.'

'We took this as pretty clear evidence that he was collecting valuable information to pass on to a Nazi agent, at what seem to be very frequent meetings,' interrupted Renton. 'And wasn't there also another book, in which he had written much sketchier lists of different information under these same dates?' asked the Inspector keenly.

'That's right, sir,' replied Bernstein. 'Our best guess is that Shaw met with his contact as part of a group of informants and that this other information was what he was able to recall of the stuff which the other informants brought to the meetings. But this information ceases after war was declared.'

'So how do you explain that?' prompted the Inspector with raised eyebrows. 'Well our best guess is that group meetings were considered too risky. It looks like one to one contact from then on,' replied Bernstein confidently.

'In other words,' summarised Renton eagerly, nodding his head in agreement, 'Shaw was part of a cell of informants which, in all probability, was pro-Nazi rather than Red. So let's deal now with the question of what Shaw was doing at that meeting in the first place.' The Inspector went on to argue that since the Nazi-Soviet Pact, it was by no means uncommon for Nazi sympathisers to attend Communist meetings and vice versa. 'However, in this case, Shaw's death and its brutal manner suggest that the Reds blamed him for the raid on the meeting. We know, of course, that he was not the informer, so it was a case of him being in the wrong place at the wrong time, I'm afraid.'

'It certainly looks that way, sir,' responded Bernstein tentatively, as if he were about to say something more. 'OK,' Renton interrupted quickly, 'the strong probability is that Shaw was part of a group reporting to a Nazi agent, Lazarus, based in London. Now, what else was there from his notebooks?'

'Well sir,' Bernstein answered without looking at his notes, 'we believe that the letter next to each of the pieces of information in Shaw's second book could be an identifier for each particular informant.'

Renton smiled at the optimism of his junior officer, but nevertheless questioned this assumption. 'Hang on, David, you know my enthusiasm for catching this Lazarus, but a lot of that last bit is pure conjecture. We don't know if the letters refer to a name or not, or whether this is an accurate first or family name, or even some sort of code name.'

Bernstein was not, however, dissuaded by this and, much to Renton's pleasure, went on to argue 'That may be so. But this is one of the best leads we have. I'm going through this information and trying to deduce anything which may help us to identify the informants. For example, we may be able to gather some idea of where they might work. We could then ask for lists of employees and look at those with the appropriate initial. It is very long and painstaking work and I've only just begun it, but who knows where it may lead?'

'Excellent, David,' said Renton encouragingly, 'keep up the good work. You're right, it may well lead us closer to this nest of vipers and to Lazarus himself. Now, what else was there?' Bernstein reminded his Inspector that, in examining Shaw's address book, they had found one address that seemed different to the rest. 'All the entries bar this particular one had a precise name and address, including the appropriate door number,' said the young Special Branch officer excitedly. 'Of course, all of these were checked out, but they proved to be family, work colleagues and a couple of friends and have all been cleared of any involvement in this case. However, the unique address simply said 'Portobello Road.' Working on the assumption that this might refer to the meeting place of this group of informants, we checked on all possible addresses on that road. We finally found one flat on a long pre-paid lease. According to the owner, who runs the shop below the flat, this had been used relatively infrequently and almost always in the evenings for a couple of hours, though he also suspected that it had not been used at all for several months now.'

'Ah yes,' recalled Renton with a wide grin, which transformed his normally taciturn features into something altogether more friendly. 'This is where your skills of detection came to the fore, if I'm not mistaken.' Renton took a paternal pleasure in watching Bernstein struggle with his mixed emotions. On the one hand, he could see that the young man felt pride that he had, in effect, contributed significantly to the enquiry. On the other hand, it was painfully obvious that he felt an associated embarrassment, caused by his natural desire not to push himself forward or stand out in any way.

'If you say so, sir,' spluttered the junior officer, 'though in truth it was just luck. It could've happened to anyone in my place.'

'Nonsense' replied Renton dismissively, fully aware that he was embarrassing his young colleague even more. 'You had the very good sense, and patience, to give the place your own thorough search. As a result of this you found, in the bottom of an umbrella stand, a note which had clearly fallen there by accident. The note said

'Lazarus, can we have a short chat after everyone else has gone. It's important. A.'

'This discovery was the first definite corroboration that I was on the right track, when I made the assumption that Lazarus is the code name of a German spy operating in Britain,' continued Renton, as he gazed thoughtfully at his steepled hands. After a brief pause, he continued in a surprisingly relieved tone, 'You shouldn't underestimate the importance of that to me, David. Many colleagues had said that I was 'spy crazy', and, to be perfectly frank, I'd begun to wonder the same thing. But that's over now and we're on his trail. For now, just concentrate on checking those names. It may be tedious, but it's probably our best lead.'

'I agree sir,' replied Bernstein, consulting his notes. 'I'm focusing more on 'A', as this is the most firm link with Lazarus. From the nature of the notes made by Shaw, on the information provided by 'A', my guess is that this person is a civil servant of some kind. Could be in the Home Office, Foreign Office, Ministry for War, or even the Cabinet Office. I've requested lists, from all of these government departments, of employees who have a first or surname beginning with 'A'.' At this point, the younger man looked in frustration at his Inspector, before continuing. 'But they're being very slow to respond. I imagine that there must be hundreds, if not thousands of such employees. And I have to give some thought as to how these individuals can be checked discreetly. After all, I wouldn't want to alert our 'A' to Special Branch's interest.'

Renton sighed with exasperation, 'Yes, it's galling how uncooperative some people are, but keep at it. To date, it's really the only clear way forward for us. If you get nothing back from any of these departments in the next two weeks, let me know and I'll try to bring some pressure to bear on them. In the meantime, let's keep our eyes and ears open too... we don't want him to slip through the net if he resurfaces.'

'That won't happen, sir,' replied Bernstein with all the confidence of youth. 'We're gearing up our networks of informants in London and the South East. If Lazarus sticks his head over the parapet again and arranges meetings with his Nazi sympathisers, there's every chance that one of our people will get a whisper. Maybe then we'll have him without even having to identify 'A.'

****

The arrival of Spring didn't merely bring a welcome rise in temperatures and the first signs of new growth among the plants, flowers and trees of northern Europe. It also delivered to the Wehrmacht exactly the conditions it required to implement its plan to invade Denmark and Norway. In common with many Britons, King had mixed feelings when, on April 9th, the BBC broadcast reports of the German invasions of Denmark and Norway. On the one hand, people were anxious about the possibility of casualties, but on the other, morale was high and the mood was very much one of wanting to get on the front foot and give Jerry a bloody nose as soon as possible. Morale was dented somewhat by the immediate, but in truth expected capitulation of Denmark, but with the Royal Navy and a British and French Expeditionary force to contend with, surely the Germans would be kept out of Norway? Despite the navy inflicting significant damage to German ships, the allied land forces proved ill prepared and equipped and, suffering a lack of artillery and air support, were all too soon forced to accept defeat and withdraw from Norway.

Chapter Twenty Seven

Thursday, April 11th 1940, New York, United States of America.

When it arrived, Joachim Brandt read the coded telegram from Prinz Albrecht Straße in Berlin with very conflicting emotions. During the months since Great Britain had declared war on Germany, he had envied those involved in the real fighting against the enemies of the *Reich*. He was excited, therefore, about the prospect that this communication was offering him the chance to do just that. However, he also had to admit to himself that he had very much relished his long sojourn in the United States, a posting of almost four years' duration.

When the offer of the move to the United States had first been made, he had harboured very real doubts as to its advisability. Having joined the SS while still a student in Heidelberg in 1933, he was ambitious to progress and had been reluctant to move so far away from the centre of power in Berlin. How wrong he had been. His official status as a diplomat had, of course, concealed his true appointment as a *Hauptsturmführer* in Himmler's SS and during his time in America, Brandt had made himself the lynchpin of links between Germany and such pro-Nazi organisations as the German American Bund. He had been very much involved in helping to organise pro-German propaganda, like the German American Bund Parade, which had marched in its thousands through New York City on October 30th 1939. However, he regarded as his greatest achievement the coordination of the huge Madison Square Garden Rally, which attracted a febrile crowd of twenty thousand on February 20th 1939. His suggestion that Bund leader Kuhn should consistently and sarcastically refer to the US President as 'Frank D Rosenfeld' had earned him admiring comments at the very highest levels of the Nazi hierarchy back in Berlin. To those with power in the SS, he was proving himself to be a devious and successful advocate of the *Reich* and had become one of Reinhardt Heydrich's favourites. Tall and slim, with a face that could at turns appear charming and positively devilish, with its deep set eyes and high cheek bones, he had also made the most of his opportunities to mix among the extremely rich, ardently pro-Nazi American families. He had even found the time to be seduced by one of their daughters, Emma de Jongh, with whom he had been relishing a sado-masochistic relationship for eighteen months and from whom he had learned how best to express his own increasingly violent sexuality.

In truth, therefore, Brandt had thoroughly enjoyed much of his time in the USA, which he saw as an extremely divided society. The Jews, to his disgust, clearly influenced many city areas such as New York, but he had come to understand that this contrasted sharply with what he saw as the much more sympathetic and traditional farming areas of the Mid West. In common with many ideologically committed Nazis, Brandt simultaneously hated and enjoyed his proximity to what he saw as the decadent aspects of New York culture. Indeed, for almost all of his time in America, he had lived a very comfortable existence, courtesy of a sympathetic millionaire, in a spacious Upper East Side flat overlooking the Metropolitan Museum of Art and Central Park.

It was in this flat, as he looked through the huge picture window of his living room towards the sunbathed green of the park, with its seasonal, bright pink cherry tree blossoms, that he opened the telegram which was to change his life. Sent in code to the German Consulate in New York, it had been immediately despatched by courier motorcyclist to his apartment. As soon as he had it in his hands, Brandt hastily opened the small wall safe, concealed behind what he saw as a typically degenerate modern painting, took out his code and eagerly translated the message.

'MOST PRIVATE. To *Hauptsturmführer* Joachim Brandt. You are to report to Room 311, Prinz Albrecht Straße, Berlin at 2pm on Thursday April 25th. Your mission in America is at an end. You are to travel to Berlin via Lisbon, where you will liaise with *Obersturmführer* Baumgartner who is taking over your role. I look forward to meeting you in Berlin. Heil Hitler! *Obergruppenführer* Reinhard Heydrich.'

He felt an immediate surge of pride at the personal order and friendly salutation from Heydrich himself. Despite his fervent wish that he could share this honour with his parents, no sooner had Brandt read the message than he followed standard protocol by burning the decoded copy in a large metal ashtray and replacing his codes in the wall safe. Savouring the moment, he then reached for his decanter of finest brandy - he had never come to like the taste of American bourbon whisky - poured himself a good measure into one of his fine, lead crystal tumblers and sat in his favourite easy chair, which afforded the best view over the park. His orders allowed him only a week or so, in which he would have to tie up any loose ends here in America before leaving for Lisbon. He was suddenly very conscious that he was on borrowed time in New York.

Brandt was, of course, well aware that with the successful German invasions of Denmark and Norway, the 'Phoney War' in Europe was well and truly over. While fighting was still taking place, according to the latest intelligence both countries would soon be totally under German control. He greatly hoped that the Wehrmacht was poised to invade France and the Low Countries, probably in the early summer. Success there would leave only Great Britain to be brought to submission. Brandt warmed his brandy in his hand, while reflecting on the Führer's masterstroke in fooling the savage Soviets into a Non-Aggression Pact. Only a genius could have effectively neutralised his enemy in the East so cheaply, thus allowing the Wehrmacht to smash his foes in the West. The alcohol was beginning to make itself felt, as his mind turned to his likely mission - Great Britain. It had to be. He was surely to be used in some assignment, vital to Germany's inevitable invasion and ultimate defeat of that weak and exhausted nation. This could be exactly what he had been waiting for. The chance to serve the Führer and to play a leading role in the defeat of Britain. He couldn't wait to tell Emma at their dinner date. Of course, he couldn't tell her everything, just that he was recalled to Berlin to undertake vital war related work. That should enthuse her, he thought with a lascivious smile to himself.

****

Sunday 21st April, 1940, Lisbon, Portugal.

The huge Boeing 314 Clipper seaplane banked steeply over the rooftops of Lisbon, its twin engine wings and fuselage glinting silver in the early morning sunshine, as it made its final approach to land on the calm waters of the River Tagus. Emma de Jongh looked excitedly out of the porthole and gasped at her first glimpse of Portugal. Of course, as the daughter of an extremely rich and politically ambitious father, she had travelled frequently to Europe, but previously always with one or both parents and always first class on one of the luxurious transatlantic liners, which plied between New York and Northern Europe. This had been both her and Joachim Brandt's first flight across the huge ocean and they had both been impressed by the quality of comfort and service on board. The speed of the crossing had been remarkable and the possibility of converting their seats into beds for the night part of the flight had been unexpectedly welcome. The fact that only thirty six passengers, each of whom had paid a very high ticket price, were on board added to the sense of exclusivity and adventure that they both relished.

During their dinner date at 'The Stork Club' in Manhattan, when he had told her of his reassignment back to Europe, she had at first pouted like a spoiled child, who was to be deprived of her favourite plaything. It had taken much of the suave charm that Joachim had picked up during his time in America to persuade her that his transfer, while necessarily secret, was a good thing for him and his career. Later, after dancing until the early hours and Emma's characteristically provocative sex games, he had found himself agreeing to her proposal that she travel with him as far as Lisbon. There, she could meet up with an old school friend who was returning from a sixth month study period at the Sorbonne University in Paris. Deep down he knew that he should have waved goodbye to her in New York, but he had to admit that she was a force of nature and, damn it all, he really enjoyed their increasingly uninhibited sex life.

As soon as they had completed the necessary immigration procedures, a German embassy official escorted Brandt and de Jongh to a black Mercedes. They were then driven to the magnificent Monte Estoril Hotel, where they were due to spend a few nights before going their separate ways. His girlfriend smiled at the commanding manner in which he ordered the Embassy driver to wait until he had completed their registration at the hotel. The driver was then to take Brandt on to his first meeting at the German Embassy. 'The luggage will be delivered immediately to our room. You just wait here for me *Schatz*,' he said solicitously. 'I may be an hour or two, but I'll be back in time for dinner.' By way of answer, Emma flung her arms round his neck and, in the busy reception area of the hotel, kissed him hard and open mouthed. 'Hurry back, darling. I'll be waiting for you,' she breathed into his ear, before giving him a playful bite. Brandt reluctantly detached himself from her tight embrace and, blowing a kiss, hastened out of the hotel and back into the Embassy Mercedes.

****

'Brandt, my dear fellow,' beamed *Standartenführer* Horst Grünewald, as he ushered his guest into his top floor office in the splendid palacio, which served as the German Embassy in Lisbon. 'Welcome to 'spy city'. Ambassador von Hoyningen-Huene sends his regards and his apologies that he is not able to greet you in person.' Brandt was directed to one of a couple of armchairs, which were placed in front of a huge window offering a wonderful views of parkland and the city beyond.

'Thank you sir,' he began, looking Grünewald confidently in the eye. Unlike the majority of deskbound officers, the older man, despite approaching fifty, was still in reasonable shape, carrying only a few pounds over the ideal weight for his six foot frame. Grünewald's face was that of a street fighter which, of course he was, being one of the first to have joined the Party and selected personally by Himmler as a rising star for his new SS movement. His career had been somewhat derailed, however, by an unfortunate indiscretion with a fellow officer's impressionable daughter, and he was now trying to rebuild his reputation and career in Lisbon. 'It's a real pleasure to meet you and to be able to speak German again, sir, after all the years in America.'

'Well, from what little I've been able to glean from my sources in the Prinz Albrecht Straße, I wouldn't get too used to that,' Grünewald said enigmatically. 'It seems that your ability in English is crucial to your next posting. But first, please tell me all the news from our supporters in the States and then, after lunch, you can brief your replacement.' Despite his sense of excitement and anticipation, Brandt focused on selecting sufficient juicy pieces of information to keep Grünewald happy. As he sat impatiently conversing and sipping his host's admittedly excellent Dao wine, his mind was racing ahead to speculate on the likely nature of his new mission. Lunch was a pleasant affair and his replacement, Baumgartner proved to be such an assiduous listener and student that, by late afternoon, he was able to excuse himself and return to the hotel and the unique charms and demands of Emma.

In some ways, the two days in Lisbon could not pass quickly enough for Brandt, eager as he was to meet with Heydrich, whereas Emma would have liked them to stretch to several weeks. Indeed, he happily conceded that the romantically Latin atmosphere of Lisbon had inspired her creativity and abandon in the bedroom to ever greater heights. It was, therefore, a contemplative Brandt who bade a tearful Emma 'Auf Wiedersehen', as he boarded the Luftwaffe Focke Wulf Condor, which was to fly him and several other passengers directly to Tempelhof aerodrome in the centre of Berlin. The flight lasted somewhat longer than it would have done in peacetime, as the Condor had to avoid flying over southern France. Instead, having crossed Spain it took its path over the Mediterranean Sea until, in the distance through his porthole window, Brandt could see the Ligurian coast of northern Italy glistening in the bright sunshine. For one unguarded moment, he imagined what life might have been like, living as a simple fisherman on some sun kissed coast; hard work, yes, but the camaraderie on the boats and, of course a beautiful, sultry wife to return to each night after much wine and song with his fellow fishermen in the local taverna. He was acutely aware that the life he had chosen was, by contrast, basically solitary. Of course he had his contacts, acquaintances and some SS colleagues, who had earned his respect. Essentially, however, his was the life and work of the loner, the person who trusts and gets close to no one. Emma had initially been fun, there was no doubt about that. She had taught him to revel in her extremely deviant attitude to what made for good sex and he had relished his instruction by a mistress of those arcane arts. But, he reflected, now that he was unsure whether or not he would ever see her again, he began to wonder if it could ever have been serious for him. As a long term partner, an American, albeit one who shared most of his political views, was an unconventionally risky choice, but one that he definitely would not rule out. For despite his characteristic, borderline psychotic disregard for the feelings of others, he had come not only to value the time they had spent together, but also to value her. However, for now it was clear to him that his work and career had to come first and he had absolutely no desire to allow himself to become, like so many of his peers, a soft and emotional type. That way led inevitably to degeneracy and weakness. For some reason he could not explain, at that precise moment an image of the Englishman King came into his mind. He involuntarily scowled at the very thought of him, such that the person in the next seat looked sideways in his direction. Having failed to find reassurance in what he saw, Brandt's neighbour edged towards the far side of his seat, as if trying to put as much distance as possible between himself and his maniacal looking fellow passenger. Brandt calmed himself by reflecting that the Englishman was dead and that at last Germany was at war with Britain. Enjoying his daydreams of the victories to come, he was finally brought out of his inner reflections by the voice of the captain instructing all passengers to fasten their seatbelts in preparation for their descent into Tempelhof and the capital of 'The Thousand Year *Reich*.'

The next afternoon, seated in the rear of an open-topped, SS staff car which had picked him up from the Hotel Kaiserhof, Brandt reflected that he had rarely felt so vital. In minutes, he had arrived at the imposing, and among Berliners universally feared Headquarters of the SS on Prinz Albrecht Straße. After making his way through the main entrance of the building, he was gratified to note that his announcement that he had an appointment with *Obergruppenführer* Heydrich roused a bored looking receptionist into grovelling solicitousness. He was immediately shown into an ante room, positioned off the large office of Heydrich and sat nervously awaiting his audience. He had met the high ranking Nazi several times, but always in the presence of more senior officers than himself. This was to be their first private meeting and he saw it as a huge compliment that he would have the sole attention of such a powerful and feared man.

As he was shown into the large office, Brandt was surprised and also a little impressed to see that it was furnished in such a Spartan manner. Heydrich had few, if any of the trappings of high office which were so beloved of many of the most senior Nazi officials. Rather, he was content with only a plain wooden desk, a few bookcases and filing cabinets and two easy chairs, positioned to face one another across one corner of the room, with a small coffee table between them. Heydrich rose from his surprisingly uncluttered desk, as he saw Brandt enter and responded enthusiastically to the younger man's *Hitlergruß*. 'Come in *Hauptsturmführer*,' Heydrich began in his unusually high pitched voice. 'I have taken a real interest in your excellent work for the *Reich* in America.'

Beside himself with pride, Brandt spent several minutes briefing Heydrich about his work and was, in turn, impressed by the senior officer's broad and deep grasp of attitudes in America. While he was determined to use this opportunity to enhance the already positive impression his commanding officer had of him, Brandt felt the omnipresent threat from his piercing eyes. He was, therefore, in some ways grateful when Heydrich turned away from him and reached to press a concealed button underneath his desk. As soon as an orderly appeared at the door, Heydrich dismissed the younger man, saying enthusiastically, 'I've enjoyed this opportunity to meet you face to face and alone, Brandt, and I can tell you that I'm very impressed by what I've seen and heard this afternoon. Alas, my other duties now require my full attention and you must join *Sturmbannführer* Schellenberg, who is waiting to brief you on the reasons for your withdrawal from New York.' Brandt stood briskly to attention and offered the perfect 'Heil Hitler', before marching smartly out of the room.

Schellenberg was about the same age as Brandt, but had progressed rather more quickly through the ranks. A slight flicker of envy flashed through Brandt's mind as he saluted the superior officer, who greeted him and set out the bare bones of his mission. 'What I'm about to say to you is top secret,' began Schellenberg crisply. 'While I'm sure that you'll not be disappointed with the reason for your withdrawal from America, I would also like to say that you were doing an excellent job there for the *Reich*. You are no doubt well aware that *Obergruppenführer* Heydrich has very high hopes for you. I'd even go so far as to say that this assignment could be the making of you.'

'Of course, sir,' replied Brandt, suppressing another surge of irritation at what he perceived to be his contemporary's somewhat patronising manner.

'You are obviously aware of our forces' successful invasion of Denmark and Norway and the humiliation of the British at Narvick,' Schellenberg continued. 'I can tell you now that this was only the beginning.' Overlooking his dislike of his superior's attitude, Brandt's attention was now fully focused on what the *Sturmbannführer* was saying. 'Within days, German forces will overrun Belgium and sweep into France. The French have no stomach for a real fight and the British Expeditionary Force is no match for our *Panzergruppen*. I'm very proud to say that I've been entrusted with the responsibility to compile '*Informationsheft GB*.' Clearly pleased at the blank expression which formed itself on Brandt's face, he continued smugly. 'Essentially it's a blueprint, by which our forces should organise themselves for a successful invasion and subsequent occupation of Great Britain. I need hardly tell you that this work will depend to a great extent on the quality of the information we receive from our agents in Britain.'

Schellenberg went on to explain that, while *Abwehr* agents do remain in frequent contact with their controllers in Hamburg and while they do provide information, much of this seems to be of an extremely low level. 'The *Abwehr* remains convinced that their networks in Britain are working effectively, but we in the SS are of a different mind. We think that there's something not quite right over there in Britain and we want someone very special to go there. His task will be to find out what has been going on and, most importantly, to provide us with the information we will need to prepare for an invasion of Britain.'

Brandt smiled inwardly and congratulated himself on the accuracy of his guess at the reason for his recall from America. 'And you believe, sir, that I have the qualities for such a job?'

'We certainly do, *Hauptsturmführer*. Of that, we have no doubts. You will operate in England, posing as an American journalist. But first things first. Because of our, how shall we say, uncertainty about many of The *Abwehr* agents in Britain, we don't want you to make contact with them when you arrive across the Channel. In fact, The *Abwehr* will know nothing about you, your cover or your mission.'

'Then how am I to proceed. Am I expected to build up my own networks? Surely that would take time?' asked Brandt cautiously.

'I can see that you are as sharp and to the point as *Obergruppenführer* Heydrich believes,' said Schellenberg with an unctuous smile. 'We have one connection which we know has not been compromised by those incompetents from the Bendlerblock. According to their previous controller, these networks have the potential to offer us a great deal of useful information. So, you will start with them.'

'I understand,' replied Brandt carefully. 'But surely I will have other duties?'

'Of course,' said Schellenberg somewhat impatiently, 'But I have arranged for you to be briefed on these networks now. So let's start with that.' The *Sturmbannführer* pressed a button on his desk and almost immediately the door opened and a dapper, middle aged man, dressed in a smart suit and tie, entered. 'May I introduce Herr Rösel, one of the most successful German agents in Britain, until his unfortunate expulsion last year. Please Herr Rösel, would you be so kind as to explain how you think your connections may be useful to my colleague here.' Rösel described how he had run a series of networks of informers, who were sympathetic to the aims of the *Reich* and that everything had been progressing well until, in May last year, he was caught up in a tit-for-tat sequence of expulsions. At this point, Schellenberg raised an arm and interrupted, 'With the demand for agents in other areas and because of 'turf wars' between ourselves and The *Abwehr*, a replacement for Herr Rösel was not regarded as a high priority. It was not until November last year, that it was agreed that The *Abwehr* should send a replacement. However, some considerable time after this agent's planned arrival in Britain, we received notification, from a very reliable source, that he had been killed in a failed parachute drop. It was quite by chance that this source was given this information and we believe it to be true because we have naturally heard nothing from any of Herr Rösel's informers.' At this point, Schellenberg indicated that Rösel should continue and the civilian gave Brandt a pen picture of each of his informants. He was very clear that Abigail Stevenson and Martha Perrygo were potentially the most significant members of his networks. 'Stevenson is very lacking in self-confidence and is easily manipulated by the right sort of man. Perrygo is the spider at the centre of a large web of informants who live all along the south coast of Britain. I believe that the intelligence you will receive from those two people could be decisive to Germany's plans. 'I suggest that you initially try to gain Miss Abigail's confidence and trust and take it from there.'

'Thank you very much Herr Rösel,' said Schellenberg with a smile. 'Now,' looking at Brandt he continued, 'are there any questions that you would like to ask Herr Rösel? ' As soon as Brandt had shaken his head in reply, Rösel was thanked for his help and assured that, should it be decided he could be of further assistance, he would be contacted immediately.

When the two SS officers were alone, Brandt looked at Schellenberg before asking sharply, 'How certain are you that Rösel's networks have not been compromised by the British? I might be walking into a trap.'

'There is an element of risk, of course,' conceded Schellenberg, with a smile that clearly indicated that he was happy that this particular mission had fallen to Brandt, rather than to himself. 'We can't be absolutely certain. But, because the replacement agent died before he could make contact, these networks have had no direct connection with The *Abwehr* at all. Neither has the SS been in contact. Had the British somehow managed to penetrate these networks, we believe that they would have sent us trivial information to keep us happy. The fact that we have heard nothing supports the view that the networks have simply remained dormant.' Brandt nodded his head thoughtfully as Schellenberg continued. 'So you'll have to tread very carefully. I agree with Rösel that you should use your cover to get close to the Stevenson woman. That should give you a good idea whether or not the networks have been turned by the British. But we have real hopes that these networks can still be made operational, especially now that the demand for information from Britain is a much greater strategic priority. It could be that Perrygo becomes more significant as your mission proceeds. The information from Rösel, though by no means perfect, should enable you to track down each of the informants.' Brandt had taken on a more troubled look, but Schellenberg ignored this and pressed on with his briefing. 'Regardless of what Rösel just said, on no account must you reveal your identity as a German agent to anyone, least of all to the people in his networks. Until you are absolutely certain of their loyalty, let them continue to think that you are the American. Don't rush things too much, but remember the information is urgently needed. Keep the informants that will be useful in producing the '*Informationsheft* GB' and get rid of the rest.'

  Brandt nodded his head in agreement, before asking the obvious question. 'How soon is it likely that I'll be going to England and what, exactly, will be my cover and my other duties there?' Schellenberg nodded his head vigourously, 'Your cover in Britain will be that of an American journalist. We've made arrangements for you to pick up your accreditation, once you're safely in London and have also organised a small office for you in a building, rented by a sympathetic American News Bureau. No one will bother you there. You will, however, have to put in some time there to maintain your cover. We've even arranged for you to be able to wire stories to America from this building, just to add to the authenticity of your cover.' He could see the momentary alarm in Brandt's expression and, uncharacteristically, he laughed warmly. 'Don't worry Brandt, my dear fellow. They'll just go to a sympathiser in New York. The quality doesn't need to be high, but just make sure you justify your presence in Britain. Anyway, I'd advise you not to make any contact with any of Rösel's people for at least two to three weeks after your arrival in Britain. If, by some chance, the British do tail you, you must be seen to be working normally. We understand that they are very stretched and will lose interest pretty quickly in yet one more American newsman. I must stress that your mission is of the utmost importance and the highest levels of secrecy must be maintained. Accordingly, you will work only through your contact at the Portuguese Embassy. No one else is to know or contact you. Understood?'

Brandt had to admit that Schellenberg, for all his unpleasantly self-important manner, was an alert and competent officer and had expressed his orders clearly and succinctly. He had, however, one further key question. 'And when do I go, sir?'

'The precise timings are not yet fixed. They'll depend on the speed at which our armies are able to crush those of France and Britain,' replied Schellenberg, his manner icily matter of fact. 'Our best guess is that you will leave towards the end of May.'

****

Monday, May 27th 1940, Hotel Kaiserhof, Berlin.

It was just after 5AM when the insistent noise of the telephone urged him from his deep sleep. As he reached drowsily to pick up the receiver, he realised with a jolt that he was not alone in the bed. Long, wavy, dark brown hair fell in cascades over the pillow and he could hear a gentle murmuring from beneath the bed covers. He had no time to try to remember the sequence of events that had led to his sharing his bed, before he heard a commanding voice barking down the telephone line. 'Report to SS Headquarters by 6AM. You will not be returning to your hotel and come in civilian clothes.' Immediately Brandt's mind began to race. He was aware that the launch and prosecution of the 'Blitzkrieg' in North West Europe had resulted in the rapid defeat of the Dutch and the outmanoeuvring of the British and French. He also knew that his controllers had been awaiting the right opportunity to get him into England. Quite how these events would help to achieve that goal, he didn't yet know. Before he could contemplate fully the significance of all this, he realised that he had to get rid of the girl. He shook her roughly, saying 'Come on Fräulein… it's time for soldiers to go to work. You have to go.' When the sleeping woman showed no sign of stirring, he pulled the bedclothes back to reveal her naked body, with its livid, red marks. As he did so, a host of memories from the previous evening and night came flooding back into his mind. Drinking with SS Kameraden in many bars; carousing in one of Berlin's more dubious nightspots, followed by a return to the hotel and a night of unrestrained sex all played before his eyes. Alas, he knew that he had no time to repeat any of those pleasures. Shouting now, he physically turfed her out of the bed and smiled as she scrambled to collect her clothes and shoes, before she was unceremoniously pushed out into the corridor. 'Please accept my apologies, Fräulein,' he laughed, before adding with total honesty, 'but duty calls.' With that, he pressed a wad of Reichsmarks into the tempting space between her breasts and the pile of clothes and shoes she was grasping to herself, before closing the door on her.

    Within forty five minutes, Brandt was in the office of *Sturmbannführer* Schellenberg, who wasted no time in explaining to him that the German Army had the British Expeditionary Force and some French units trapped in and around the Channel port of Dunkirk. 'Luftwaffe reconnaissance suggests that the British are probably attempting to evacuate as many of their men as possible. Reports suggest a chaotic situation, with literally tens of thousands of military personnel being evacuated in hundreds of ships, some of which appear to be privately owned pleasure craft.' Schellenberg's face creased into a wintry smile as he steepled his fingers in concentration. 'Where better to hide you, as you cross to England, than in plain sight among the remnants of the British Army?' He then let out a grotesque cackle at his own joke, while Brandt, evidently unconvinced by this scheme, asked sharply, 'Wouldn't it be easier simply to parachute me in, sir? I've done some training.'

    'Yes, that would be an alternative, Brandt,' conceded Schellenberg with ill-disguised irritation. 'But our recent record of success in landing agents in this way is, as you are aware, rather poor and we expect the British to be on red alert, in case of an invasion. No, this is a perfect opportunity for you to slip into England with the help of the Tommies, disguised as a Canadian member of the RAF. You have a wholly convincing American accent, so that'll help. Also many British personnel have only the clothes they stand in. Few, if any papers or identity documents at all, other than the normal identity discs… the

British, you see Brandt, are effectively being routed.'

Schellenberg temporarily halted his narrative to light a cigarette, before continuing, without having had the courtesy to offer one to Brandt. 'We are taking this opportunity because one of our SS units, operating near the front line, has captured a downed pilot officer. This man's identity fits the bill perfectly. He's a Canadian flying a Spitfire which was destroyed by one of our fighters. You'll have his uniform and identity tags, and our staff has pieced together a dossier on the plane he flew, where it was probably based and so on. This will be very useful to you in the unlikely event of you being interrogated. Once in England, we imagine that everything will be in chaos, so it should be easy for you to slip away by train to London, where you will go to one of our safe houses. There, you will be able to get out of your uniform and rendezvous with our agent from the Portuguese Embassy. You'll be provided with identification papers as Joe Brand, an American journalist stationed in Britain, wallet, keys to a flat etc. All the details are in this file, which you should read, memorise and then destroy. You leave for the front from Tempelhof in one hour. When you arrive in France, you'll be met at the airfield and driven to somewhere near the town of Bethune. There, you should report immediately to *Hauptsturmführer* Knöchlein of the 14th Company SS Division *Totenkopf*. Good luck, Brandt. Heil Hitler.'

The formalities at Tempelhof were very brief and, within half an hour of his arrival at the aerodrome, Brandt was looking down on Hitler's capital city and wondering if and when he would see it again. He thought back fondly to his luxury trans-Atlantic flight with Emma, as he squatted uncomfortably among boxes of medical supplies and a handful of military passengers on the flight to the outskirts of Lille. The airstrip proved to be a less than perfectly flat meadow, hastily improvised by hard pressed engineers, in order to maintain the supply of essential medical and other military supplies, as the army advanced rapidly towards the Channel coast. Feeling rather bruised from the bumpy landing, Brandt was pleased to see an SS *Unterscharführer* smoking by his Volkswagen jeep. He was obviously waiting to drive him further towards the front line and Brandt was surprised by the tone of his first words. 'You must be pretty damned important that I've had to leave my unit at this time, just to offer you a ride,' said the sergeant, with ill humour.

'Thank you for your assistance, *Unterscharführer*,' replied Brandt with a smile, before adding curtly, 'by the way, I may not be in uniform, but it's *Hauptsturmführer* to you. Get that cigarette out immediately and take me to *Hauptsturmführer* Knöchlein.' The sergeant immediately jumped to attention and began to drive the jeep expertly, weaving among the flood of military vehicles and swarms of civilian refugees. Eventually, the sergeant said rather shamefacedly, 'My apologies, *Hauptsturmführer*. I meant no offence. It's just that we've been battling the Tommies hard over the last couple of days and we've lost quite a lot of men. Things are building to a climax and I didn't want to leave my boys.'

Brandt looked carefully at the driver, a tough looking man in his mid- thirties, who bore the evidence of several days uninterrupted fighting. 'Forget it, *Unterscharführer*,' said Brandt, handing the man a cigarette by way of a peace offering. 'Let's see if you can get us back in time to join in.' Gratefully accepting the already lit cigarette, the driver turned to Brandt, grinned broadly and shouted 'Yes, sir!' over the roar of the engine.

****

Monday, May 27th 1940, Thames Embankment, London

King had been staring out over the River Thames for a full five minutes before he realised that it had started to rain. From his bench on The Embankment, just downriver from the Houses of Parliament, he had not been aware of the familiar shapes of County Hall or St Thomas's Hospital on the opposite bank. Rather, his mind had been filled with hellish images of thousands of defenceless and desperate men, trapped on the beaches of Northern France, as Stuka dive bombers ruthlessly attacked them from the sky. Eventually, the typical British rain, a fine drizzle that seemed to wet clothes to a far greater extent than seemed logically possible, had brought him back from his nightmarish visions. He stood rapidly and left the bench, heading off in the direction of the Westminster Underground Station and home.

King had, some two hours earlier, been summoned to an urgent meeting at The Embankment with Professor Pym. The older man had looked extremely grave as they shook hands before sitting down. The cause of his depressed mood had soon become clear to King, as the older man had explained the true extent of the dire circumstances in which the BEF found itself across the Channel. 'Of course, the BBC has given a rather different picture of what's going on over there, but in the next couple of days everyone's going to find out what's really happening,' he had said glumly. 'The point is, John, that it's very likely that the Germans will mount an invasion of Britain as soon as practicable.' He reinforced this view, by emphasising that not only was the British Army in serious disarray, but that it must of necessity leave all of its heavy equipment in France. 'The Chiefs of Staff think we'll be lucky to extract twenty thousand men out of a total complement of well over three hundred and fifty thousand still out there. In such circumstances, the retrieval of equipment is unthinkable'

King had blinked hard at these bald statistics, which outlined what was likely to become one of the worst military disasters in British history. Of course, he had been aware that the campaign was not going well against Guderian's new 'Blitzkrieg' form of warfare, but he had no idea things were as desperate as Pym had just outlined.

'Then, sir,' he had answered slowly and clearly, 'I suppose it's up to we that remain to do our damnedest to stop the Nazis setting one foot on British soil. And if they do succeed in achieving that, to throw them back into the sea as soon as possible.' It had been very quickly agreed that King must contact, as a matter of some urgency, several of his key informants. Now, more than ever, it was vital that these be kept under his close control, to prevent any sensitive information finding its way to German ears and, thereby, possibly helping to shape their invasion plans.

*****

Monday, May 27th 1940, near Lille, Belgium.

Progress was frustratingly slow as the roads were crowded, both with military vehicles making for the front line and with bedraggled civilians, who seemed to be heading in all directions. 'If you think this looks chaotic,' said the sergeant with grim satisfaction, 'just think what it must be like on the other side of the line. Those Tommies are running out of land... they'll get their feet wet in the Channel soon.' The driver made use of every opportunity, including many reckless gambles, to overtake slower moving vehicles and it was perfectly obvious to Brandt that the sergeant really was very eager to get back to his men. However, the advantage gained by his daredevil driving was invariably eliminated by the lengthy stationary periods caused by gridlock ahead, or some cumbersome wreckage of a military vehicle being manoeuvred off the road. There was much evidence of the recent fighting; a great deal of burnt out British armour, tilted at crazy angles where it had been pushed off the road and the terrible number of fresh, tell-tale mounds, barely covering the hastily buried casualties. Increasingly frustrated by their lack of progress, the driver stopped abruptly on several occasions to peruse a worn map, desperately calculating their chances of making use of quieter side roads to arrive more speedily at their destination. On each occasion, however, his muttered *'Sheiße'* indicated that they had no alternative but to remain on the overcrowded major roads.

Finally, after some hours of painfully slow driving, the last couple of which took place against the ever growing sound of both artillery and smaller arms fire, the sergeant was flagged down near the Bois de Paqueaut woods. 'What's been happening, since I left this morning, Hofmann?' he barked at the exhausted looking SS soldier.

'We got them cornered in a farmhouse, just the other side of the woods, Sergeant. It was tough going this morning and afternoon and we took a lot of casualties. I heard a few minutes ago that the Tommies have surrendered, so it's safe for you to go on towards Le Paradis. *Hauptsturmführer* Knöchlein is waiting for you there.'

The sergeant looked shaken by the news and merely grunted *'Sheiße*. I should've been there for my boys.' With little care, he ground the jeep's gears violently, as he drove around and then through the woods. Eventually, he pulled up in front of what once must have been an attractive farmhouse. Now, it was almost a total ruin, having taken considerable mortar fire and with walls that were heavily pock marked with bullet holes. Brandt looked about him and saw soldiers running in all directions and that universal aftermath of any battle: a great many wounded being treated in makeshift field hospitals. He also noticed a bedraggled column of disarmed British soldiers being marched down the road, away from the ruined farmhouse. 'Where will I find *Hauptsturmführer* Knöchlein?' Brandt asked a passing soldier. 'He's up there with the prisoners, sir,' replied the young man before hastening off.

Brandt marched quickly towards the column of prisoners, which was shuffling slowly along the lane. He easily overtook them and presented himself to Knöchlein, who was deep in conversation with one of his men. Brandt was struck by his cold eyes and his thin, mean looking face which broke into a cold smile. 'Well, *Hauptsturmführer*, you've turned up at very auspicious moment. You're about to see the fruits of victory and the consequences of defeat. Indeed, you may wish to apportion some of these consequences yourself.' Uncertain what was meant by this, Brandt merely responded, 'I'm happy to assist in any way I can.' Knöchlein gave him a sideways glance, smiled bleakly and indicated that Brandt should follow him. The prisoners had now been marched into a meadow and told to line up along the wall of a barn. Knöchlein seized a sub-machine gun from one of his soldiers and threw it to a perplexed Brandt, sneering, 'Join in, if you have the stomach.' The SS Commander then gave the order for two heavy machine guns, set up in the meadow facing the barn wall, to open fire on the prisoners. Rather than look at the slaughter of the defenceless men, he stared at Brandt, a smile of challenge playing around his lips. It was clear to Brandt that these field soldiers held him in little regard, the attitude of the sergeant and now this explicit questioning of his stomach for the fight. He had never been in such a situation before. Beating up and hurting unarmed prisoners in the cells, yes; but executing unarmed soldiers, after they had fought bravely and surrendered, that was something quite different. He had an instant to make up his mind what to do and rapidly released the safety catch of the machine gun, after which he swept the prisoners, who were still standing, with a deadly burst of fire. Far from being appalled or disgusted at his actions, to his surprise as his fingers pressed on the trigger, he felt a burst of adrenalin so powerful that he almost felt that he was floating above the scene, looking down on the massacred prisoners and their executioners, including himself. He was amazed that he felt absolutely no remorse, indeed, he wished that there had been ten times as many prisoners to shoot. Incredibly, most of all, he regretted that it was all over so quickly. The looks of terror, incomprehension and, finally resignation, which had passed over the faces of the British prisoners as they realised their fate, was something that he would never forget.

Afterwards, he felt different; he knew instinctively both that he had crossed some kind of Rubicon in that French meadow and that there was no possibility of ever going back. Of course, since he had first joined the SS he had held the correct opinions and had mouthed the right words. But now, he felt that he had become one of that select band which was unafraid to take the most appalling actions to achieve the aims set by the Führer. For perhaps the first time in his life, he truly felt that he belonged somewhere, that he had a genuine cause and, above all, that he had been authentically empowered by his actions. In effect, he now felt himself to be a superman who could never be stopped by the weak British or the feckless French.

'Well done, *Hauptsturmführer*,' declared Knöchlein, at the same time clapping Brandt on the back like an old friend. 'See boys,' he shouted at the many young SS troops within earshot, 'even the desk men of the SS have got guts. That's why we'll smash these British and French back into their damned Channel and let them drown there.' A few 'Sieg Heils' and 'Heil Hitlers' followed Knöchlein and Brandt, as they moved away from the site of the execution and back towards a waiting car. 'Oh, and don't waste too many bullets on any still alive. Bayonets are good enough for them, eh?' he ordered the *Untersturmführers*, who were in charge of cleaning up after the massacre. 'And get those damned French peasants to bury the evidence or they'll get a dose of the same medicine.'

Once they were seated in the rear of the car, Knöchlein took off his gloves and offered his hand to Brandt. 'Welcome to the front line of the *Reich, Hauptsturmführer*. I hope you enjoyed your introduction to the real fight for Germany. Now, as soon as we get back to my headquarters, you'll have to explain what it is that we can do for you. I've only received the order to offer you every possible assistance, but I know nothing more of your purpose here.' Brandt was, he had to admit, very impressed by Knöchlein and listened attentively as he explained the latest military situation in the Pas de Calais.

After a good thirty minute drive, and as the light of the day was beginning to fade, the driver pulled off the road and into the yard of a moderately damaged farmhouse. 'Welcome to our Company Headquarters – at least for now,' Knöchlein quipped. 'With the speed of our advance, we're sure to be somewhere much nearer the sea tomorrow, so we don't have time to get too comfortable.' Brandt was ushered into what looked like a small office and, once the door was firmly closed, he briefly and succinctly outlined his requirements. 'I thought it might be something like that,' said Knöchlein with little enthusiasm. 'So I've delegated this task to one of my sergeants. He spent a lot of time in this area when he was younger and he knows it like the back of his hand. He's the best man to help you get through the British lines. I'll send him in now and leave you to it.'

Left alone for several minutes, Brandt took the opportunity to survey the room. It was sparsely furnished with what looked like the farmer's old desk, a couple of chairs, one cabinet and, squashed into one corner, a camp bed. Just as he was about to inspect the quality of the bed, the door burst open to reveal the sergeant who had driven him from Lille. *'Unterscharführer* Kaube, at your command, sir,' he said, with an entirely different attitude to that which he had displayed on first meeting. Indeed, as Brandt looked him in the eye with a sardonic expression, he was pleased to notice wariness, a suspicion, perhaps even a fear of him, which had totally replaced the previous irritation. Once Brandt had explained his requirements, Sergeant Kaube took a map out of one of the cupboards and, with a nicotine stained finger, pointed out their current location to the west of Lille.

'As you know, sir, over the last couple of days we have fallen a little behind the front line, because we had to deal with very tough pockets of resistance in this area.' Indicating Ypres on the map, he continued, 'Our best guess is that the front line is around here, which is also close to the section on our right flank which faces the Belgian Army. The Belgians are just about finished and have approached us to surrender. That means that tomorrow will be even more chaotic on the Tommies' front line. Tomorrow night, it should be fairly easy to get you across the line, find you a nice spot to wait for dawn and then you attach yourself to one of the massive lines of stragglers heading for Dunkirk. That's the best way to do it, in my view. I'll pick a couple of my men to accompany us and we'll set out after breakfast tomorrow.'

'Perfect. Thank you,' replied Brandt in a formal voice, to which Kaube merely gave a curt nod, before adding, 'Now, sir, may I suggest that you come with me to the temporary mess to get some food and that you then try to get some rest in this office.' Brandt noticed something of the sergeant's initial insouciance return as he smiled,

'You'll need it where you are going; all our guns are soon going to be pointing in your direction.' The two men nodded briefly and, just before leaving, Kaube, said flatly, 'I'll send someone over straight away with your RAF uniform and identity tags. He'll show you to the mess.'

****

Monday, May 27th 1940, Charing Cross Road, London.

As soon as he had returned to his flat, King set about summoning his informants to 'most urgent' meetings. It was highly likely that the essentially political intelligence offered by Abigail Stevenson was now of lesser significance to that which related to the actual deployment and organisation of forces on the south coast of England. This could provide vital and unanticipated advantages for the invaders and he was determined to gather and quarantine as much of this as possible. He first demanded a meeting with hotel owners Jane and Peter Lambton, who had many pro-German friends in Kent and Sussex. He needed a list of the names and addresses of these people and he had decided that he would use the pretext that he had to provide the names of such high level sympathisers to The *Abwehr*, which was compiling a register of those who could help govern a defeated Great Britain. He also arranged to meet Martha Perrygo, whose large group of informers possessed a great deal of information about defence organisation in the South and South East. Finally, he contacted both goods train controller Joe Watkins, who could give very sensitive information on night time train movements, and Spitfire production worker Fred Beach.

****

Tuesday, May 28th ,1940 Northern France.

Brandt was awake the instant the door to the office clicked open and, through the gap between the ragged curtains and the wall, he saw immediately that it was bright daylight outside. 'Time to get up, sir, if you want something to eat before we set off. I wouldn't have too much, though. You're supposed to be an RAF man who was downed three days ago. I doubt that he would've been fine dining,' said Kaube, in a voice that sounded both exhausted and stressed. Brandt quickly dressed in his RAF uniform which, though suitably damaged from the crash, was a remarkably good fit. Only the trousers were a little short, but that didn't matter as they were tightly tucked into the downed pilot's perfectly fitting flying boots. He was also able to conceal the Webley revolver, which Schellenberg had given him 'just in case', before he had left Berlin. As he followed Kaube to the mess to take breakfast, he reflected that he must cut an incongruous figure, enjoying his meal with a troop of SS infantry. He was full of nervous tension and jumped up like a shot when, shortly before eight, Kaube indicated that it was time to leave.

The sergeant took the wheel of the jeep, Brandt sitting beside him and the two troopers squatting in the rear. Because they were heading North East towards Ypres, rather than more directly North towards the Channel coast at Dunkirk or Calais, they found that the military traffic was not as heavy. This advantage, however, was eliminated by the fact that there were only minor roads running in the desired direction and these were crowded with refugees. Brandt felt little or no pity for these shambling columns of dispossessed humanity and firmly believed that they should have stayed where they were and prospered under German rule. Fleeing in this way simply inhibited the essential movement of men and materials and had it been up to him, he would have had them all forcibly pushed off the roads. He shouted this opinion to Kaube over the din of the engine, but the sergeant merely grunted something incomprehensible by way of reply. By midday they had reached Armentières, about halfway to Ypres, and Kaube pulled the jeep over to speak to a couple of SS Panzer crews, who were enjoying lunch in the sun by the roadside.

'Let's have a break for a few minutes, while I find out what's going on up ahead,' he said as he screeched to a halt and went over to the nearest tank crew. Brandt took the opportunity to stretch his legs by the roadside and, after provoking very odd looks from the members of the tank crews, who recognised his RAF uniform, he wandered off into the meadow bordering the road. Within five minutes, Kaube had returned to the jeep and shared the news that, as predicted, the Belgian Army had surrendered. This had created a huge gap in the eastern flank of the defence line of the enemy. He also reported that the front line was now at Ypres and would, by nightfall, be some kilometres beyond that town. 'It's perfect, sir,' he said to Brandt, 'just what we hoped for and expected. The tank crew says that progress will still be slow, but we're now on a main road and should reach Ypres by late afternoon.'

Brandt congratulated the driver, 'Excellent, Kaube. Keep this up and I'll write a most favourable report on your actions.' In response, Kaube nodded vaguely, as if that mattered little to him, engaged first gear and the jeep moved off towards Ypres. As they came nearer to the town and to the front line, the detritus from the very recent fighting became ever more apparent. Many military vehicles were still ablaze and Brandt noticed with contempt the huge amount of equipment and weaponry that had simply been abandoned by the British, in their haste to retreat. Here, also, it was commonplace to see the bodies of dead soldiers and civilians simply pushed unceremoniously to the side of the road. Many of these had started to rot, in that part of the warm, late May sunshine that was not blocked out by the dark, oil filled smoke which still rose into the deep blue sky.

As they entered Ypres, it was immediately obvious that this had been the scene of fierce fighting between the retreating British and the advancing Germans. 'It looks like the Tommies put up much more of a fight here sir,' said Kaube. 'The town must only just have been taken by us.' Brandt merely nodded his mute agreement, as they drove on past buildings in the city centre which had suffered badly from the effects of shell fire. Finally, they reached the main square which was totally impassable, its centre comprising a massive crater, dug by the heavy shelling of the previous day. Many of the remaining buildings had holes punched into their front walls, which looked like the dark gaps where teeth have been knocked out. Kaube cursed, as he realised that it would be impossible to cross the square in the jeep, but Brandt's concern at this was short lived, for it soon became apparent that his driver knew his way around Ypres, even in its current ruined state. 'I spent many summer holidays near here at my Belgian grandmother's,' he explained with a grin at Brandt's look of amazement, as he darted the jeep down a succession of much smaller streets to emerge quickly on the northern side of the town.

'Halt!' shouted a Military Policeman, holding up his right hand in the universal sign of policemen the world over. 'You can't go any further up here.' Kaube immediately got out of the jeep and produced the written orders brought by Brandt from Berlin. These seemed to impress the policeman, but he still insisted that they could go no further by jeep.

'As far as we know, the front line's about fifteen kilometres north of here. We've been told the road is impassable up ahead, so best to leave the jeep here. It will only take you about three hours to walk.' In response, Brandt leapt out of the jeep and confronted the policeman. 'That is not acceptable! We will take the jeep as far as we can and then go on by foot. *Unterscharführer* Kaube, if this man makes any attempt to stop us, you have my full authority to shoot him where he stands.' Kaube nodded to the two soldiers in the jeep, who immediately jumped out and, grinning at the policeman, prepared their sub-machine guns to fire. 'Well, what's it to be? My lads are damned good shots.' The policeman's face was by now drained of all colour. He certainly didn't like the look of this person dressed in an RAF uniform, who seemed to be in command of these SS soldiers. Not wishing to die in such a futile cause, he sullenly raised his simple wooden barrier to let the jeep through. As it sped past him, he contented himself by spitting openly on the ground and muttering, 'With luck, it'll be your funeral, you bastards! I hope a Tommy shell blows you all to hell.'

Brandt and Kaube soon discovered that the policeman had been correct; the road became more and more clogged and airplanes of the Luftwaffe frequently roared overhead, heading towards the sea on yet another mission to strafe the retreating British and French. Luckily for Brandt, a motorised column of Wehrmacht reinforcements was just ahead of them and their accompanying panzer made relatively light work of pushing most of the wreckage off the road. The four men in the jeep fell more and more silent as they approached the vast clouds of heavy black smoke, which hung over the current battle zone and the port town of Dunkirk. Tapping one of his hands on the windscreen, in the direction of the smoke, Kaube muttered, 'Some poor swine are really taking a pounding over there.' One of the young soldiers quickly asked in a nervous voice, 'Where is that, *Unterscharführer*, and are we heading there?' Kaube laughed and turned around, even as he continued to drive forwards. 'That's Dunkirk over there, son. It's where the British are trapped. And, yes, God willing we will be going there and indeed across the Channel and all the way to London itself. But not today.' This seemed to reassure the soldier, who sat back with a sigh and continued to polish his machine gun.

They had just passed through what remained of the hamlet of Woesten, when the road ahead was blocked by the now stationary vehicles of the infantry column. The soldiers were jumping down from their trucks and lining up in the meadows at the side of the road. 'We must be very near the front now sir,' said Kaube to Brandt. As he jerked his thumb back towards the soldier who had just asked the question about Dunkirk, he continued. 'I think this is where we'll leave the jeep with him and proceed on foot. I know this area fairly well, but I'll just have a quick word with the officers of this lot. They may know the actual situation up ahead.' When Kaube was away, Brandt ordered the two soldiers out of the jeep and addressed the one, who had been told to stay with the jeep. 'I know what Kaube said. But I think you need to get some stiffening in your backbone. So you'll come with us across the lines. And you,' pointing at the other soldier, 'will stay with the jeep. Understood?' The two soldiers stood to attention and almost shouted 'Yes, sir!'

  The warmth of the day was fading, when Kaube returned. 'We'll carry on along this road for a little more than two kilometres and then strike out northwest across the meadows. We'll then lay low until midnight, just east of the village of Krombeke and then get you into enemy territory there. The roads up ahead are full of Belgian troops who have simply thrown away their weapons and are running westwards, away from our advance. The fools don't realise we have this area totally surrounded. The British are trying to hold the line around here, but they're struggling. Unless we're very unlucky, we shouldn't encounter any enemy presence tonight.' Kaube, noticing the soldier waiting by the jeep, rubbed his chin and said 'Something going on here?' Brandt immediately responded. 'This fine young soldier here volunteered to accompany us tonight, *Unterscharführer*. I hope you're happy with that.' Kaube knew that Brandt was lying but merely saluted and murmured 'Of course, sir.'

  Once they had struck away from the road, Brandt was surprised at how untouched by war much of the countryside still was. Apart from the unmistakable sounds of conflict, both nearby and further distant, it was the kind of place and weather, in which it would have been pleasant to walk out with a willing Fräulein. Finally, they approached a deep, dry ditch which was sheltered by a thick hedgerow and Kaube indicated that Brandt and the soldier should rest there. 'I'll have a quick look what's up ahead. Keep quiet and don't light up,' he whispered. 'We don't know how near the Tommies are.' Several minutes later, he returned with the information that the British had a string of defence positions just on the far side of the meadow, which began on the other side of the hedge. 'The positions are at least a hundred metres apart, so we'll slip through the lines at midnight, find you a good spot to hide and then we'll get back to our side before Tommy is any the wiser.'

Brandt was pleased to note that, as evening gave way to night, the sky became cloudier, 'This should make our jaunt across the lines somewhat easier,' he said to Kaube, in a doomed attempt at familiarity. Shortly before midnight, they set off in single file at a low crawl across the two hundred yard expanse of meadow, which constituted the 'no man's land' between the British and German controlled zones. Only once did Kaube, who was leading, indicate urgently that they should lie face down and make absolutely no noise. On that occasion, they were embarrassed by a family of rabbits, which was rummaging through the nearby grass, totally oblivious of the armed men all around. Once through the British lines, the three Germans moved quickly and silently until, about a hundred yards away from the edge of the meadow, they came to a dry ditch leading westwards and slightly north.

'This is where we leave you, sir,' whispered Kaube. 'This ditch will take you in the direction of the French border. After a couple of kilometres, you'll come across a minor road. Keep heading in a generally north westerly direction and you'll intersect with the main road, running northwards towards Dunkirk. The less time you spend on that the better, as it's bound to be a target for the Luftwaffe. So try to keep heading north-west, rather than west. We'll return the way we came. Good luck sir.'

'Thank you for your help Kaube,' replied Brandt, though the darkness prevented the sergeant from seeing the lack of sincerity in his eyes. 'Take care on your return journey.'

Brandt waited until the two soldiers were a good seventy yards away, before he very carefully began to follow them back towards the German lines. Kaube and his young comrade were too focused on possible dangers to the front and side to pay too much attention to the man who was now trailing them. When Brandt reached the edge of the meadow, he judged that the two Germans were about half way across. Without hesitation, he took out his revolver and fired three times into the sky, before immediately making haste back towards the ditch. His shots, however, had had the desired effect. The British immediately focused all their attention in the direction of the German lines. Fearing the possibility of a night attack, they sent up flares which illuminated the whole of the meadow. Caught out in the open, the two Germans dropped to the ground and tried in vain to conceal themselves in the short grass. They were both dead before Brandt had moved back into the ditch. 'Leave as few people alive as possible, who know anything of your mission, Brandt,' Schellenberg had said before he left Berlin. Well, it had been a pleasure to rid the *Reich* of the cowardly soldier and the insubordinate sergeant, he thought contentedly, as he moved as quietly and quickly as possible towards The English Channel.

Chapter Twenty Eight.

Wednesday, May 29th 1940, Near Roesbrugge, Belgium

After less than an hour's hard, but undisturbed progress along the bottom of the dry ditch, Brandt came to its intersection with the dirt track, which Kaube had mentioned. He had not heard or seen anyone, since leaving his escort to its fate in the fire-fight he had caused in the meadow. As he carefully approached the culvert, through which the ditch went underneath the track, Brandt paused to catch his breath and to prepare to climb up. It was still pitch dark and he cursed frequently as, unable to see clearly what he was doing, he dragged himself slowly and painfully up the bank of the ditch. Having reached the top, he lay motionless and listened for a full three minutes. Having heard nothing, he silently got to his feet and started walking westwards towards Roesbrugge, a village about one kilometre from the French border. It wasn't a great surprise to Brandt that he had not met any British troops, as they had been conducting their retreat by falling back to successively prepared defensive lines. He had been told that, in all likelihood, these would intensify at the concentric canals, which pointed the way to the coast and that it would be much better for him to have attached himself to a retreating column before reaching these.

He was grateful for the continued cover of darkness when, after a good hour and a half walking, he was close to the junction with the main road from Lille to Dunkirk. He could hear British military vehicles some two hundred yards distant, as they whined and rumbled their slow way northwards and he could see, much more clearly now, the glow of the flames from the besieged port of Dunkirk. The road was heavily congested, not only with vehicles, but also with horse drawn equipment and many soldiers and civilians on foot. As he squinted through the dark, he swore in frustration at the firm order from Schellenberg that he was not allowed to carry a pair of good binoculars. Despite the poor visibility, however, Brandt was just about able to see a detachment of Military Police directing the traffic at the junction with the main road. He decided to stay in the fields while he could still enjoy the protection of darkness and, cutting the corner to stay well away from the junction, he began to move parallel to the main road, which he would attempt to join later. He found this to be relatively straightforward, as people were frequently leaving the road and returning shortly afterwards, having presumably answered a call of nature. Brandt simply waited for a suitably large gap in the retreating column, slipped out of the shadows at the side of the road and started his long trudge to the coast. Very soon after joining the road, he was passed by a motorised troop carrier heading towards the coast and had to endure the good natured taunts of the soldiers, once they had recognised his RAF uniform. Relieved at having passed his first 'inspection' with flying colours, he pulled down his cap and focused both on trying to ignore the now unmistakable stench of rotting and burning flesh and on trying to catch up with those walking ahead of him in the column.

By the time the first signs of dawn were appearing in the sky to his right, Brandt had caught up with, and been befriended by a platoon of Royal Engineers, who were very happy to have been joined by a 'real life' Canadian. The first Luftwaffe strafing run occurred shortly before seven in the morning, luckily at a time when Brandt and the Royal Engineers had left the road to rest and enjoy whatever breakfast they could find. The German watched with morbid fascination, as first the Stuka dive bombers attacked the column, closely followed by Messerschmidt fighters which raked the desperately fleeing soldiers and civilians with machine gun fire. It was all over in less than five minutes, yet the carnage created by the attack was indescribable in its horror. The road was temporarily impassable, as burning vehicles littered its course for a length of some four hundred yards. But what struck Brandt most was the dozens of people; men, women and children, who were lying on the road and its verges and in the immediately adjacent fields. Many were clearly dead, their broken bodies either left in the grotesque contortions created by bullet fire, or left without limbs, which had been blown off by the blast of the bombs. Despite the evident slaughter, Brandt was amazed at how many people, once the attack was clearly over, began to emerge from their impromptu, yet effective hiding places. The soldiers were quickly organised by the few officers and NCOs present and ordered to begin the dreadful task of removing the dead from the roadway and clearing it, as quickly as possible, of the irreparably damaged vehicles. Brandt had little option but to join in this endeavour and was relieved when, after a half hour's hard work, the Royal Engineers once more were able to begin their journey north.

'You must be prepared to be questioned by many about your

experiences,' Schellenberg had warned him in Berlin. 'Just keep your answers short and based on the back story we have provided.' In fact, since he had joined the retreating column, Brandt had been surprised at the almost total lack of interest in anything to do with his supposed exploits with the RAF. Rather, in what Brandt took to be acts of pure escapism, they were much more interested in his 'home' in North America, what life was like there and so on. He had not been in any way specifically prepared for this line of questioning and more than once he was glad of his knowledge of American life and society and of the Tommies' almost total ignorance of the difference between that country and Canada.

     Progress towards the coast was always slow, but by turns it was also tedious, dangerous and horrific. During the day, the retreating column was subjected to a series of attacks by the Luftwaffe, each successively more deadly and effective than the one before. He had seen some poignant sights, such as mothers weeping by their dead children and burned out shells of troop transporters, which had suffered direct hits while full of people. He had also come across members of the Royal Indian Army Service Corps Mule Company who, he discovered in conversation, had lost many of their men and animals during the retreat. Brandt was on the one hand disgusted that such inferior races should be part of the British armed forces, but on the other, he could not help but be impressed by their loyalty. As he was passing, he heard the order being issued to the mule handlers that, as they approached the coast, they must destroy their animals, because nothing useful was to be left for the Germans. Brandt was astounded to hear the officer accept, after much discussion with his men, that, should they be able to find a home for their animals on any of the French farms they were constantly passing, the animals could be permitted to survive. What kind of fighting army is this? he wondered, that cares so much about dumb animals? Towards the end of the day, Brandt was approaching the outskirts of Dunkirk and many of the army personnel had been extracted from the column to help boost the numbers in the lines of defence around the port. On more than one occasion he had been grateful for his RAF uniform, which prohibited him being deployed in this way. He decided to settle down for the night in one of the roadside buildings that appeared still to have a roof and, having found a place among the dozens of military and civilian people with the same idea, he prayed that, for once, the Luftwaffe would not engage in too many night raids.

****

Wednesday, 29th May 1940, Scotland Yard, London

David Bernstein sat gazing out of his office window, reflecting on the irony that security and police forces were arguably among the greatest hotbeds of rumour and gossip. Like many of his colleagues in Special Branch, he had heard whispers and 'sure things' in the canteen of Scotland Yard about what was 'really going on' in Belgium and France. Such reports invariably contradicted flatly what the overwhelming majority of the British public believed to be the military situation across The Channel. Of course, the BBC had reported the German Blitzkrieg through the Low Countries, but had also maintained the fiction that the BEF and the French were successfully resisting its onward advance. The reality was that, compared to the Panzer Divisions of General Guderian, the British army in France was numerically inferior, woefully inexperienced, under prepared and relatively poorly equipped. The general consensus of opinion among those 'in the know' at The Yard was that the allied forces had been comprehensively outmanoeuvred and outfought and it was really only a question of how many men and how much material could be saved from the wreckage.

Bernstein was roused from these not altogether pleasant thoughts by the loud ringing of his desk phone. The familiar voice of Inspector Renton ordered him to report immediately to his office adding, with little enthusiasm, that he was being reallocated from his current duties. As he entered the Inspector's office, he found Renton crouched over a map of The English Channel, which was spread over his unusually clear desk. The grey pallor of the older man betrayed the effects of a chronic lack of sleep and the stress which he was clearly suffering. The Inspector nevertheless smiled weakly at his young subordinate. 'I'm afraid that there's a hell of a flap on,' he began with little enthusiasm. Noting the younger man's obvious interest in the map, Renton continued, 'If I know anything at all about how The Yard works, I'm sure you'll have heard the stories about what's happening in Belgium and France.'

'Yes, sir, I have,' replied Bernstein seriously. 'Is it as bad as they're saying, sir?'

'I'm afraid not, David. It's actually far, far worse. Effectively, the BEF and the French have been surrounded by the Nazis. They're just managing to hold on to Dunkirk, but they won't be able to do that forever. They've taken, and are continuing to take, a fearful battering.' Renton couldn't help but notice the look of horror covering Bernstein's face, before continuing. 'It's a bloody mess. But the Navy, and anyone who can be pressed in to help, is trying to evacuate as many as possible from the beaches and the port before it falls. It's definitely not good. The top brass think we'll be lucky to get twenty thousand out.'

'My God, sir,' shouted Benstein in horror. 'But there's over three hundred thousand of our blokes out there. What the hell will happen to them?' Renton shrugged helplessly to indicate that he did not have any answer and both men fell silent for a moment, as they contemplated the likelihood that the overwhelming majority of these men would be lost, killed or captured.

'But there's nothing we can do about that,' Renton stated glumly. 'And it's not directly the reason that we're being involved. As I said, it's an absolute shambles, both over there and back in Blighty. Literally thousands of troops and others are being brought back on hundreds of ships. There's little organisation, because many of the men were scattered from their units during the retreat. There are people purporting to be Dutch, Belgian, Polish and French, as well as some other nationalities, all mixed up with the remnants of the BEF. Many of the men can't be identified by their uniforms, as these have suffered during the march back to Dunkirk and the intelligence boys are very concerned that 'Jerry' might try to slip some of their own agents into Britain, under cover of the evacuation. It wouldn't take much for them to pose as Dutch or Pole or whatever. I need hardly stress that such agents would most probably be tasked with organising the 'Fifth Column', in preparation for a possible Nazi invasion of Britain.'

Bernstein slowly nodded his head in understanding, while Renton carefully refilled and relit his pipe. 'Basically, you'll have to leave your pursuit of Lazarus for the time being and get yourself down to Dover as quickly as possible. You are to join a specialist screening team for all those returning from France who don't seem straightforwardly British. You'll focus initially on those claiming to be Dutch and try to weed out any infiltrating Nazis hidden among them. You're to report to

Major Brown at Dover Castle with immediate effect. Good luck, David. We'll miss you here but, for God's sake do your best down there.'

****

Wednesday 29th May, Near Dunkirk, France

Brandt awoke with a start, just as the first hints of dawn were showing themselves in the Eastern sky. As he stumbled out of the relatively intact building which had served as his shelter for the night, he saw immediately that the road towards Dunkirk and the coast was already teeming with military personnel. The lucky ones were in vehicles, the rest of the desperate looking soldiers and civilians on foot, like himself. As he fell in on the march towards The Channel, he noticed with great satisfaction that many of the retreating British could scarcely look the civilians in the eye. It was obvious to him that even this feeble rabble was ashamed of their rapid retreat in the face of the Panzers. As they shuffled through each successive half destroyed town or village, where the stony faced French stared at them with barely disguised contempt, one or two of the more cheerful types were loudly promising that, 'We'll be back to finish the job!' Brandt was outraged by such arrogance and had to struggle to stop himself yelling at such men that they should have fought harder, rather than flee like scared children.

As he finally approached the outskirts of Dunkirk, for the first time he noticed signs of a proper attempt by the French and British to resist the German advance. What looked to him like much more organised and well equipped units were digging in on the seaward side of the various canals which surrounded the port. It was here, he reasoned, that the British and French would attempt to hold off the Panzers, until the bulk of their comrades had escaped back to England. Perhaps for the first time, he began to see clearly how massive a victory this could be for Germany. Even if some of the British did escape the trap in Northern France, they would have very little equipment with which to fight off an invasion. And once the battle for France had been successfully concluded, it was obvious that hundreds of thousands would become prisoners of war.

Buoyed by such thoughts of victory, Brandt almost smiled as he saw at first hand the enormous battering that Dunkirk had taken both from the air and, as the Wehrmacht closed the noose around the port, from heavy shelling. The unmistakable stench of burning flesh hung over the town and craters of various sizes pockmarked the roads, many of which had tram tracks twisted upwards like crazy modern sculptures. The roar of collapsing buildings and the frequent surge of hot air, as walls fell to the ground, reminded everyone that they should make rapid progress while they were able. The column, in which Brandt was hiding himself, was now close to the docks and to the port itself. 'Come on lads,' shouted one of the soldiers to no one in particular. 'The docks're just over there. I can smell the sea and with it, our freedom!'

'Not so fast!' came the surprisingly commanding voice of a small and wiry NCO, who was directing the column towards the right and therefore away from the port. 'You have to go in a north easterly direction, parallel to the coast, until you reach the beach. It's a couple of miles or so. You'll have to take your turn up there with all the rest of the men. Good luck.'

The tired and hungry soldiers, having registered initial disappointment at being made to walk yet further, fell into line and obeyed the orders they had been given. Brandt was unhappy that he would have to spend more time at risk of being killed by his own side, but he recognised that he had little option but to retain his place in the column of men as it shuffled away. It was late afternoon by the time he and his column reached the beach, where they were greeted by the dreadful sight of a defeated army, surrounded by yet more of its now destroyed equipment and huddled down on the beaches awaiting rescue by boat.

To a groan of protest from the British, another young junior officer revealed that there was no chance of their disembarkation that day. 'The ships will come in on the tide later today and take off as many as possible. My guess is that you lot will be lucky to get out tomorrow. So, my advice is that you make good use of these sand dunes and dig yourselves in well … the Stukas are bound to be back soon.'

Brandt found a suitable spot, but before he started digging into the soft sand, he stood up to survey the scene. A little further along the beach, in the direction of the docks, he could see the burning wreckage of a destroyer which had evidently been the victim of a dive bomb attack. Also at the edge of the water, several deserted ambulances stood motionless, seemingly abandoned after delivering their last cargo of wounded for evacuation. In the distance, the pier or mole of the harbour was visible through the smoke and he guessed that this would be where the larger ships would come to receive directly their human cargo. He was, however, genuinely surprised to see lines of men, stretched out across the beach and right up to the water's edge. He had no idea what they were doing. As night began to fall, he was amazed to see a flotilla of craft, from rowing boats to fishing vessels and even what looked like pleasure craft come as close to the beach as possible. As soon as they appeared, the lines of men began staggering from the dunes, drunk with exhaustion, across the sand and into the shallow water of The English Channel. The most forward of the men, as they progressed away from the shore, were almost neck deep in water before they were hauled into the nearest small vessel. All of this activity, Brandt saw, was being directed by junior officers, who were also in the water. Once full, the small vessels, many of which were listing dangerously under the weight of people, made their way out to sea where the larger vessels were waiting to gather in their human harvest. Despite his contempt for the British, Brandt was deeply impressed by the unexpected sense of calm and order prevailing on the beach. Settling himself into his recently dug foxhole, as the sky grew darker he could see the blazing oil tanks just outside the port. Indeed, the whole of the seafront of Dunkirk was one long continuous line of burning buildings, which made the scene seem wholly hellish. For the first time since crossing into allied territory, Brandt began to feel truly afraid. He wondered whether or not this had been a sensible route into Britain and found himself hoping that the Luftwaffe would not attack.

  His prayers went unheeded, however, as less than one hour later the ominous drone of aircraft engines could clearly be heard. Parachute flares were dropped over the beach and dock areas to facilitate the air attacks which followed shortly afterwards. The dense smoke hanging over the beach and the need to try to hit larger targets meant that the bombers' main activity was centred on the ships lying just offshore or tying up on the harbour mole. Brandt was transfixed at the sight of the various ships of The Royal Navy, desperately firing their anti aircraft guns into the night sky in a clumsy, but seemingly not wholly unsuccessful attempt to ward off the dive bomb attacks. Eventually the air attack subsided and the beach became relatively still and calm, until a huge noise came from the direction of the mole. Brandt leapt up and saw that a troop ship, which had been tied up to the mole and was just about to start embarking soldiers, had received a direct hit, probably from shell fire. One or more of these shells had evidently hit the ship's boilers, for it exploded and was all but destroyed in seconds. Eventually, a sort of peace began to descend on the beach area and, shivering despite his flying jacket, Brandt was able to settle into an uneasy sleep among the remnants of The British Expeditionary Force.

****

Thursday 30th May, 4a.m. Dunkirk, Northern France

'Come on, Yank!' shouted the British infantryman urgently, as he shook the sleeping RAF officer by the shoulder. 'Time to wake up. It looks like we might be on our way.' Brandt woke with a start and automatically began to reach down to his right flying boot which concealed a deadly knife. He quickly realised there was no danger and replied with a smile, 'I'm Canadian. How many times do I have to tell you that I'm not American. It would be like me calling you Scottish.' The British Cockney laughed and clapped Brandt on the back as he struggled to his feet in the sand. 'Listen, mate. You can call me a bleedin' Jerry, if it helps us get off this bloody beach... now come on!' Brandt clumsily followed the wiry Englishman, in what was still almost total darkness, deepened by a sea mist which seemed to cover the entire area. As they moved further down the sand dunes, marshalling officers were organising the men into groups of around fifty, each of which would snake down across the wide beach to the water's edge and thence into The English Channel. There they would await rescue by one of the huge number of small craft, which had made the perilous journey from the south coast of England to help with the evacuation.

As dawn broke to a grey and misty morning, Brandt realised immediately that such weather would probably ground the Luftwaffe for much of the day. The British, it seemed, were preparing to make the very most of this stroke of luck to save as many men as possible. As the murky day wore on, Brandt and the other mixed bag of troops in his group edged, desperately slowly, nearer and nearer to the shoreline. He was again surprised at the orderliness and calm of the British as they moved in their turn, for all the world like some huge bus queue awaiting the arrival of the number 49, which would take them home from work. Only the odd shell, fired by the German artillery further inland, caused occasional alarm, but order was soon restored by the organising officers. There was little chatter to draw attention away from the continuous sound of small arms and artillery fire, which was clearly audible from the direction of Dunkirk town. To the great relief of those on the beach, however, this did not seem to be getting any closer. 'Those lads in the final defences are putting up a great fight,' murmured one wounded soldier. 'If we get out of this in one piece, we'll owe our lives to them.'

Each run of the small boats to the larger craft offshore seemed to take an excruciatingly long time and, for a period in the early afternoon, no pick-ups took place at all. Evidently, the larger ships had reached their quota of men and had set off back to England, to be replaced by other vessels with large, troop carrying capacity. By the onset of dusk, Brandt found himself, together with the other members of his group, edging into the cold waters of The English Channel. As the sky darkened progressively, the fires raging all along the front of Dunkirk cast everyone in an infernal glow, as they patiently awaited their turn to be picked up. After a good hour in the water, the last minutes up to shoulder height, Brandt was beginning to realise that his flying jacket, soaked and thus weighing a great deal, was becoming more of a hindrance than a help. Just as he was contemplating jettisoning it into the sea, a large rowing boat emerged out of the gloom and, to his great relief, he was dragged out of the sapping cold of the sea. 'Come on son,' said a burly, middle-aged man with arms like tree trunks. 'Let's get you on board and off back to Blighty'.

Chapter Twenty Nine

Friday, May 31st 1940, The English Channel and Dover, England.

Brandt had certainly never, in his wildest dreams, imagined that his first approach to the famous White Cliffs of Dover would have taken the form that it had. At least the steady sea breeze was managing to take away some of the worst of the smell of hundreds of men packed close together on the deck of HMS *Icarus*, most of whom had not had the opportunity to wash in over a week and were wearing soiled and damaged uniforms. He had been transported by rowing boat from the beach at Dunkirk to the destroyer, which had taken on-board as many men as could stand upright together on the deck. Initially, he had been disappointed that he had not secured a place below decks, but this space had been reserved for the wounded. Now, he was hugely relieved to be on the open deck, as all too frequently he caught a whiff of the indescribably foetid air which wafted over him, each time the nearby door was opened. There had been little or no conversation since the *Icarus* had finally steamed away from the catastrophe that was Dunkirk. Evidently each of the rescued soldiers remained locked in his own memories of the retreat and evacuation. Once the glowing fires had all but disappeared into the swirling sea mist and the sounds of explosions and gunfire had been replaced by the altogether more pleasant sound of seawater, as it swished against the side of the ship, Brandt felt able at last to utter a silent, unconditional prayer that the Wehrmacht would sweep the remaining British and French forces into the sea. In truth, he had found the whole experience, of masquerading as an allied airman and leaving France with the remnants of this defeated rabble, thoroughly unsatisfactory. His anger began to focus on Schellenberg and his intelligence people who had massively underestimated the degree of danger he would face from German shells, bullets and bombs. He still felt very uncomfortable that, at times over the last thirty six hours, he had been forced to hope that the German advance would stall or even, dreadful to think now, be thrown back from Dunkirk. As the first glimpses of the English coastline came into view through the early morning mist, he felt an absolute conviction that he should not again place any trust in his controllers in Berlin. He would run this mission as he saw fit, not according to the whims of someone like Schellenberg. Feeling at ease for the first time since his exhilarating participation in the shooting at Le Paradis, he reminded himself that, unsure what kind of screening mechanism would be in place in Dover, he must be extra vigilant on his arrival.

As the *Icarus* entered between the breakwaters of the port of Dover, he could see the incredible number of destroyers, cruisers and other large vessels, each absolutely packed with men. The ships were berthed two or even three abreast along the jetties. As his ship pulled nearer to its designated docking position, he could see hundreds of men using dozens of gangplanks to leave the various ships moored at the dockside. Gangplanks had also been placed between the inner and outer lying ships to allow men to cross, as space on the decks of the innermost ships was released by those who had finally reached the safety of the dry land of Britain. He was disgusted to see several men, on reaching land, drop down onto their knees and make a show of kissing the ground. They'd have been better fighting harder in Belgium and France, he thought. Such womanly emotionalism appalls me.

The *Icarus* finally tied up on the outside of another destroyer and gangplanks were quickly put in place between the two ships. Officers were positioned at each plank and held the men back to allow the prior disembarkation of the men on the innermost ship. Perhaps it was the enforced delay so near to their final goal of reaching home; perhaps it was the realisation that they had actually escaped the hell of Dunkirk, Brandt never knew what exactly sparked off the hostility towards him. But now, having reached Dover, for the first time he found himself on the receiving end of the open anger of some of the men. Standing in the crush, some feet away from the gangplank, he felt a rough punch on his shoulder and, turning round in surprise, he was confronted by a red faced, overweight sergeant. The furious soldier shouted at him. 'You shouldn't be here, you swine!' For one dreadful moment, Brandt thought that this ugly and abusive creature had somehow seen through his disguise and was frantically wondering what he could say in answer to his seemingly inevitable denunciation. To his relief, however, the sergeant continued, 'You bloody cowards! Where was the damned RAF when we needed it? Me and my lads were shot to bits by the Luftwaffe all the way from Lille to Dunkirk, while you and your lot cowered at your safe airfields.' This intemperate outburst was followed by several shouts of encouragement and a few more pushes and attempted punches aimed at Brandt.

'Stop that immediately, Sergeant!' rang out the authoritative voice of the officer who was controlling movement across the gangplank. 'Just use your bloody head, man. How do you think this chap got here? By sitting on his backside at his airfield? He was one of the few, who damned well did try to help and was shot down for his pains, you idiot. Now, any more of this nonsense and I swear by God that those responsible will face a court martial.'

This threat occasioned a muttering of objection, but also several cries of, 'He's right, sarge. You're shouting at the wrong man. He tried to help.' The sergeant and his supporters were not altogether appeased by this, but they grudgingly accepted the officer's reasoning and moved away somewhat shamefacedly. Brandt carefully wiped away the specks of spittle that had flown into his face during the sergeant's outburst and turned back to the gangplank. Men were already making their way between the ships and, when his turn came to leave, the officer suggested with a sad smile. 'You'd better stay with that group of Dutch and Polish flyers who've just left the ship. Safety in numbers, what?' Brandt nodded his head in agreement and pushed his way through the crowd until he was standing with the group of RAF personnel.

'You Dutch and Polish airmen, over there please!' instructed an officer with a clipboard, at the same time pointing towards a civilian, who was accompanied by a detachment of Military Police. Brandt had the strangest feeling that there was something familiar about the civilian, his dark, wavy hair and his general expression. Worryingly, he also observed that this man had also noticed him and was peering directly at him with a quizzical look. 'What's going on?' one of the airmen asked the officer. 'Why do we have to go with those Military Police?'

'Don't worry,' replied the officer soothingly. 'It's only routine screening for all Europeans. Detective Sergeant Bernstein will be finished with you in a jiffy.'

Bernstein! Brandt realised with panic. Of course. The younger brother of that Jewess, back in Heidelberg, who ran away to England. He was always a cunning and inquisitive little brat. I would've dealt with both of them, if that interfering Englishman King hadn't helped them to emigrate. Christ! What terrible luck that he should be a policeman here in this spot right now. Brandt was cursing this dreadful coincidence that now, at the last moment, had put his whole mission at risk, when the officer spoke to him directly. 'Stay with your comrades, please. Over there with the Military Police.'

'But I'm not European, I'm a Canadian member of the RAF,' Brandt replied in his best North American drawl. 'I should report directly back to my unit at Kenley. I somehow think that experienced fighter pilots are going to be needed now more than ever.' For a moment the officer seemed undecided, almost talking to himself in his confusion. 'Well, our orders do only concern Europeans. There's no mention of Canadians....' After an excruciating wait, which seemed like hours, but must have been less than a minute, the harassed officer said, 'OK, you go with the Brits. Go straight along the dockside, through the building at the end and collect your rail warrant.'

Brandt saluted and replied, 'Yes, sir.' As he moved along the dockside, the merest of sideways glances told him that the damned Jew boy was still staring in his direction. Tension still flowing through him, he walked briskly, but not so fast as to arouse suspicion. He was again overwhelmed by the poor state of the rescued soldiers; most with helmets, but very few carrying weapons of any kind. Many were sitting on the dockside, enjoying a cigarette which they had no doubt obtained from one of the dock workers or sailors. All in all, they looked like a thoroughly defeated army, with little fight left in them. What a total rabble, he thought happily. He would look forward to transmitting this information back to Berlin. It may actually help them to decide on what must surely be an imminent invasion. At the end of the dock, he was passing a building, in which many men were changing out of their ragged uniforms into utility clothes, which had been provided for them. On the spur of the moment, and perhaps thinking of the risk of a repeat of the attack which he had suffered on the *Icarus*, he decided to discard his RAF uniform and adopt this anonymous clothing.

****

When he had arrived in Dover the day before, David Bernstein had been appalled at the chaos which seemed to pervade the whole screening operation. It had been intended that he should help with the checking of those evacuees who claimed to be Dutch. Such was the shortage of foreign language speakers, however, that he was ordered to screen any Europeans who arrived in the port. He had found the work tiring, but interesting, as he spent at least several minutes with each evacuee, trying to get them to tell him how they came to be in Dover. Conscious of their recent experience, he really did not like to refer people for further questioning and out of hundreds people he had interviewed, he had only selected two for further investigation. In the cases of a middle aged Dutch infantryman and a young Polish airman, something in their stories had not quite added up and he had felt the tell-tale prickling of the short hairs on the back of his neck. Oddly, he had felt the same thing just now, when he awaited his next group of Dutch and Polish airmen. It was the one bringing up the rear that interested him. He couldn't really say why, but there was something about him. Could he possibly know him from somewhere or did he just remind him of someone? When this particular man had been ordered off in another direction, he had been unable to do anything about it, surrounded as he had been by his new group of interviewees. Nevertheless, during his years as a police officer, and especially since his transfer to Special Branch, with its opportunity to work with such a gifted and perceptive officer as Inspector Renton, he had learned to trust these hairs on the back of his neck. 'With me, it's my fingertips,' Renton had confided in him. 'When these start to tingle, I know there's something not quite right. Trust your signs, David. Whatever they are, son, trust them.'

He therefore had no reservations about sending a runner to the main dock exit points, with the instruction that anyone in the uniform of an airman was to be detained, pending interview with Special Branch. There were indeed, as the sergeant who had accosted Brandt on HMS *Icarus* had suggested, precious few of those passing through Dover and he was sure that his order would not cause too much difficulty.

****

As Brandt shuffled slowly through the reception hall, he noticed a final guard point, before he would pass out towards the railway platforms and his escape to London. Just as he was approaching the gateway, a guard shouted, 'You there! You, in the RAF uniform. To one side, please.' Initially, Brandt thought that the order was directed at him, but he quickly remembered that the intemperate attack on him by the sergeant on the *Icarus* had caused him to change into this plain utility clothing. Thank God I did, he thought, that young Jew's not so stupid after all. Perhaps I owe my life to that oaf on the ship. No one gave a second glance to Brandt, as he made his way through the control point and onwards into what seemed to be large customs sheds. In turn, the soldiers made their way to one of the many sets of desks, which were positioned some fifty yards away on the far side of the shed. Brandt took his turn to be asked his name, issued with a rail warrant and advised where to go to catch an appropriate train. Of course, no one at these desks had been alerted to be on the lookout for an airman. As a consequence, he was able to identify himself as a pilot stationed at RAF Kenley, and to receive his warrant to return to his base via London. 'Thank you very much,' he offered in exchange for the warrant, thinking slyly to himself, 'it's a pity that I'll never make it to Kenley. I have more urgent business in the capital.'

The trains operating from Dover to London were stretched to their full capacity, repatriated soldiers crowding into any available space, including corridors, luggage vans, dining cars and even toilets. The mood, it seemed to Brandt, was a mixture of happiness and relief to be back in Britain and shame and embarrassment at the scale of their defeat by the Wehrmacht. The German had managed to find himself a part of a seat in a compartment which was designed to transport eight people, but which now carried twelve men. He was rather uncomfortably sandwiched between two sweaty corporals, who chain smoked their way through Kent and engaged in the most banal of chatter. Somewhere between Dover and Ashford he nodded off and was awakened by the juddering of the train, as it came to a halt in a medium sized station. Through the grimy window of the carriage, he caught sight both of the sign proclaiming the station as Maidstone, but also, to his amazement, of people thronging the platform. The majority of these were waving Union Jacks and cheering at the top of their voices. 'Will you look at that?' said one of the corporals in amazement. 'You'd think we'd won rather than been roundly thrashed by Jerry.' Brandt sensed the unease among his fellow travellers at this show of support from the public. Indeed, their embarrassment was dispersed only when a very young looking private shouted, 'Well, we may've lost this time lads, but we live to fight another day. And, by God, I swear we'll repay these people's support for us by going back over the Channel and putting things right.' 'Hear, Hear!' cried several of the soldiers before the oldest looking man, nursing an arm in a sling and with one eye heavily bandaged, said quietly. 'Right you are. It may take us a year; it may take two, or even longer, but we'll go back and give Jerry a damned good taste of his own medicine.' Inspired by these defiant words, those seated nearest the windows promptly opened them and leaned out to smile at and laugh with the surging crowd.

Having silently observed these events, Brandt had the uneasy feeling that he was perhaps beginning to understand something more of the resilience of the British mentality and why it was held in such esteem by many Germans. To him, this characteristic had seemed so lacking in France, but it was now becoming more obvious, as the British adjusted to being on home soil. For the first time, he began to wonder whether defeating the British here might be an altogether different proposition to defeating them in France. The most he could muster in support of the changed mood in the carriage was a thin smile, as he reflected that if these people can turn an utter rout into a cause for great celebration, pride and confidence, what might they make out of an actual victory?

The initial euphoria from the reception given to the soldiers at Maidstone Station was being severely tested by the lack of any further movement. The train had been standing for a good twenty minutes and some of the men were becoming impatient to make further progress towards London. Their spirits were, however, somewhat restored by the sight of a great army of Women's Institute volunteers, marching along the platform. It soon became clear that they were passing cups of tea and stamped envelopes through the train windows. 'Better if you seal the envelopes and use them as a kind of postcard, dearies,' said the middle aged, buxom lady, dressed in her classic English country tweeds. 'They're for you to let your nearest and dearest know that you're safely back home. Either post them yourself in London or write them quickly now and we'll post them for you.' All the soldiers in the compartment now had beaming faces, as they enjoyed their first taste of 'proper British tea' and composed their postcards for home. 'Better not put anything too saucy, if you're writing to your missus or girl, lads,' said one happy lance corporal. 'Remember they're postcards. Wouldn't want to embarrass the poor postie, now would we?' In response, the whole carriage burst out in laughter, to such a degree that they didn't even notice that the train had resumed its way to London.

Their arrival in Victoria Station could not come soon enough for

Brandt. He had had enough of the new found confidence of his fellow travellers. At last the train cruised slowly into the London terminus and, as he waited his turn to alight, he went over his plan once again. He would find a public telephone and put in a call to his contact at the Portuguese Embassy where he would use a pre-arranged code to request the safe house address, also in coded form. There he would find all the information, clothes and documents that he would need to start his life in Britain as Joe Brand - American newspaperman. At least he was content with this part of Schellenberg's plan, not having to meet anyone in person would certainly reduce the risk to himself.

Everything went like clockwork and he found the safe house, situated just off Cannon Street, with plenty of time to spare. He knew to wait until after nightfall and then approach the house from the rear, where the back door would be unlocked. Once inside, Brandt was pleased to see everything he needed, including a fine spread of food and drink to sustain him through the night and, perhaps most welcome of all, a wonderful bathtub in which he could wash away the grime of Dunkirk. He felt like a new man, as he sank back into the welcoming warm water. Relaxed for the first time in days, he soon found his mind turning back to Emma. He felt a surge of desire, as he pictured her on their last night together in Lisbon and his recollections of the exquisite pain she had inflicted did nothing to dampen this urge. As he let himself float away on a cloud of erotic memories, perhaps it was his recent proximity to death that caused him also to hope that they may after all have a future together.

*****

It was the end of what had been a dreadfully long day for David Bernstein. Exhausted, he collected the sheaves of notes he had made during the day and totted up with the senior Military Policeman exactly how many men had been processed and what his decision on each had been. When they had finished, he turned to look at the soldier, a doubtful expression on his drawn face. 'And you're sure that those we inspected before are the only men in RAF uniform to have come through Dover since my instruction?'

'I'm sure, Detective Sergeant,' replied the 'Redcap' earnestly. 'Your order was given immediately. He couldn't possibly have avoided being in the twenty odd we intercepted.'

'But he wasn't Sergeant,' sighed Bernstein heavily. 'He damn well wasn't.'

'Why is he so important?' asked the MP. 'Who on earth is he?'

'That's just it,' replied the Special Branch man with exasperation. 'I don't know. I fear that I may have recognised him and that, somehow, it was important that I intercept him. But... ah well... maybe my eyes were deceiving me.' The Military Policeman noted the faint smile on Bernstein's face and, though he didn't believe a word of what he was about to say, he nevertheless made the following suggestion. 'That's right, sir. So many faces. Mind playing tricks on you.'

'Yes, probably,' replied Bernstein. But he, too, didn't believe what he had just said.

Chapter Thirty

Wednesday, June 5th 1940, Central London.

King had arrived early at the Lyons Strand Corner House for his scheduled meeting with Martha Perrygo and had chosen a quiet table for two, situated well away from the windows at the front of the establishment. He ordered tea and a slice of sponge cake and sat down to read his copy of *The Times*. All the newspapers had, of course, reported Prime Minister Churchill's speech in The House of Commons the previous day. This had struck a grave tone and, despite its rousing finish, in which he had declared that Britain would resist a German invasion on the beaches and landing grounds, in the fields, streets and hills and that Britain would never surrender, its references to Britain now 'fighting alone' had greatly worried people. Moreover, the speech, while acknowledging the incredibly high number of British and French soldiers evacuated from Dunkirk, had also sought to remind everyone that 'Wars are not won by evacuations.'

The café was barely half full, but nevertheless a pleasant background hum of conversation reminded King of happier pre-war days. He was soon brought back to the grim present, however, by a heated discussion which broke out between two middle aged men seated at a nearby table.

'I tell you, Winston is saying that we can't rely on the French at all. They've caved in, just like they always do,' exclaimed a bald man, his face puce with anger and his girth straining the seams of his ill-fitting, pin striped suit.

'Come on, old man,' his equally paunchy companion replied with exasperation. 'It was only yesterday that you sat here and expressed sympathy with the French, after the Paris Air Raid.' King was unable to hear how the discussion progressed because, at that moment, Martha Perrygo came through the front door of The Corner House, strode purposefully over to his table and sat down opposite him. King was happy that the argument was still in full swing, as it claimed all the attention of those sitting at nearby tables. 'As long as we exercise some caution, we should be able to hold our meeting here,' he said in a low voice. With a brief nod of agreement, Perrygo began by outlining her difficulties in getting a train from Sevenoaks. 'They've reduced the service enormously. It seems that the vast majority of rolling stock has been directed to ferry the evacuees back towards London. While I was waiting, I counted at least a dozen trains passing through the station. It's a hell of a shame that so many managed to get out.' The brutality of this last statement shocked King and he wondered what on earth his fellow customers would think of such sentiments. Hang, draw and quarter the old bag, he imagined with a grim smile. As he was contemplating how deserved such an end might be, the young waitress appeared at the table with King's order and made a note of Perrygo's selection. As she wrote the order in her book, she kept glancing and scowling at the two arguing men, 'You'd think those two would just give thanks to God that so many of our lads got back safe and sound, instead of arguing about it.' King gave her a warm smile and she quickly turned away and left to take another order.

'Poor, ignorant soul,' sneered Perrygo. 'Defeated men will be no match for the Wehrmacht, when it lands on the south coast, as it surely must within the next few weeks. Don't you think so?' King leaned part way across the table, so as to be able to speak in a soft voice. 'That's why I wanted to see you. I've been informed by my *Abwehr* controller in Germany that I must gather as much information as possible about the fixed defences on the South Coast, especially the section from Margate to Brighton. We also need up to date intelligence on the disposition of military units in this area, especially those with artillery and tanks at their disposal. Do you have people who can help?'

'Of course,' gushed Perrygo, clearly extremely excited at the prospect of the invasion occurring on her doorstep. 'I have literally dozens of people who are prepared to provide accurate information. Some of them are even ready to engage in sabotage. I'll get on to my network immediately. Does this mean the invasion is being planned for the Straits of Dover?'

'I can't possibly say,' replied King noncommittally. 'Remember, I'm only one of many agents operating in the south of England. You must emphasise to your people the need for absolute discretion. Speed, secrecy and accuracy should be their watchwords.' As soon as the waitress had brought Perrygo's pot of tea and was safely out of earshot, King came to one of the principal reasons for the meeting. He had had a frank discussion with Pym, in which the possibility of invasion was considered. Both men had accepted that, should the Luftwaffe be able to defeat the numerically inferior RAF and thereby neutralise the Royal Navy, by keeping it well away from The Channel, an invasion before the end of the summer was extremely likely. 'You must consider, John,' the Professor had said gravely, 'the British Expeditionary Force not only lost a lot of men, but almost all its equipment in France. 'Jerry' will never have a more opportune time to finish us off.' It was, therefore, agreed that, in the event of an invasion being imminent, it would be essential that the authorities should be able to arrest and intern as many as possible of the Nazi sympathisers in Britain. King had suggested that he use the heightened possibility of invasion, as a pretext to instruct his informants that The *Abwehr* wished to issue each of them with an identification document that they could show to the German forces, when they arrived in Britain. By this ruse, King would be able to obtain an up to date list of the names, addresses and dates of birth of all those Nazi sympathisers known by Perrygo. 'An excellent idea, John,' Pym had enthused. 'I like it a lot. It simultaneously reinforces your status with them and gets us the information we want.' Perrygo's reaction to the suggestion of German identity cards was even more enthusiastic. She quickly fell for the ruse, believing it to be official Nazi recognition of her network's loyalty, and promised to get the information as soon as possible.

King's next week was taken up with meetings with further informants who, without exception were taken in by The *Abwehr* identity card and had given the necessary information or undertaken to provide it at their next meeting.

****

Wednesday, June 12th 1940, Highgate, London

As he basked in the sunshine pouring in through the large bay window of his Highgate flat, Brandt had to admit that life was much better in London than he could possibly have imagined. He had been initially appalled, but later cynically amused that he should be living so close to the cemetery in which Karl Marx was buried. But there was no doubt about it, this pleasant and airy flat, located close to The Archway underground station, would serve his interests perfectly.

Indeed, as he reflected back on the last few days, he decided that things could hardly have gone better. The safe house off Cannon Street had proved to be the perfect place to stay for a few days and he had had to admit that the arrangements for his arrival in London had been ideally planned. The three suitcases full of used American clothes, his genuine looking American passport, press identification card and permission to stay in Britain had exceeded his expectations. He had found the Highgate area pleasant, leafy and, above all, discreet; indeed he had barely seen, let alone spoken to any of his neighbours, a situation he was happy to maintain. His first days had been spent in orientating himself in the city and in familiarising himself with the agreed means of communication with SS headquarters in Germany. It would have been far too dangerous to send messages by radio and so he had to pass information via a Post Office Box number used by the agent employed at the Portuguese Embassy in London. He had already confirmed, in code, that he had arrived on schedule and that he would be starting work at the office which had been arranged for him. Schellenberg, of course, had insisted that he made Perrygo his priority and that he should waste as little time as possible in contacting her. He just wants the information to put in his damned invasion book, Brandt had thought bitterly. And he doesn't care if I give my life to get it. To the obvious irritation of his controllers in Berlin, Brandt had advised that, as planned he would act as a genuine American newspaperman for at least two weeks, but would keep his eyes open for a British 'tail'. He would not, therefore, be making any surveillance of, or attempt contact with Rösel's informants until he was sure that he was 'clean'. He also kept to himself his decision to make the first approach to Stevenson. He was acutely aware that any, or all of the network may have been blown and turned by the British and if that were the case, a false step and he could find himself in front of a firing squad. He had resolved that whatever the careerist Schellenberg might prioritise, he would focus on Stevenson. With his cover, a romantic approach would seem very natural and would conceal his true purpose. If she seemed unturned, then he could assume that the British were ignorant of the networks and he could proceed with the others.

****

Monday, June 17th 1940, Dover, England.

'Yes sir. I agree, sir. It's very annoying, but I'm afraid there's not much I can do about it,' David Bernstein said into the telephone receiver for what seemed like the hundredth time. He had just broken the news to Inspector Renton that he was likely to be needed in Dover until the end of July. 'The screening is taking far longer than we anticipated, sir. There are so few good German speakers here and most of the 'high risk' candidates, being Poles and Dutch are sent to me,' replied Bernstein with weary resignation. He had had precious little sleep since his arrival in Dover and he could see no likelihood of any improvement in the near future. 'The backlog is already huge, because we are being urged to be very thorough, what with the heightened threat of invasion.'

'I understand, David,' sighed Renton. 'It's just that we are also short staffed here. Anyway, keep up the good work and stay in touch.' Bernstein was in two minds whether or not to say anything to the Inspector about his strange experience with the unknown man in RAF uniform. His feeling that he should have recognised this man had not faded. Yet however much he ransacked his over tired memory, to try to recall anything about him, he came up with a blank. Perhaps he would have shrugged it off as a trick of perception, but he was unable to explain why he was not among the men intercepted by the Military Police. He couldn't possibly have got out into the Customs Sheds before the guards had been alerted to stop all men in RAF uniform. Therefore, he reasoned, the only explanation was that he had changed out of this uniform. He knew that there was a facility on the dockside for men with badly damaged clothes to change into utility uniforms. But why would he do that? His uniform had seemed to be in reasonably good shape. It's a pity that we missed being able to go through the discarded uniforms, before they were sent away to be sorted, he thought grimly. No, he definitely recognised me and then changed out of his uniform to make himself more inconspicuous. I just wish I could figure out who the hell he is and why he did that.

Chapter Thirty One

Saturday, July 13th 1940, Central London.

'Is this seat free, ma'am?' asked the good looking man in a marked American accent. 'Oh, er, yes. Yes, it is....' stammered the pretty young woman as she nervously flicked back her long blond hair. 'Then with your permission, I'll just sit myself down here and sample one of the coffees.'

'Oh, I'm not sure that I would do that,' the young woman smiled broadly, 'I'm afraid the quality here will be nothing like you're used to.'

'Well, I'm fairly new here in London,' the man said as he removed his expensive looking raincoat and hat and sat down in the crowded café. 'What would you recommend? Tea, perhaps?' The young woman blushed as she looked self-consciously at her own pot of tea for one. God! she thought miserably, I must look like some blasted maiden aunt to him, sitting here with my tea. The man stared at her with a quizzical expression, until she eventually raised her head from the table. He then burst out in a huge gale of laughter, 'Hey! That's fine. Tea'll be just fine by me.' A strange, almost predatory expression crossed his face as he saw the utter misery vanish from the young woman's face to be replaced by a relieved smile.

This may well be easier than I'd dared to hope, thought Joachim Brandt, as he settled himself to wait for the waitress to arrive and take his order. As he had planned, and much to the increasing irritation of Schellenberg if his decoded instructions were anything to go by, Brandt had initially spent three weeks both establishing himself in his American identity in Britain and ensuring that he was clear of any British 'shadow'. For the past couple of weeks he had been following Abigail Stevenson from her workplace at the Foreign Office to her flat in Maida Vale and had observed that, apart from work, she led a fairly solitary existence, more often than not making her way straight home from work. It was good that there didn't appear to be any potentially jealous man friend on the scene, something which could have meant real trouble that he would have had to deal with. Despite the excitement and pleasure that the disposal of such a fellow might offer him, it would have been a definite complication. No, he had reflected contentedly, all things considered, it's a stroke of luck that she seems to be unattached. He had only seen her socialise in two ways; first the standard quick drink with her fellow secretaries after work on Fridays and what appeared to be choir practice on Wednesday evenings at a nearby church. He had ruled out both as acceptable opportunities to engineer a first meeting with her. He had also decided that an approach, while she was eating her lunchtime sandwiches in St James's Park, was equally inadvisable. He had seen no evidence of any clandestine meetings and had concluded that either he had had her under surveillance for an inadequate amount of time, or that since Rösel's expulsion she had decided to lay low. Having immediately noted with appreciation her slim body, good clothes sense, long blond hair and pretty face, he had silently declared himself happy to be the one to 'bring her back into the fold.' Waiting for her to emerge from her flat that morning, Brandt recognised that he had not had any definite plan to effect an introduction. However, when she had entered the crowded café and had sat at a table for two, he had waited outside for several minutes to make sure that she had not arranged to meet someone there. Stimulated by his uncharacteristic lack of planning, he had decided immediately to seize the opportunity that had now presented itself.

When the waitress returned to their table, he took the liberty of ordering tea and cake for two and overrode Miss Stevenson's attempted objection with an utterly charming, 'You'll be doing me a great favour, ma'am. I'm new in this city and still trying to learn how you do things here.'

'You said that you've only just arrived in Britain?' she asked, arching her eyebrows in a way that he found very appealing.

'That's right, er … say, what can I call you? By the way,' he continued, smiling broadly and reaching his hand across the table in innocent greeting. 'The name's Brand, Joe Brand. Nice to meet you, I'm sure.' The young woman looked flustered, as if she were unused to being offered and shaking hands with men and she failed totally to notice how the dark cold of his eyes contradicted his friendly smile. 'Oh', she spluttered nervously, 'I'm Abigail, Abigail Stevenson.'

'Right then, Abigail. If I may presume to call you Abigail that is….' he continued with an old world charm which she found most attractive, 'You asked how long I've been here.' Brandt went on to explain that he had arrived at the beginning of the previous week, by ship from New York. 'I'm working as a reporter for one of the biggest East Coast News Agencies. There's a lot of interest back home in how Britain will cope, especially now that it looks as if you are on your own against Hitler.'

Brandt was not at all surprised that the young woman's expression initially showed wide-eyed interest which rapidly changed to indifference. He reasoned that she was probably intrigued by his work, but also acutely conscious that she would have to be on her guard, when discussing the current political situation. He judged it to be strategically advisable to change the subject completely and put on his most disarming manner. 'But, say. That's not what I should be talking about. The first chance that I get to talk to such a pretty girl here in London and there I go with work stuff.' He interpreted her blush and immediate looking away as a further indication that he should tread carefully and slowly, in order not to unduly scare the woman. The two strangers spent the next half hour talking about his first impressions of London and the British and where one could go to get a good meal and some sophisticated entertainment. It was clear to him that Stevenson was by no means an expert on London's nightlife, but she did suggest a couple of restaurants. When it was clear that she was preparing to leave the café, Brandt used all his flattery and charm to extract her telephone number. Putting on his most naïve smile, he promised her that he would be in touch soon '...if that would be okay with you.' The woman simply smiled and offered her hand before standing and walking towards the door to the Strand.

A most satisfactory first engagement, Brandt congratulated himself, as soon as she had disappeared from the café, a lascivious smirk crossing his face.

****

Throughout the rest of July and the first half of August, Brandt ensured that, despite still having to work significant hours as a reporter, he found sufficient time to meet Abigail Stevenson on a regular basis. During this time, he was very careful not to ask her about her work, maintaining a disingenuous acceptance of her description of it as 'a pretty boring office job, where nothing much happens.' As a description of The Foreign Ministry of a nation fighting for its very survival, this seemed to him to be a singularly misleading description. On the other hand, his cover as a journalist did afford him considerable scope to discuss the latest events, rumours and public opinion as the war moved inexorably towards its first anniversary. Brandt had thought that it would be prudent to keep things fairly easy going and while he could tell that she was becoming more attracted to him, he was well aware of her inexperience and her nervousness around men. He therefore set about cementing their friendship with a series of unthreatening weekend lunch dates, walks in the park and the odd visit to the cinema. It was after such a visit to see Alfred Hitchcock's recently released film 'Rebecca', with its melodramatic emphasis on the secrets which surrounded the death of Max de Winter's first wife, that she suddenly posed a totally unexpected question. 'Tell me, Joe', she asked, her pretty face screwed up with concern. 'Do you believe that each of us has our secrets? And do you think that having secrets inevitably stops us from really becoming close to someone?'

While Brandt was fairly certain that this was a genuine and characteristically naïve question and while it may have offered the perfect opportunity to start to probe Stevenson for her secrets, something told him that he should treat this subject rather lightly. 'Heck, yes, Abby,' he answered with all the homespun sincerity he could muster and using a pet name to which she had not objected. 'Of course we do. But the point is, are these really important or not? Now you, for example, I simply can't imagine that you have any deep dark secrets. You're much too pretty for that.' Abigail Stevenson smiled, as if pleased with his answer, while Brandt was convinced that a necessary bridge had been crossed. He was fairly certain by now that Stevenson had not been 'turned' by the British, but for reasons he could not explain, he also suspected that, somehow, she was still operating as an informer. However, he hadn't been able to observe her meeting any possible controller, and he felt sure that such a person could not be another German agent. All in all, it was a puzzle for him. He was, however, certain that before too long she would be ready to tell him all about her secrets

Since he had started to meet with Stevenson, Brandt had, of course, sent a number of reports to Berlin, which outlined his thoughts on how he should proceed with Rösel's old networks. He had received replies which, while they expressed some satisfaction with the progress he was making, consistently urged him to try to gather the information that was urgently required for the *'Informationsheft GB.'* Indeed, the last message from Schellenberg had hinted that planning for an imminent invasion was well under way. Given the uncertainty surrounding Stevenson, it was with limited enthusiasm that he finally accepted that he could not put off any longer the need to engineer a meeting with Martha Perrygo.

****

Monday, August 5th 1940, Whitehall, London.

'How did The *Abwehr* Identity Cards go down with our friends, John?' asked Professor Pym with a huge grin on his face. 'Bloody well, if I'm any judge.'

'I should say so, sir,' replied King, his eyes twinkling with amusement. 'I really do think that it's partly the romance and thrill of being involved in something secret that's a key factor in the appeal of being an informer. They were like a membership card for an exclusive club. They loved them.'

King was sitting with Pym in a quiet corner of The Red Lion, a pleasant and conveniently positioned London pub on Parliament Street and a safe place for the younger man's latest report. King outlined how he had been given the names and contact details of over one hundred Nazi sympathisers across the South of Britain. 'Martha Perrygo had definitely not been exaggerating when she said that she had a large network of like-minded people', King laughed while shaking his head in seeming disbelief. 'She alone has given us over ninety names, many of whom are very respectable members of a range of communities in Kent and East and West Sussex. She's also given us lots of information about the operation and organisation of the LDVs, as well as detailed maps showing the positions of the pillboxes along the coast and the nature of shore defences there. All in all, that stuff would've been deuced useful to the Germans in planning an invasion,' he concluded with evident satisfaction, before enjoying a mouthful of his beer.

'And what of the others?' asked Pym with interest. In response, King gave a succinct account of the intelligence provided by his other sources. This had included information from Fred Beech about the Spitfire factory in Southampton and a detailed account of night time train movements from Joe Watkins. 'Both of these would've been of immense value to the Luftwaffe, in its planning of night raids to the south-eastern counties,' he added with emphasis, before taking another taste of his ale.

'Right, John,' beamed Pym, 'everything seems to be going very well. But you've not mentioned our star pupil, Abigail Stevenson...'

'No sir, I haven't', the younger man began with uncharacteristic hesitation. 'That's because, frankly, I'm not sure what to think about her.' A frown spread across the Professor's face as he prompted an explanation, 'Really? Why's that?' The older man patiently allowed King to take a full half minute to compose his answer. 'It's just that, for the last couple of meetings, she seems different in a subtle, but quite definite way. She's a little more reserved, a little less cooperative. I don't know sir, I can't put my finger on exactly what the issue is, but things've certainly changed.' The two men agreed that for the present, the cause of this altered behaviour would remain unknown. Further, they resolved that King would maintain contact with Miss Stevenson, but would withdraw immediately, if he felt the situation was becoming dangerous or unpredictable. In such circumstances, she would be arrested by Military Intelligence.

****

Wednesday, August 7th 1940, Scotland Yard, London.

At the sound of the purposeful knocking on his door, Inspector Renton raised his eyes from the mountain of paperwork littering his desk and couldn't help but smile broadly. 'I thought I recognised the rhythm of that knock,' he said warmly, rising from his desk. 'It's very good to have you back, David. Very good indeed.'

On the previous day, David Bernstein had finally been released from his temporary, though unexpectedly lengthy transfer to Dover. 'Thank you, sir,' he answered brightly. 'It feels good to be back. Not that what we were doing down in Dover was a waste of time. It had to be done by someone, I imagine. But we more or less drew a total blank.'

Renton decided to use the return of his sergeant to take a break from the tedium of reading files and reports and quickly invited the younger man to sit down. 'I'm not really surprised, David,' he continued, while cleaning out the bowl of his pipe. 'I suppose that the speed of the advance to the coast caught 'Jerry' out as well. I can't believe that they were so organised that they were able to use the evacuation as a cover for infiltrating spies into Britain.' Seeing the doubt on Bernstein's face, he shrugged his shoulders. 'I can see from your expression that you may not agree. Anyway, let's get some tea ordered and then we can discuss that and how you are going to get back on the hunt for Lazarus.'

Bernstein groaned inwardly – back less than two minutes and the old man was going on about him again – it certainly didn't look as if his obsession with this particular agent had declined at all. Doing his best to ignore this minor irritation, Bernstein went on to argue cogently that it was by no means beyond the realms of possibility that the Germans had used the chaos, both in France and back on the South Coast of England, to try to slip some agents into Britain. 'After all, sir, what better way of getting them in, than letting us do the job for them?'

Seeing the Inspector's genuine interest in what he was saying, he continued by pointing out that the enhancement of the Nazi presence in Southern England was probably a vital precursor to invasion. However, he did accept, in response to Renton's observations, that there was no concrete evidence of this as yet. The conversation then turned to a comparison of the public mood in London, with that among the population of the South Coast. Renton reminded his sergeant of the universally felt relief at the rescue of so many more men from Dunkirk than had been expected and the facts that the imminent German invasion had not yet taken place and that there had also been something of a lull in the fighting. 'In a funny sort of way,' the Inspector mused, 'our Home Intelligence reports suggest that, for many people, the war seems to have moved to a position, which is 'somewhat in the background' of their concerns.' Shaking his head in apparent disbelief, he commented that 'the crowds out on the recent Bank Holiday were absolutely enormous.'

Bernstein's eager young face broke into a sad smile as he agreed. 'It's amazing, sir. It's very similar on the South Coast. They seem to think that, because the invasion didn't happen immediately after Dunkirk, that it isn't going to happen at all.' In contrast to the widespread public opinion, both men readily agreed that Britain was probably now about to enter the most dangerous phase of the war.

'It's obvious that Hitler would be a total fool, if he didn't move quickly to invade and inflict a knock-out blow on us,' Renton said, while puffing his pipe contentedly. 'But, in order to protect his armies on The Channel, he'll need air superiority. Our intelligence boys are telling us that the next big battle to be fought will be that for control of the skies over southern England and The Channel. Lose this, and things will be very, very hard.' As if to take their minds off Renton's rather pessimistic analysis, both men took a cup of The Yard's steaming tea, before discussing Bernstein's priorities for the coming weeks. As the sergeant had expected, he was to continue his search for the agent Lazarus, initially by uncovering the contact known to them only as 'A'. He had already eliminated all likely candidates from the Ministry for War and the Cabinet Office and he was now turning to the much larger Foreign Office. Bernstein explained that it would take him a few days to go through the list of those with 'A' as an initial to identify likely suspects. He would first select likely candidates who lived alone, subject each to a week's surveillance and see where that would lead.

'I know that it's like looking for a needle in a haystack, David', the Inspector offered in a most sympathetic tone. 'But it's vital work. Good luck and keep me posted.'

As he walked out through the doors of Scotland Yard and into the bright sunshine of a late summer's day in London, David Bernstein could almost have forgotten all about the war, Special Branch, Inspector Renton and this damned 'Lazarus' – almost, but not quite. He knew where his duty lay.

****

Friday August 23rd 1940, Sevenoaks, Kent,

Why the hell couldn't the stupid old bitch have a telephone? This question had resurfaced in Brandt's furious mind more times than he cared to recall. And why didn't Rösel chance smuggling a written record of the full addresses of his informants out when he was expelled? By God, if the smarmy fool had shown a bit more courage it would have saved him so much wasted effort. All he could remember about this Perrygo woman was a rough age, a reasonable description and that she lived in Sevenoaks. He was beginning to doubt the accuracy of this last piece of information, as he was now coming to the end of a day's tramping around that wretched town, trying to pick up any trace of the woman. It's not as if she's called Smith or Jones, for God's sake, he fumed, as he prepared to enter yet another newsagents to buy a packet of cigarettes that he didn't want and to pretend to be her long lost nephew from the States. People seem so stupidly trusting here, he thought contemptuously, as he pushed open the door and heard, once again, the tedious tinkling of the shop bell. They're prepared to believe almost anything, if it's said with a smile.

'What's that you say, dearie?' the ancient looking woman serving behind the counter of the small shop in Bank Street said with an expression of embarrassment. 'You'll have to speak up, love. I'm a bit hard of hearing, you see.' Brandt, happy that no one else was present, once again repeated his patter, this time much louder and more slowly. He had no expectation of any success at all, so was astonished when the old woman began to nod her head vigorously. 'Oh yes, dear. Yes, indeed.'

Come on, get on with it, you stupid old crone, thought Brandt irritably, simultaneously smiling affectionately through gritted teeth.

'You must mean Martha Perrygo... it's a funny sort of name, isn't it, love?' Brandt was almost beside himself with impatience and had to struggle very hard against his urge to pull the old fool out from behind her counter and shake the information out of her. Indeed, the old lady had stopped talking, seemingly having forgotten what she had been asked, or perhaps believing that she had already offered a sufficient answer.

'But please, ma'am', Brandt pleaded in his most artificially pleasant way, 'could you just tell me where she lives. I've come a long way to see her.'

'Of course, lovey', she answered, much to the further irritation of Brandt. How he was coming to hate this endless supply of British pleasantries. 'She lives just around the corner on the High Street. It's a semi-detached. You can't miss it. It's the one with the black door.'

'Thank you very much ma'am,' Brandt smiled, as he touched the brim of his hat in salute. 'Now, you won't spoil things by mentioning me, will you? And you won't tell your husband?' A look of uncertainty and sadness briefly crossed the old woman's face, as if she couldn't quite understand what this charming young American meant, before the penny dropped and she replied with a wink. 'Oh no, darling. I won't say anything to Martha and my Albert, God bless him, has been dead these past ten years. I'm quite alone here now. No, love, I wouldn't dream of it. You can trust me.'

Brandt made his way back out onto Bank Street, thinking to himself that he would arrange things so that trust didn't come into it. He quickly found the house that must belong to Martha Perrygo. It certainly was a fine looking home on the High Street, with a pleasant, though small garden at the front. As he walked by, he tipped his hat at the somewhat masculine looking middle-aged woman who was working there. She barely acknowledged his salute and returned quickly to her digging and weeding, wielding her spade more like an Irish navvy than a forty something spinster.

It was early evening and, having decided that he needed somewhere to have a quiet bite to eat, Brandt was pleased to find a bustling inn some three hundred yards further down the High Street. The Sennockian, a black and white, Tudor style building with leaded windows and a wood lined, smoke filled interior would suit his purposes perfectly. It was crowded with people and he was fortunate to find a relatively quiet corner, where he sat to consume his beer and cheese sandwich. Enjoy is hardly the word I would use to describe this dark, flat slop that the British call beer, he thought morosely. And as for this cheese... Having taken the precaution of ordering his food and drink in his best English accent, he was pleased to observe that no one was paying him the slightest attention. While waiting to be served at the bar, he had heard snippets of various conversations, which were taking place among some of the other customers. Many of these had concerned the belief that, somehow, Dunkirk had been a victory, the RAF were defeating the Luftwaffe in the air above southern England and that, therefore, 'Hitler's not going to try to invade us. He'd never dare!' How Brandt hated the British! It was true, he grudgingly had to admit, that Goering's much vaunted air-force didn't seem to be having the swift victory over the ramshackle RAF that he had vaingloriously predicted. The conflict, which that old drunk Churchill had dubbed 'The Battle of Britain', had been raging for the past eleven days and he felt sure that the weight of numbers and superior skills of the Germans would eventually win the day. He would love to be here, in this very pub, when the invasion is heralded by the first paratroopers descending from the sky and 'Blitzkrieg' rolls its devastating path across this overly confident little nothing of an island.

Turning his mind back to his plan, he decided that he would put the Perrygo woman under surveillance for some days, in order to discover whether or not she had been turned by the British or, like Stevenson, she still seemed active in the interests of the *Reich*. This delay would, of course, necessitate the elimination of the gossipy old woman in the newsagents. Despite his belief that she had probably already forgotten the conversation, he couldn't possibly trust her not to blab about 'Martha Perrygo's nice young American nephew.' Brandt was very relieved that, as the early crowd began to leave the pub for their homes and dinners, they were more than adequately replaced by the Friday evening drinkers, none of whom seemed interested in him. Consequently, he was able to leave it until dusk was falling, before leaving and making his way to the rear of the newsagents shop in Bank Street. The rear door was hopelessly secured; indeed, it took him less than a minute to gain entry and to find his way through the very neatly organised store room to the foot of the stairs, leading to the old lady's first floor flat. He could hear the radio from the bottom of the stairs and he gave silent thanks as he remembered that the woman was hard of hearing. This is going to be simple, he muttered, as he silently crept up the stairs. The door into the small living room was open and he peered in to see the old lady, sitting in an armchair in front of an unlit fire, her back to him. From the sound of the quiet 'put putting' emanating from her open mouth, he deduced that she was asleep. He quickly moved to the rear of the chair, reached over and around her head and, before she knew what was going on, snapped her neck like the old twig it was. He felt pride in his SS taught skills and enjoyed the momentary adrenalin surge as he despatched the old woman. Working quickly now, he picked her up and took her to the top of the stairs, where he stood her on her feet before letting her body fall in an ungainly heap. He was pleased to see that, lying now in the hallway, her broken body looked just as it would have, had she fallen down the stairs. Leaving everything else as it was, he quickly made his way back through the rear door, secured it as badly as it had been when he arrived and returned anonymously to the railway station, where he caught the next train back to London. He was so exhilarated that he didn't even mind having to stand in the corridor, much of the packed train being taken by squaddies off to London for a weekend's leave.

Chapter Thirty Two

Friday, August 30th 1940, The Foreign Office, London.

Ever since mid-August, when the decisive air battle between the RAF and the Luftwaffe had begun, most British eyes had been focused anxiously on the skies over Kent and Sussex. Bernstein, however, had been wholly occupied putting under surveillance each of those Foreign Office employees who he suspected of being Lazarus's contact. He had eliminated two from his list of six people and was on his fifth day of observing a young woman called Abigail Stevenson. As a relatively junior member of the secretarial staff, he had had little expectation that she would prove to be anything other than a total waste of his time for a week. As was his pattern with the other suspects, he had observed her over the lunch hour and again from her time of leaving work until midnight, or even later.

The first four days of his observation had, as he had fully expected, yielded nothing of interest and the Friday's lunchtime surveillance had been equally insignificant. He now found himself unenthusiastically waiting for her to emerge from The Foreign Office building. As he stood in the warm afternoon sunshine, he allowed his mind to wander back in time to the happy days before Germany had succumbed to the collective madness of Nazism. When he and his sister had left their home in 1933, he had also left behind many good and loyal friends who were as appalled as he at the increasing violence towards, and discrimination against Jewish Germans. He wondered idly what had become of those people in the intervening seven years... had they come to believe the rantings of the Führer and his henchmen? Had they, in turn, become willing participants in the Thousand Year *Reich*? Perhaps more likely, had they simply come to accept Nazism and its hideous characteristics as 'how things are now' and, therefore, unchangeable? He rather hoped that some of his friends had had the moral and physical courage to become part of the internal opposition to Nazism. He knew that such heroic people existed in Germany and this, as part German himself, meant a great deal to him.

He quickly snapped back to the present, as he saw the young woman emerge in company with several other secretarial staff. The group was smiling and chatting, as it first made its way towards Trafalgar Square and then entered The Silver Cross pub on Whitehall, for what he guessed would be the traditional end of the working week drink. It was just after seven, when the group began to disperse and Bernstein felt sure that his target would simply make her way home to her small flat in Maida Vale. To his surprise, however, she moved so quickly to catch a Number 9 bus in Trafalgar Square, that he had to dash out in front of traffic which, justifiably outraged at his behaviour, hooted its various horns in unison. Ignoring the blasts directed at him, he ran after the departing bus and leapt athletically onto its rear platform. 'Nearly missed us there, son,' said the middle aged bus conductor with a smile. 'Anybody would think you were in some kind of a hurry. Late for a date with your girl, eh?'

'Something like that, yes', replied a red faced Bernstein, pretending to be struggling to catch his breath, in order to give himself some thinking time. He had no idea where Abigail Stevenson was going, but he had won the time to rack his brains to recall that the Number 9 route went towards Hammersmith. Unsure where the woman would leave the bus and not wishing to show his warrant card to the conductor, he played safe by buying a ticket to the route's terminus. He took a seat three rows behind his target and waited for her to get up to leave the bus. Within fifteen minutes she rose from her seat as the bus approached Hyde Park Corner. Once again, Bernstein waited until the last minute before he leapt off the bus as it pulled away from the stop. The bus conductor simply shook his head in confusion. 'Young 'uns these days,' he said to no one in particular, as he made his way down the carriage to collect fares. 'How will we ever beat the bleedin' Jerries with lads who don't even know where they're going?'

Bernstein paused, pretending to tie his shoelace, while Abigail Stevenson crossed the road and started walking up Park Lane towards Marble Arch. It was a fine warm evening and many Londoners, having taken their pleasure in Hyde Park, were now happily strolling arm in arm in the failing daylight. Because of the cover provided by these crowds, he found it the simplest of tasks to fall in unobtrusively behind her as she made her way purposefully along the busy pavement. None of his other suspects had behaved in this uncharacteristic manner and, for the first time in his long pursuit of the mysterious 'A', he began to feel a twitch of excitement. As the young woman approached The Dorchester Hotel, she was met by a tall, slim man, dressed in a fashionable suit topped off by a dark-coloured hat, and whose bearing, if not his general appearance, looked oddly familiar to Bernstein. The man gave Stevenson a quick peck on the cheek and they both made their way into the Hotel's restaurant. Bernstein softly whistled in surprise. Surely The Dorchester would be far too expensive and select an establishment for Abigail Stevenson and very much out of her normal everyday experience? And who was this man? Determined to find answers to the first really interesting questions which this surveillance had thrown up, Bernstein settled down on the opposite side of the road to the hotel and patiently awaited their reappearance. Conscious, as he was, of the fine food and wine they would no doubt be enjoying in the restaurant, he regretted bitterly his decision not to equip himself with at least sandwiches to eat.

****

Brandt had decided that, in light of the increasing pressure on him, he must use this British bank holiday weekend to strengthen his relationship with the woman Stevenson. It was essential that, in the very near future, he should pass some information to Schellenberg, which would be useful in the creation of *'Informationsheft GB.'* After all, it had been made clear to him in Berlin, that the SS was looking to him to provide the kind of speedy, valuable and accurate information, which seemed beyond the efforts of The *Abwehr*. Having spent the previous week observing Martha Perrygo, he was convinced that she was still active in gathering intelligence and that she had a wide network of potentially valuable informants based in the south east of Britain. Whichever way he looked at it, he couldn't work out what had been happening to this network, since the deportation of Rösel and he decided that the quickest way to solve this mystery must surely be to question her.

For this evening, however, he intended to focus his attention on another of the women informers. At his first sight of Abigail Stevenson, breathlessly approaching him, he gave thanks that the ugly hag Perrygo was safely away in Kent. Indeed, he was relishing what the evening may offer him as, having experienced Stevenson's increasing fawning over him, he was certain that she was ready for their relationship to move to a different stage. In fact, his plan for that evening had been to wine and dine her in the extremely luxurious setting of The Dorchester, followed by a return to her flat, where he planned to have her. This change in the nature of their relationship would make it easier for him to begin moving their discussions towards her Nazi sympathies and her actions as an informer.

'I've never had dinner in anywhere like this,' beamed Stevenson, as they followed the meticulously dressed Maitre d' towards a table, which was positioned in a discreet part of the dining room. 'But you should have told me so that I could have gone home to change. I'm still in my work clothes.'

'And mighty pretty you look in them, too,' replied Brandt, utilising all his charm. 'You know, Abigail, we Americans don't set too much value on fuss and show. Believe me, you look great.' He squeezed her hand and she smiled happily in return as they strolled across the luxurious, blue patterned carpet and between the various circular dining tables. Once seated, the young woman gazed, wide eyed, at the splendid panelled ceiling, the upholstered wooden furniture and the stylish, yet discreet lighting before whispering, 'Now I understand why they call this 'The Spanish Room', it's just beautiful.' Touching his hand across the table and, unusually for her, looking him squarely in the eye, she breathed, 'Thank you for this treat, Joe. It's marvellous ... and so are you.'

'You're worth it, and a whole lot more besides', he replied with a smile which did not quite reach his eyes. 'Now, what about a cocktail while we consider what we should eat?' By way of reply, Abigail Stevenson asked him to order for her, as she needed to 'powder her nose'. He watched her, with rising sexual interest, as she walked with a natural elegance out of the Grill Restaurant and into the main hotel lobby. When she returned to the table, her face still flushed with excitement, a heavy cut glass tumbler occupied each of their place settings. Both glasses contained a good measure of a pale orange coloured liquid and were garnished beautifully with a twist of fresh orange peel.

'Whatever's this?' she asked excitedly, lifting her glass and breathing in the heady mixture of alcohol and fruit. Picking his glass up, ready to propose a toast, he answered. 'It's called 'The Bronx' and, in my opinion, it's the classiest cocktail for a very classy lady.' Brandt could see her eyes twinkle with joy and, somewhere in their deepest recesses, he suspected perhaps also with something like desire.

They both chose Chicken Caesar Salad to start, followed by Beef Tournedos from the Grill and Orange Soufflé for dessert. Without consulting her, Brandt chose a crisp, dry Chablis to accompany the salad, a much fuller bodied Chateauneuf-du-Pape for the main course and a rich Sauternes for the dessert. 'Goodness me!' Abigail Stevenson cried, in a sweetly girlish manner, 'How on earth will I cope with all that?'

Brandt smiled reassuringly. 'Relax, honey. The night's very young. We've lots of time to enjoy the meal and wine and for me to find out all about you.' He was interested to see a fleeting look of suspicion enter her eyes, before it was quickly banished by a much more open and happy expression. 'Very well,' she countered. 'But I want to know much more about you first!' They both laughed, as young people often do when they find themselves on the verge of some deeper, probably sexual attachment. In order to maintain the open and revelatory mood, Brandt bargained, 'OK.OK. You win. But let's each of us say something in turn about our self. That way, you won't get too bored, having to listen to a lot of dull stuff about me.'

The first part of the meal passed very quickly, with Brandt offering humorous anecdotes from his fictitious back-story. In return, Abigail Stevenson told him of her childhood and youth in Hertfordshire and her pride in gaining employment at The Foreign Office. As soon as her workplace was mentioned, Brandt seized the opportunity by asking if she liked working there. She replied, enigmatically, that perhaps it was not good to be so close to those making very important decisions, as one is all too aware that they are mere mortals, with all their weaknesses. Just as they finished the Entrée, Brandt leaned across the table and said earnestly, 'You know, Abby, I've been surprised that in my time here, I've come across quite a few people who aren't convinced that you guys are fighting the right enemy...' In reply to her shrug of the shoulders and non-committal 'Really?' he continued. 'Yeah, that's right. Many feel that the real enemy lies further East. In Soviet Russia.'

'But surely they're now allied to Germany... to fight one is to fight the other,' countered the young woman with unexpected clarity.

'Well, yes. But of course, that's just an alliance of convenience, isn't it?' Brandt argued persuasively. 'No one in the States thinks that will last long once Hitler knocks out Britain.'

Abigail Stevenson looked startled by this assertion. 'You really think that will happen, Joe?' He put down his wine glass, looked her in the eye and said in his most sincere voice. 'It's inevitable, Abby. Dunkirk was a disaster, whatever your Prime Minister says, and you surely cannot hold out for long. My employers are concerned about the threat of invasion here. They want me home. And, by the way, many at home think that an invasion here would be no bad thing.'

The young woman's expression shifted from startled to shocked and worried, but the cause was not obvious to Brandt until she opened her mouth to reply. 'Oh no, Joe!' she cried, her eyes filling up with tears. 'Please don't say that. Don't say you're going back to America.'

'Hey! Sweetheart,' he said consolingly, 'no one's going anywhere just yet.' With this reassurance, Abigail Stevenson seemed to calm down a little and looked at Brandt with a quizzical expression. 'You said that a lot of people in America wouldn't be worried by a German invasion of Britain?' While this was the taking of the bait that he had been working for, he took the precaution of waiting until the waiter had removed the dinner plates, and he had indicated that they would take a short pause in their meal, before continuing. 'That's right. Don't forget that there are a great many people of German extraction in the USA. They don't see this as their fight at all and if they did, a lot of them would support Germany. I've spent some time among the members of the German American Bund.' Genuine pride lit up his face, as he recalled his key role in what he was about to describe. 'You should've seen their rally last year at Madison Square Garden. There must've been twenty thousand there, uniforms, swastikas, the lot.' The young woman's eyes widened, as he continued, 'And also, it's true that most Americans see Stalin, not Hitler, as the real threat to the world. No, Abby, honestly, it's not as simple as just supporting poor little Britain.' He felt that now was the moment to really cast his net on the waters and whispered, 'You know, I've been speaking with some folks here who are frankly against what they see as Churchill's pointless war making. I just wish I could meet more. There's a great story there for the readers back home.' Seeing her expression become more cautious, he decided now to make a strategic retreat. Changing the subject deftly, he cried in mock horror. 'But, hey! We've talked enough about that kinda stuff for one evening... what say we have dessert and then decide what to do next?' Abigail Stevenson smiled with relief and nodded her agreement.

****

David Bernstein was heartily tired of waiting outside The Dorchester. No amount of celebrities and famous people entering and leaving what had become one of the most stylish and popular luxury hotels in London, since its opening in 1931, could compensate for his discomfort and boredom. Just as he was trying to get the circulation in his left leg moving again, he saw the woman emerge from the hotel with the tall stranger. Before he could move to get a closer look, they had leapt into an obviously pre-ordered taxi and sped off towards Marble Arch. He could feel the hairs on the back of his neck prickle in suspicion and consoled himself with the belief that he had quite possibly found the 'A', who had written the note to Lazarus.

****

The 'what to do next' proved to be quite simple. They both left The Dorchester in a taxi and, despite the blackout, within a few minutes they were standing outside Abigail Stevenson's home. She had clearly made up her mind that she did not want the evening to end with a chaste kiss on the pavement and, having unlocked the door, led him by the hand up the stairs to her flat. Once inside, Brandt fell on her, showering her with kisses and hastily beginning to undress her. 'Come, my darling. We'll be more comfortable in here,' she whispered as she led him into her bedroom. She was self-evidently not an experienced or, Brandt reflected ruefully afterwards, a particularly skilful lover, though he readily conceded that she was a very pretty girl and had a firm young body. Long after they had made love, Abigail Stevenson snoozed contentedly on his chest while Brandt lay staring at the darkness above his head. He reached carefully for his jacket, which had been thrown carelessly on the floor next to the bed and, having found his cigarettes and lighter, he lay back, enjoying the sensation of the nicotine. The evening had gone well, their relationship was advancing nicely and he would very soon be in a position to get much more of the information he wanted out of her. He was more and more certain that, from the date of his expulsion, something had not been right with Rösel's networks. The British were obviously not aware of the informers, otherwise they would have already been arrested. He couldn't rid himself of the belief that someone was still running the networks. But who? Not a German... so who? He burned with the desire to solve this puzzle. The key to his success, however, was clearly going to be the degree of patience exercised by his masters in Berlin.

Chapter Thirty Three

Tuesday, September 3rd 1940, Central London.

'You off to see the show in the sky?' asked the grinning ticket inspector at the entrance to the platform at Charing Cross. 'Our boys are giving Goering's lot a right bashing, you mark my words.' Brandt mumbled a quick, 'Something like that,' in response, but looked with barely disguised disdain at the eager face of the weakling in the uniform. Given what he had planned for that day, he was certainly in no mood to take any unnecessary chances and had deliberately timed his arrival at the station such that he had to walk briskly to reach the train, just as the whistle signalling its departure was sounded by the platform master. Having leapt on board, he immediately leaned his head out of the window to check that he had been the last to pass through the ticket control. Having verified this, he quickly found an empty compartment and selected a window seat before carelessly throwing his medium size case onto the netting luggage rack above his head and making himself comfortable. There were still many commercial travellers or, more prosaically, door to door salesmen operating in Britain and a case full of junk gave him a pretty good disguise for his trip to meet Martha Perrygo. Once the train began to steam out of the station, he began to review the events of the weekend and what they signified.

He had spent much of the Bank Holiday weekend playing the part of Abigail Stevenson's lover. While she certainly did not possess the skills to satisfy him, as the American Emma de Jongh could, he had found her innocence and classic 'Englishness' something of a thrill. With a sense of some superiority, he reflected that this was much the same, though in his view not as distasteful, as the way that several of his most fervent SS comrades enjoyed taking their pleasure with young Jews. He shook his head in cynical amazement at her naïveté, especially in answer to his mock jealous question about previous male friends. He had said that he could not believe that someone as beautiful as her did not have any number of male admirers, ready to be her love interest. She had thought about this for a few seconds before replying earnestly, 'No, not really. There is no one special. There is someone, who I thought I was interested in, until I met you... But that could never have been, whereas with you, I knew right away.'

Brandt spent a few minutes, as the outskirts of London flew by, pondering whether or not this other man could have some connection to her activities as an informer for the *Reich*. He decided that, while he didn't like the sudden appearance of an unknown man, this was not likely. As the train pulled into Bromley station, Brandt groaned as he saw that, despite there being relatively few people standing on the platform, he would have to share his compartment. Indeed, the door to the corridor was soon pulled open and four people entered, including a young, bespectacled schoolboy, who was clearly excited that the train would pass fairly close to RAF Fighter Command's strategically important base at Biggin Hill. Sliding across the bench seat, so as to be sitting by the window and facing Brandt, he was beside himself with excitement. 'Do you think we'll see some Spitfires, mummy?' he almost shouted to a harassed looking young woman. 'Oh I do hope we will. And I hope they shoot all those nasty Germans down out of the sky.' Brandt offered a pained smile as, using a crudely made wooden model of a Spitfire to wave around the 'sky' in the compartment, he began to enact imaginary dogfights, which to Brandt's extreme irritation the British pilots always won. Little did he realise that the youngster's games were fairly true to the reality of what was actually taking place in the skies above Southern England.

Thinking again about his weekend with the English woman, he recalled his huge excitement when, quite out of the blue, as they were walking in Regents Park on the Sunday afternoon, she had said, 'Joe... You know you were talking the other day about people who are not so keen on Churchill. Well, I myself am not so keen on him.'

'Come on, Abby,' he had replied lightly. 'You know that you don't have to say things like that to make me keen on you.' He had squeezed her hand and, releasing it suddenly, had jogged away from the path onto the grass. He was rather pleased with himself, as this had seemed to be a purely spontaneous action, but of course, he had wanted some privacy for what she might have said next.

'No, no really, Joe,' she had insisted, panting to catch up with him, inhibited as she was by the flowing skirts of her bright, yellow summer frock. 'If I told you what I had been doing, you'd never believe me in a month of Sundays. No one would.' Brandt had pulled her down onto the warm lush grass, sensing that this was the moment that she would confess to having been Rösel's informant. His excitement, however, dissolved into pure fury as she then said quickly, 'But not now, Joe. Not now. I've said too much. Let's leave it.' Despising himself for sinking so low, he had tried to recoup the situation by wheedling, 'Come on, Abby. You can't leave it like that. That's not fair.' She had, however, made up her mind and closed the subject firmly for the day. 'No, Joe. I'm not ready to say anything more just yet. But I will soon, I promise.' He felt the blood start to pound in his head, as he recalled how he could have strangled the idiotic bitch there and then.

The train was now moving through what Brandt recognised as the outskirts of Sevenoaks and many of the passengers in the compartment prepared to disembark. Hat brim pulled down well over his face and disguised in an appropriately shabby suit, he reached Martha Perrygo's house after fifteen minutes of brisk walking. As there was no other person within sight, he strode purposefully up to the front door and knocked, willing her to answer the door. After what seemed like an eternity, he heard a shuffling followed by a turning of a key and the door opened a quarter to reveal the craggy face of Martha Perrygo. She quickly, if totally erroneously, summed up Brandt and barked, 'No hawkers here! Did you not see the sign attached to my front gate? Now be gone with you before I summon assistance.' Brandt could see that he had taken her by surprise, as he stood his ground, smiled sardonically and said, 'I'm no door to door salesman, Mrs Perrygo. In fact, I bring greetings to you from one of your dear friends, Parsifal. I know that you've not seen him since the early summer of last year, but I can assure you that he is in fine health back in his home town of Berlin.' Brandt was gratified to see both the shock register on Perrygo's face and her slight backward stagger. 'May I be of assistance,' he smirked, as she reached out for the door frame for support. 'Perhaps you are feeling faint?'

Despite the undoubted shock that he had caused to the older woman, she recovered impressively quickly. 'I don't know anyone of that name. Now, please, I would like you to leave before I call a constable.' Brandt merely chuckled at this empty threat, 'Come now, Martha. We're friends here. How can I convince you of my bona fides? Let me think... yes, I know...' He proceeded to give Martha Perrygo sufficient details of her meetings with Rösel and, more importantly, information she had given which only her controller could know. He was not surprised to see her expression change from suspicion and hostility to incredulity.

'For heaven's sake be quiet, man,' she hissed. 'Do you want to get us both arrested? Careless talk costs lives and I don't want mine to be one of them.' With this admonishment, she hurried Brandt into the hallway of her house and, with a final look to ensure that no one had witnessed this exchange, she firmly closed the door. Brandt was aware of the unmistakably unpleasant smell of cat in the house and he made a mental note not to forget its presence, as she ushered him into the rear facing room. From here, he could see the doorway into a small kitchen, with a back door opening onto a short walled garden, which had a high gate at the rear.

'Who on earth are you and what are you doing here? How did you find me?' she demanded, suspicion returning to her flushed and perspiring face.

'It's quite simple, Martha,' he said, as if to reassure a frightened child. 'May I call you Martha? Good. Now, as I was saying, Parsifal and his friends in Berlin wanted to contact you. You must be aware that an invasion is imminent. We need all the help we can get from our loyal friends.'

'Of course I understand, Mr....?' she asked pointedly. 'Just call me Joe for now', he replied smoothly.

'Very well, Joe,' she continued, 'I've been gathering all kinds of information from my informants over the last weeks and months, some of which could be very useful to our forces when they arrive. 'Here,' she went to a florid looking Gainsborough print on the wall and lifted it off its hook, revealing a small door, set into the wall. She then produced a key from the pocket of her very English looking tweed skirt and opened the door, lifted out a thick folder and whispered, 'I know it's not strictly allowed. But I saw no harm in keeping copies of all the information that I've passed on, as well as details of those who have provided it. It's been perfectly safe here and I wanted some kind of insurance, for when our troops liberate Britain from Churchill and his warmongers.' Brandt's eyes lit up at this treasure trove, but he sensed there was more to come from the old hag. 'I mean, those *Abwehr* Identity Cards we got are useful. But there's nothing like a dossier of proof to demonstrate my loyalties.'

'Naturally,' Brandt purred, 'A very sensible precaution, if I may say so. I can see why Parsifal was so impressed with you.' His crass compliment had the desired effect, causing Perrygo to preen in self-congratulation before speaking. This short pause allowed Brandt's racing mind some time to try to make sense of what he had heard. Could it really be that The *Abwehr* was still running this network? Schellenberg had been clear that his sources in that bunch of amateurs had assured him that that was not the case. So what the hell was going on here? He was beginning to like this mission less and less. Perrygo brought him back from his contemplation, by saying the last thing that he would have expected. 'I believe you are who you say you are Joe,' she began haltingly. 'But surely you must know Lazarus? After all, he was sent out to replace Parisfal. I've been giving him information for more than a year now. I did the right thing doing that, didn't I?'

'Of course you did, Martha' he replied reassuringly. 'Have no worries on that score. I should've explained that I am a member of the SS, whereas Lazarus is certainly a member of The *Abwehr*. I know it sounds crazy, but sometimes we are so hell bent on secrecy that we each do not know what the other is doing.' Brandt laughed at his own humorous comment, before promising her, 'I'll contact Berlin as soon as possible, in order to get this confusion cleared up. After all, preparing for the invasion is all that matters now.'

'Yes, you're right, Joe,' agreed Perrygo readily. 'But this has all been a bit of a shock... would you like a cup of tea?' Brandt almost burst out laughing at this. The English person's absurd solution for any problem or crisis ... a damned cup of tea! He was, however, glad to accept the offer, as it would mean that she would be busy preparing this for a couple of minutes. This was time, which he desperately needed to collect his chaotic thoughts.

In many ways things could not have gone better. He now had all the recent information gathered by Perrygo and her network, as well as the names and addresses of all her informers. But who the hell was this Lazarus? It didn't make sense that he was an *Abwehr* agent; yet, what else could he be? He would have to check with Berlin, but he was becoming increasingly suspicious of Rösel's networks. He decided that he would immediately take over Perrygo's informers and concluded, therefore, that apart from any more information on Lazarus, she had outlived her usefulness.

When she returned with a tray set for tea, Martha Perrygo's face was set in a severe expression, which Brandt interpreted as an indication that, having had time for reflection, she was far from happy with his appearance at her door. This confirmed the wisdom of his plan to get as much information out of her, before silencing her. He began by asking matter-of-factly, 'It's really urgent that I get in touch with Lazarus as soon as possible. I can do this via my contacts in Berlin, who can get his contact information from The *Abwehr*. However, if you have a faster method of communicating with him, that would save me a great deal of time, which might be critical in helping to plan for the invasion.' Perrygo was still pouring the tea and did not have to look him in the eye, as she began to answer in a regretful tone. 'Yes, Joe. I can see that would be better. But unfortunately Lazarus always contacted us. We never had a means to communicate directly with him. Security, I imagine.'

She's a tough old bird, thought Brandt, admiring the believable way in which she had finally looked at him and smiled sadly, as she reached her inevitable conclusion. Unfortunately for Perrygo, he was already aware that Rösel's informants could get in touch via a post office box number. She clearly has some suspicions, or she's playing a game of her own, he reasoned silently. Either way, I think I have everything that I'm going to get out of her. It's time to wrap things up here.

The sense of this decision was immediately confirmed, when Mrs Perrygo asked him to return her dossier. 'I must keep it in my safe as proof of my support of the *Reich*. I do hope you understand.'

'Of course, Martha,' he replied agreeably, handing it back across the table. 'And while we're at it, you might as well have a couple of my samples, which I've brought here as part of my cover.' The middle aged woman was nobody's fool and smiled uncertainly. 'Oh no. That's not necessary.' Brandt ignored her and carefully opened his suitcase, from which he produced a British service issue Webley revolver to point directly at her head. Martha Perrygo simply nodded her head in quiet resignation, rather than any sort of surprise or shock. He carefully took out from his case some rope, which he used both to tie her hands behind her back and her feet by the ankles. Fearing that she may try to shout for help, he stuffed a silk scarf into her mouth, before closing the curtains of the room. He had already noticed a wooden clothes dryer suspended from the ceiling by two strong looking hooks. Working silently and quickly, he took a coil of much thicker rope, which he fastened around one of the hooks. Perrygo's eyes widened in terror and she involuntarily gagged as she realised what he had planned for her. She began to struggle madly, trying to free her hands and feet, but he had fastened the rope expertly... it neither gave an inch, nor tightened, so as to leave tell-tale marks on her ankles and wrists. Recognising the inevitable, she finally slumped back in resigned defeat. Brandt had now almost finished his preparations and, having placed the noose round her neck, he hauled her up onto a dining chair and pulled the rope tight. 'Just so you know, Martha,' he spoke almost kindly, 'I don't know what has been going on here, but I have told you the truth. I am a genuine SS agent.' With that, he expertly cut the ties on her wrists and ankles and removed the scarf from her mouth, while simultaneously kicking away the chair. 'No... I can hel....' were the last sounds uttered by Martha Perrygo, as she dangled and twitched violently at the end of the rope. Brandt sat back in his armchair, poured himself another cup of tea and enjoyed watching the life drain out of her.

Once he was absolutely certain that she was dead, he washed and dried the tea cups and saucers and placed the rope, ties, scarf, revolver and dossier in the hidden compartment at the bottom of his case. He then locked the safe and replaced the painting and put the safe key back into her skirt pocket, as her body swung grotesquely in death. He had previously locked the cat upstairs and, just as the light had faded completely from the day, he opened the door to allow it back into the room. He then silently sneaked out of the back door, leaving it unlocked, and made his way under cover of darkness into the alleyway and away from the scene of his handiwork.

Once safely seated in a second class compartment of a train to London, he planned his next steps. He must, of course, contact Berlin to check out this Lazarus with those bunglers at The *Abwehr*. But he was also beginning to suspect that he could be the man that Abigail Stevenson was talking about, the other man. Whatever the truth, his only way to this man was through the woman Stevenson and he would have to pursue that route as soon as he had a clear reply from Berlin.

Chapter Thirty Four

Saturday, September 7th 1940, Tower of London, London.

Abigail Stevenson, a hopeful expression on her pretty face, squinted into the distance towards the unmistakable shape of Tower Bridge. For one bizarre moment, she wondered whether she was looking for a sign, such as departing ravens, to help her divine the future. With a slight, almost imperceptible shake of the head, she realised how ridiculously out of character that would have been, for she had never been a superstitious person. In fact, she had been noteworthy among many of her female contemporaries, on account of her evident rationality. Were she to be given a problem to solve, then she had the perseverance and mental capacity which was required to reach a solution, often when this seemed impossible. As a young girl, she had loved sitting with her father trying to solve the crossword puzzle or a brain teaser in the daily newspaper. That was long ago, however, her father having taken his own life after being held responsible for a terrible mistake at The Treasury, where he had been a mid-ranking clerk. He had been blamed for the leaking of market sensitive information, immediately before the Budget of 1931, even though the police could find no firm evidence to point to his involvement. Everyone had said after his death that a more reliable and hardworking clerk would be almost impossible to find. But the most senior civil servants in The Treasury hushed the matter up, by blaming an innocent man. It was some years after his death that Abigail, looking for a sense of purpose, had turned to fringe movements that worked against the British Government. Rightly or wrongly, she firmly held the amorphous British Establishment to be responsible for her father's suicide. It was through such involvement that she had been introduced to Parsifal and had begun her secret life as an informer for Germany. Parsifal had initially seemed so urbane and charming and what she was doing had given her a sense of repaying something for the injustice served on her father. But that had been in peacetime. Now Britain was at war with Germany, and especially since the start of the Blitz, she was having doubts as to whether she should carry on. Of course, she had also met and fallen in love with the lovely American reporter. For the first time since her father's suicide, she had begun to look forward to the future with eager anticipation.

She had been summoned to one of her regular briefings with Lazarus and they met at 3PM at The Tower of London. She liked Lazarus very much; he had such a calm and gentle manner, especially for a German, and his face somehow looked younger than his general appearance suggested. If only he would get rid of that hideous moustache, she had often thought, he'd look so much more handsome. She spent a pleasant half hour strolling with him around the perimeter of The Tower, watching the gardeners tend the vegetable patches that had been planted to make use of its moat. They discussed the likelihood of an invasion and what appeared to be the success of RAF Fighter Command, in preventing the Luftwaffe from destroying its fighting capability. In a way that she couldn't really explain, neither of them seemed so disappointed at the evident failure of Goering's numerically superior air force. She also passed on to him some routine information concerning morale in the British Armed Forces, which she had committed to memory from a report she had typed.

Although he was scarcely an expert in the interpretation of the moods of women, throughout their meeting King could not help but notice that her manner had once more changed... perhaps happy was the best way to describe it. She was smiling much more than usual and seemed more open and confident. She had chosen to dress in vibrant summer colours, which accentuated the blondness of her hair and her trim, yet very feminine figure. 'You seem happy, Abigail... has something changed?' he asked as naturally as possible. 'You seem full of the joys of life.' She immediately blushed and looked away. 'It's nothing, Lazarus, really,' she said, rather too quickly and too firmly.

'Have you met someone?' enquired King, playing a hunch that perhaps she had decided to join the very many young people who, aware of the uncertainties facing them in war time, were nevertheless determined to get the most out of life. If so, his first reaction was to be pleased. To him, Abigail had always seemed such a serious and lonely young woman, needy even, and he was very taken with this new version, which seemed in contrast so full of life and playfulness. Yet, at the same time he could hear Professor Pym's warning voice in his ear, 'You can't afford to react as you would normally, John. You must think how an agent would think and act accordingly.' It was obvious, he supposed glumly, but nevertheless he just wished he could innocently enjoy Abigail's evident happiness, without having to consider it from the point of view of the twilight world he now inhabited.

'That would be telling,' she replied pertly. 'Why? Isn't it allowed?'

'Of course I can't stop you,' reasoned King with a half-smile. 'But you should be very careful, Abigail. In our line of work, relationships with the wrong person could be very dangerous.'

'Don't worry,' she had reassured him, 'I'm in control. But now, I really must be going. I'll be in touch.' Having offered him a beaming smile as farewell, she began to walk hastily towards the City of London, her long, blond hair streaming out behind her in the sunlight. Despite the fact that she was a traitor, King had always had a soft spot for Abigail Stevenson and he smiled at her, before making his way down to the riverbank.

As he stood staring down river towards the huge Port of London, with its labyrinth of docks, he could see formations of dark specks in the distant sky. What on earth could they be? he wondered, only to be very quickly answered by the loud drone of the air raid sirens. The evident size of the raid surprised him, as since the fall of France, the major targets had been the airfields of Fighter Command far to the south of the city. Transfixed, he stared at the huge formations approaching the capital, the sound of their engines increasing as they grew nearer. Within a few minutes, the first bombers were clearly visible, twin engine Heinkels with their unmistakable black cross markings. They had already started to deposit their deadly cargo over the dockland area and both the sounds of nearby explosions and the dreaded palls of dark, heavy smoke began to fill the air. He wasn't very familiar with the positioning of shelters in this part of London and, while he realised that he could be very much at risk by staying out in the open, he found himself unable to take his eyes off the bombers and the carnage which they were wreaking. A new wave of the monstrous planes was approaching the target zone every two minutes, such was the ferocity of the attack. Despite the number of aircraft, King was amazed that their engines gave off a sound that was more like a grinding or deep buzzing than the expected roar. For one ludicrous moment, he actually thought that a swarm of bees was circling around his head, such was the odd nature of the sound of the attackers. By now, it was clear that the docks and the East End of the city were the principal targets and he could hear the frantic clang of fire engines, as they rushed eastwards to deal with the worst of the fires. The anti-aircraft defences had also opened up, making a ferocious counterpoint to the sounds of the aircraft engines and the all too frequent explosions caused by bombs finding their targets. He had no real idea how many aircraft were taking part in the raid, but felt safe in estimating their number in the hundreds, rather than dozens. The spectacle went on for almost two hours, before an end to the incoming waves of bombers offered some brief respite to the emergency services. It had been King's introduction at first hand to the might of the Nazi war machine and what it could do. He shuddered involuntarily at the thought that this may be what London and other cities in Britain might face in the weeks and months to come.

Without making a conscious decision, King found himself walking quickly northwards and away from the river, rather than in the more obvious direction of westwards and back towards The City of London. He was, therefore, moving towards Whitechapel and the East End, with its densely packed working people's housing. His suspicion was soon confirmed that this area had borne the brunt of Goering's first major daytime raid on the capital. As he walked deeper into the narrow streets, he could feel rather than see the numerous fires which had broken out across a wide area of East London. He turned a corner into a mean and narrow street and immediately saw that a bomb had exploded, more or less in the centre of a long row of tenements on the side facing him. His first feeling was one of utter fury, a futile, though arguably natural reaction to the bomb leaving the street looking horribly violated. He was acutely aware that while it may look desperately poor and deprived to his eyes, these were people's homes, and he felt outraged on their behalf. He was still brimming with anger, when he heard a woman shouting to him. 'Please, can you help? You must help... it's my baby girls. They're both still in there. They're only four and three. They're too young to die...' The woman was pointing frantically at the standing half of one of the bombed tenements. 'I tried to get us out and to the shelter, but they came so quickly. I never heard the sirens and it was too late...' she shrieked. 'They're still in there, on the top floor. There's no one else. Please can you get them out?'

Without pausing for thought, King crashed into the fiercely burning building, taking off his jacket and using the cold water tap in the downstairs kitchen to soak it. Holding his new shield in front of his face and against the increasing heat and smoke, he began two at a time to run up the stairs. He was hardly aware of the dreadful creaking and cracking noises which filled the air as parts of the structure of the tenement began to take the strain and prepare to collapse. Rather, he was only conscious of the desperation he had seen in the terrified mother's eyes. As he moved further up the stairwell, he could see the doors on one side of the landings start to blister, as the fire which was raging in the bombed out part of the tenement threatened to break through. One door had been blown open and, as he passed the gaping space, he could see the inferno raging just a few feet away from him. This was greedily and rapidly consuming the pathetically shoddy furniture and desperately few possessions, in what had evidently been a kitchen and living room. For a second he paused, remembering that in a lecture he had attended on what to do in case of bombing, the speaker had said that, on no account should people venture alone into burning buildings. The risk of asphyxiation and even gas explosion was far too great. Too late to remember that now, old son, he thought grimly, as he approached what he hoped was the topmost landing of the building. Reaching this, he paused and, to his enormous relief he could hear, over the pounding of his own heart and the raging of the fires all around him, the sound of children whimpering. He threw open the smouldering door and was immediately thrown back onto the landing area by the blast of hot air. The children, who had had the good sense to hide underneath a very substantial sideboard, began to scream with terror. King clambered back to his feet and approached the girls, shouting, 'Come on, darlings. Your mummy's waiting outside for you. She sent me to fetch you. There's nothing to be afraid of, I promise.' The sisters quickly climbed out from under the furniture and rushed to King, who picked one up under each of his arms. Having covered their heads as best he could with his still damp jacket, he immediately plunged back down the stairs. Just as he reached the half way point of his descent, the upper landing, totally consumed now by fire, started to rain burning wood down onto them. The girls, though terrified, seemed to trust that this fearless man would save them and simply hugged ever closer into his chest. King, however, had been hit by a large piece of wood and staggered down the next flight of stairs, almost coming to grief when he reached the landing. His lungs were now bursting with the effort and the smoke and heat were making him feel increasingly light headed. One more flight of stairs to go, he desperately urged himself through gritted teeth. Come on, man. You can't give up now. His jacket was smoking, and the muscles in his arms and legs were screaming as he made one last rush down to the ground floor and safety. Once he reached the narrow entrance hallway, which was now filled with dense black smoke, he flung off the now burning jacket and half ran, half fell through the front door. He didn't see the sudden burst of the press photographer's flash bulb freeze the three of them, covered in ash and dust, but mercifully not seriously injured, as he moved slowly away from the now wildly burning building. Indeed, just as he reached a safe distance away, the whole front of the tenement collapsed in an inferno of dust, flames and smoke. The woman ran up to King and hugged her two daughters, neither of whom wanted to leave the care of this unknown man. 'Come on, girls,' said King in a voice made rough and hoarse by the choking smoke. 'Here's your mummy.' The two girls allowed themselves to be prised away from King and were taken up by their now weeping mother, who hugged them so tight that it seemed she would never allow them out of her sight again. Once the sisters had become calmer and the fire brigade and ambulance crew had arrived, the woman looked around for King, but he had already disappeared.

'Where's that man gone?' she asked an ARP Warden desperately. 'The tall one who was covered in ash and dust?'

'He's gone,' replied the Warden with distaste. 'I told him that he should have left well alone. Fool that he was going into a building like that. Alone and with no equipment. Shouldn't be allowed.'

'But he saved my girls,' the mother shouted hysterically, as if unable to grasp the attitude of the Warden. 'Don't you care that, without him, they would've been killed? He'll always be a hero to me.'

After a respite of no more than a couple of hours, a second Luftwaffe attack was visited on the burning city. The formations of bombers had little difficulty finding their targets in the failing light, as the East End of London was by now a mass of flames. Unbeknownst to King, lying in the bath in his flat on Charing Cross Road, this was to be the first of fifty seven consecutive days on which the Luftwaffe would launch attacks on London – the Blitz had begun.

Chapter Thirty Five

Monday, September 9th 1940, Paddington Station, London.

Henry King was a relieved man as he settled himself into the first class compartment of the 6.15PM train to Gloucester. His wife had been concerned, when the German bombing raids over London had begun just before her beloved husband was due to make a business trip to the capital. However, like most women of her generation, she recognised that duty could not be subordinated to self-interest, or worse still to fear. So she had dropped him off, and given him her usual peck on the cheek, at Gloucester station that morning, never for one moment showing any fear that he would be at risk.

Henry had completed his legal business on time and had rung his wife to say that he would be on the early evening train from Paddington. Having stopped only to buy that day's *Evening Standard*, he now turned to read the news of the latest casualty figures and damage suffered in the capital. As he began to read through the inside pages, which reported more local news, his attention was drawn immediately to a small, but very clear photograph under the headline; *'Unknown Hero Saves the Day.'* He quickly scanned the story, which concerned the rescue of two young sisters from a bombed tenement by a mysterious passer-by who, afterwards, had simply disappeared. While the story might well have been that which engaged most of the newspaper's readers that evening, Henry King couldn't take his eyes off the close up photograph of the tall man, his hair lightened by dust and ash, who was carrying the two young girls, one in each arm, out of the burning wreck of the tenement. The photographer had caught the man square on as he was moving directly towards the camera and Henry King's heart began to lurch as he frantically reached for his reading glasses to study the photograph more carefully. 'My God', he whispered, 'My God, it's him. I'll swear it's John!' Without taking a second to consider the wisdom of what he was about to do, he rapidly gathered up his possessions and jumped down off the train, just as it had started to move away from the platform. 'Now you didn't ought to be doing that kind of thing, if you forgive me for saying so, sir,' said the Platform Master, whose whistle had just sent the train on its way westwards. His kindly voice and sympathetic smile disarmed Henry King. 'You're absolutely right. I'm sorry. I've just realised there's something very urgent that I need to do.'

Ever the considerate husband, he immediately telephoned his wife to let her know that something had come up at the last minute; that he would be staying in London for at least one and possibly two nights and that she was not to worry at all. He had just finished reassuring her that he was fine, when he could hear the first wails of the air raid sirens signalling another stage of Hitler's attempt to bomb Britain into submission. That damned little Austrian corporal knows nothing of the British mentality, he thought as he proudly followed the orderly stream of people towards the nearest shelter. In a strange way Henry was glad of the raid, as it gave him the time he needed to calm himself and decide what to do. He'd always suspected that his son had not died on a Swiss mountain and now he had the proof! When the all clear sounded at just after 8.30PM, he reached into his briefcase and breathed a sigh of relief as his fingers closed around his small address book. In fact, these days he rarely left home on business without it, as his memory for phone numbers and addresses was now so poor. He quickly found a vacant telephone box, looked up the number of Professor Pym and, his hands shaking with tension, phoned the St John's Wood number.

****

Apart from the use of dense blackout curtains, which hid the magnificent view towards the Lord's Cricket Ground, the flat of Professor Pym looked perfectly normal. A pleasant, relaxing light was produced by a combination of stylish art deco standard and table lamps. Mozart 'Divertimenti' were issuing from his gramophone player and the academic was sitting in his favourite armchair, pondering the unexpected telephone call that he had just received. Apart from a quick visit the previous Christmas, he had not heard from Henry King since the Summer of 1939, when he had had the unpleasant duty to visit him and his wife in their lovely Gloucestershire home to inform them that the Swiss authorities had given up the search for their son John's remains. 'They say that, in such cases, it's not at all unusual that nothing is ever found,' he had said quietly, but firmly enough to dissuade any objection. He knew from Gerhardt Rösti, the local Swiss mountain guide, that both parents had made a sentimental visit to the place of their son's accident. Afterwards, the Swiss had reported his uneasy feeling that

Henry King seemed somehow doubting of the whole episode. Indeed, Pym had left the family home with the distinct sense that the mother had accepted the loss of her son stoically, but that the father still did not entirely believe in the truth of his son's unfortunate walking accident in the snows of the Bernese Oberland.

Henry King arrived shortly after 9.30PM, the sounds of yet another bombing raid over the relatively distant East End of London clearly audible, as Pym opened the door of his flat to welcome his guest. Henry King entered the flat and thanked his host for agreeing to see him at such short notice. 'Not at all, Mr King. It's my pleasure. Though I'm not sure how I can help you,' the Professor responded somewhat cagily. 'But, anyway, do come in and sit down please. Would you take a brandy with me?'

Henry King nodded his assent, before saying quite brusquely, 'I'll get straight to the point, Pym. Have you seen this?' He exchanged the *Evening Standard*, opened to the page on which the photograph appeared, for a beautiful balloon glass of fine cognac. Pym looked at the newspaper in some bafflement. 'This evening's edition... no, I don't think I've seen it...'

'Just look carefully at the photograph on that page, would you? The man carrying the children.' Pym picked up his reading glasses and studied the newspaper. Of course, he recognised John King immediately and struggled to suppress his sense of alarm. In order to give himself time to think, he moved the newspaper towards the light, as if to get a better view, before saying in his most academically eccentric way. 'I'm not sure what I'm supposed to be looking at, Mr King. Other than the man shows some similarity to your son, John.'

'Some similarity... some similarity!' Henry King thundered. 'My God, man. You must be able to see, it is John, no question about it!'

Pym recognised that this could quickly get out of control and he tried to pacify his guest. 'Look, Mr King,' he said soothingly, 'he does look like John, I agree. But we both know that John, tragically, is dead.'

'I'm disappointed in you, Professor,' replied King scathingly. 'I really thought that you were a man of moral fibre. I understand that you needed to create this fiction of John's death, presumably because he is involved in some kind of secret war-related work. He more or less implied that to me at our last meeting, just before he left for Germany. But, come on man. Face facts! The cat's out of the bag now! You might as well tell me the whole story.'

Pym inwardly cursed John King for his naïve failure to accept the rules by which he had to operate as an agent in the field. What on earth had he been thinking of? Rushing into that house to rescue those children and, as a direct consequence, causing his own exposure and with it risking the whole operation? Did he not understand that some casualties are inevitable in war? Henry King took further advantage of the Professor's silence to interrogate his host further. 'Does it not strike you as odd that this man, injured as he probably was, simply disappeared without trace? Why would he do that, unless he had something to fear from publicity?'

'I can't explain any of this, I'm afraid,' Pym responded firmly. 'But I can assure you that this man is not your son.'

Henry King, his bitterness and fury subsiding by this time, merely sat shaking his head sadly. 'I suppose I should've expected this kind of response from you. You have no children, have you, Pym? You're a sad excuse for a human being. Anyway, thank you at least for listening to me. I will go to the offices of The Evening Standard tomorrow to obtain a clear print of the photograph. I shall then run a series of advertisements in the press, asking for information on my son's whereabouts. In the meantime, sir, I will bid you good evening.'

Pym was shocked by Henry King's determination and recognised immediately that he could not let him leave in this way. Damn John King! he thought angrily. Damn the day I ever thought of him for this mission. What a blunder that was. Just as his guest was preparing to leave, Pym cracked. 'All right, Mr King,' he said in an uncharacteristically defeated tone. 'You win. I'll tell you what you want to know.'

For the next ten minutes, Pym gave Henry King a brief outline of the deception of his son's death and the reasons for it. 'Of course, you may not say anything of this to anyone,' Pym said firmly, in an attempt to regain something of his composure. 'Not even, I'm afraid, to your wife. I must insist on that.'

Henry King studied his host with what was almost a look of disdain. 'Please do me the courtesy of withdrawing that insistence. I can assure you that I know my duty and I would do nothing to jeopardise John's safety. Even to the extent of keeping my beloved wife in ignorance.' Pym had the good grace to look shamefaced as he realised that he had both totally underestimated Henry King and unfairly cursed his son. The pressure of this damned war was starting to get to him, and he told himself that he must, at all costs, try to retain his humanity. If that is lost, what on earth was he fighting for? In a strange way, he had to admit that it was a relief to have been able to tell the truth to King's father. He could now acknowledge that he had dreaded having to tell him of an actual injury to his son, or even of his death whilst on active service. 'At least you're now fully aware of the risks John is running and of the vital nature of his work. This is, of course, especially the case now that Britain stands alone and in imminent danger of invasion.' Looking at his straight-backed and principled guest, Pym realised that, after the deception of the last year and more, he owed him his best attempt at rebuilding trust. 'It would give me great pleasure, if you would stay here tonight,' he said tentatively. 'I rarely go down to the air raid shelter. If my name's on one of those damned Jerry bombs, then it's on it. But I can show you to the shelter if you prefer.'

Henry King recognised his own ex-serviceman's approach to danger and, despite his lingering annoyance, smiled before replying, 'Yes, Professor, it would be good to see out this raid together. And by the way, I realise that it would not be sensible for me to meet John until this is all over, but I would also ask that you do not tell him that I now know he is alive.' Pym readily agreed to this condition and, making a mental note to arrange for *The Evening Standard* to be instructed to destroy all copies of the photograph, he set about pouring them both another hearty glass of cognac.

****

Brandt had experienced an extremely frustrating week waiting for the information on Lazarus to be returned from Berlin. Security had been tightened up enormously in view of the invasion threat, and his Portuguese Embassy contact was extremely nervous about undertaking the role of messenger. Such irritations were soon forgotten, however, when he received definitive information that 'Lazarus' was not an

Abwehr or any other form of German agent.

****

'*Standard*! Get your *Standard* 'ere,' cried the newspaper seller as Abigail Stevenson approached Trafalgar Square underground station for her journey home from work. Contrary to the widespread media reports, most of her colleagues and neighbours were very frightened by the Luftwaffe's obvious targeting of London. 'They may well be losing the Battle of Britain, but it's a certainty that Adolf will make us pay for that,' seemed to sum up the gallows mood. She, herself, was terrified during what now were the daily and nightly air raids and she had decided, over the previous weekend, that it would be safer to travel home by underground rather than by bus. As if to justify her fear, the moaning of the air raid sirens began as she was entering the station. A collective groan rose from the dozens of commuters who realised that, depending on the length of the raid, they may have to spend an uncomfortable night squatting down wherever they could find a space within the tunnels and stations of the tube system. Stevenson, fearing that it may indeed be a long night, paused at the station entrance to buy a newspaper, before hurrying down to track level. Trafalgar Square was not one of the nearest stations to the densely populated parts of the city. Nevertheless, as she moved into the station and down towards the platforms, she saw that much of the passage and platform space had already been staked out, by means of blankets rolled up lengthways and placed against the wall. An adult, or more frequently an older child, had evidently been assigned to patrol the space earmarked for the later use of the whole family. The noise of exploding bombs had not penetrated down to track level by the time her train rattled into the station. It was crowded with mainly office staff on their way home from their jobs in central London, most of whom appeared grey and tense in the artificial light. 'Looks like Jerry's having another go at us tonight, eh my dear?' said a middle aged man in a bowler hat. Gallantly, he had decided that it was his duty to protect the attractive young woman from the worst of the crush of people behind him. She smiled in acknowledgement at his ruddy, well- meaning face and he took this as encouragement to advise her. 'Don't worry. We're far too far beneath ground level to be in any real danger. Try to think of something nice, which will take your mind off things. I think about my lovely rose garden at home.'

Suddenly the lights went out, plunging the whole carriage into pitch darkness as the train screeched and swerved, causing many people to stagger and some to fall. Several people screamed, either in pain as they were trodden on by others, or in fear that the train would crash. Gradually, however, the train steadied itself and began to pick up speed and the people in the packed carriage began to calm down. When the lights were restored a minute or so later, Abigail Stevenson was amazed to see someone else in the place of the middle aged man to whom she had spoken.

At last she reached Maida Vale station and with considerable relief left the train, only to find the platform crowded with people sheltering from the raid. She managed to find a relatively quiet spot on a set of stairs, where she could wait for the sound of the all clear. Even though she knew that the bombing was probably an essential preface to an invasion by the Germans, she resented the way it was reducing the possibilities of meeting Joe. She had been at home alone since her appointment with Lazarus and, especially with the now much heightened risk from the Blitz, she felt more and more acutely the need for company, specifically Joe's company. Still, she supposed, he must be very busy reporting this shift in German tactics and she would just have to be patient. In truth, however, she was tiring more and more of her role as an informer. Since the fall of France and Dunkirk, she had begun seriously to question the validity of her rationale for betraying her country. It had all seemed so clear at those first meetings of like-minded people before the war. Soviet Russia was the real enemy and Britain could surely have worked with Germany, had it not been for Churchill and his fanatical anti-Hitler stance. But since the Nazi-Soviet Pact and the stories spread by refugees about what life is like for some in Germany, she had begun to have doubts. She felt sure that Lazarus also harboured some concerns. She could tell from the look in his eyes at every one of their meetings as he asked her to keep up the good work. She had been planning to speak to him about ending her role as an informer, but things became even more complicated with the arrival of Joe Brand, her growing feelings for him and his seemingly sympathetic stance on Germany. Giving up on the conundrum of what to do for the best, she turned to her copy of The Evening Standard. She had put it in her bag and forgotten all about it until she had been searching for her cigarettes. 'Sorry, Miss,' advised a nearby policeman regretfully. 'You can't smoke here, not while there's a raid on... risk of gas explosion.

Hope you understand.'

'Of course, officer, I'm very sorry. Should have realised,' she answered hurriedly, glad of the distraction of being able to hide behind the newspaper to conceal her embarrassment. As soon as she saw the photograph of the dust-covered man carrying the two young girls out of the bombed tenement, she gasped in recognition. Almost before she had recovered herself, the all clear sounded and she patiently waited her turn to exit the station.

Chapter Thirty Six

Friday, September 13th 1940, Scotland Yard, London.

David Bernstein sighed with frustration, as he stared at the pile of paper which covered one half of his desk, before addressing Colin Trench, the colleague with whom he shared the office. 'We surely can't be expected to deal with all of these, Colin. It's impossible. I'll have to talk to the Inspector.' It was true that since the Dunkirk Evacuation and the Fall of France, fears of a German invasion of the south coast of Britain had increased enormously. And with such fears, there had been an exponential increase in reports of 'Fifth Column' activity in London and the South East. From bitter experience, Bernstein knew that almost all of these were misguided, some even malicious in that they were often directed at those who didn't quite fit in, who lived alone, who kept themselves to themselves or who had unusual habits. Nevertheless, each and every one of these reports had to be checked and, given the difficulties of travelling which the now daily bombing raids were causing, this work was taking an increasing amount of his time. Inspector Renton had initially tried to protect him from exposure to such cases, to allow him to focus on the pursuit of Lazarus. This new pile of reports on his desk, however, suggested that his boss was also fighting a losing battle.

On entering the Inspector's larger office, he could see immediately that, if anything, Renton's desk was even more piled high with papers than his own. 'Sit down, David and tell me what progress you're making,' said the Inspector setting aside his profusely smoking pipe. Bernstein knew immediately what he meant; he didn't want to know about all the other reports and cases, he desperately wanted news of some progress in the search for Lazarus. Nevertheless, the younger man began by explaining that he had been bogged down with more and more specious reports of 'Fifth Column' activity.

'Do you know, sir, that working people in the shelters around Knightsbridge have complained that those who don't work talk all through the night, thereby preventing them from getting any sleep. They actually believe these gossips are Fifth Columnists. I wasted a whole afternoon on that.'

Renton groaned in sympathy, 'I know it's frustrating, David. But orders have come from the highest level. We have to investigate each and every report, however idiotic it seems.'

Bernstein nodded in resigned agreement, before turning to his report on the Lazarus case. 'I've kept the woman Stevenson under observation during this week and have managed to discover that the man at the Dorchester is one Joe Brand, an American journalist assigned to provide reports from Britain to his news agency in the United States.'

'Does his story check out?' asked Renton sharply.

'As far as I can make out, yes it does and to be honest, he seems a most unlikely Lazarus. After all, would Lazarus appear so publicly with someone who may well be one of his key informers?'

Bernstein saw the disappointment cloud the Inspector's face, 'Yes, David. You have a pretty good point there. OK, then let's work on the basis that he isn't our man... what ideas do you have to progress the case?'

'Well, sir,' began Bernstein hesitantly, 'I still have the feeling that she's our 'A', so I think I should take a look around the woman's flat. Try to pick up some sort of lead…. She always goes out with colleagues after work on Friday, so I thought I'd try it next Friday. Early in the evening.' He had always had the confidence to say what he thought to his Inspector, but this was something different and, while not illegal, he did not know how Renton would react.

Renton looked worried by the suggestion. 'I don't like it, David. What if it goes wrong? It could be very embarrassing.'

'I'm prepared to take that risk, sir,' countered an obviously confident Bernstein. 'I'm pretty good at picking locks and I should be in and out in a few minutes.' Renton finally agreed that, if no further progress had been made in the case by the next Friday, he should put his plan into operation.

****

Friday 13th held no superstitious terrors for Abigail Stevenson, so she saw nothing untoward in Joe Brand waiting outside The Foreign Office to meet her after work on that date. Granted, he had never done such a thing before, but after a tiresome day of the other women quizzing her non-stop about her love life, she took great satisfaction in being swept off by this handsome American. Of course, she realised that her colleagues meant nothing serious by their questions; with the Blitz and the war going so badly, they needed a simple diversion and her love life happened to be it. However, it somehow fitted perfectly that they now stood in line, mouths agape and eyes flashing with jealousy, as she rushed towards Brandt. On catching sight of her, he immediately hailed a passing taxi and ordered the driver to take them to Abigail's flat. 'We're going out somewhere really special,' he drawled with a glint in his eye. 'So maybe you'd like to go home, freshen up and get changed after work? Not that I think you need it, of course,' he added, while reaching over and pecking her cheek. 'You always look sensational to me.'

Abigail Stevenson looked down at her functional pleated skirt and sensibly flattish shoes and laughed out loud. 'Though, perhaps,' he teased, 'you may be interested in this…' Brandt indicated the flat cardboard box lying on one of the empty seats and Abigail Stevenson's eyes widened at the name of the couturier emblazed on its upper side. Eagerly anticipating the box's contents, she squeezed Brandt's hand tightly before eagerly returning his kiss.

As soon as they were inside her flat, Brandt's surprise was revealed to be a stylish dress. 'I saw it in the shop window and could only see you wearing it. I hope you don't mind.'

'Don't mind?' she gasped. 'Oh Joe it's beautiful! I can't wait to try it on.' Brandt stared at her as she made her way towards her bedroom to change, unfastening the back of her skirt as she moved. Aroused by this simple action, he crept after her. Stepping out of her skirt, she turned in surprise as he came towards her, picked her up in his arms and carried her to the bed, where he laid her gently down.

Once again, he found their lovemaking banal in comparison to his preferred style, but he recognised that this was as much business as pleasure. She, on the other hand, lay back on the pillow afterwards with a dreamy, satisfied look on her face. 'You know I was saying the other day, that you wouldn't believe me if I told you some of the things that I'd done, Joe?' she asked with a mixture of excitement and anxiety. Suppressing his eagerness, Brandt merely raised his eyebrows in a quizzical expression. 'Well, now that we love one another, I don't think we should have any secrets. Do you?' It took what remained of Brandt's self-control not to laugh in what he saw as her deluded face. Rather, he responded as she would have wanted, 'Of course not, honey. You can tell me anything.' Stevenson seemed to settle herself for her confession, before continuing. 'Well, I have a particular friend who is sympathetic to Germany and we have had lots of discussions on many themes.'

'Really?' replied Brandt in a casual manner far removed from the eager anticipation he now felt. 'Who is he, and what do you talk about? Remember, Abby, my country is not at war with Germany and I'm interested in reporting all sides of this war to the folks back home.' Abigail Stevenson reached for a cigarette, but he held her hand back, leaning over her so that she was looking him straight in the eye. 'It's OK honey,' he murmured softly. 'Really. It's OK. You can tell me. You know you want to tell someone. So best it's someone like me who has feelings for you.'

This seemed to destroy Stevenson's final inhibitions and she explained simply, and with tearful eyes, her recruitment by the agent Parsifal, who she now knew to be a German called Rösel. She went on to describe her passing of information to him, his expulsion from Britain and then his replacement by a new German *Abwehr* agent known only by the codename Lazarus. Brandt's heart was pounding now. He was so close to being able to confront this imposter that he could almost feel him in trapped in the sights of his gun. 'It's OK Abby, I understand,' he said, with an earnest expression. 'I think what you've been doing is very brave.' She laughed harshly as she replied, 'Not half as brave as him... just look at this.'

She handed him the copy of *The Evening Standard* containing the photograph of King. 'What's this, Abby?' asked Brandt in genuine confusion. 'What am I looking at here?' She sat back and smiled like the cat that had got the cream. Finally, after what for Brandt was an excruciating pause, she explained very slowly. 'That's him, Joe. That's Lazarus there. The man carrying those girls. I couldn't believe it when I saw it...' Brandt squinted at the photograph in the poor light of the bedroom, but could not see the man's face clearly. 'Would you mind switching on your bedside light? I can't really make him out.' As soon as the light had improved, he could see the man's features quite clearly and was immediately struck by a sense of familiarity. Could it possibly be that he knew this man? But how and when?

'He's so brave and good, Joe... I think you'll like him,' said Stevenson in gushing admiration. Somehow, the woman's fawning attitude towards this man hit him like a thunderbolt, as memories of similar reactions from young women to the Englishman King came flooding back. King, he thought savagely. This man reminds me of King and this stupid woman's bleating about him reminds me of how he was always the brave and the good one. The one who all the best girls in Heidelberg liked. Pity the poor fool never realised how attractive he was to women. His brow puckered with concentration, as he tried to recall the details. But surely King is dead. Killed in a walking accident in Switzerland. After their final meeting in The Bendlerblock in 1938, he had happily put King out of his mind when he'd read the report of his death.

Suddenly, the scales fell from his eyes and he could see the whole incredible deception. Lazarus, he thought dismissively. Just like King to choose such a codename. Now I come to think about it, his body was never found. How damned convenient and how typical of those traitorous Swiss to be involved in faking his death. In his mind, he could see how King had replaced Rösel and had run the expelled agent's networks since mid-1939. That's why we never got any reports after that time and why none of them tried to get in touch with us, he concluded, his mind racing to keep up with the insights crashing into his consciousness. They use a bogus *Abwehr* agent called 'Lazarus' to gather this intelligence, which the informers think is going to Germany, but which is in fact helping British Intelligence to identify risks to national security. Damned clever!

'Joe, Joe, are you all right?' He suddenly became aware of the woman's concerned voice, interfering with his train of thought, damn her! 'What? Oh yes, Abby, I'm fine thanks,' he answered reassuringly, though she could not help but notice the cold fury in his eyes.

'You seem disturbed by something, darling. Are you sure you're OK? Have I upset you?' she persisted, much to his irritation. 'Yes, honestly. I'm fine. I suppose I was just thinking what a heroic man Lazarus must be, to risk his life and his anonymity to save two children from the country he is fighting against.' Speaking these words almost made Brandt retch, but he realised that he couldn't afford to do anything which would cause this woman to be suspicious. She was, after all, his one and only route to King and he was determined to track him down and confront him.

'You're right, he is,' said Stevenson dreamily, thereby stoking Brandt's anger even more.

'Then I'd dearly love to meet him. Would that be possible?' asked Brandt eagerly. 'I'm sure my readers would be really interested in his story and, of course, I'd reveal nothing that could allow the British authorities to identify him. What do you say, honey?' Stevenson looked genuinely torn; on the one hand, she would have liked Lazarus to gain some recognition for the man he undoubtedly was and, of course, she would like to please Joe. But on the other hand, even to her naïve mind, it all seemed rather unlikely. An American writing a story about a German agent operating in London. 'I'm not so sure, Joe. It's difficult.'

'OK, darling, forget it,' he responded quickly and sharply. 'If I'm not to be trusted, then that's fine. We won't mention it again.'

'No, you're right, Joe. Of course I trust you. How could you suggest that I don't?' she said miserably. 'And it's only right that the people in America get an accurate picture of both sides in this war. It's just that, ever since meeting you I've been thinking that I want to stop giving him information.' She was speaking very quickly and nervously now, as if she wanted to get all this said before she had the chance to change her mind. 'In fact, I almost told him the last time we met. But now that it's clear that we've fallen in love with one another, I realise I must tell him. Since the war actually started and Dunkirk and now the bombing, it's all so horribly real. I just don't want to go on. What do you think, Joe, darling?'

While Brandt was repulsed by what he saw as the self-serving, weak drivel being spouted by Stevenson, especially that nonsense about them being in love, he realised that he could now more or less get her to do whatever he wished. 'I think you're right, sweetheart,' he said, smiling at the thought of his own imminent triumph over his old enemy. 'But I want to be there when you tell him. Just in case he tries anything on with you.' Abigail Stevenson snorted with derision, as she rejected that possibility out of hand, to which Brandt, declared that he would never forgive himself if anything were to happen to her. Relishing the supreme irony, he made the key point, 'after all, this guy is a German spy. He could be dangerous.' It was immediately obvious to Brandt that he had played things just right and he felt euphoric when Stevenson, wrongly interpreting his motives as ones of love and concern for her, agreed to request a meeting with Lazarus. She would, of course, give him no indication that she was planning to withdraw from his network of informants.

'OK, Abby. That's a deal!' said Brandt, a gleam of triumph in his eyes, which again Stevenson misinterpreted as the happiness of someone in love. 'Now. Shall we stay in bed, or would you like to put on that new dress I bought and come dine at The Ritz?' He was gratified to see Abigail Stevenson's eyes widen in excitement, before she replied with uncharacteristic suggestiveness. 'But, Joe. Why can't we do both?'

Chapter Thirty Seven

Monday, September 16th 1940, London.

On emptying the Post Office Box, to which his informants sent their routine information and requests for meetings, King was a little surprised by its contents. It had been some time since Abigail Stevenson had requested a meeting and now, just over a week since they had last met, she wanted 'to discuss a very urgent issue as soon as possible.' Intrigued, but wanting to give himself time to discuss this directly with Pym, he replied in the normal coded way, offering her a meeting at 8.15PM the following Tuesday at The Bandstand on Hampstead Heath.

****

Friday September 20th , 1940, London

Abigail Stevenson had been barely able to contain her excitement since receiving confirmation that Lazarus was indeed able to meet her. She was sure that Joe would be pleased with her and that her willingness to do this for him would cement their love even more. She did, however, have mixed emotions about her decision to inform Lazarus that she could no longer continue to supply him with information. Sitting at her ancient dining table and eating her usual breakfast of toast and butter accompanied by a pot of weak tea, she thought back over the months that she had known him. She had definitely come to like him a great deal; he was not at all like that odious Parsifal. What a revolting man he had proved to be, especially after he started to make suggestive comments and to leer at her in a totally unashamed way. He had hardly met her expectations of what the new Germany should stand for. But Lazarus, on the other hand, he was obviously very intelligent but also kind and sensitive, in a way that intelligent people rarely are. She thought briefly of some of the highly gifted colleagues at the Foreign Office and their almost complete lack of any form of social competence or grace. Lazarus was different; she thought him quite handsome, but also liked that he seemed totally oblivious to this. How unlike the strutting arrogant peacocks she had encountered, especially since the outbreak of war. 'Put a uniform on them and they think they are God's gift to womankind,' she snorted with derision. For a short time, she reflected with embarrassment, she had even had vague hopes that her relationship with him might have developed into something altogether more personal. But, despite being a caring man, Lazarus was far too professional for anything like that. Anyway, she would definitely be sorry never to see Lazarus again, but her life had taken on a whole new and better meaning since she had met and fallen in love with Joe.

In a total daydream now, she thought of how considerate and charming, yet at the same time how strong and assertive he is. She knew that, at present, it was highly likely that she did not satisfy him in bed, but, she told herself, she could be a quick learner. All things considered, she couldn't wait to see his face at their meeting after work, when she would tell him that he had his chance for a scoop with Lazarus. Her mind went racing on in a whirl of romance, fine dining, dancing and lovemaking to such an extent that she completely lost track of the time. Emerging from her reverie and realising that she would almost certainly be late for work and have to suffer a severe telling off by her miserable manager, she left the remains of her breakfast and put on her lightweight coat. Carelessly, she grabbed her handbag from where it lay on the sofa and, smiling broadly because today of all days not even Mrs Tripe's ill humour could affect her happy mood, she left the flat as quickly as possible. She was so preoccupied that she did not notice that her handbag was unfastened and that, as she snatched it up, a small blue book fell to the floor and skittered away under her old sideboard.

****

David Bernstein had spent another frustrating week responding to what had frequently been preposterous reports of 'Fifth Column' activity in and around London. As a consequence, no progress had been made in the pursuit of Lazarus and he had spent the last couple of hours at work preparing himself to break into the flat of the Stevenson woman. His deep, dark eyes were focused on the set of thin metal hooks that he would use to pick the flat's lock. One of his grandfathers, back in Heidelberg, had been a very successful locksmith and had, unknown to any of the women in the family, taught him how to pick locks. 'You never know when such a skill may come in handy, my boy,' he had chuckled with a mischievous glint in his eye. As he thought of his grandfather and their happy times together, a bittersweet wave of sorrow mixed with pleasure washed over him.

Returning to the task in hand, he once again went over his plan. He would make his entry in the early evening, when the woman would normally be enjoying either an after work drink with her colleagues or a night out with the American journalist. His calculation was that most of the other tenants in the house would, at that time, either be still on the journey home from work, or would be engaged in preparing or eating their dinner. At five thirty, he left Scotland Yard in Special Branch's own 'Black Cab', which parked in a side street near The Foreign Office. 'You wait here while I have a quick look at what's going on,' he said to the paunchy young officer who was his driver. The man looked bleary eyed and not quite alert, but Inspector Renton had assured him that this man was 'the best in the business' at tailing other vehicles. Bernstein immediately recognised the tall American journalist lounging by the entrance, carrying a large bouquet of flowers and with a taxi awaiting his instructions. He dodged back into the side street before he was spotted and updated his driver. 'It looks like our girl's going to be leaving in a taxi with her American boyfriend. Keep your engine running and I'll keep an eye on things. When I see her emerge and they get in the taxi, I'll jump in and we can follow them. The job's off if they go back to her place.' The driver simply nodded his head in understanding and went back to reading his Daily Mirror. As Bernstein waited for the woman to emerge from the depths of The Foreign Office, he prayed that the Luftwaffe's daily raid on the city would not arrive in the next hour. That would make following their taxi virtually impossible.

****

Abigail Stevenson was even more delighted than normal to see Joe Brand waiting for her with a bunch of flowers and a taxi, especially after her wretched day at work. She had been severely told off for lateness by that old trout Mrs Tripe and had been picked on by her the whole day. And there was also her diary. As soon as she had got on the tube to work, she had realised that it was not in her handbag. She was not overly concerned, as she had noticed that her handbag was open as she left her flat. She had immediately closed it, which, she reasoned, meant the book must still be somewhere in the flat. She was determined that now she should put behind her any lingering concern over its whereabouts and enjoy the evening with Joe. A thrill of excitement sped down her spine, almost making her shiver despite the relatively warm early evening, as she bade a hasty farewell to her work colleagues and ran into the waiting arms of Brandt. 'Oh Joe, thanks for picking me up,' she gushed. 'I've had a beast of a day. But now it feels much better.' Brandt made sure to give her a lingering kiss for the benefit of her co-workers, before ushering her carefully into the taxi and giving the driver his instructions. 'I've got such a lot to tell you, Joe,' she gabbled. 'I think you'll be very happy. You'll never guess...'

'Let's talk about that later, honey,' said Brandt, in a tone that allowed for no disagreement. 'After all, we have all the evening and we'll be there in a minute.' Slightly deflated by her lover's manner, Abigail Stevenson gazed at the flowers, before saying happily, 'Oh, Joe, they're beautiful. Thank you. But where are we going?' Brandt leaned across to kiss her and murmured, 'I thought we'd have an early dinner and go straight back to your place.'

****

Bernstein had to admit that Renton was correct about this driver; he had kept Brandt's taxi in sight all the way to the small restaurant, without ever running the risk of being spotted. It really was driving of the highest skill. Smiling, he tapped the driver on the shoulder. 'Thanks, it looks like they'll be in there a while. Can you take me to the Stevenson woman's flat and then I won't need you any more.'

'But I'm scheduled to be on duty till 2am...' the man protested.

'Don't worry about that. You'll still get paid,' Bernstein reassured him. 'We can say you were on call for me.'

'Thanks, guv,' the man replied happily, already clear in his mind what he would do with the rest of the evening.

Bernstein had come prepared to force an entry through the front door of the building, if necessary. He knew how to do this without leaving a trace and he had just arrived at the steps leading up to the front door, when a young couple, totally engrossed in one another, was emerging. He quickly reached the door before it closed and, with a muffled 'Thanks', went unchallenged into the bright and tidy hallway. From there he silently ascended the stairs until he reached the door to her flat. He smiled to himself, as he noted that the hallway smelled of various types of cooking and music could be heard from the flat opposite Stevenson's. His hunch about the other residents being engaged with their evening meal seemed to be a good one. He rapidly took out his tools and, using them deftly to avoid leaving any tell-tale scratches, had gained entrance to the flat in less than a minute.

Despite his belief that the woman would not return for a least a couple of hours, Bernstein resolved to get his search completed as quickly as possible. He removed his shoes, so as to make as little noise as possible, before he set about methodically searching the flat. The bedroom was a fairly small, though pleasant space with a double bed, wardrobe, chest of drawers and small dressing table. He swiftly looked under the bed and through the wardrobe, taking out any item with pockets and rifling through them. He then turned his attention to the chest of drawers and, having gone through the various underwear, blouses and sweaters, he carefully extracted each drawer in turn and verified that nothing was attached to the underside. Having done the same with the dressing table, he had again turned up a blank. A quick look on top of the wardrobe and behind the chest of drawers and a more thorough check for any loose floorboards and he had basically finished with the bedroom. This left the living room, kitchen and small bathroom. His first thought, as he turned to review the living room, was that Stevenson had left in a hurry that morning. The uneaten toast and half full cup of tea on the table stood in marked contrast to the neat and tidy bedroom. He felt a tingle of hope that perhaps the urgency of her exit that morning may have caused her to make some small mistake that would give him the information he craved. Without success, he looked through the small bookcase, taking out each book for inspection and felt under the cushions of the small sofa and chair. Once again, he checked carefully for any loose floorboards which might conceal a hiding place. The kitchen yielded nothing and he was about to move into the bathroom, when he realised that, while he had done a thorough search, he had omitted to look under the sideboard. His heart began to race as he caught sight of the small, blue book pressed right up against the skirting board. However, he proceeded with caution, in case it had been placed there deliberately as some sort of check on whether the place had been searched. He doubted that very much and carefully picked up the book, which he soon realised was Stevenson's diary. He could hardly believe his luck and came to the immediate conclusion that she would not have left such an important item here deliberately. No, he reasoned, somehow this must have been dropped in her haste to get out of the flat this morning. Almost laughing at the absurdity of it, he realised that, had she not been late for work, he would in all probability have been wasting his time in searching the flat.

He sat down at the table and began to leaf through the book, from back to front so as to see the most recent items first. It wasn't long before he found what he was looking for. In the section for Tuesday 24th September, she had written: *'L. 20.15 H.H. B.S.'* While he was not sure what the last part of the entry meant, he was instantly certain that 'L' referred to Lazarus and that the figures represented the time of the meeting. He swiftly made an exact copy of the note in the diary and then began to review previous entries. Almost all the most recent ones referred to 'Joe', who he assumed was the American journalist. There were also frequent mentions of 'L', followed by a time and abbreviated location. Feverishly, he searched through the address section of the book for anything that might look like contact details for 'L', but he could not find anything. Having ensured that there was nothing else of value in the book, he carefully replaced it in exactly the same spot he had found it, completed his search of the rest of the flat and quietly exited both the flat and the building. He was sure that Renton would want him to call with this information as soon as possible, even if it meant disturbing his evening's entertainment. He would no doubt now be sitting in his favourite armchair, puffing that dreadful pipe, with his family all around him listening to the radio. Nevertheless, for the first time they had a definite lead to Lazarus and, with luck, they would soon decipher the location and thus know where he was going to be on the following Tuesday evening. Bernstein's fresh young face grinned at the prospect of his Inspector's likely response to his 'fishing expedition'.

****

Brandt's spirits had lifted considerably, as soon as the woman had told him about her arrangement to meet King on the coming Tuesday. He had chosen the restaurant well, as there were very few other diners and no one within earshot, as his dining partner excitedly recounted details of the planned meeting. In response, his face covered itself with a broad smile, his dark eyes flashing in the candlelight, which was virtually the only illumination in their part of the romantic cellar. In truth, he was beginning to find the whole business of romancing this woman increasingly tiresome, but he reassured himself that it would be worth it, when he had King in the sights of his pistol. 'That's great, honey,' he replied, touching her hands across the small, square shaped table. 'I really appreciate it. But you didn't mention anything about me, did you?'

Abigail Stevenson looked almost hurt. 'Of course not, Joe! I'm not completely stupid. I merely told him that I have something very important to discuss with him. I really don't know how he'll react, when he realises that I've brought you to meet him. I must admit that I am concerned about that.' Abigail Stevenson's pretty face creased into a worried frown at the thought of this, but in contrast, Brandt almost laughed out loud. He had no difficulty in imagining how the Englishman would react. Once more he had to suppress his genuine feelings and responded, 'That's no problem, Abby. I understand he may not want to talk at all. That's fine. Just a chance to pitch the idea to him, that's all I want.'

The young woman seemed to be put at her ease by this reply and, smiling, squeezed his hand. 'I'll be so happy when I'm out of this whole business, Joe. Then we can start our lives together properly. I was thinking, I may even leave The Foreign Office. Try my hand at something different. After all that's gone on, it wouldn't seem right to me, staying on there.' She looked at Brandt, for all the world like an unhappy child, craving the basic reassurance that everything would be all right. Brandt knew exactly what she wanted to hear and, with an earnest expression on his face, said, 'Of course. It's a big strain on you, honey. And I'm sure you'll be glad when you don't have to see this guy ever again. But let's not make too many big decisions too quickly. You can quit, if you like, but there's plenty of time for that.'

At that moment a very small waiter, with thinning black hair, slicked back to reveal a narrow, rodent-like face, appeared noiselessly at their table to take their orders. Despite his obsequious manner, Brandt despatched him fairly quickly to bring a bottle of Chianti and to place the food order with the kitchen. Brandt found the wine to be of mediocre quality, but he was happy enough to toast long life and happiness, to the evident delight of his dining partner. In the pause between the starter and the main course, he approached the one question, over which he still had some concerns. 'Hey, Abby,' he began lightly, 'You've told me when you're going to meet Lazarus but not where. In some crowded place, right?'

Abigail Stevenson looked pleased with herself, as she was able to reply in the negative. 'Not at all, Joe,' she said smilingly. 'We are to meet at The Bandstand on Hampstead Heath. It's on Parliament Hill and at that time of the evening, it should be quite private. I wouldn't say it's remote, but it's a good spot for a clandestine meeting.'

Brandt's heart leapt at this news. It meant that this whole thing might be resolved with far fewer complications than he had expected. Fading light, in a remote place. He would surely be able to arrange things to look like she shot King and then turned the gun on herself. He should have plenty of time to get away and with any luck, those idiotic police would think it was a crime of passion. But, crucial to all this would be the location itself. Somehow, he had to get to see it before the confrontation on Tuesday. He masked his face with an air of concern, before saying, 'I'm not so happy with that, Abby. You being alone with him in a remote place. Do you know where it is?' On seeing her nod and noting the mounting worry on her face, he made his suggestion. 'Let's take a cab out there, right now, after we've finished here. It'll be near the time of the meeting and we can plan how we're going to play it.' Reaching over to squeeze her hand, he managed to make himself sound extremely concerned. 'You see honey, we don't know how this guy will react when you tell him that you want out.' He was pleased to see her nodding in agreement and went on to insist. 'That's settled then. We'll finish up here and then go see how the land lies. Now, let's talk about something else. How'd you like to go away for a weekend?' He knew, of course, that this would never happen, but they were able to discuss the possibilities, excitedly, until the end of the meal.

The evening, Brandt reflected, had gone perfectly so far; the arrangements to meet King could hardly have been better; the meal rather better than he had expected after the first sip of that wine and, miraculously, there was a taxi just outside the restaurant, as he and Abigail Stevenson had emerged into the pleasant evening air. The driver dropped them off in good time at Dartmouth Park, from where it was a short walk onto The Heath. The light was beginning to fade as they walked briskly across Parliament Hill and the famous old Bandstand came into view. Abigail Stevenson was having trouble keeping up with

Brandt as he moved swiftly down the pathway, her shoes not being the most appropriate for such speedy walking. 'Joe! Slow down, please. I can't keep up with you,' she wailed, as he forged ahead, totally caught up in the moment. He saw the paths, coming from all directions to meet at The Bandstand, which was a simple, open construction of wrought iron overlooking the sequence of Highgate Ponds. The area around The Bandstand was relatively clear, only two clumps of bushes about twice the height of a man to the north and south west, the nearest about six yards away. Having taken in and assessed the scene, he turned to see a wretched looking Abigail Stevenson hobbling towards him. 'I'm so sorry, Abby,' he said rushing to help her, 'I just wanted to work out how best we should approach this.' He put his arm around her slim back and under her arms so that he could support her weight. 'Oh that's better, Joe,' she said with a tight grimace. 'I didn't dress this morning for hiking, you know.' Brandt grinned wolfishly at her, 'Don't worry honey. I'll make it up to you when we get back to your flat. But now, I want you to listen very carefully to me. This is how we're going to play things on Tuesday.'

****

Much, much later that night, after he had pretended that their mundane lovemaking had met his every desire, she had fallen asleep in his arms with a peaceful smile playing on her face. He, in contrast lay fully awake, listening to the distant explosions, as the East End and the docks took yet another hammering from the Luftwaffe. His black eyes were glinting with hatred, as he contemplated his final revenge on King.

Chapter Thirty Eight.

Saturday, 21ˢᵗ September 1940, Scotland Yard, London.

'You did excellent work on Friday, David,' said Inspector Renton with a generous smile, before raising both palms of his hands in a gesture of frustration. 'But, blast it! Knowing when Stevenson is going to meet with Lazarus does us no good, if we don't know the location.'

'We could always try following her,' Bernstein replied, conscious that they were no nearer to deciphering the final part of the message he had copied from the woman's diary. Renton had been delighted when he had been told of the success of the breaking and entering. But, having agreed to meet on the Saturday morning at The Yard, and having spent a couple of fruitless hours trying to make sense of the last part of the message, his optimism was beginning to fade. 'I think I'd like to keep that as a last resort,' he reasoned. 'Too many things could go wrong too easily. We lose her in crowds or our man Lazarus runs his own check that she's not being followed, sees us and scarpers. No, we must try to work out where the hell they're meeting.' The older man punched his left palm with his right fist in irritation. Not even a good pipe full of his favourite tobacco was easing his growing anxiety that this may be their one chance to catch Lazarus and that the blighter may yet slip through their hands.

'Would you mind nipping down to the canteen and picking us both up a cuppa and a sandwich,' he said, more as an order than a request. 'Maybe salmon would be good, huh? We could both use a bit of brain food.' David Bernstein was glad to recognise something of his guv'nor's natural humour reassert itself and with a laugh and a 'Coming right up, sir,' jumped to his feet and made for the door.

The canteen was a large, airless room in the basement of Scotland Yard, its long refectory style tables rapidly filling up with noisily chattering police officers, as the time approached midday. In his relatively brief period at The Yard, the easy going and optimistic Bernstein had become a popular colleague with many officers and, as he joined the queue to be served, he nodded and acknowledged several waves and friendly greetings. Predictably, salmon was once again off the menu and he settled for two rounds of cheese and egg sandwiches, accompanied by two sizeable pots of tea. His tray being heavily laden with the two lunches, he was grateful that the canteen door was held open for him, and he raised his eyes to thank the officer. To his pleasure, he saw that it was the driver from the previous evening and Bernstein called out to him, over his shoulder as he passed out of the canteen. 'Good Morning! I hope you enjoyed your early finish.'

    To his surprise, the officer replied brightly, 'Actually, I didn't finish early after all.' There was something in the officer's tone of voice that made Bernstein pause. He stopped a police cadet on his way to lunch, thrusting the tray into his hands saying, 'Sorry, mate. Can you just hold onto this for me for a minute or so? Thanks.' Leaving the hapless young cadet holding his lunch tray, Bernstein hurried back into the canteen to catch up with the driver. Touching him gently on the shoulder, he asked, 'Excuse me. Sorry to bother you. But what did you mean that you didn't have an early finish?' The heavy man grimaced and rolled his eyes before leading Bernstein away to a relatively quiet corner of the canteen, shouting over his shoulder, 'Sorry, lads. Be with you in a minute. There's just something I have to do first.'

    Once they were out of earshot of his friends, the driver said, 'Sorry about that. But you know how it is? I don't want my mates to see me as some sort of a teacher's pet.' Bernstein was by this time totally confused. 'I'm afraid I don't understand... all I wanted to know is why you didn't finish early after you'd dropped me off at the woman's flat yesterday.'

    'But that's exactly it,' replied the driver. 'I decided to go and see if I could track our couple after they left that restaurant.' Seeing the look of astonishment cross Bernstein's face, he went on to explain. 'Since being a nipper, I've always wanted to be a detective. As a uniformed plod, I don't get much chance to try myself against the job, so I thought I'd give it a go and I didn't want my pals to know. Especially as it was basically a waste of time.' Eager to hear everything now, Bernstein said quickly, 'You mean you didn't see them again? Tell me everything that happened.'

    'Oh no!' the driver replied, his usually bored and exhausted looking face lighting up with interest and excitement. 'As luck would have it, there were no other cabs around when they came out, so I picked them up.' Bernstein gaped at his beaming face. 'You did what?'

'Yes. But the American simply told me to take them to Holland Park. You know, not far from the edge of Hampstead Heath and I dropped them off there.' Looking somewhat crestfallen, he added, 'I'm afraid that's all there is. As I said, bit of a waste of time.'

The young driver was astonished to see the beaming face of Bernstein laughing out loud, as he punched the air and shouted 'Hampstead Heath! Of bloody course!' He then heartily clapped the confused driver on the back and cried, 'Now you come with me, my lad, and tell all this to Inspector Renton. Don't worry about your lunch. You can have mine. And the Inspector's too, I'll bet.' Totally bemused and thinking perhaps it was true what everyone said about Special Branch – that they're all a bit mad – he allowed himself to be ushered out of the canteen. Stopping only to pick up the tray from the still bewildered cadet, Bernstein led him quickly to the Inspector's office.

Once the driver had retold his story, Renton's face creased into a huge grin. 'So you want to get into detective work, eh my boy? Well, you'll do for me! I like such initiative. I'll have a word with your guv'nor and get you transferred over here.' The driver almost choked on his half of Bernstein's sandwich, 'You really mean it, sir? That'd be excellent!' Renton, all thoughts of lunch now far from his mind, pulled from his bottom desk drawer a large map of the area of Holland Park and Hampstead Heath. As he spread the map out on his desk, everything else having been pushed to one side, he said almost to himself, 'Now. Let's see, the American got you to drop them in Holland Park... so the meeting point is probably in that part of the Heath. Remind me, David. What exactly did the note say?'

Almost as soon as Bernstein had replied, 'the letter 'B', sir,' the driver's face lit up again. 'Begging your pardon, sir, but that's got to be The Bandstand.' Pointing to the map with the last part of his sandwich, he continued rapidly. 'It's just there, on Parliament Hill. I grew up in this area and it was always a favourite meeting place, you know, sir...' His face now glowed bright red, as the two Special Branch officers looked at him expectantly. Swallowing his last piece of bread, he muttered 'meeting girls and that, sir.'

Renton sat back happily in his chair, his hands clasped behind his head, a sure sign that all was right in his world. 'Well, David and ...?' 'Catesby, sir, Derek Catesby,' replied the driver. 'Well, David and Derek.

It looks like we've cracked this message and we owe it all to you, Derek.' After further thanks and congratulations, Catesby was dismissed, with both the order that he keep to himself everything he had heard about the case and the promise from Renton that he would do all in his power to expedite his immediate transfer to Special Branch.

Once Catesby had left the office, Renton and Bernstein immediately began discussing the implications of what they had learned. They were especially interested in why the American had been involved in reconnoitring the meeting spot. 'I just don't get it sir,' said Bernstein, running his hand through his mop of unruly black hair. 'Unless he plans to go to the meeting as well.'

'But that makes no sense at all, David,' countered Renton firmly. 'Why on earth would Lazarus agree to meet him? It'd be a terrible risk. And why would the woman want him to be there? She is committing treason, after all.'

Bernstein gazed, unseeing, out of the famous round windows of Renton's tower room office. 'Unless, sir,' he suggested, 'Lazarus doesn't know anything about the American.' The Inspector looked sharply at his subordinate, who went on to develop his line of thought. 'Let's just suppose that Lazarus thinks that he's meeting only Stevenson. But for some reason, she has involved the American journalist. Maybe the Yank thinks that he'll get a story, she's besotted with him and has offered this to please him. Who knows? Maybe she's scared to meet Lazarus alone, in such a place at such a time? Maybe she needs her buddy there to ride shotgun for her? Whatever the reason, I think we must operate on the assumption that Lazarus doesn't know about the American.'

'I see your point, David,' said Renton thoughtfully. 'Right, let's work on that basis. But it does, of course, add a complication. There's something not quite right with all this. It doesn't smell right to me. After all, the American is also taking a great risk, consorting with a German agent and a traitor... and she must have told him she's a traitor, mustn't she? Would he really do that?'

'Yes, I see that, sir,' replied Bernstein pensively. 'But let's not forget that America isn't yet at war. As a neutral, representing people in a neutral country, he might be interested in the Jerry side of things. But I agree, he's running a tremendous risk and I suspect that there's more to his motivation than we understand.'

'Agreed, David,' concluded Renton decisively. 'But fore-warned is fore-armed, as they say. And for sure, we'll find out on Tuesday what's going on. In the meantime, I suggest we visit The Bandstand this evening to plan our strategy for then. We mustn't lose sight of the fact that Stevenson and the American are bit part players. It's Lazarus I want. And I won't be happy unless we get him alive.'

Chapter Thirty Nine

Monday, September 23rd 1940, St James's Park, London.

The sun was beginning to lose its warmth as King approached the park bench where he was scheduled to meet Professor Pym. His memory might have been playing tricks on him, but he could have sworn that it was this self-same bench, on which he had given his agreement that he would take part in the operation. Hardened by his experiences of the past months, King was increasingly inured to the attraction of coincidence and quietly opened his copy of *The Times*. Before starting to read, he noticed the feverish anti-aircraft gun crews going through their drills, in preparation for the next German raid. These had come every day or night and frequently both for over two weeks now and Londoners, especially in the East End, were having to get used to the grim business of spending the night in whatever shelter they could find. King had had to spend some time in the East End and was horrified at the scale of the destruction there. On the other hand, he was also hugely impressed by the increasing resilience being shown by many Londoners. Of course there were problems; the rest centres for those made homeless by the bombing, especially in areas such as Bethnal Green, were finding it increasingly difficult to accommodate all who needed shelter. The result was that, as soon as the air raid sirens sounded, more and more people were seeking shelter in the underground stations. King wasn't entirely sure what the change in German tactics meant; he would have thought that, in order to prosecute a successful invasion, they would certainly need control of the air over The English Channel. The bombing of London seemed to him to have little strategic value, other than to try to undermine morale, a goal which to date it was definitely not achieving.

He was considering this issue, when Pym arrived. Despite the sunny afternoon, he looked decidedly older and more careworn than he had when they had last met, less than two weeks previously. His usually tanned features were pale and drawn, his hair appeared to be thinning at an alarming rate and King thought that he looked like he hadn't recently enjoyed any fresh air and had had little sleep. 'Are you feeling alright, sir?' he asked in a concerned voice. 'Only you look a little peaky, if you don't mind me saying.' Pym had sat down on the bench with an uncharacteristic groan, very unlike his typical, energetic and lively self.

'I'm fine, thanks, John. I surely can't complain about a few nights' lost sleep, when one considers what some people are having to put up with. Anyway,' he continued, clearly making an effort to remain purposeful, 'I didn't ask you here to talk about me and any tiny problems I may have. I'm afraid I have some bad news for you, John. You remember that you reported that you had tried without success to contact Martha Perrygo?' King nodded in acknowledgement before the Professor continued, 'Well, I've seen a report from the Sevenoaks police. Apparently, she committed suicide by hanging almost three weeks ago.'

King's face drained of all colour. 'I don't believe it!' he protested. 'She was as tough as old boots. She'd never have done such a thing. She'd have seen it as a coward's way out. And one thing Martha Perrygo was not, was a coward. And anyway, why? Why would she do such a thing now, when she was firing on all cylinders, desperate to give us information that she hoped fervently would assist a German invasion?' Shaking his head emphatically, he concluded 'It just doesn't make sense. There must be another explanation.'

'Yes, John, it worries me too,' agreed Pym, a frown wrinkling his face. 'And that's not all. Apparently the old biddy who ran the newsagent just around the corner from Martha Perrygo's house fell down the stairs and broke her neck just before the suicide. Coincidence, don't you think?' King now looked even more concerned, 'I should say so, sir. And also both are methods of murder which could quite easily be faked, one as suicide, the other as an accident. But who would do such a thing and why?'

'That's just it, John,' replied Pym with some exasperation, 'I haven't a clue. I just know that it's odd and, until we know what's going on, you should be even more careful.' Having taken a couple of minutes to digest all he had just learned, King gave a brief verbal report on his recent and future activities. Pym interrupted him, only when he mentioned the planned meeting with Abigail Stevenson. 'She asked for the meeting, you say?' the Professor asked with evident concern.

'Yes, sir. She said that she had something very important to discuss with me,' replied the younger man while swatting an irritating bee with his newspaper. 'And what might that be, do you think?' prompted Pym. King paused before replying, 'I'm not really sure. To be honest, the significance of what she reports from The Foreign Office has declined somewhat over the past couple of months. Obvious, I suppose, as the war develops and other types of information become a priority. The only thing I've come up with is that maybe she wants to stop acting as an informer.'

'What on earth makes you think that?' asked Pym urgently, 'Could she have been approached by a genuine German agent who managed to slip through our net? If so, this changes everything.'

'Well, as you know,' began King in response, 'I've felt that her enthusiasm for supplying information has declined markedly in recent weeks. I put this down to her genuine horror at the fall of France and now the Blitz. But I also think something has changed in her private life... maybe she has met someone and this has changed things for her.'

'Well,' intoned Pym ominously, 'if that's the case, we shall have to consider what we do about Miss Stevenson. We'll have a much clearer idea after Tuesday, but I must say I don't like this at all. Maybe I should ask McNair to keep an eye on you?'

'That's absolutely unnecessary, sir,' said King lightly, 'I've arranged to meet her in a safe place and I don't see her as dangerous. I'll get to the bottom of it and report back. Now, what do you make of the Luftwaffe's shift in strategy? Other than as an attempt to destroy British morale before an invasion, I can't make sense of it.'

'But that's it, John,' Pym replied with renewed energy. 'Our latest intelligence tells us that the 'Huns' have halted any preparations for an invasion. They seem to accept that they've achieved neither control of the air nor of The Channel and they won't risk their army in such circumstances. Of course, it's a bit early to be absolutely certain, but we believe the invasion has at least been postponed, if not cancelled.'

'But that's marvellous news,' King said, a great grin spreading across his face. 'Because we all know that this was their big chance. Our army has men, but very little else with which to resist an invasion, but next year that would be very different.' For several minutes, the two men discussed the possible implications of this for King's mission. It could be that he would have to work hard to maintain the morale of his informants, who would face the disappointment of a postponement, or even a cancellation of the expected invasion. Eventually they parted, just as the first air raid sirens began to sound over London, Pym still very uneasy about King's imminent meeting on Hampstead Heath.

****

Bernstein and Renton spent much of the day disagreeing about how they should handle the operation. The Inspector argued that, in order to minimise the risk of frightening Lazarus off, they alone should deal with it. They could easily conceal themselves in the nearby shrubbery and the two of them should be more than sufficient to overcome the German agent who would be taken totally by surprise. They discussed again what the likely role of the American journalist might be in all this and Renton remained certain that he was only after a great scoop for his newspaper syndicate. 'Just think, David,' he argued persuasively, 'How big a hit would a story on *'The War in Britain from a Nazi Agent's Viewpoint'* be in the many areas of the USA, which are sympathetic to Hitler's *Reich*?' While Bernstein could see the logic of his Inspector's opinion, he also felt a nagging doubt in the back of his mind that this was a misreading of the reason for the American's presence. Something didn't quite feel right about the whole thing, but try as he might, he had been unable to articulate this cogently enough to convince his superior. 'Forget the American,' Renton said dismissively, 'He's a bit part player in this. Just focus on Lazarus. He's the big prize.' Recognising the look of disappointment on Bernstein's face, Renton eventually compromised. 'Look, David,' he had said sympathetically, 'I can understand your concerns, so how about this? We deploy officers at every entrance and exit to The Heath, but they move into position only ten minutes after the planned time of the meeting. We want to give them time to show their hands, but if it all goes wrong at The Bandstand, there's a good chance that we'll still get our man. We can alert them to move in by police whistle.' Having reached agreement, Renton excitedly set about organising his back up teams for the operation on the following day.

Chapter Forty

Tuesday, September 24th, 1940, London.

After receiving the Professor's instruction to observe King's meeting on Hampstead Heath, McNair had decided to leave nothing to chance. The 'old man' had seemed uncharacteristically agitated and concerned and McNair had therefore decided to follow his young protégé all the way from his flat. He knew the time and location of the meeting which, he reasoned, would allow him to conduct his pursuit at a comfortable distance. His plan was to watch King enter The Heath and then quickly make his way to approach The Bandstand from the opposite direction. He knew the area around The Bandstand and was aware that a couple of dense clumps of bushes would afford him the screen to observe the meeting at close quarters and to intervene, if necessary. The Professor had been absolutely adamant on that score, 'Take your Webley, Mac and if it looks like things might be going pear shaped, make sure he's unharmed. I don't care about the Stevenson woman.' Like King, McNair had felt that Pym was over reacting, Stevenson could hardly constitute a real threat, surely. But there was something in the Professor's anxious look that had caused him to take his warning seriously.

From his vantage point on the opposite side of the road, McNair observed King as he left the bookshop and turned towards the nearest underground station. He was just about to copy his target's movements, by turning the corner out of Charing Cross Road, when a section of scaffolding, erected to enable repairs to a bomb damaged property, fell onto his head, immediately rendering him unconscious. King, without ever knowing he should have had one, had lost his protective shadow.

****

Having issued the final instructions to the back-up squads, Renton and Bernstein equipped themselves with firearms from the official store at Scotland Yard, before making their way to Hampstead Heath. A thin mist was starting to gather as they hid themselves in the bushes a few yards away from the deserted Bandstand, both men very aware of that tingle of excitement that comes at the end of a long pursuit. Some twenty-five minutes after they had taken up their stations, Renton tapped Bernstein gently on the arm and indicated the figure of a man approaching The Bandstand. Over six feet tall, dressed in a thin overcoat and wearing a hat over his black hair, the bespectacled and moustachioed man first walked past The Bandstand, before turning back and heading straight for it.

As he had made his way towards Hampstead Heath, King had felt more troubled than for some time. Since the previous day's meeting with Professor Pym, he had been considering whether or not the Professor had been right to be so concerned about this meeting. Approaching The Bandstand, he felt a shiver of anxiety slip down his spine as he remembered turning down the offer of McNair's support. Relax, old chap, he encouraged himself with a grin, a bit of mist and you get all in a funk. Having used his normal procedure of first passing and noting that the place was deserted, he turned to enter the meeting place.

****

'OK now Abby, let's go over it one last time,' whispered Brandt, with a sense of pent up urgency that Abigail Stevenson had rarely, if ever heard before. 'I know it's tedious, but we have to get this right. I simply can't let you walk into danger.' In fact, Brandt was inwardly cursing the woman's inability to grasp a set of simple instructions. Impatiently, he kept repeating to himself, 'I can't let her mess the whole thing up now. King shouldn't be too dangerous, but it would be much better if I can take him totally by surprise.'

Looking pale and drawn, Abigail Stevenson recited slowly by rote, 'I will approach The Bandstand from the direction of Dartmouth Park. My main task is to get Lazarus to position his back towards Highgate Ponds because, five minutes after me, you will approach from that direction. This will allow you to remain unseen and he'll not be scared off, before you get the chance to speak with him.' Secretly fingering the grip of his pistol, which was securely hidden in the deep pockets of his trench coat, Brandt replied, 'Excellent, honey. You've got it. Now, let's go see this Lazarus guy.'

****

Thankfully, the mist had not thickened as Renton and Bernstein gazed towards the solitary figure, leaning on the wrought iron railing of

The Bandstand. The younger officer could sense the tension in the posture of his superior and would not have been surprised, were the Inspector to have ordered that they pre-empt the meeting by rushing Lazarus there and then. He still had the uneasy feeling that there were aspects of the meeting which were unknown both to himself and to Inspector Renton. Moreover, his initial sight of the German spy Lazarus had, in a way that he couldn't readily explain to himself, disturbed him even more. If he felt on edge, however, he was acutely aware that as the minutes passed, Renton was looking ever more stressed and was seemingly at the end of his patience. As he leaned towards him, Bernstein feared that he was about to give the word to take Lazarus without delay. This possibility was aborted when Stevenson gradually came into view through the mist, as she made her way slowly towards The Bandstand from the eastern edge of the Heath. He heard a frustrated sigh from his Inspector, whose body slumped back from its alert state and silently gave thanks for the woman's timely appearance.

As he peered through the gloom towards London, King felt a surge of feeling for the embattled city, preparing itself not for a quiet and peaceful sleep, but to be revisited by the squadrons of Luftwaffe bombers which would surely come during the night. He caught sight of Abigail Stevenson walking, it seemed to him rather jerkily, as if being pushed towards a meeting against her will. He raised a hand to her in acknowledgement and, as she joined him in The Bandstand, he was concerned to note that she seemed to have reverted to a closed, almost furtive demeanour. 'Hello, Abigail,' he began warmly. 'It's good to see you again. But I must say that I'm intrigued by what it might be that you have to tell me.' He was disappointed to see that she would not look him in the eye, as he gazed at her sympathetically. He was taken by surprise when, instead of replying, she moved carefully around The Bandstand. In order to continue speaking with her, he had to mirror her movement and was now facing away from the Ponds below. He thought this a rather odd and pointless thing to have done, but, being more concerned to discover the purpose of the meeting, he gave it little attention. Finally, she began in a voice hoarse with emotion. 'Thank you for agreeing to see me at such short notice Lazarus. And yes,' looking him in the eye now, with a mixture of sadness and relief, she continued, 'There is something important that I wish to discuss with you.'

Abigail Stevenson's manoeuvre in The Bandstand meant that

she was now standing with her back to the bushes, which concealed the two Special Branch officers. Perhaps more pertinently, Lazarus was now directly facing them. 'Damn!' muttered Renton softly. 'Why the hell did she do that? For us, it's the worst possible position for the blasted German to adopt.'

The answer to the Inspector's question was soon evident, when a third figure began quickly to approach The Bandstand from the direction of The Ponds. He was walking on the grass, rather than the gravel of the pathway, a strategy that had the effect of softening the noise of his rapid footsteps. 'Looks like our American friend is putting in an appearance, David,' whispered Renton excitedly. 'Keep your eyes and ears open. Things are sure to speed up now..'

King's entire attention was focused on Abigail Stevenson, as she prepared to unburden herself to him. He looked on with an understanding smile as she at last began her explanation. 'As you know, I've been loyal to Germany for over two years now and I've offered you a great deal of information.' King nodded in agreement as she continued. 'But now, Lazarus, I hope you can understand that things are different. The return of the wounded from France and this terrible bombing of London and the other cities have made what I'm doing seem much more real in its consequences and, frankly, unjustifiable. I had my reasons for what I've done and I don't regret anything, but I don't see them as valid any longer.' The woman was sobbing openly now and, without thinking, King began to move across The Bandstand to offer her some comfort. He was just passing a handkerchief to her, when he was shocked to hear, coming from behind him, an oddly familiar voice speaking German.

'Hello, John. It's been a couple of years, hasn't it? I do hope that you don't mind if we speak in German. I'd rather this woman doesn't understand everything that we're saying.' Stunned by the use of his real name, King spun round, his eyes quickly taking in the gun pointing directly at him and a smiling Joachim Brandt. 'Who'd have thought John, all those years ago in Heidelberg and more recently in Berlin, when I swore that I'd have my revenge on you, that we'd meet again here, in the heart of London? But, of course, I forget my manners,' he continued smoothly, 'Perhaps I should call you Lazarus? That seems to be your preferred name these days. I'm sure that you can imagine how much

I've been looking forward to this moment, especially when I'd thought that your 'accident' in the Alps had denied me this pleasure. I suppose to call yourself Lazarus was some kind of pathetic joke?'

Before King could offer any reply, Abigail Stevenson, her face a picture of fear and betrayal, shouted. 'What's going on here? Joe, I don't understand. Why are you speaking in German and why do you have a gun? Oh God! What have I done?' King had to react quickly to catch the distraught woman as she fainted, an action to which Brandt responded harshly. 'Ever the British gentleman, eh John? You should have left the love-struck fool to fall onto the floor. The blow might have knocked some common-sense into her.'

'What the hell's going on?' hissed Renton, his normally calm face a mask of confusion and uncertainty. 'What're they saying?'

'I can't hear every word because of the distance,' replied Bernstein urgently, 'But the American is definitely speaking in German and the Stevenson woman has fainted with shock. She's obviously no idea what's happening. And it looks to me like the American has Lazarus covered with a gun. Why the blazes would he do that?' Bernstein was now absolutely certain that neither he, nor the Inspector understood fully what was taking place in The Bandstand and he whispered to his superior. 'I can't hear enough to understand everything. I'm going to crawl a bit nearer, to the edge of the bushes to try to get a clearer picture.'

'I'm very tempted to go in now, David, but I'll give you five minutes. Then we move.' Bernstein nodded grimly, before carefully crawling his way forward and to the very edge of the bushes.

King realised that he was now in a hopeless position; his decision to prevent Abigail Stevenson from falling to the ground had eliminated any opportunity he might have had to tackle Brandt. Now, as the woman started to regain consciousness, he found himself defenceless and prepared himself for the worst. Much to the Englishman's surprise, however, the German did not immediately shoot him, but shook his head with a wistful smile, as if he had just realised something of great importance. 'You know, John,' he began in an almost sad tone, 'right from that day in Heidelberg in '33 up to this last second, I really thought I hated you. I was absolutely convinced that I did, because you always seemed so sure of who you are, where you belong and what you stand for. Did you never realise that all I wanted was your acceptance of me and the path I've taken? Would that really have been so difficult for you?'

King was suddenly transported back to a far simpler time, when he and the man now facing him with a gun had been the closest of friends. A great wave of sadness for lost fellowship and innocence broke over him as he softly admitted, 'I simply couldn't do it, Joachim. Not even for your friendship. We'd become opposites you see...' Eagerly Brandt interrupted, 'But that's just it, John! That's exactly what I've just this minute realised.' King looked at his old friend, a frown of uncertainty covering his face. 'Actually,' the German continued, confident in his own opinion and clearly wanting to persuade his old friend of this now self evident truth, 'we are two sides of the same coin. Mirror images of one another. You could say even brothers.'

'I'm afraid I don't understand,' said King in genuine confusion, 'what do you mean.'

'Don't you see, John? It's obvious really. You are an Englishman pretending to be German, and I am a German pretending to be an American. Both of us are what we have been made into by such deceptions and neither of us really knows who or what we are any more.'

As soon as he heard Lazarus address the American as Joachim, Bernstein's brow furrowed in concentration. The man seemed deucedly familiar and, for that matter, so did the name. Infuriatingly, he still couldn't bring to mind who the man might be and how he, himself, might know him. Full understanding began to dawn, however, as soon as the person they had taken to be the American journalist called Lazarus 'Dr King'. The Special Branch officer's heart began to pound and he felt quite lightheaded, How could this be? he thought in panic, I know only one Dr King, who has any connection to Germany and he was killed in a mountain accident in '39. Squinting through the mist and the fading light, Bernstein focused on the man Special Branch knew as Lazarus. He had thought that there was something familiar about him when he had first caught sight of him. To be sure, the hair colour and moustache had in some odd way seemed wrong, as was the fact that he had been wearing spectacles. Well, the glasses had fallen off somewhere and he tried to imagine the man with fairer hair. Within seconds, he recognised with a start that Lazarus was none other than John King, the person who had been instrumental in helping himself, his sister and his parents to leave Nazi Germany. Almost instantaneously, it also dawned on him that the 'American' was, in fact, the SS officer Joachim Brandt, who he had also known in Heidelberg. Moreover, he now realised that Brandt had been the man he had seen some three months ago in RAF uniform in Dover. Silently cursing his own stupidity for not recognising the Nazi at that time, he quickly realised both that Brandt was an SS agent and that he had infiltrated Britain during the retreat to Dunkirk. But why was John King acting as the German agent Lazarus? And why was Brandt pointing a gun at him? Looking quickly at his watch, he saw with a start that his five minutes were almost up and that he had no choice but to return to the Inspector and discuss what to do in light of these revelations.

****

King was initially shocked and outraged by his former friend's conviction that they were alike and he responded dismissively, 'You can't be serious! You've come to represent everything that I hate. How can you say such a ridiculous thing?' Again Brandt wrong footed King with his almost sympathetic reply, 'Of course I understand that it's hard for you to accept, John,' he said with a smile. 'I felt exactly like that until just now, when I realised that we may have chosen opposite sides in this war, but we, ourselves, who we are as people and what we do in the name of our values and beliefs, are very much the same. It's this that makes us brothers.'

King suddenly felt dizzy and disoriented. Brandt's assertions had reawakened in him the real doubts about the moral justifiability of his actions as a spy, with which he had been grappling since the death of Albert Shaw. Surely, he reasoned desperately, it can't be true. I must be better and completely dissimilar to him. It can't be possible that we are in any way alike. The two former friends stood staring at one another in silence for a full two minutes, the one holding the gun smiling benevolently, as if waiting for the other to catch up with his blinding insight. King, however, was acutely disturbed by the thought of having to confront such an uncomfortable truth about himself and determined to try to turn the conversation in what would, for him, be a much safer direction. He calculated that Brandt's concern with wanting to convince him of his newly acquired opinion, may well distract him from the obvious necessity to kill him. Surprising and simultaneously appalling himself with the coolness, perhaps even cynicism of his reaction, King began to consider how he might make use of the German's unexpected reflectiveness to turn the tables on him. He decided that he must do everything he could, both to prolong the conversation and to try to influence its direction. If he was able to impose himself on the German, he might disturb his seeming equanimity and even irritate him to such an extent that he would lose his composure and make a mistake. King recognised grimly that this tactic offered very little chance of success. But, in contrast to the German, who inexplicably seemed to want some sort of reconciliation, he had realised immediately that the only logical outcome to this confrontation was a fatal bullet. 'So tell me, Joachim, what are you doing here? I never had you cut out for a spy.'

'Well, that's where you're wrong,' replied the German smugly. 'I was sent here by the SS to find out why those bunglers in The *Abwehr* were producing next to no useful information from many of our best informants in Britain.' Smiling, as if what he was about to say confirmed the truth of his analysis, Brandt continued, 'You see, John how alike we are. We are both masters of deception.'

Feeling increasingly uncomfortable with this insistence on their similarity and wanting to maintain his attempt to direct the conversation away from this theme, King again interrupted quickly. 'And how did you get here, parachute, U-Boat?'

'Oh come now, Herr Dr. King. Surely you can imagine a more innovative approach? No? Well, I suppose that now we see the truth of our brotherhood, there is no harm in telling you. As it happens, for me, that was one of the most significant parts of the operation. Witnessing at first hand the utter chaos of your army's retreat to Dunkirk and having the opportunity to serve my country fully at a little place called Le Paradis. What we did there will be the stuff of legend in The Thousand Year Reich.' The sheer power of this recollection seemed to force a perhaps unwelcome inner resolution on Brandt, and his face twitched as he steadied his gun hand.

Recognising that Brandt's period of reflection was over, King attempted to postpone the fatal shot by asking in desperation, 'So how did you get on to me, Joachim, I'd really like to know.'

The German seemed in some way relieved to be able to withdraw, if only momentarily from the brink and he relaxed his posture a little before replying matter of factly, 'It wasn't so difficult. You just couldn't resist being the hero, could you?'

'Ah,' interrupted King, with a sad smile. 'The photograph in the newspaper? That was just bad luck.'

'Of course you would say that, John. I prefer to see it as the consequence of sentimental weakness. You will now see how real men deal with things.' Brandt once again cocked his revolver and steadied his hand with the barrel pointing directly at King's head.

King sought one final time to deflect Brandt from the inevitability of shooting him by pleading, 'But wait, please, Joachim. You still haven't explained to me how you come to be here with Abigail?'

Brandt tilted his head to one side, as if balancing the strength of an argument, before smirking and replying, 'Yes, John. I think that you deserve to know that. After all, it will be the last thing that you ever learn.' Noticing that Abigail Stevenson was now fully conscious and struggling to her feet, Brandt effortlessly switched to his American drawl. 'In fact, I had a very interesting conversation in Berlin with Herr Rösel, whose networks you took over for the British.' At this revelation, the woman's tear filled eyes widened in shock, as she took in its implications. 'Yes, honey,' Brandt said, looking at her with utter disdain. 'You're so stupid that you've been giving information to the British for the last eighteen months.' It hardly seemed possible to King, but it was actually the case that Stevenson's face grew an even whiter shade of the extremely pale colour it had already taken on.

'So that's how you got the contacts here in Britain?' asked King, attempting to keep Brandt talking, in the hope that Abigail Stevenson might say or do something that would distract him long enough to allow him to attack. 'And I suppose it was you, who killed Martha Perrygo and the newsagent in Sevenoaks?'

'I can't deny it, John,' replied Brandt with a conceited smile. 'But never fear. I have the details of all her contacts safely in my little black book.'

****

Bernstein, having returned to his original position, attempted to explain to Renton, 'I know these people, sir, but I'm still not sure what's going on. The American is, in fact, an SS officer and Lazarus is an Englishman called John King, who was presumed dead. Let's both get closer so we can hear more of what's being said.' Recognising the grim determination of his sergeant's expression, Renton chose not to argue or to question, but simply followed the younger man to the edge of the bushes. They arrived just in time to hear John King's voice, bravely challenging Brandt. 'You may have the upper hand here, Joachim, but you must be as aware as I am that it's over for you here.' Encouraged by the first signs of doubt flickering across the German's face, King continued. 'The invasion, Joachim; Germany's one and only chance to deliver a quick knock-out blow to Britain. And guess what? You've fluffed it.'

'What do you mean?' demanded Brandt, simultaneously hitting King on the side of his face with the pistol. Gratified that he was at last getting under the German's skin, King wiped the blood from his cheek, before continuing calmly, 'If you don't already know, I can tell you that your troops are being withdrawn from The Channel coast. The Luftwaffe has failed to win air supremacy and the invasion is off. Even someone as intellectually limited as yourself must have realised that the shift from attacking RAF fighter bases, to this barbaric and random bombing of cities, means that the invasion is not going to happen.'

'For the time being, perhaps, that may be true,' Brandt said hesitatingly and King seized the opportunity to emphasise the point. 'Come on, Joachim. You say you were at Dunkirk. You saw how much equipment the British Army left there. If Germany was going to invade Britain successfully, it would have had to be now. By next year, our Army will be re-supplied and we'll throw you back into the sea, if you try it.'

King's tactic had worked. Brandt was now beside himself with frustrated anger. How can it be that this Englishman, who is totally within my power, can act with such confidence and reject my generous identification with him, his uncomprehending mind fumed. However, before King could seize the chance to attempt an attack on a distracted Brandt, Abigail Stevenson looked at the German and asked, sadly, 'So, it was all a lie, Joe? Or whatever your name is. You had no interest in me at all?'

This seemed to tip Brandt even further out of control as he shouted, 'Of course not, you fool! And now, see what will happen to you very soon.' With these words, he raised his revolver, pointed it straight at King's heart and pulled the trigger.

It's strange, Brandt thought calmly, as he fired his pistol, I could have sworn that I heard a shot just before mine....

****

No one knew for certain whether or not Abigail Stevenson had deliberately placed herself in front of John King, in those desperate split seconds around The Bandstand on Hampstead Heath. As soon as he had aimed at Brandt and discharged his weapon, David Bernstein had struggled out of the bushes and rushed towards the wrought iron enclosure shouting, 'Special Branch! Stay where you are and put down your weapons!' Renton, surprised by his subordinate's sudden action, had little alternative but to follow him towards the chaotic scene. The person he had known as the American journalist, Joe Brand, was face up on the ground, his head covered in blood and his eyes gazing sightlessly into the fading light of the evening sky. His face, so often sneering, now simply wore an expression of vague bewilderment, as if he couldn't quite work out how this had happened to him. On the far side of The Bandstand, Renton could see the person he knew as Lazarus, the German agent he had been pursuing for months, kneeling on the floor and cradling the head of the woman Stevenson. It was immediately obvious, both that she had taken the bullet intended for him and that he was struggling in vain to staunch the rapid flow of blood from her chest, as her life rapidly drained away before his eyes. At last, Renton became vaguely aware of Bernstein's urgent voice shouting, 'Sir, sir! You must go quickly for help. Get an ambulance. She's very badly wounded.' When the Inspector didn't immediately respond, the younger man shook him roughly by the shoulder and repeated his instructions. 'What's going on here, David? I don't understand.'

'There's no time for that now, sir,' the younger man replied urgently. 'We have to try to save Miss Stevenson. For God's sake go and get help! Here's my police whistle to alert the back-up. But it's an ambulance we need.' This seemed to bring Renton to his senses and, after giving several long blasts on the whistle, he stumbled off towards the entrance to The Heath at Dartmouth Park.

King's anguished and blood streaked face looked up at Bernstein, as the Special Branch man crouched down next to him. A faint hint of recognition flitted across his eyes, before he turned back to gaze forlornly at the deathly pale face of Abigail Stevenson. 'What happened? Why is she dead and not me?' King asked with a dull, defeated voice.

'She's not dead, John,' replied Bernstein calmly. 'We've sent for help. There's still hope.' King looked sharply up at Bernstein, as he registered the use of his real name, his eyes now showing full recognition of the young policeman. 'And why did Joachim wait so long to shoot? He could've killed me at any time.'

'I don't know, John,' replied Bernstein shaking his head gently. 'I honestly have no idea. But it definitely saved your life and cost him his.'

King nodded, as if he had finally understood something important about both himself and his former friend, who now lay a few feet away. His confused attention was drawn back to the dying woman as she stirred in his arms and attempted to speak between coughing up mouthfuls of blood. 'He... he called you John,' she said, looking weakly up at King. 'Why?'

'Because that's my name, Abigail,' replied King softly. 'I work for British Intelligence. He was a German agent. I am not.' King could almost see the woman's brain processing this information, as her eyes darted right and left in their sockets until, like the sun emerging briefly from behind the darkest grey clouds, a smile spread across her face. 'Then that means....' She was unable to continue, her mouth again coughing up blood. So King did all that he could for her. He finished her thought. 'Yes, that's right, Abby. You didn't betray your country. Nothing that you said to me ever went to help the Germans.' This seemed to take a huge weight off the young woman's shoulders and she relaxed into King's arms, as if she no longer saw any reason to cling on to life. 'Hold on, Abigail,' King said desperately. 'We've sent for help.

Don't talk now. You'll be fine. We'll all be fine now.' It was obvious to Bernstein that the woman's wound was fatal and he muttered a silent prayer of his old religion as she smiled at King, nodded her head slowly and mouthed the words 'Thank you'. As the first wailing sounds of the air raid sirens began, Abigail Stevenson slipped quietly away from life.

ABOUT THE AUTHOR

A.P. Martin was born and spent his entire working life in the North West of England, where he was a university lecturer. After taking early retirement, he and his wife made the decision to leave England and move to the Swiss Alps, where they have lived since 2013. Now also a Swiss citizen, he spends his time enjoying the beautiful mountain scenery and writing.

'Codename Lazarus' is his first novel and he is now working on his second. For more information about A.P. Martin, please go to his website at www.apmartin.co.uk.

Printed in Great Britain
by Amazon